Aged fourteen, Rosie Mullender decided that her top five life goals were to work for *Cosmopolitan* magazine, have her name printed on a film poster, write a novel, buy a dog, and get married. Although she's spent the last thirty years working through the list, she's still not quite there yet. In her twenty years as a journalist, she's worked on both 'real-life' weekly and glossy monthly magazines (including reviewing films at *Cosmopolitan*), and she currently works as a freelance writer. Now she's finally ticked off number three, her next plan is to tackle the last two goals on the list. You can follow her @Mullies on Twitter to find out how it's going.

By Rosie Mullender

The Time of My Life
Ghosted

THE TIME OF MY LIFE

Rosie Mullender

SPHERE

SPHERE

First published in Great Britain in 2022 by Sphere
This paperback edition published in 2023 by Sphere

1 3 5 7 9 10 8 6 4 2

A CIP catalogue record for this book
is available from the British Library.

ISBN 978-0-7515-8524-7

Typeset in Caslon by M Rules
Printed and bound in Great Britain by
Clays Ltd, Elcograf S.p.A.

Papers used by Sphere are from well-managed forests
and other responsible sources.

Sphere
An imprint of
Little, Brown Book Group
Carmelite House
50 Victoria Embankment
London EC4Y 0DZ

An Hachette UK Company
www.hachette.co.uk

www.littlebrown.co.uk

For Mum, Dad and Dookie,
and all the fun they had

What if there is no tomorrow? There wasn't one today.

Phil Connors

Chapter 1

'Where are my Converse? And are you sitting on my bra? I know you're pretty, but can you at least try to make yourself a bit more use than a candy floss bikini too, please?' Jess pleaded.

Nate grinned at her lazily from her dishevelled bed and blew a handful of perfect smoke rings in Jess's direction.

Despite investing enough in Marlboro Lights to buy a small house, Jess had never quite learned how to blow smoke rings, even though other people – irritating ones, like Nate – made it look easy. It was like those old magic eye pictures, which everyone had told Jess turned into fish or the Statue of Liberty if you stared at them for long enough, when they just looked like a mess of squiggles to her. 'Stop showing off and help me, you monster!'

Sighing, Nate removed a muscular arm from behind his head, leaned over the edge of the bed, and looked underneath.

'Here you go, Your Majesty,' he said, propping his cigarette in the corner of his mouth and saluting as he handed Jess a battered pair of red sneakers with wonky red hearts drawn in Sharpie pen on the toes.

'Thank you, Sir Butthead,' Jess said, grabbing them from his hand and pecking him on the cheek.

'Why don't you come here and thank me properly?' he said, grinning, as he wrapped his arms around her waist and pulled her onto the bed, which made her squeal.

As Nate kissed her, Jess groaned, making their lips vibrate. She had such little willpower when it came to Nate's love of early-morning, work-bothering shags. The sight of his perfectly toned lower half wrapped in the tiny, tatty towel she purposefully gave him to use whenever he stayed over made her melt. Which, in turn, made her feel like a terrible, horny cliché. Wasn't she supposed to be attracted to men's brains and stuff, rather than their bits?

Still, with that body, and his twenty-four-year-old enthusiasm for her relatively ancient, thirty-two-year-old arse, it was almost a shame she was going to have to give him up soon. They'd been dating for six weeks now – *was it really that long?* – and seeing the same guy for more than a month or so wasn't in the spirit of the article she'd read in *Bijou* magazine on 'Dating, New Yorker Style!'

Although Jess knew she'd never be a true *Bijou* girl, the idea of casually trying on a few different men for a while to see how well they fit, before swiftly moving on to pastures new, sounded like a lot of fun.

Of course, a *Bijou* girl wouldn't live in a falling-apart flat the size of a postage stamp, fix her shonky IKEA coffee table with gaffer tape, and mostly eat dinner straight out of a saucepan using one of the bumper pack of plastic sporks she'd bought at a car boot fair. But still. A girl could dream, couldn't she?

And although she wouldn't know an eyebrow pencil if it bit her on the bum, the latest *Bijou* dating trend suited Jess down to the ground. Juggling two men at once meant the relationships were both strictly temporary and wouldn't bring up any dreary conversations about 'us'.

Jess was determined to stretch the fun of her twenties as far into her thirties as possible. While the thirty-somethings around her started caring what colour the hallway was painted, their parties gradually morphing from 'house' to 'dinner', Jess wanted to grab every opportunity for fun that was thrown her way.

No ties, no chores, no responsibilities.

Dating like a New Yorker suited her carefree blueprint down to a tee, which is why, as well as Nate, she was currently seeing Tom, a slightly nerdy but extremely tall and sexy book-binder who shared her taste in films.

The perfect movie-night companion, he was happy to play the Big Spoon to Jess's Little Spoon as they inhaled popcorn on the sofa together, even if he did spend far too much time trying to persuade her that old-person plans could actually be more fun than going out clubbing, as long as you bought the right snacks. Jess thought he was being ridiculous – when you went out clubbing, you had no idea what might happen to you, but the sofa was completely, boringly predictable. No one had ever woken up with a hangover, someone else's shoes and a stranger in their bed after a night in.

She was having fun, but Jess knew she'd have to move on soon, before they – or, god forbid, *she* – got too attached. Jess hadn't actually told either of the men she was dating about her New Yorker project, or that their relationships were strictly temporary. Both men had qualities that she'd miss once she'd worked out how to ease her way out of their relationships – but, still, they had to go.

I'll definitely miss this, she thought, as Nate whispered his fingers tantalisingly up her leg. Jess started returning the favour, sliding her hand up the inside of his toned, tanned thigh and towards his . . .

'*Balls*,' she muttered, as her phone started beeping urgently from its spot on her bedside table. She'd already ignored her 'time to leave for work' alarm and her 'no, really, get your arse in gear' alarm, and this – her 'oh-my-god-are-you-kidding?' alarm – was her final warning.

'I've got to go,' she groaned, flicking the alarm off. 'I can't be late for work again, or Maggie will have my guts for garters, and I've got to take Alfie for a walk on my way.'

'That's such a strange expression,' Nate mused. 'Who would want to make a garter out of somebody's guts?'

This was the sort of chat that passed for philosophy when you were in your early twenties. Jess strongly suspected Nate was the kind of man who wouldn't hesitate to pull a guitar out at a party to 'jam', and would be oblivious to how weary everyone looked when he did it. Those abs, though . . .

'It's a threat from Tudor times,' Jess said, as she plucked yesterday's outfit up from her floordrobe and found her bra dangling off the bedroom doorknob. 'When they used to dis-embowel people for doing stuff like stealing bread or trying to blow up parliament.'

Jess frowned as she realised she was regurgitating one of Tom's facts, of which he seemingly had hundreds stashed in his brain.

'At least turning a pile of free guts into garters is thrifty, I suppose,' she added. 'Waste not, want not, and whatnot. On which note, those fags cost sixty-five pence each, you know. You're literally burning my money.'

Nate grinned, rolled over, and stubbed his cigarette out in the Foster's ashtray on her bedside table.

Sniffing the armpits of her favourite maroon playsuit, Jess slipped it on. All her favourite outfits had already been flung into the washing basket once, and now she was onto Phase Two: fishing them back out and wringing one more (slightly musty) wear out of them before she was forced to go to the launderette.

'Anyway,' Jess added, scooping her bee pendant necklace up from the bedside table and carefully fastening it around her neck, 'there will be no gut removal needed if I skip having a shower. I should just about make it in on time.'

'No shower? It's a good job you didn't have a load of filthy sex last night then, innit?' Nate grinned, leaning across the bed and squeezing Jess's bum. She slapped his hand away.

'I thought you were supposed to be a feminist?' she said, adding a black leather belt to her playsuit, and pushing her bare feet into her Converse trainers. She'd noticed that even the most deconstructed men claimed to be feminists these days, hoping it would help get them laid. And, sadly, it often worked.

'Feminists can be into bums too, you know,' Nate said. 'Votes for bums! Free bums for all! Et cetera.'

Jess laughed, despite herself. Picking up her handbag and phone, she read the text her best friend had sent her first thing.

Mel: What's up, Buttercup? Got any gossip?

Mel texted Jess every single morning, without fail. It was their 'thing' – one of a hundred little habits only they knew about. They'd known each other since school, and as teenagers they'd delighted in their myriad in-jokes, as if they were the only friends on earth who spoke their own, private language.

On the surface, they seemed like chalk and cheese. Mel was quiet, thoughtful and moderate, while Jess was loud, impulsive and a big fan of Pot Noodles, and, as well as being different on the inside, they looked completely different, too. Mel was all angles and clavicles, set off beautifully by her sharply fringed bob, which was about five luscious shades of brown thanks to an expensive dye job. She wore large round glasses, which made her look a little like Miss Honey in *Matilda*. Meanwhile, Jess was a good five inches shorter and three sizes bigger than Mel, all curves and boobs, with a freckled nose. She never remembered to bring a hair elastic out with her to tame her wavy, red-brown hair, which she inevitably got annoyed with every few months and hacked with the kitchen scissors, and her preferred look was to wear what the barman at their local referred to as 'grungy Avril Lavigne shite'.

Yet, despite their superficial differences, Mel and Jess had been best friends since their teens, were fiercely loyal, and fit together like two slightly wonky puzzle pieces that had been made especially for each other.

Jess pinged Mel a photo of Nate, who was lazily scratching the line of blond hair on his stomach that led to her favourite body part.

I'm currently trying not to shag Nate's brains out so I can get to work on time. It's not

Mel: I mean yes, he's quite easy on the eye,
isn't he? So what I think you should do is . . .

Mel: . . . GET TO BLOODY WORK!

OK! God, Grandma

'I'm off,' Jess told Nate as she threw her phone into her
bag. 'You can let yourself out, right? And don't nick any of
my food; I'm completely skint until payday. You can go to
McDonald's for breakfast if you're hungry. You young people
still eat McMuffins, right? Or is it all about the revolting pro-
tein shakes these days?'

'We still eat McMuffins. Some of us even do it unironically.
Sad that I'm not allowed to eat one of your mouldy, half-eaten
jars of Dolmio or out-of-date Weetabix though,' Nate said,
sticking out his lower lip and pressing his palms to his cheeks,
which were razor-sharp and sexily dusted with stubble. 'How
ever will I survive the winter?'

'No need for sarcasm,' Jess said, flicking his bare thigh with
the strap of her bag. 'And make sure you take all your stuff
with you, too. I woke up to find one of your horrible shell
necklaces digging me in the bum the other day. Until you
stop buying your accessories from the Southend Shell Shack,
you'll have to learn how to tidy up after yourself.'

'Meh meh meh meh *meh*,' Nate said, in a squeaky parody
of Jess's voice. Seriously, what was she thinking shagging
someone so young? She'd have to reread *Bijou* and check New

7

Yorkers didn't have a lower age-limit rule, determined by doubling his age and subtracting it from your IQ or whatever.

As she stepped out of the bedroom, Alfie leapt up from the spot where he was curled on the carpet in the hall next to the blobs of breakfast that had been flung out of his bowl, casualties of his usual enthusiasm, and started leaping up at her shins. He barked indignantly, clearly unhappy with being banished from the bedroom.

A small, fluffy white rescue dog, Alfie seemed to be a cross between a Maltese, a terrier and a tiny idiot, and Jess loved him as much as she loved any human. He usually slept next to her bed, so she could leave a hand poking out from under the duvet for him to lick if he got scared in the night. Unfortunately, he tended to assume gentleman callers were attacking her, and after he'd grabbed her ex's wobbly man-bun with his teeth mid-act, she'd been forced to send him into the front room when anyone stayed over. Although, secretly, she'd agreed with Alfie's oblique critique of her ex's hairdo.

Clipping a lead to his collar, Jess slammed the door of her flat behind her. The pair skittered down the steps, crammed in a speedy walk around the block and a fast-walk to the Tube, Jess running down the escalator with Alfie in her arms before stepping onto a carriage heading for central London just as the carriage doors shut.

As she swayed along with the jerky movement of the train, holding onto the rail above her head with one hand and Alfie's lead with the other, Jess promised herself, for the umpteenth time, to set a deadline for telling Tom and Nate it was over.

Nate would probably take it pretty well. One of the great things about Gen Z, apart from their youthful hotness, was that they seemed to take these things in their stride. It was like they had all the time in the world to find someone new to shag. Which, Jess supposed, they did.

Tom might be a bit trickier to deal with. His sexiness was less earthy than Nate's, and largely based on how swoony she felt when he grabbed things for her on high shelves, and she'd learned over the past few weeks that he was quite sensitive. At the end of watching *Marley & Me*, when she'd turned around to wipe her tear-streaked face on his shirt, she'd discovered he was crying even harder than she was.

He was also the first man she'd ever met who thought nothing of replying to texts within a few minutes rather than a few days, which made her wonder if he might take a break-up badly.

Whatever, it had to be done – because the last thing Jess wanted was an actual boyfriend. Although Mel, happily coupled up as she was, regularly suggested that Jess might want to give a proper relationship a go, she had no intention of going there. As far as she could see, relationships mainly involved interminable conversations about bin day that no one had the answer to, and the phrase, 'If you don't know what's wrong, I'm not going to tell you'.

Still, she'd definitely miss Nate's abs and Tom's Big Spoon Energy when she finally did the deed, and she wasn't looking forward to the 'it's over' conversations either. Maybe she could just pretend to have moved house? Or died?

As she emerged from the Tube, she noticed the usual queue outside the hipster café by Old Street station wasn't there. Which probably wasn't a great sign in terms of how late she was going to be for work after she'd taken Alfie to the patch of grass on Hoxton Square for his daily safety wee, but did present an opportunity to buy Jasmit a coffee by way of apology – after which she headed for Aevum House, the tall, shiny glass building that housed *Real Talk!* magazine, where she worked as a features writer.

Clutching her recycled cardboard tray of coffees in their recycled cups, she scooped Alfie up with her other hand and shouldered her way backwards through the heavy revolving doors and into the building.

A brand-new copy of *Bijou* magazine was lying on the table in reception, next to a bowl filled with sweets wrapped in dusty cellophane. Apparently, the type of people who visited Aevum House didn't eat sugar.

Bijou, whose glossy offices were on the floor below *Real Talk!*'s, advertised itself as the bible 'For women who know where they're going!'

Jess stole one of the copies that Aevum's receptionist, Ashleigh, carefully fanned out on the visitors' table every single month. She might not have a clue where she was going – where was the fun in having life all mapped out in advance? – but she still read every issue from cover to cover. It was like a glimpse into another world.

She couldn't imagine what it might feel like to be one of the uber-together girls who worked at *Bijou*, a laptop permanently balanced on a slender forearm as they swept to the top floor for meetings with the CEO, wearing pin-thin heels that never seemed to hurt their feet or get trapped in escalator slats.

When the lift doors opened on the fourth floor, it was like getting a glimpse into the magazine equivalent of Willy Wonka's factory: everything seemed to be bathed in an ethereal glow. All the staff looked so perfect, and their hair was so shiny. Just like in Jess's favourite movies when she was growing up, it seemed that in *Bijou* World, harried-looking women really *did* spend their days pushing rails of gorgeous clothes across a giant, light-filled office.

But instead of working towards a job at *Bijou*, like most of *Real Talk!* magazine's senior writers before her, Jess had been happily ensconced in the same role for nine years. Her position slightly above the bottom rung of the ladder meant she got to pick all the juiciest stories, but without any of the hassle of having to sort things out when they went wrong. Which, thanks to the editor's fondness for borderline-libellous headlines, often featuring the word 'bonkathon', they frequently did.

Behind the lurid splashes, Jess tried her best to capture the humanity of the people she interviewed and take the reader on a journey alongside them – even if her job wasn't quite what she'd had in mind when she'd decided as a child that she wanted to be a writer.

It had been her dream ever since she'd seen her nan's favourite film, *All the President's Men*, for the first time. She was only eight, and the political intricacies of the Watergate scandal had gone completely over her head. But she'd insisted on watching it again the next day, and the next. After that, her favourite game was playing Being An Editor, which involved making fake newspaper front pages with headlines like, NANNY MAKES YUCKY DINNER AGAIN, and NEIGHBOUR'S DOG POOS IN GARDEN!!

Then she'd stomp around the front room, pressing the TV remote to her ear, yelling 'STOP THE PRESS!' at volumes that startled Alan, her nan's cat, off the back of the sofa.

Later, as a teenager, she'd devoured films like *How to Lose a Guy in 10 Days* and *Never Been Kissed*, and decided her dream job was to be a writer on a glossy magazine. Instead of dressing in her cousins' cast-off clothes, she'd throw outfits snaffled from the fashion cupboard into a simple and casual but stunning look, go undercover at a school/beauty pageant/whatever, to engineer some lighthearted high jinks, then write two pages of copy a month in exchange for an enormous sum of money.

She'd also live in a huge, but cosy, detached cottage that was somehow reachable via the Northern Line and always got snow at Christmas, *à la* Kate Winslet in *The Holiday*.

Unfortunately, she didn't grow up to be much like the glamorous Adult Jess of her fantasies. She preferred the ease of a job where nobody expected you to know how to transform a look effortlessly from day to night, and she couldn't reach too high and fall flat on her face. Instead of free designer clothes, the *Real Talk!* features desk's biggest perk was the occasional visit from a disgraced former soap actor dressed as a peanut handing out free snacks.

Still, in her own small way, Jess felt like she'd made it. She might not be working in 'serious' journalism, but she felt a buzz knowing she was writing for a living. She had a National Union of Journalists membership card that she hadn't made herself using a cut-up cereal box and some glittery felt-tip pens, which she kept in the see-through pocket of her wallet so people would see it when she paid for stuff, and hopefully ask what she did for a living. And her nan radiated pride whenever she talked about her granddaughter's job, cutting out Jess's Totally Hot Top Tips! page every single week, which was reward in itself.

So no, Jess's life wasn't shiny and effortless, like she'd just fallen out of the pages of *Bijou*, but whatever her younger self might think if she'd been able to glimpse the future, she was still having the time of her life.

Stealing a glance at Ashleigh – who was busy pouting at her phone, giving a double peace sign and meowing, which meant she was either on TikTok or having a nervous breakdown – Jess stuffed a handful of sweets in her pocket and swiped a copy of *Bijou*.

She spent her short journey in the lift to the fifth floor carefully peeling the PLEASE DO NOT REMOVE FROM RECEPTION!! sticker from the front, then flicked straight to the relationship pages and started boning up on sex tips.

Chapter 2

'Did you know that a woman *deserves* her orgasm, and there are a hundred and one new ways she can get it?' Jess asked Jasmit and Ian as she dumped her handbag among the piles of debris on her desk. 'Apparently, one of them involves grabbing a mirror and getting to know your body inside *and* out, so next time you see him you can, "give him a geography lesson he'll never forget". So that's nice.'

Jasmit, *Real Talk!*'s features editor, glanced up from her laptop and snorted, while Ian, the silent-but-deadly-delicious subeditor whose chief forms of communication were lifting weights and facial expressions, raised an eyebrow.

While Alfie made himself comfortable on the fluffy cushion under her desk, circling it three times before sitting down, Jess handed out the coffees; a double espresso for Jasmit – who'd decided her unborn twins 'might as well get used to caffeine sooner rather than later' – and an oat-milk latte for Ian, who, mysteriously, exercised for fun.

He kept a spare gym kit under his desk so he could run both to and from work, and his favourite mantras came straight from the walls of his local gym: 'Pain is weakness leaving the body', and 'I find comfort in discomfort'. Jess's motto, meanwhile, was: 'You can never have too much cheese.'

She slid her own coffee – an iced vanilla latte – under a coaster that had ZERO FUCKS GIVEN written across it in neon pink, which had been a gift from Mel. When she'd received it, Jess had exclaimed, 'That is precisely my number of fucks!' and felt a warm glow at being so well understood.

Plonking herself into her chair, she adjusted it down then up again, in a doomed attempt to stop it slowly deflating throughout the day like a punctured bouncy castle. Across the way, she could see Jasmit frowning at her coffee, presumably wondering why it was already cold, and attacking the pink frosting on her second doughnut of the day. Since conceiving the twins, she'd transformed from a 6 a.m. SoulCycle devotee into someone who thought licking the icing off doughnuts before tossing them back into the box, naked and glistening, was perfectly reasonable.

'You know that's disgusting, right?' Jess asked, as Jasmit tried, cross-eyed, to remove a blob of frosting from her nose with her tongue. 'You're aware of that right now, even as you do it?'

'It's allowed. I'm preggers,' Jasmit said, which was her answer to everything these days. To be fair to her, she could get away with almost anything if she rubbed her stomach and looked sad, unless she was talking to Maggie, who claimed not to believe in babies.

'You look like you're practising for tip number thirty-five: Become a Cunning Linguist,' Jess said now, as Jasmit swirled her tongue around the doughnut hole, tapping the

15

article she was reading. It was titled, '101 Ways To Achieve Your WOOOOAH!'

'I don't know how those *Bijou* girls come up with this gold dust,' she added. 'I've heard plenty of euphemisms for "orgasm", but "WOOOOAH" with four Os is a new one on me.'

'People in glass houses, Jess . . . ' Jasmit said darkly, tossing her doughnut back into the box. 'You're hardly about to win a Pulitzer for this now, are you?'

She waved a copy of that week's issue of *Real Talk!* in the air. The main line on the cover screamed, 'BUSTED BY OUR BURGER KING BONKATHON!' The story was about a couple who'd gone on the run after trying to hold up a branch of Greggs, and got caught when they'd stopped off to have a quickie in the loos at Knutsford services.

Jess wasn't even sure whether the loos at Knutsford services were anywhere near the Burger King, but, at *Real Talk!*, facts rarely stood in the way of an attention-grabbing headline.

'You make a fair, but depressing, point,' Jess conceded, bringing up the features list. 'Although at least at *Bijou* they get press trips in exchange for coming up with their rubbish headlines. What do we get?'

'I've been sent a bottle of head lice lotion and some Vagisil this morning, if you're interested?' Jasmit said.

Ian turned bright red and ducked his head below the top of his monitor.

Letting out a small sigh, Jess scrolled through the features list. *Real Talk!* offered its readers eighty tissue-thin pages filled with 'real-life' stories every week; a litany of human highs, lows and rock-bottoms, punctuated by the occasional funny story about a hamster. Each week, the cover was plastered with neon-bright headlines that screamed about murder, love rats and betrayal.

The printers worked a couple of months in advance, so mid-August meant the magazine's small team was busy pulling together October's Halloween Spooktacular bumper issue. Which, in a nutshell, meant Terrence the art director would add cartoon cobwebs to the cover, and all the stories on the features list would have a spooky theme shoehorned into them.

Tradition dictated that at least one feature in each Spooktacular issue would be headlined, 'Halloween House of Horrors!' in a melting green font. Last year, it was about a guy dressed as a mummy who'd been caught shagging his sister-in-law (who was dressed as a sexy cat) by his wife (also a sexy cat).

This year's story was about a woman who'd somehow managed to glue her eyelid shut while applying spooky false nails to complete her Halloween costume (yes, you guessed it: sexy cat).

Flicking through her options, Jess considered each story as it scrolled past. Even though she loved animals and leapt at any chance to talk at length with owners about their pets, she'd generously let Rachel, the magazine's junior-writer-slash-web-editor, nab that week's 'Crazy Critters' story.

Rachel tended to cry even more than her interviewees if she was given anything gruesome, romantic or tragic to write, so Jess had taken pity on her and let her have 'My Haunted Pussy From HELL', which was about a cat who'd behaved a bit oddly in the run-up to Halloween, causing its hysterical owner to get a priest in to exorcise it. (It turned out to have swallowed some Lego.)

Jess took her time browsing through the rest of the list, looking for something juicy to write about.

'My Night of Lust with Willy Wonky' was about a woman who'd snapped her boyfriend's penis during sex when he was dressed up as an Oompa Loompa. 'Doctor! I've Got a Freaky Frozen Fanny!' featured a girl who'd stopped to do a wee on her way home from a party and got frostbite somewhere delicate. Jess really wasn't in the mood to discuss a bloke's banjo string or lady's labia before lunchtime in case it put her off her Boots Meal Deal, so she was left with the issue's main cover story: 'Hands Off My Halloween HUNK!'

It was a classic age-gap love story – the kind of thing *Real Talk!*'s readers lapped up and was the magazine's bread and butter. Donna, a reader in her fifties, had met a younger man called Alejandro in Tenerife the year before. She'd been quickly seduced, and, a few months after returning from holiday, he'd followed her to England, moved into her tiny flat in Hackney, and promptly proposed.

Jess's heart sank. She'd written dozens of stories like this one in the past, and they all ended the same way: with the man in question buggering off with his new wife's life savings. She could already imagine Donna claiming her man was 'different to all the others', firm in her belief that he was the key to a new and exciting life, when all she was being sold was a lie.

Perhaps this one really will be different, Jess thought, crossing her fingers without much hope.

She'd soon find out, anyway. As Donna lived in London, Jess would go to her house to interview her in person, rather than over the phone. Seeing people face to face always made them more open, and Jess always got her best stories that way.

Firing off an email to see if Donna and Alejandro might be available that afternoon, she pulled the story summary up on her iPad and headed for Maggie's office.

Although she was a genius editor, Jess's boss made Meryl Streep in *The Devil Wears Prada* look about as threatening as an egg and cress sandwich with the crusts cut off. Talking to her was a bit like having a smear test – an unavoidable but thoroughly unpleasant experience that made your shoulders shoot up around your ears.

Knocking gently, Jess peered around Maggie's office door.

'What?' she barked, not looking up from the *Sun*.

'I just wanted to know what angle you had in mind for the Donna Wilson story,' Jess said.

'Donna Wilson?' Maggie snapped, finally looking up and somehow managing to look disappointed without changing her expression. 'Oh, you mean the Halloween Heifer?'

Jess's eyes widened. 'Umm ... I guess? Although ... do we need to call her that? She's really not that big ...'

Maggie referred to all the stories in the magazine by a quick shorthand, and insisted the rest of the office did the same. Unfortunately, they were usually less than flattering to their subjects, despite Jess's attempts to steer Maggie towards less evil nicknames.

'Come on, Jess, she's a size fourteen if she's a pound,' Maggie said. 'That kind of dress size looks just about OK on you because you've got huge tits, but most women can't pull it off.'

'Right. Good to know,' Jess said, her cheeks turning pink. It was just like Maggie to be able to determine someone's dress size at a glance, and to deem size fourteen unacceptably elephantine. Looking down at her playsuit, Jess wished she'd worn her favourite baggy jeans and vintage T-shirt combo instead.

'OK, let me think about this,' Maggie said thoughtfully, tapping her teeth with a biro. 'She's fifty-two, as well as wobbly. By all accounts, this Alejandro is a babe, which means the engagement is definitely a scam.'

Tapping at her iPad screen, Jess brought up a selfie of Donna and Alejandro, which they'd emailed to the features desk. Even though the photo was a bit out of focus, Jess could see Donna looked friendly and kind, with one of those rare faces that radiates optimism. It reminded her of that Roald Dahl quote from *George's Marvellous Medicine* – or was it *The Twits*? – about good thoughts shining out of your face like sunbeams, and making you look lovely.

'We could do a bit of digging, bust him now, and get the love-rat exclusive to shift some extra copies of the Halloween issue,' Maggie pondered. 'Or we could stick with the age-gap romance angle, keep tabs on her, then do a follow-up later, when it all goes tits-up. Two stories for the price of one. What do you think?'

'Sure,' Jess mumbled. This was definitely *not* the kind of story she enjoyed writing, but it was part and parcel of the job. She'd learned long ago that complaining too loudly simply led to Maggie pulling the story and challenging Jess to replace it with something better, usually with only a day or two to spare.

'I like the headline "Hands Off My Halloween HUNK!",' Maggie mused. 'I thought we could dress them up – something funny. Like, he could be a sexy Dracula or topless Frankenstein, and she could be ... an egg.'

'An egg? What, like a scary one?'

'You know what I mean,' Maggie said impatiently,

drumming her fingers on the desk. 'Just something unflattering, to emphasise that he's a sexpot, while she's this dowdy, puddingy type of person. I'll leave you to deal with the details. Just make sure you make a big deal of how in love they are, so we can milk it when it all goes kablooey.'

'Kablooey?' Jess echoed, her cheeks burning.

'Yep, that's the one,' Maggie said briskly, pointedly picking up her newspaper and putting her feet back on the desk. 'Now, stop looking like I've asked you to put down a fucking puppy and shoo.'

Chapter 3

Jess left Maggie's office, daring to close the door with a single middle finger, before dropping her iPad with a loud sigh onto the teetering pile of old newspapers she really needed to get around to throwing out. Despite the fact it was only about ten feet from her desk, the recycling bin always felt so far away ...

'Ian, do you fancy chucking these out for me?' Jess asked, slumping into her chair. 'It'll give your ... *glutes*? ... a lovely workout.'

'Nope,' Ian said, as Rachel finally arrived for work, late as always.

'Morning, darlings,' she said warmly, quacking her hand like a duck in the general direction of everyone. Jess assumed this was the latest posh-person way of waving hello. Maybe someone on Harley Street had announced that it preserves the collagen in your fingers.

'Morning, princess,' Jess waved back, turning to her laptop and pulling up her emails.

'Look, Jess, Rachel's here!' Jasmit gasped, with sarcastic

delight. 'You might know her from such shows as *Who Needs To Be At Work On Time?* and *Junior Writers Need Their Beauty Sleep.'*

Rachel let out a long-suffering sigh, as if having her lateness pointed out was a terrible inconvenience, and sat daintily at her desk, blinking slowly at the papers scattered across it like it was her first day on the job.

Jess rolled her eyes and picked up her mobile phone as it lit up, telling her BRIAN DO NOT ANSWER!!! was calling. She grimaced. Partly due to the purchase of a pair of side-splittingly hilarious cushions printed with cats that looked like David Bowie, but mostly thanks to her inability to resist buying Alfie anything she thought his tiny heart might desire, Jess currently owed her landlord two months' rent.

She felt bad about it, but pushed away the guilty thoughts by reminding herself how grossly rich Brian must be. She was a skint writer living in the modern equivalent of a grotty poet's garret, while he was a property owner. He was obviously rolling in money – perhaps literally, for all Jess knew, diving into a pool full of it, like Scrooge McDuck. While Jess really couldn't afford to go overdrawn yet again, it wouldn't cause Brian any real problems to wait for his money a little bit longer, would it? Pay day was just around the corner, after all, and she could pay what she owed him then. Well, some of it, at least.

Hitting the reject button, Jess quickly turned her phone face down on her desk and pretended to feel totally chill about the whole situation, instead of a bit sick.

Turning to her email, she saw she'd already had a reply from Donna Wilson.

Subject: RE: Your story
From: Donna Wilson
To: Jess Janus

Hi Jess were here from 1 p.m. for the interview if u wanna cum over? And we luv dogs! Alfie is v. welcome.

As always, Jess tailored her reply to match the interviewee's writing style. It helped them warm to her, even before they'd met.

Subject: RE: Your story
From: Jess Janus
To: Donna Wilson

Hi Donna great! C U at lunchtime. xx

It was one of the first tricks Maggie had taught her when she'd arrived at the magazine as a fresh-faced young hack.

'If you go to their house and they offer you a fag, you take it, even if your grandad died of emphysema,' Maggie had lectured every trembling new writer. 'If they're drinking Special Brew at eleven a.m., you join in. Anything to get them onside and spilling their guts out. Just don't come crying to me about lung cancer or liver disease. I've got full indemnity, and lawyers with all the scruples of a politician during a pandemic.'

'It was exactly like *All the President's Men*!' she'd lied to her nan after her first day of work.

After spending a pleasant morning replying to a slew of emails from PRs telling her about the latest super-mops and vinegar-based cleaning tips, Jess beckoned Alfie out from underneath her desk, where he was nibbling at a chew-toy that was clutched between his paws. 'Right,' she said, slapping her thighs. 'I'm off to grab some lunch then interview Donna Wilson, aka the Halloween Heifer.'

'Christ, is that what Maggie's calling her?' Jasmit muttered, shaking her head as Jess tugged her jacket from the back of her chair.

'Well, be reasonable, Jas, she *is* a size fourteen. It's a miracle anyone that huge can get through normal-sized doors, let alone find an *actual man*.'

Before she'd even reached Donna's front door, Jess had guessed which one belonged to her. Her flat was housed in a 1960s block – the kind of concrete tower that had a covered walkway on each floor with plain wooden doors leading off it, most of which were painted with a thin layer of flaking maroon paint.

Donna's door, meanwhile, was a bright, fresh, glossy yellow, with a little window set into it and a tiny flowery curtain hanging inside. Her doormat was pink, with 'Live, Laugh, Love' written on it in a dangerously curly red font.

Inside the front living-room window, below the scalloped edge of a pristine patterned net curtain, was a line of faded gnomes, one of whom was pulling down a pair of moss-green trousers and mooning at passers-by.

Pressing the doorbell, Jess smiled as she heard a tinny rendition of 'Happy Birthday' playing inside the flat. The little curtain was pulled back, and a nervous-looking face peered through the window.

'Hi Donna, it's only me. Jess, from the magazine.'

'Oh lovely!' Donna said, her voice muffled through the

glass. Swinging the door open, she beamed delightedly, like Jess was a dear and long-lost friend. She had curly, fluffy blonde hair, blue eyes, and a plump face with the smooth skin of someone a decade younger, apart from a cluster of well-used laughter lines around each eye.

'Is it someone's birthday?' Jess asked, gesturing at the doorbell.

'No, no! That's just my musical doorbell,' Donna laughed. 'It plays all sorts. Thirty different tunes. See?' Leaning around the door frame, she pressed the bell with a frosted-pink painted fingernail, setting off a brave rendition of *Greensleeves*.

'Nice,' Jess nodded, approvingly.

'Come in, come in,' Donna said, waving Jess through the door. 'Alejandro is just getting dressed, but he'll be out in a mo.'

'This is Alfie, Donna. Alfie, meet Donna. And be nice to her, OK?'

Alfie wagged his tail as Donna bent down to meet him, her face lighting up as he attempted to lick her left and right hands simultaneously.

'Oh, isn't he *sweet*?' Donna exclaimed delightedly, letting Alfie sniff her hand to check she was friend not foe before stroking him.

'I bought us something to drink, Donna, I hope you don't mind,' Jess said, shutting the front door behind her and waving the black carrier bag she was clutching. 'Although I'm afraid it's just bog-standard Chateauneuf-du-Offie,' she added, pulling out a slightly dusty bottle of white wine. She'd grabbed it from the local corner shop and wouldn't have been surprised if it had been lurking on the shelves since the 1990s.

Offering up free alcohol to encourage interviewees to spill the beans was another of Maggie's expert tips, even though it sometimes meant Jess's notes became slightly wobbly by the end of an interview. One time, after chatting to a woman with a wine club subscription, the last three pages of her notebook had been filled solely with wobbly outlines of her hands, drawn in blue biro.

'Oh, not for me love, thank you all the same,' Donna said, examining the label. 'I only drink on high days and holidays. Alejandro will join you though, I'm sure. He loves a tipple. Here, let me put that in the fridge for a sec to cool it off. It's so bloody hot! Chafing bras and rubbing thighs will be the death of me, I swear. Make yourself at home,' she added, ushering Jess towards the living room.

The front room was small and dark, thanks to the gnomes blocking much of the light coming in via the front window. But it was cheerfully decorated, with multi-coloured fairy lights draped over a set of old-fashioned mahogany shelves, which were littered with mis-matched ornaments.

Peering at the cluster of random objects, Jess smiled to herself. There didn't seem to be any rhyme or reason to Donna's collection of loved objects. A brown ceramic splodge that was attempting to be a squirrel sat on its hind legs next to a porcelain-headed Pierrot doll in a dusty white silk costume.

A green glass vase held some orange and yellow plastic roses, and a picture frame decorated with tiny seashells had a Polaroid photo of Donna and Alejandro Blu-Tacked to the front of the glass.

They were sitting opposite each other at a small round table, the sky behind them bright blue, and a huge goldfish-bowl glass of a green, pond-like drink between them. It was festooned with umbrellas, slices of fruit and cocktail sticks decorated with bits of tinsel, and on the paper panel at the bottom of the photograph, someone had written 'Donna + Alejandro 4 Eva!!!', the dot above the J a tiny heart.

'Handsome, isn't he?' Donna said behind Jess, making her jump. 'I couldn't believe it when he made a move. I think I'm the luckiest woman alive. Or in Hackney, at any rate.' Donna let out her generous laugh. 'Here, let me take your jacket.'

An exercise-bike-come-coat-rack was parked in front of the TV, a couple of handbags and an umbrella dangling off the handlebars. Donna took Jess's jacket from her arms and added it to the pile of clothes draped over the seat.

Jess wondered what Alejandro had made of Donna's flat when he'd arrived here from Spain. It didn't quite live up to the image he might have gleaned from the London of Richard Curtis films; a fantastical land where booksellers can afford to live in enormous Notting Hill flats, and the Prime Minister is an absolute babe.

'I reckon I've only done about two miles on this bloody thing,' Donna said, patting the exercise bike. 'I told myself I could get fit while watching *Loose Women*, but it turns out I enjoy it a lot more with a cuppa and a Jammie Dodger. Shocking, eh?' She laughed. 'But Instagram can be very persuasive when it wants to be, can't it?'

Jess thought about the two Bowie cat cushions decorating her sofa, their furry faces bisected by red zig-zags, and nodded in solidarity. 'I can't say I blame you – it's like having a personal shopper who can read your mind. I don't care if it reads my emails, I *love* the algorithm.'

Donna chuckled and gestured for Jess to take a seat on her small, two-seater sofa, which was upholstered in a dingy flowery print that was so ancient, it had passed straight through 'vintage' and was fast approaching 'antique'. Alfie ducked into the small space underneath it, shuffled in a circle, and poked his head out, giving Jess's ankle a reassuring lick.

'Oh look, here he is!' Donna beamed, as a young man in his mid-twenties came into the front room. He was tanned and wiry, with curly black hair, bright brown eyes and muscular arms. Jess loved a good arm – when Nate held her, she could almost feel herself melting, like the heroine on the cover of a Mills & Boon novel – and she could certainly see what Donna saw in Alejandro. But she still cringed slightly as he swept Donna into his arms and kissed her wetly on the lips.

'*Mi amor!*' he said breathily. 'This is the journalist who will be giving us money to speak of our love, yes?'

'Yes, love, this is Jess. Do you want biscuits? I've got some Party Rings in the cupboard.'

Jess nodded. It would be good to get a bit of alone time with Alejandro before the interview, to try to suss him out. 'I'll get you two some wine, and put on the kettle then,' Donna said brightly.

'Would you mind getting Alfie some water too, please?' Jess asked, pulling a collapsible dog bowl from her bag.

'Of course,' Donna said, wiggling her fingers at Alfie and shuffling back into the kitchen.

'Do you mind if I start?' Jess asked Alejandro, pulling out her notebook and phone, which she set on the small coffee table in front of the sofa. He nodded, squeezing next to Jess. He was wearing the same kind of tapered, spray-on jeans Ian enjoyed wearing, and which Jess had never quite understood. Surely they just crushed men's balls into peanuts?

The denim strained across Alejandro's muscular thighs,

29

then stopped abruptly above his ankles, which ended in a pair of bright white trainers. They looked brand new, and Jess wondered if Donna had paid for them. Shaking her head, she reminded herself to give the couple the benefit of the doubt before jumping to mean conclusions, and pulled on a smile.

'So how did you meet Donna, Alejandro?' she asked, switching on the recorder on her phone. 'Can you tell me what happened? Describe the big moment.'

'You can call me Al,' he said, grinning, and showing off a row of very white teeth. 'I met Donna on the beach. She was sunbathing and reading a book. She looked strong, intelligent. A big woman, with a big beautiful body. And I thought straight away that here was a woman I could fall for, you know?'

'Weren't you worried about the age gap?' Jess asked.

'Not at all,' Alejandro said, shaking his head firmly. 'An older woman has the beauty of wisdom. She is ... *especial*. And knows how to treat a man.'

'Fair enough. That sounds pretty cool. And what happened when you got chatting? What do you have in common?'

'I asked about her home here in England, and about her work. She is a ... personal assistant?' Jess nodded. 'I pictured her booking flights for wealthy businessman, nice lunches, things like this, you know? But no, she works in small office. Her boss can't get his own Greggs sandwich. He is simply what you people call a "lazy bastard".' Alejandro burst into laughter.

'Ah, OK. I see, yes,' Jess said, shifting in her seat. 'Anything else? Do you have any similar interests?'

'Before I answer your question, Jess, I think I have a question for you.'

'Go on ...'

'Where is it that you live? Here in London?'

'Yes, East London. Not too far from here, really.'

'And do you live in a house, not a flat? You are a journalist and must earn good money, I think.'

'Well, a flat. And not really. I mean—'

'And tell me, Jess. Are you single?'

'*Technically*, but . . .'

'Ah. I see. That is interesting to hear. This is a country of very many beautiful women.' Alejandro leaned over, looking Jess in the eye, and squeezed her knee. She assumed it was supposed to be seductive, but shivers of revulsion rippled all the way up her leg. 'They have all the curves that a red-blooded man looks for. Like Donna, and like you, yes?' Alejandro added, moving his hand higher up Jess's bare leg and squeezing again.

'Well, that's not really the point, is it? I'm here to talk about Donna,' Jess said stiffly, plucking his hand off her thigh. She nervously adjusted her phone on the table. 'And um, when was it . . . when was it that you realised you were in love with her?'

'I think I realise when I find out she lives in London,' Alejandro said, then roared with laughter. 'The women here are all independent, they can work. And to me you seem like an independent lady also, Jess. Only . . . and I have to tell you this, Jess . . . much more attractive.'

Alejandro leaned over and put his hand back on her thigh.

'And you seem like a prick,' Jess hissed, slapping his hand away and standing up. From beneath the sofa, Alfie let out a low growl and peered out nervously, his eyes flicking between them.

Alejandro frowned. 'I'm not familiar with this word.'

'You're *uno bellendo*, OK mate?' Jess said, shaking. 'Keep your horrible greasy paws off me.'

'Here we go, I've brought you two some wine and biccies, and a cuppa for me,' Donna said, suddenly appearing in the doorway with a tray in her hands. 'Shift your phone, love, and I'll put these things down and grab Alfie's water. Do you want to bring over another chair, Alejandro? Is everything OK?' she added, seeing Jess standing, pink-faced and panting, by the sofa.

'I just . . . suddenly need the loo,' she muttered, glaring at Alejandro as he stood up and pulled a chair out from underneath a small round table in the corner of the living room.

'I understand. The heat plays hell with my bowels,' Donna said happily.

Alejandro looked Jess in the eye and smiled at her mildly, as if groping young women when your fiancée was next door making the tea was just par for the course for a Thursday afternoon.

Spinning his chair around, he sat on it with his legs spread as far as they'd go, his arms resting loosely on the back.

'Oh god, really?' Jess muttered. It was like he'd been reading *How To Be A Total A-Hole For Dummies*.

'The bathroom's just on the left as you come in,' Donna said, smiling. 'Help yourself. I'll keep an eye on Alfie for you.'

Scurrying into the bathroom and away from Alejandro's creepy stare, Jess leaned on the small sink, splashing her face with water from the limescale-stained tap, and taking some deep, calming breaths. Her hands were shaking, and her stomach was rolling.

It hadn't taken long for her to find out that Alejandro was, as suspected, an enormous, scamming douchebag. And it wasn't

32

the first time one of her interviewees had crossed the line so fast that they risked a nasty case of whiplash. But, in this case, she wasn't sure what to do next. Usually, she would just pull herself together and move on. But there was something different about Donna. She was . . . well, so *nice*.

The people she interviewed usually fell into two camps: those who told their stories for money, and those who wanted to share their lives, for better or worse, and inspire other people. And while Alejandro might have giant pound signs in his eyes, Donna believed she'd found her happy ending, and wanted to share the good news with women like her, who might be worried it would never happen for them.

Telling Donna that her fiancé was a cheating scumbag would be the right thing to do, but it would almost certainly cause the feature to implode. Maggie would be furious if Jess let her conscience get in the way of a good story, and she'd definitely be left to find a new story to fill the missing pages on her own.

In short, being honest might help Donna in the long run, but it would cause Jess a world of pain. And it was hardly her fault if Donna couldn't see Alejandro for the ratbag he was, was it? She was a grown woman. She was old enough to make her own choices, and her own mistakes. It wasn't Jess's job to stop her from making them, was it?

No, Jess told herself. It was probably best all round if she just carried on with the interview, keeping a safe distance from Alejandro's hairy hands.

Swiping her face dry with the back of her hand, Jess took a deep breath, told the knot of guilt gnawing at her stomach to do one, thank-you-very-much, and pushed open the bathroom door.

Chapter 4

'And when he swept me into his arms on the dancefloor, I knew at last I'd found my prince,' Donna beamed. 'I've never met anyone so romantic in my life. And now look!' She held out her left hand, which sparkled with a giant rock that looked more like George at Asda than Tiffany & Co., which was where Alejandro had claimed to have bought it.

Jess blew her nose into a tissue, feeling a bit weepy. Despite knowing Alejandro was a total creephole, she'd become absorbed by Donna's story as it had unfurled during the interview.

'And what about the age gap?' Jess asked carefully, looking at Alejandro, who was suddenly finding the back of the chair he was straddling very interesting. 'Did you ever worry that Alejandro might not be genuine?'

'I'm not an idiot, I know he's young,' Donna said, firmly. 'But he's from a different country, and they're more mature over there. He really gets me, and for the first time in my life, I've found true love.' Her eyes glistening with happy tears, Donna leaned over and squeezed Alejandro's hand.

He gave her his 1,000-watt smile back, and Jess realised that even if she decided to do the honourable thing and tell Donna about Alejandro's sleazy come-on, nothing she could say would burst Donna's happy bubble. She just hoped that when he inevitably let her down, he'd do it gently – and without stealing too much of her money.

By the time the interview was over, Jess and Alejandro had somehow got through the whole bottle of wine. Suddenly, Jess was feeling warm, relaxed, and a lot less guilty about covering up the truth.

'You're OK for me to take this with me for the art department to scan, yes?' Jess asked, waving the fishbowl photo and carefully sliding it into her bag. 'I'll give it back to you tomorrow morning when we see you for the photo shoot. Is nine forty-five still good for you? Because it's for the Halloween issue, you'll be dressing up in costumes.'

'Ohh, what are we going to be?' Donna asked excitedly. 'I love fancy dress!'

'It's, um, a surprise. I'm sure you'll love it,' Jess said awkwardly.

She'd have to email the art department when she got out of here, and ask Terrence to order a new costume. He'd probably already called in a giant Humpty Dumpty outfit, or something even less flattering, for Donna to wear. But even if Jess wasn't quite brave enough to tell Donna the truth, she could at least help her retain some dignity.

'That sounds exciting,' Donna said, squeezing Alejandro's arm. 'Will you see Jess out while I tidy up, love? We'll see you tomorrow. It's been ever so nice chatting.'

'After you,' Alejandro bowed, ushering Jess towards the

front door, before following far too close behind for comfort. As Jess turned to say goodbye, he loomed over her, his face just a few inches from hers.

'I'm already looking forward to seeing you again, Jess. It has been a pleasurrrre.'

Purring the last syllable and grabbing her hand, he pressed his greasy lips to it, then opened the front door, his hand sliding down the small of her back and towards her bum as she turned to go. Once the door was closed, her whole body shuddered with revulsion, as if she'd just survived being trapped in a box full of bugs on *I'm a Celeb*.

And, although she was already a little bit drunk, Jess decided she really needed another glass of wine.

An hour later, Jess was happily ensconced in the Bush Tavern, sipping wine in her and Mel's usual spot by the window. It was almost 4 p.m., and she'd decided that there was no point schlepping all the way to the office just to leave again half an hour later, when she could send emails from the pub instead. As a producer on a TV breakfast show called *Wakey, Wakey, Britain!* Mel started work at oh-my-god o'clock, but was usually finished by lunchtime, too. So, grabbing her phone, Jess texted her.

Come to the pub. Pleasepleasepleasepleaseplease.
I IMPLORE you

She didn't need to specify which pub. Although it was nowhere near Mel's swanky flat in Limehouse Basin, or Jess's crappy one in Walthamstow, the Bush had become 'their' pub when they'd stumbled across it when they were seventeen after a trip to the big Topshop, and thought its name was hilarious.

They'd been attracted by its retro old-man vibe and horse brasses, and had since become part of the fabric of the place, just like the nicotine stains on the wallpaper and the beer embedded in the carpet, which looked like they hadn't been cleaned since the 1990s.

Over the years, they'd grown to genuinely love it – right down to the inexplicable collection of *Pulp Fiction* memorabilia Mark kept behind the bar, and Arthur, who looked about a hundred years old and spent three hours every afternoon sipping his way through two pints of stout while reading the *Sun* from cover to cover.

He always sat in the window seat downstairs, forcing Mel and Jess upstairs if they wanted a nosy view of the shoppers below, and was fond of swearing liberally at the tourists who came in for a drink after shopping on Oxford Street. Jess had once considered matchmaking him with her nan, who was equally attached to earthy language, until she realised she definitely didn't want Arthur as her step-grandad.

Jess smiled as three wobbly dots told her Mel was replying to her text.

> Mel: OK, but I can only come for one.
> Busy day tomorrow. See you in fifteen?

> Excellent. I've got a juicy story for you
> and need your advice. It involves a
> hairy, greasy man in spray-on trousers
> and a delicious plate of biscuits

> Mel: Oh, grim. And: yum! On my way xxx

Next, Jess's finger hovered briefly over Nate and Tom's names in her phone, before she decided to text Tom. Although Nate was big on performative acts of feminism (which mainly involved letting her pay for their takeaways), she knew Tom would be more sincerely annoyed about Alejandro's behaviour.

Ugh, I had the grossest interview today. A Lothario called Alejandro touched me up. So much for #MeToo

Tom: Was he wearing those jeans that make men's thighs look like massive chicken drumsticks?

Yes!! He was mega sleazy. It was like he'd learned about romance from a frozen pizza advert

Tom: I apologise sincerely on behalf of my kind. And I hope you're OK

Apology accepted. Although you clearly owe me a back massage next time I see you, to make up for the patriarchy

Tom: I guess it's only fair :)

Jess smiled to herself. Tom's premium phone-flirting was another thing she'd miss about him when she finally got her act together and ended Project New York Dating. Tossing her phone onto the table, she opened her laptop and shot off an email to Terrence about the new costume for Donna's photo shoot, then started tapping out an email to Jasmit about the disastrous interview.

'Here she is!' Mel said, her head arriving at the top of the stairs first as she walked carefully up them one at a time, her knuckles showing white on the top of her cane. She was wearing a gorgeous floaty yellow dress that somehow managed to be both diaphanous and incredibly well cut at the same time.

'We can always sit downstairs, you know,' Jess said, getting up to pull Mel's seat out for her. 'Seeing as Mark refuses to get a bloody lift installed.'

'First of all, he can't get a bloody lift installed because this is a listed building, as he's told you a million times,' Mel said, wincing slightly as she sat down and leaned her cane against the windowsill. From underneath the table, Alfie sniffed Mel's ankles, and woofed happily in greeting. 'And secondly, I like the window seat. The window seat is *our* seat. The only way you'll get me downstairs is by persuading Arthur to relinquish his spot, and good luck with that.'

'You're probably right. The man might be as ancient as all hell, but he's part-human, part-Rottweiler. I hope I'm that feisty when I reach ninety or whatever.'

'He's seventy-three,' Mark said, as he arrived upstairs carrying a bottle of wine in a cooler and a glass for Mel. 'He's just had a hard life, that's all. Trust me, I could recite every one of his hair-raising stories, I've heard them enough times.'

'Buy him a drink on me, will you?' Mel nodded.

'Is all that wine for me, then?' Jess said, eyeballing the wine cooler. 'I thought you had a busy day tomorrow?'

'Yeah, well. Not *that* busy.' Mel shrugged, pouring both of them a glass.

'What's happening? Anything juicy? Is someone going to fake a big on-air strop? What's the tea?'

'Jess, you're thirty-two, which makes asking "What's the tea?" generational appropriation,' Mel scolded. Jess sulkily stuck her bottom lip out. 'Believe it or not, our presenters really do have that many actual strops. Although we might sometimes fake things like falling off the sofa to make the Christmas blooper shows.

'The meeting's nothing that important, anyway. Just budget planning, that's all. I need to be on top of my game, though, what with being hugely important and indispensable and everything.'

'I'm sure you'll smash it,' Jess said. 'You always worry about work, but you're amazing at your job and you know it.'

'Thanks,' Mel said, looking relieved. 'How about you? What's the "tea"?'

'Well, hold onto your tits, because this is truly terrifying.'

After Jess told Mel all about Alejandro's wandering hands, and Donna's heartbreaking optimism, Mel looked thoughtful.

'Ahh, so this is why we're knee-deep in wine, is it? I thought you must be feeling guilty about something.' Jess stared into her glass, and Mel sighed in sympathy. 'I agree it's a tricky one. I get that you can't risk the story by telling Donna, but it's horrible all the same. Have you told Jas about it? Share your monkeys, as Aya says.'

'What's this got to do with monkeys?'

'I'm not too sure. I think it's her version of "a problem shared is a problem halved".'

'Of course it is,' Jess said, trying to hide her irrational annoyance at Mel dropping her girlfriend's name into the conversation in the middle of her crisis. 'I was just writing an email as you arrived, actually. How does this sound?'

Hi Jas, just to give you a heads up that Donna's boyfriend is a gross sleazeball who tried to feel me up THREE TIMES during our interview. He's obviously just in it for the money. But it does still work as a story – Donna's a bit naive, shall we say (to put it mildly), and has seriously fallen for his slimy charms. And, between you and me, I'm not keen on finding another story to fill four pages. Over to you, boss . . .

'Well, I guess it's to the point.' Mel shrugged. 'Poor Donna.'
'Yes. Poor Donna,' Jess agreed as she headed up her email.

Subject: "Halloween Heifer"
To: Donna Wilson
From: Jess Janus

Feeling better already, Jess hit Send, closed her laptop, and grabbed the bottle of wine for a top-up.

41

Chapter 5

'*What's new, Pussycat, woah-ah woah-ah woah-ohhh*!' Jess sang softly, reaching down the side of the bed to stroke Alfie's head as she read her morning text. Thanks to Mel's early starts, it was usually waiting on her phone when her alarm went off at 7.45 a.m.

> **Mel: What's new, Pussycat?**
>
> Since yesterday at 7 p.m. approx, when
> we wibbly-wobbled out of the pub?
> Not much. Good luck with your work
> meetingy thingy thing though! xxx

Picking up her cigarettes from their spot on her bedside table and giving the packet a firm shake, she drew a cigarette out with her teeth and lit it with her pink plastic lighter. Then she grabbed her ashtray – the blue Foster's Lager one she'd nicked from the Bush as a souvenir on No Smokes Eve, the night before the smoking ban – and balanced it on her chest.

Inhaling deeply, she popped her lips and blew a wonky smoke blob towards the ceiling, which was covered in yellowing swirls of Artex.

Scrolling through Twitter and Facebook, allowing herself her usual five minutes to warm up to the idea of being awake, Jess stubbed her cigarette out, swung her legs over the side of the bed with a groan and pushed her feet into a pair of slippers shaped like giant, fluffy unicorn heads.

These had been a gift from Mel: since Jess had voiced her theory that grown women who love unicorns and mermaids need to seriously reconsider their life choices, it had been Mel's single-minded aim in life to make sure every item Jess possessed was covered in them. By now, she looked like the world's biggest mermaids-and-unicorns fan, and had to sheepishly admit to herself that she actually really liked them now that they reminded her of Mel.

In her hand, her phone buzzed to life again.

Tom: See you later. Looking forward to our date! xxx

Jess tutted and smiled. Tom had absolutely zero chill when it came to dating. Surely the men in New York would at least *try* to feign indifference towards the many women they were simultaneously bonking in order to look sexy and hard to get? Nate had got the hot-unavailable-young-buck act down to a tee, but with Tom, what you saw was what you got, and he was about as hard to get as herpes.

Making sure her reply was strictly neutral – she was *excellent* at New York dating – she added a kiss without thinking, before hastily deleting it.

Heading into the kitchen, Alfie trotting at her feet, Jess went through the motions of her regular morning routine: opening the back door so Alfie could bound out into her flat's tiny shared garden, and emptying a tin of posh dog food, which she'd been unable to resist due to the pooch on the front looking just like Alfie, into his bowl.

Next, she unwound the sock she kept wrapped around the tap to stop it dripping, filled and put the kettle on, and added two teaspoons of coffee and three of sugar to her favourite mug. She'd found it in a charity shop, and it said 'Doug's Mug' on the front, which she thought was hilarious, what with her name not being Doug.

Waiting for the kettle to boil, trying hard not to look or even glance at it out of the corner of her eye (as a kid, she'd taken her nan's insistence that 'a watched kettle never boils' a bit too literally), she pulled open the cereal cupboard.

As she opened the door, a packet of butterscotch Angel Delight fell onto the counter. Maybe this was the cosmos telling her she should eat dessert for breakfast? It wouldn't be the first time. Except Angel Delight took far too long to set, and she had the patience of a saint: the Patron Saint of Impatience.

Pulling out her last two Weetabix (noting that they were actually in date – take that, Nate!), she tipped them into her Tony the Tiger breakfast bowl, flung the empty box into the carrier bag hanging off one of her cupboard doors that served as a recycling bin, and covered them in milk.

Tearing open the Angel Delight, she sprinkled the whole lot with butterscotch-flavoured powder, before adding a handful of pink and white mini marshmallows from the open bag on the counter – 'For that little *je ne sais quoi*,' she told herself – before pouring her coffee.

Shuffling to the sofa, the gold glittery horns on her slippers wobbling back and forth, she held her mug and cereal bowl in the air to keep them steady, then flumped backwards into the soft cushions.

One benefit of living in a flat furnished at the Landlord's Emporium of Generic Second-Hand Crap was that her ancient sofa had been worn smooth by countless bums, like a much-loved pair of jeans. It was super-soft, like sitting in a big bowl of corduroy-upholstered marshmallows. It also meant she could let Alfie sit there without worrying about him ruining the high-end furnishings.

Gripping her mug between her thighs, she pulled the remote from its usual home – wedged between two of the sofa cushions, among the sweet wrappers she'd shoved down there – and switched on the TV. For once, she was right on time.

'Good morning. It's Friday the thirteenth at eight a.m.,' the presenter said soberly, from her spot on the *BBC Breakfast* sofa. 'Welcome to *Breakfast* with me, Naga Munchetty.' Jess munched her way through her Weetabix as Naga read out news pieces about a cheating politician, a campaign for disability rights, and a lighthearted piece about Morris dancers, which Naga ended with a wink and a wry, 'And let's hope they don't get too much *stick* for it.'

As Jess cleaned her teeth after breakfast, her phone lit up again, with a message from her work WhatsApp group. Originally called 'Work Crap', it had since morphed into a platform devoted to bitching about Maggie behind her back, and was renamed 'The Devil Wears Primark'.

Jasmit: Jess, can you pick up a copy of the
Sun and the Mail on your way in? I think
the Bijou girls have nicked ours again.

Jasmit: Oh, and chocolate. Maggie's already
in a foul mood, and I need extra supplies.

'Marvellous,' Jess muttered as she sent her reply – although Maggie's foul moods and her normal ones tended to be indistinguishable.

Quickly getting ready, she threw on her baggy jeans, belted tightly at her curvy waist, and favourite vintage T-shirt. She added her red Converse, and a long, slouchy cardigan that was the exact same colour as Oscar the Grouch. Tom called it her 'Nana or Nirvana?' look.

After taking Alfie for a trot around the block, stopping off at the patch of grass near her flat that doubled as a park, Jess headed for the Polski Sklep at the end of the road to get Jasmit her chocolate and papers. Pushing the door open, she jumped as the electronic bell above it let out a strangled but ear-splittingly loud buzz, like a dying bee with a megaphone.

Borys, the shopkeeper who never seemed to have a day off – Jess wasn't even sure he had legs as she'd never seen him leave his spot behind the counter – smiled widely as Jess appeared in the doorway.

'Morning,' she saluted, picking up copies of the *Sun* and *Mail* and sliding them onto the counter, before piling three grab bags of Maltesers on top. 'Could you put this on my tab?' she added. 'I get paid soon, but I'm a bit brassic right now. You know – skint.'

'It is possible, but tabs are to be paid one day, yes?' Borys sighed, digging out a notebook from under the counter. 'Initial here, please. And don't forget to pay. My shop has bills too.'

'I promise, Borys,' Jess said, crossing her heart with a forefinger and gathering up the pile of newspapers and sweets in her arms. 'Imagine what I'd do if I couldn't buy any more potato waffles from you?'

'Shop go out of business. Close for ever,' Borys said, seriously. 'You're my best customer for ready meal for one. Plus wine. Lots of scratch cards on pay day. Very lucrative for Borys.'

'OK, Borys, don't rub it in,' Jess muttered, as she headed outside and towards the Tube.

On the escalator, Jess stood behind a woman with a black spaniel puppy with huge brown eyes peering back over her shoulder. From Jess's arms, Alfie poked his nose towards him and wagged his tail in greeting. The puppy had an extremely boopable nose and Jess loved making friends with Tube pooches, but her arms were full of newspapers and dog. After taking Alfie to Hoxton Square, where he pretended to be brave by running quite close to some pigeons, Jess headed towards Aevum House.

Stepping out of the lift into the office, Jess waved hello to Terrence, who sloped past her clutching a cup of tea. 'Morning!' he trilled, before coughing, dropping his voice a couple of octaves, and trying again. 'Ahem. Morning.'

Jasmit appeared to be attempting the splits in front of the photocopier.

'Um, are we OK here?' Jess asked.

'Trying … to reach … Can't … bend,' Jasmit panted, pointing at a pile of paperclips she'd spilled into the carpet.

'This is a terrible idea. Do you want your mucus plug to pop out right here and shoot across the room? Here, take these and let me do that,' Jess said, handing the papers, chocolate and Alfie's lead to Jasmit.

'How the hell do you know about mucus plugs?' Jasmit grimaced. 'I wish I didn't, and I'm the one who's pregnant.'

'I've been reading up,' Jess said, sweeping the paperclips back into the box. 'You know, just in case you go into labour at work. I quite like the idea of being the first person the twins set eyes on. They might imprint on me, like baby ducklings, and you'd have to let me take one home.'

'You are so weird,' Jasmit said, letting Alfie off his lead so he could take up his spot on the fluffy cushion under Jess's desk.

'Eleven! Woop!' someone on the advertising desk cheered as June, who had terrible hay fever, finished a string of sneezes. A smattering of claps rang out as she blew her nose loudly into a tissue.

Back at her desk, Jess opened her laptop. A pink Post-it note fluttered out and landed on the floor by her feet. Jess scooped it up. She'd written it last night before leaving the pub, so she wouldn't forget to chase the email she'd sent to Jasmit.

Ask Jas what to do re: Donna sitch.

Her arms prickled, remembering Alejandro's sleazy overtures.

'Did you see the email I sent you after the interview last night?' Jess asked, crumpling the Post-it up and aiming it at the recycling bin. It bounced off the rim and onto the floor, so she raised her eyebrows meaningfully at Ian, who shook his head. 'They'll be here for the photo shoot soon. What do you think we should do?'

'Nope, I didn't get an email.' Jasmit frowned, double-checking her inbox. 'Is it lurking in your unsent folder with all the other urgent emails you forgot to send?'

'I definitely sent it,' Jess said, shaking her head. 'It was the last thing I did before shutting my laptop. I remember waiting a few moments to make sure it'd gone through.'

Jess opened her sent emails folder and scrolled to the top. And that's where she saw it – her last sent email.

To: Donna Wilson

'Oh no,' Jess muttered, hot and cold panic rippling through her. 'No no no no no ... Oh *shit*, Jas, what do I do?'

'Please tell me you didn't send an email *about* Donna Wilson *to* Donna Wilson,' Jasmit said, the blood draining from her face. 'And if you did, tell me it was about what a wonderful interviewee she was and how fantastic her story is?'

Jess felt queasy. 'It was about her boyfriend trying to touch me up. And the subject line was "Halloween Heifer". Oh god, I think I'm going to be sick.'

'Oh Jesus, Jess,' Jasmit said weakly, looking pale.

'If Maggie finds out she'll totally fire me.'

As Jess rubbed her face with her hands, the doors to the lift pinged open. Ashleigh walked out, followed by a sullen-looking Alejandro and a beaming Donna.

'These two are yours, I presume? I found them in reception completely failing to work out how to use the lifts,' Ashleigh said archly, glaring at Jess and stalking off.

'Thanks, love!' Donna said, smiling at Ashleigh's retreating back. 'What a lovely girl.'

'How have you both been?' Jess asked, trying to appear calm while her heart hammered in her chest. Donna didn't seem to have skin thicker than a rhino, which meant she couldn't have read the email yet. Jess felt a wave of relief. She still had time . . .

'Talking to you about our romance had a bit of an aphrodisiac effect, actually,' Donna giggled. 'We spent most of yesterday afternoon in bed.' From underneath her desk, Alfie let out a sleepy growl.

'That's . . . nice,' Jess managed, shivering at the thought of Alejandro's sleazy willy. 'Let me introduce you to Terrence, the art director, and he'll show you your costumes.'

As she ushered Donna and Alejandro ahead of her, she hissed, 'Phone the IT department,' over her shoulder to Jasmit, who gave a double thumbs up. Which had turned into a double thumbs down by the time Jess led Donna and Alejandro back to the features desk.

Alejandro gave Jasmit a muffled, '*Hola, señorita*,' through a pair of pointy fake teeth.

She ignored him, muttering, 'No luck,' to Jess. 'You'll have to find a way to get to that email before she does.'

'Shall we go down to the studio, then?' Jess said, hoping her chirpiness sounded less fake to Donna than it did to her.

'Ah, this must be our two lovebirds!' Maggie said, suddenly stepping out of her office. She had an uncanny knack of seeming to appear out of nowhere, scaring the bejesus out of everyone, like a charmless vampire.

'Lovely to meet you both,' she said, a weird look on her face that Jess realised was her attempt at a smile. Maggie never expressed genuine joy, unless she was watching YouTube videos of people injuring themselves.

'And what's this?' she added, fingering the wig clutched in Donna's hands as if it was a clump of hair pulled from a drain.

'I'm going to be Elvira! Isn't it exciting?' Donna grinned.

'Yes, isn't it just?' Maggie said, flashing Jess an icy glare that said, *Why isn't she dressed as an egg?*

'It is an honour to meet you,' Alejandro said, slipping his vampire teeth out and grabbing Maggie's hand to kiss it.

'And you,' Maggie simpered. Jess had never seen her trying to flirt before, and it was revolting. 'This is such a pleasure. Which part of Spain are you from, Alejandro? My family have spent so many wonderful holidays there.'

As Alejandro liberally applied his 'charms' to Maggie, presumably because she earned more than Jess and Donna put together, a muffled 'ping' came from the direction of Donna's bag.

'That'll be my reminder to check my lottery numbers,' she said cheerfully, pulling out her phone and tapping on her email app.

Jess froze, and briefly considered staging an accident so she could knock the phone out of Donna's hands. Then she realised she wasn't Sandra Bullock and this wasn't a cheesy romcom: this was actually happening. Although Jess could have sworn everything actually went into slow motion as Donna looked up from her phone, frowning.

'Oh! I never saw this email you sent me, Jess, love. What's it about? I wasn't supposed to bring anything with me, was I?'

'It's nothing,' Jess stuttered, reaching her hand out in the hopeless expectation that Donna might actually give her the phone.

'Hold on. "Halloween Heifer"? What's this?'

Suddenly, the room went very still. From across the desk, Jasmit looked like she was going to faint. Ian's face was frozen in a cringe. As Donna read the email, her cheeks turning pinker, Jess could see Maggie out of the corner of her eye, slowly turning to face her. Even without seeing it, she knew her face looked like thunder.

'Alejandro tried to feel you up? And ... I'm naive, to *put it mildly*?' Donna whispered. 'What is this?'

Jess sat heavily in her chair and put her face in her hands. She waited for Donna to explode, to shout and scream and call her every name under the sun. But what happened next was much, much worse.

She started sobbing.

'Alejandro, tell me this isn't true? Please? You didn't try anything on with this girl, did you?'

Alejandro looked nervous. 'Of course not, *mi amor*!' he said, unconvincingly. 'I would never hurt my love in this way.'

'And Jess? I don't understand,' Donna said, tears spilling down her cheeks. 'I thought you liked me. You were so lovely to me when you came to my flat.'

'I'm sorry,' Jess croaked. 'I do like you. I just ... thought you wouldn't want to know about what happened, that's all. And Halloween Heifer is shorthand for ... something,' she added weakly. Jess wanted to throw up. She'd felt bad enough after convincing herself to hide the truth from Donna. But watching her find out this way was too much to bear.

Jess looked up. The whole office was staring at the features desk. The food editor had pulled out a free packet of popcorn she'd been sent by a PR and torn it open. And, thanks to Jess, Donna looked like her entire world had just been blasted into pieces.

'How dare you treat our valued readers this way, Jess?' Maggie said, stonily. 'I can assure you, Miss Wilson, this isn't the way we do things here at *Real Talk!*' Jasmit stifled a snort. 'I think it goes without saying that you're fired, Jess, effective immediately. You can pack your things right now and get out ... Donna, Alejandro, please step into my office, won't you, and let's see if we can sort this out. We can't let a moron like my *former* senior features writer stand in the way of true love now, can we?'

And, with that, Maggie swept a sobbing Donna and flustered-looking Alejandro into her office and slammed the door.

Chapter 6

After Maggie's office door had stopped reverberating, the office remained silent for a full minute before Rachel broke the tension by stepping obliviously out of the lift, talking loudly on her phone.

'I don't know what you think about it, but I said if he's not prepared to buy her a ring at Tiffany's he might as well go to Costco and have done with it ... Exactly, darling, that's what I said. What next? A buffet at the wedding? She has *got* to put her foot down.'

Looking up, Rachel noticed everyone was staring at her. 'Better go, poppet, I'm at work. I know, right!? *So* cute. We'll catch up at Dean Street. Byeee!' Hanging up, she looked around at everyone's silent faces. 'What's happened? Has someone died?'

'No. I've just destroyed someone's life and been fired,' Jess said, heavily.

Rachel laughed. 'You're joking, right? You haven't really just ... and you haven't actually been ...'

'No joke,' Jasmit interrupted, heaving herself out of her

chair and easing her way to Jess's side of the desk to give her a hug.

'When did this happen? And who's going to write everything if Jess isn't here? I can't do it all on my own,' Rachel gasped, pressing a palm to her chest.

'Or something a bit more supportive, maybe?' Jasmit said, leaning down to squash Jess's head into her newly enormous bosom.

'Of course. I'm sorry, Jess. What a ... shitshow, I suppose.' Rachel looked distraught, and Ian nodded, impressed. Rachel hadn't been heard swearing since Princess Eugenie had rudely married the man she'd had her eye on.

The door behind Jasmit suddenly swung open and Maggie stepped out of her office. 'I'll leave you two to chat,' she said soothingly over her shoulder, before carefully closing the door and hissing, 'What the fuck are you still doing here?' at Jess, who was nestled in Jasmit's cleavage.

'It's only been five minutes, Maggie,' Jasmit said bravely, stroking Jess's hair. 'We need time to adjust.'

'Has it? Those five minutes were the longest of my life. Flirting with that horrible arsehole to persuade him not to go after us for defamation. He seems to know an awful lot about UK privacy laws for a Spaniard. And even if you only slandered him in an email, he can still go after us, seeing as you sent it *to his fucking fiancée*.' Jess lifted her head from Jasmit's chest and put her face in her hands.

'He was practically slobbering at the thought of wringing some more cash out of us, even while what's her name ... the Halloween Heifer, was sitting there wailing. You were right, Jess – he's a nightmare, and she's about as simple as a paint-by-numbers of a grape, but that doesn't make your cock-up OK.'

'I know, I'm so sorry. I can't believe I did that,' Jess said, tears sliding down her face. 'Poor Donna.'

'Poor Donna, my arse – you should be worrying about committing gross misconduct, not about that simpleton. If they decide to go ahead and sue us, the whole magazine could fold. You need to get your stuff and get out. Preferably before those two in my office kiss and make up and start bonking on my desk. She's already making goo-goo eyes at him again. These people . . .'

Shaking her head, Maggie pulled a cigarette out of the packet clutched in her hand, stabbed it between her lips and stormed off, muttering, 'Cretin,' under her breath. Jess wasn't sure whether she meant her, Donna or Alejandro.

'I'm so sorry, Jess,' Jasmit said, looking tearful, which is when Jess realised she was in serious trouble. Jasmit was usually completely unflappable, to the extent that when she'd found out she was expecting twins, she'd simply shrugged and said, 'I've got two tits, haven't I?' But now, she looked distraught.

'So what do I do now?' Jess asked, helplessly. 'Pack my stuff? I don't have anything to put it in.'

Wordlessly, Ian pulled the box he kept his spare gym kit in from under his desk and emptied it onto the floor. 'I know this doesn't help, but here you go mate.' He shrugged. 'Sorry if it smells of sweaty socks.'

'Thanks, Ian,' Jess said miserably.

'There has to be something we can do about this,' Rachel said, her nose turning prettily pink – the closest she ever got to ugly-crying – as Jess reluctantly started filling the box. In went the framed picture of her, Alfie and Mel on her thirtieth birthday, their heads pressed together with Alfie's in the middle, her ZERO FUCKS GIVEN coaster, and the glittery plastic mug she used as a desk tidy that said 'Be More Mermaid' on the side.

'I'm not sure there's anything we can do,' Jess said numbly. 'I fucked up and that's that. So will you all come down the Bush later? I suppose I'm having a leaving do.'

Her friends nodded numbly, watching Jess helplessly as she headed for the lifts, the box balanced on her hip and Alfie's lead looped around her wrist. She gave the office a small wave as she stepped inside and turned to see the doors shutting on their shell-shocked faces.

On the ground floor, she pushed her way through the building's revolving doors and tried to ignore Ashleigh's face, which was alight with the joy of a born gossip who'd assessed Jess's situation in seconds, like an ASOS-clad Terminator, and couldn't wait to spread the news.

Outside, Jess dropped her box on the ground, wincing before she even heard the muffled tinkle of broken glass that told her she'd shattered the photograph of her, Alfie and Mel. Alfie rested his paws on the edge of the box and peered inside, wagging his tail and searching hopefully for treats.

Leaning against the NO SMOKING sign stuck next to the door, she pulled out her cigarettes and lit one, failing as usual to blow even a wonky smoke ring on her first shaky exhale.

Taking a deep breath, she tried not to cry. She was no stranger to being fired – there was the job at the pick 'n' mix sweet shop where she'd been caught refilling the plastic bins with a generous 'One for you, one for me' approach. And the temping role where she'd altered the settings on her technophobe boss's phone so it autocorrected to 'Spank me hard' whenever he typed 'Kind regards'.

But this time, it felt different. She loved this job and had messed it up completely. And she *needed* it, too, if she was ever going to pay Brian the rent she owed. She desperately wanted a drink, and to see Mel, so as she finished off her cigarette she pulled her phone out of her bag.

While she'd been busy getting fired, she'd had a text from her nan, randomly asking if Monty Don was married. And while she was reading it, a text arrived from Tom. At least he'd be sympathetic about her plight, and she could let him know that their romantic dinner had been swapped for a leaving do. Jess swiped open his text.

Tom: I know about the other guy. It's over. I thought we had something special, but I guess not

'Oh, for god's sake,' Jess groaned. Despite her secret hope that Tom and Nate might both decide to ghost her of their own accord, she'd been planning on doing the decent thing and letting them down gently. But apparently, Tom had found out about Nate before she'd had the chance. Which should, technically, be impossible, seeing as neither of them knew the other even existed.

Had they somehow bumped into each other in the street, started talking, and magically worked out that they were shagging the same Jess? It seemed unlikely.

She was also taken aback by how upset he seemed. She'd been trying to keep things strictly casual, but Tom '*thought we had something special*'. She'd never pretended what they had was something it wasn't. But apparently, he was more attached to her than she thought, which made him finding out about Nate feel ten times worse.

Dialling Tom's number, it rang once before he quickly declined the call. Jess pictured JESS DO NOT ANSWER!!! flashing up on his screen and felt a stab of sadness. If she had the chance to find out what had happened, perhaps she could persuade Tom he'd made a mistake. Although, she wondered, why would she even want to change his mind? Shouldn't she be happy that he'd ticked a job off her to-do list?

On her second attempt to phone him, the call went straight to voicemail, and she had to listen to Tom's painfully chirpy answerphone message.

'Hi there! It's Tom! I'm rubbish at answering these things, so drop me a text. Thanks!'

As she hung up without leaving a message, she felt a strange sinking sensation in her chest. One that reminded her of the feeling she got when she realised her takeaway pizza had arrived without any BBQ dip. Was she *disappointed*?

Tom had dumped her, but instead of feeling relieved, she felt guilty for hurting him, and sad that he was avoiding her calls. The thought of never seeing him again or getting to be the Little Spoon while he regaled her with nerdy, but really very interesting, facts made her feel even worse.

So did this mean she actually *liked* Tom?

Well, it's a bit late to realise that now, brain, she thought angrily, crushing her cigarette under her trainer and leaning her cheek against the NO SMOKING sign. It was lovely and cool, but didn't stop her somersaulting brain, heart and stomach battling to win some kind of organ gymnastics.

She'd always enjoyed living her life like it was a demolition derby, never slowing down, cramming as much fun in as she could. Despite having a tendency to let the kinds of things bad people might describe as 'adulting' slide – from her haphazard finances to committing to a relationship for more than five minutes – she'd always avoided serious trouble, surfing above it, untouched by responsibility, and happily telling herself she was winning at life.

But now, thanks to her own carelessness, things had suddenly fallen apart. Dialling Mel's number, Jess sighed as the phone went straight to voicemail, and she remembered today was the day of Mel's Very Big Meeting. Jess knew it had probably gone well, because Mel always landed on her feet.

Well, almost always, Jess thought, wincing as she remembered the night of the accident.

But she also knew how to get her best friend to drop everything with a single message.

'Mel, it's me, I really need your help,' she said, not trying to hide the wobble in her voice. 'Remember, you're my perfect slice of pizza.'

Chapter 7

October 2004, Langley High School

Jess noticed the halo of space around the tall girl waiting with the other kids in the corridor before she noticed Mel herself. Although she didn't want to be caught staring, something about this awkward-looking girl drew her attention. She seemed to be trying to make herself smaller, bringing in her limbs and ducking her head in an effort to force her willowy frame to match the others.

Jess knew exactly how this new face in the sixth form at Langley High felt – like a piece from a puzzle that's found itself in the wrong box. At primary school, Jess had fallen out with her best friend, Amy. They'd always vowed to stand by each other no matter what – sealed with a pinkie promise, the most solemn pact any eight-year-old girl can make.

But as soon as one of the most popular girls in school had invited Amy to a sleepover, erasing Jess from the equation, she'd been unceremoniously ditched.

It meant that while everyone else had entered Year Seven

with their best friends in tow, Jess had been on her own. And she'd soon discovered that, while being raised by your dear old nan didn't mean much in primary school, when it came to being cool enough to make new friends in high school, it was a different matter.

She and her nan, Pamela, watched things like *Gardeners' World* rather than *The Simpsons*, so Jess felt excluded from her classmates' conversations. They never went on posh holidays to Center Parcs, or to France to stock up on duty-free booze, and they were locked in a constant battle about when Jess would be old enough to graduate from wearing a training bra.

'If you're not flashing your bazongas to every Tom, Dick and Harry, what does it matter?' was Pamela's sympathetic stance on the subject.

Although Jess wasn't bullied, she was ignored, which almost felt worse. After five years of negotiating school without a best friend by her side, she'd almost forgotten how it felt to have someone in her corner other than her nan. Who, let's face it, was kind of obliged to love her.

Even her sixteenth birthday two weeks earlier had been spent watching TV with a takeaway pizza, rather than at a party with her friends. But now, as Jess watched Mel sloping into the classroom, looking awkward, bemused and slightly terrified, she saw a glimmer of hope.

Through some casual stalking, she discovered that Mel was a promising young runner and had won a few local tournaments. She'd chosen to transfer to Langley High thanks to its prestigious sports programme, which had even turned out a few famous faces. Jess also discovered that Mel liked to smoke on her way home from running practice – which seemed a bit crazy to her, what with running involving your lungs and everything.

But at least now she had a way in. Buying a packet of Marlboro Lights, she tried one before realising they were disgusting and giving up after two puffs. Then, switching her usual lunchtime reading spot from the steps outside the sports hall's fire exit to the bench outside the PE changing rooms, she finally plucked up the courage to collar Mel at the end of one of her training sessions.

'Do you smoke?' she blurted, holding her long hair awkwardly in bunches at either side of her head as Mel paused beside Jess to adjust her shoelaces. She was wearing a long black dress with rose-gold brogues, which were the coolest things Jess had ever seen.

As Mel glanced up, Jess noticed how blue her eyes were behind her wire-rimmed glasses. Her brown hair was cut into a shoulder-length bob, with a fringe that brushed her eyebrows, and she wasn't wearing any make-up.

'Yeah. Maybe. Who's asking?' Mel said, straightening up and cocking her head at this strangely forward but nervous-looking girl with thick, long reddish-brown hair, dark-brown eyes, and jeans so baggy they threatened to swallow her up.

'Me ... me is asking. I just wondered if you fancied hanging out. I'm not, like, a honeytrap sent by your running coach or anything, I promise.' Mel snorted, and Jess couldn't tell if she was laughing with her or at her. 'Meet you after school, outside the gates?' she finished, feeling like a quiz contestant about to find out whether she'd blown her chance to win a million pounds.

'Sure.' Mel nodded once, and shrugged her backpack onto her shoulder.

Jess felt wobbly with relief. She didn't know until later that as Mel walked towards her history class, she'd had to will herself not to look back, in case this potential new friend decided she wasn't worth talking to after all.

Like Jess, Mel had pretended that her social exile didn't bother her, but it hurt more than she let on. She'd also noticed this strange kid staring at her when she thought she wasn't looking and had been intrigued. Although Mel was one of the sporty kids, she thought all the others were a bit dull. Jess looked far more interesting – and didn't smell of mud and sweaty polyester.

Jess, of course, didn't know all this yet, so she was happily surprised to see Mel waiting for her when she left her English literature class after the last bell rang, playing keepy-uppy with a pine cone.

'I'm Jess,' she said.

'Mel.'

'Park?'

'Sure.'

They headed for the swings in the park that sat on the steep hill running down from the school towards town. Finding them occupied by some teenage boys who were spinning around, trying to plait the metal chains right to the top, they decamped on the empty roundabout instead.

Parking their rucksacks in the middle, Jess sat cross-legged in one of the roundabout's four quarters, her knees hanging over the edge, while Mel sat in the quadrant beside hers and stretched her long legs out, using her heels to gently propel them around.

'So what do you think of Langley then? Shit, innit?' Jess started.

64

'It would be OK if it wasn't for the people and the lessons and the break times. And the buildings,' Mel said.

Jess snorted. 'What were the kids like at your old school?'

'Pretty much the same as here. Only I had friends over there. I didn't really notice all the cliques and stuff when I was in one, but I guess there were kids hovering on the outside there too. I just wasn't one of them, so I didn't care.' Mel looked troubled.

'Do you still see your old mates?'

'If I'm not at school, I'm training, or Mum and Dad are forcing veg down me and making me have an early night. Most of my friends are into sports, so they're always training too. I mostly saw them on the track, so not really. How about you? What made you break the unspoken rule to not talk to the new kid? Didn't your mum teach you never to speak to strangers?'

'I was brought up by my nan, actually. She was a pretty good bringer-upperer though. Just don't try to lure me into your car with poisoned sweets and feel me up, and I reckon we'll be OK.'

Mel laughed. Embarrassed, Jess leaned forward and started weaving tiny plaits into her hair. Why did this feel so much like the times she'd tried to talk to boys?

'What about cigs?' Mel said, raising her eyebrows and peering at Jess through the curtain of her hair. 'Technically they're already a poison, so they don't count. And I promise not to touch you up. Pinkie promise.'

Jess laughed, and started to relax. Reaching into her backpack, Mel pulled out a packet of cigarettes and placed one between her lips.

She waved the carton in Jess's direction, and she eyed them

warily. 'Thanks,' she said, trying to sound confident as she plucked one out and stuck it in the corner of her mouth. Mel leaned over and lit Jess's and then her own with a pink disposable lighter. Jess inhaled hard, then immediately descended into a coughing fit.

'Not a real smoker, then?' Mel laughed, waving at the blue plume of smoke that had grown between them.

'Give me time,' Jess said, sticking out her tongue in the vain hope that fresh air would cleanse it. 'So have any of the delicious Langley dicks caught your eye yet?'

'You're kidding, aren't you?' Mel said, stopping the roundabout with her feet and gesturing to the boys on the swings. They were the same age as Jess and Mel, and had abandoned trying to break the swings in favour of trying to smash each other in the face with them. 'It's horrifying that those twats are actually old enough to get married. They'll be driving in a year. I mean, Jesus. I wouldn't let them near me.'

'Some of them are fit though,' Jess pouted. 'The one over there with the blood on his face and the spiky brown hair is Craig Thomas. He's in my drama class and really funny.'

'Funny. Is that it?'

'Well, he's quite clever, too.'

'By that, do you just mean not completely thick?'

'I suppose,' Jess frowned. She'd never thought about expecting more than that of boys before. Mel began spinning the roundabout with her heels again. Jess leaned down and trailed her fingers against the springy tarmac, grabbing any tiny pebbles in her way as she floated past and piling them beside her.

'I need more than that,' Mel said, leaning back on her elbows. 'I've got this theory that to find the right person for you, you've got to think of them like a pizza.'

66

'What? Doughy and thick, with a crusty cheesy knob? Gross.'

Mel yelped with laughter. 'No! You pick your three basic essentials, which are like the cheese and tomato and dough, see? They're the things that make a pizza *pizza*, that you can't do without. Like for me, it's someone who's laid-back, funny, and into sports and stuff like I am.'

'In that case, mine are good hair, funny and kind,' Jess said, arranging her pile of stones into a smiley face.

'No no,' Mel said, sitting up straighter. 'Nice hair can be one of your toppings – three things you'd like, but aren't totally essential. Like, if Matt out of Busted had shit hair, you wouldn't say no, would you?'

Jess wrinkled her nose. 'I'm more of a Charlie Simpson kind of girl, to be honest.'

'OK, OK. Well, if *he* had shit hair then. What I'm saying is, good hair isn't as essential as, say, being a nice person. You don't want someone who's racist, or hates puppies, do you, even if their hair is amazing?'

'Definitely not,' Jess agreed. 'OK, I'll go for funny, nice, and into the same music as me. I couldn't date anyone who didn't agree that "Year 3000" is a total banger.'

'Fair enough. So, once you've picked the ingredients for your basic pizza, you choose your three toppings, which can include stuff like good hair – the things you quite fancy at the moment but aren't make-or-break, like pepperoni, or mushrooms.'

'Oh, Jesus. Who puts mushrooms on pizza?' Jess said, wrinkling her nose. Mel laughed, and Jess felt a warm glow spreading through her chest. 'I think you might be a genius,' she added, taking another reluctant puff of her cigarette. The nicotine, coupled with the spinning of the roundabout, was making her feel a bit sick. She flicked her cigarette onto the asphalt, laid down, and watched the sky revolving above her. Lifting her feet, Mel joined her, their hair mingling in the middle of the roundabout.

'So how come you're not in any of the school gangs?' Mel asked. 'Did you move here from somewhere else too?'

'Nah. I fell out with my best friend in primary school. She went off with one of the popular kids, and apparently I was too fat to be in their gang. And not enough of a slag, I reckon.'

'Ohh, *burn*.' Mel grinned. 'Which one is she? Do I know her?'

'I think you're in her history class, actually. Although I definitely wasn't stalking you. Amy Amstell.'

'The one with the gross whale tail, who thinks having good hair is the same as having a personality?' Mel laughed. 'I might have to rethink talking to you if she's your type.'

'She was all right before she got tits,' Jess said, defensively.

Mel laughed, a proper, throaty bark, and Jess grinned to herself. She knew that today had changed everything. She finally had a friend – one who already felt like she was Jess's perfect slice of pizza.

And from today, she vowed to do everything she could to keep her.

Chapter 8

'Twice in two days? And before lunchtime, too. To what do I owe the pleasure?' Mark said, raising his eyebrows as Jess pushed open the door to the Bush and slapped her cardboard box down onto the bar. 'Ah,' he said, peering into the box, and assessing the tell-tale signs of being unceremoniously fired. 'White wine?'

'Yes, please, Mark. In fact, I'm in the market for an entire waterfall of booze to make me feel better,' Jess said, as Mark reached for an unopened bottle of house white. 'Not only have I been fired after ruining someone's life, I've been dumped. *Dumped!* Me! Can you believe it?'

'It's a shocker, all right,' Mark said, holding a wine glass up to the light and giving it a quick polish with a tea towel. 'Which one was it? The Paddington-looking guy who always orders blue WKD?'

Jess nodded, hoiking herself onto a barstool and looping Alfie's lead around one of the handbag hooks above her knees. From behind the bar, John Travolta gave Jess a sideways peace sign as he danced intently to 'You Never Can Tell' at Jack Rabbit Slim's.

'I assume Mel's on her way?' Mark asked. Jess looked anxiously at her phone. It was almost midday and she hoped that Mel's meeting – what was it, something boring about budgets? – would be over soon.

It was 12.15 p.m., after Jess had already had a few too many white wines, by the time Mel called back. It sounded like she was outside, and Jess could hear a bus engine idling in the background.

'Sorry I didn't answer, I was tied up,' Mel said, her voice raised over the sound of traffic. 'What's up, are you OK?'

'Not really. I kind of got fired. And dumped. And I could really do with a chat. If you're not too knackered.'

'Are you mucking me about? What the hell, Jess?'

'I told you it was urgent. I wouldn't invoke the Perfect Pizza Slice Code of Calamity otherwise, would I?' Jess said. 'Please?'

'Of course,' Mel said, sighing. 'I'll hop in an Uber and be there in half an hour.'

'Before I say this, I want you to know I totally love you, OK? But you do also know you're an absolutely enormous idiot, right?'

'I do know! I'm totally that absolutely enormous idiot!' Jess wailed, looking up from the beer mat that she was carefully peeling into layers. Then flinched, as a balled-up paper napkin flew past her face from behind and landed in Mel's drink.

'Shit, sorry, girls!' a group of boys across the pub called, snickering.

'Grow up, dickheads!' Jess snapped, plucking it niftily out of Mel's glass. Mel looked at her wine dubiously.

'Three-second rule,' Jess shrugged, poking the glass towards her encouragingly.

Mel and Jess were huddled in their seat upstairs by the window, their bags and jackets dumped in a careless pile, and Mel's cane leaning against the sill. A bag of pickled onion Monster Munch was torn open in the centre of the table, between two half-drunk glasses of wine, and Alfie was curled beneath it, lapping happily at a bowl of water.

Already, Jess felt ten times better about her disastrous day, having shared it with Mel. They had a knack for making each other laugh through even the gloomiest disasters – although, admittedly, Mel had to deploy this talent a bit more often.

Sometimes, Jess felt like the portrait in the attic to Mel's Dorian Gray. They'd started out at the same place, but as Mel's life became more grown-up and successful, Jess's seemed to descend even further into chaos.

'You've absolutely got to start checking who you're sending stuff to before hitting Send,' Mel said. 'Remember when you texted me about your ex's dick and sent it to him by accident?'

'He was so angry, but it was all true!' Jess laughed. 'It was seriously *so* tiny. It was like being glared at by a furious, one-eyed cocktail sausage whenever he took his pants off.'

'And you say Tom dumped you, too? What happened there?'

'He says he found out about "the other guy". Which I presume means Nate. I have no idea how, though.'

Mel shifted in her seat. 'Weren't you going to get rid of them both eventually anyway? Problem solved, surely?'

'Well, yes, but here's the weird thing,' Jess said, as earnestly as if she'd discovered gravity. 'Once Tom said it was over, I was actually upset. It's like when you can't choose between two dishes on a menu, and you genuinely think it's a fifty-fifty choice. Like, if it's pulled pork macaroni cheese versus a bacon cheeseburger. That's a totally level playing field, right?'

'My equivalent would probably be avocado toast versus poached eggs, but I get the gist.'

Jess tutted fondly. 'But then if, as soon as you order one of your options you feel disappointed, you know it's because your brain secretly wanted the other thing, right? I'm pretty sure I wouldn't be bothered in the slightest if it had been Nate wailing about another guy and dumping me. Not that he would, to be honest. He's so laid back he's practically horizontal. So do you think maybe my brain secretly wanted to carry on dating Tom?'

'What, like he's a delicious bowl of macaroni cheese?'

Jess considered for a moment, then nodded.

Mel groaned and sank her head into her hands. 'Oh, Jess. Why do you have to be so . . . *Jess* about everything?'

'As far as I'm concerned, "being Jess about everything" means being absolutely awesome absolutely all of the time. But I've got a funny feeling you don't mean it like that.'

'You know what I mean,' Mel said, looking terribly serious all of a sudden. 'Keeping people at arm's-length. Mucking stuff up if it looks like you might have to commit to literally anything for more than a nanosecond. And all the while telling yourself that's the way you want things to be.'

'I didn't muck things up on purpose, though, did I?' Jess said, stubbornly, picking at a patch of scuffed varnish on the table. 'I've only just realised I might like Tom properly, rather than just as part of my amazing dating experiment. I mean, my ideal man shaves with sandpaper, chops wood and wrestles bears, and Tom's got a moisturising regime, for Christ's sake. When we order pizza, he scrapes off the toppings and eats them first, *then* the dough. He's hardly Desperate Dan, so it's no big surprise that I didn't have him earmarked as Mr Right, is it?'

'The thing is, it was pretty obvious to everyone but you that you liked Tom. You talk about him *way* more than the other guy.'

'Only about how annoying he is. He's such a nerd, always spouting facts at me. He's all, "Did you know selfies are more dangerous than sharks?"; I mean, *really.*'

'Come on. If you hate his special facts so much, how come you're always relaying them back to me? You love that about him really. All I know about Nate is that he's incredibly sexy and makes your vag tremble—'

'They're called fanny flutters, actually.'

'—but I know plenty about Tom because you're always talking about him. Even Jas managed to work out that you secretly like him, even though her bladder was being used as a football by two foetuses at the time.'

'You know I hate people talking about me behind my back,' Jess scowled.

'It wasn't anything we wouldn't have told you in person. Which I'm doing right now, you muppet. We could just see that you liked Tom. Like, properly liked him. And he liked you too.'

'How do you know that?'

'Never mind that for now. I just do. But I knew that you liking him and him liking you back meant you'd probably sabotage it somehow.'

'Reminder: not my fault he found out about Nate,' Jess said, trying to hide behind her wine glass by taking an unnecessarily long sip.

'Weren't you about to dump both of them? That doesn't exactly smack of devotion, does it?'

Jess opened her mouth, thought better of it, and closed it again.

'Look, I'm not going to have a go at you on your worst day ever,' Mel said, reaching over and holding Jess's hand, 'but maybe just think about what you're doing with your life. Everyone wants you to be happy, but sometimes you're your own worst enemy. You're so busy running away from responsibility, you forget that there's a reason people choose to have things like savings accounts and stable jobs and committed relationships.'

'Oh, oh, I know this one ... Is it because they're old and crusty and have decided to abandon fun for ever?'

'Charming,' Mel said. She let out a laugh, but as she took a sip of wine, Jess could see she looked hurt.

'Sorry, that was out of order,' she said, squeezing Mel's hand. 'You're not old and crusty, and you haven't abandoned fun. You're the best. And of course, I totally love you and Aya. You're the cutest couple ever.'

'Oh my god, you don't have to go that far. I know you're not Aya's biggest fan.'

Mel was right: even though they'd been together for nearly fifteen years, Jess had never taken to Mel's girlfriend. A gorgeous and fiercely intelligent paediatrician with a thing for reality TV shows and an acerbic sense of humour, Jess could *technically* see what Mel saw in Aya. But she still found herself rebelling against the fact that they were expected to get along, simply because they both loved the same person. Aya was just so perfect, and so *annoying*. But Jess would never have risked hurting Mel by telling her that in a million years.

'I am! You're great, she's great. You're both great. What's not to like?' Jess grinned and waggled her eyebrows. Mel laughed again, more genuinely this time.

'Thank you for pretending, anyway. She really is lovely, you know. And she makes me happy. And she likes you, for some reason. God knows why. So whether you like the idea or not, here's to you joining the Old And Crusty Club.'

'If I can persuade Tom to take me back,' Jess said.

Mel held up her glass, and Jess clinked hers gently against it. As she sipped her wine, her phone lit up on the table between them. It was an 0208 number, which meant it was a London landline.

'Do you think it's Tom calling to say he's made a terrible mistake and wants me back immediately?' Jess asked, peering at her phone suspiciously.

'It's probably a robot telling you you've been in a car accident that wasn't your fault, but there's only one way to find out,' Mel said, reaching over and hitting the answer button.

'Tom, is that you?' Jess said, glaring at Mel and switching on speakerphone so she could join in.

'It's not Tom, actually, it's Brian,' the voice at the other end said.

Jess felt herself turning hot and cold. Hadn't she suffered enough already today, without being cornered by Brian?

As far as Jess was concerned, the right of Millennials to avoid people they didn't want to talk to on the phone, especially their rent-chasing landlords, should be enshrined in law. But Brian had tricked her into answering, so it was a bit late now.

'Glad I've caught you. You've been avoiding my calls, haven't you? Look, I'm sure you're a lovely girl, Jess, but it's been two months and I really need your rent money, so I'm sorry, but I'm going to have to ask you to leave the flat.'

'Oh, hi Brian, I, er, I've just been a bit tight on money lately, you know,' she said, her voice rising to a panicked squeak. 'What with the ... thing, and the ... stuff. But I'll get it to you by the end of the week. Pinky promise.'

'Unfortunately, I'm not an eight-year-old girl, so pinky promises aren't much use to me, Jess,' Brian said, with a sigh. 'What *is* of use to me is your contract, which states that you have to pay me your rent on time otherwise you have to move out. So I'm afraid this is your notice. You've got a month to pack up your things and find another landlord to plague.'

'But I've just lost my job! What am I supposed to do without a job or a flat?'

'If you've lost your job it seems even more unlikely that you'll be paying me the money you owe any time soon, doesn't it?'

'Rats,' Jess muttered.

Across the table, Mel mouthed *'Fuuuuuck!'* in solidarity.

'I'm sorry, Jess. But my decision is final.'

Brian hung up the phone, and Jess rested her forehead on the table, groaning.

'What am I going to do, Mel? And what the hell's going on? I woke up this morning all happy – tra-la-la, twiddly-dee, isn't life special? – and now I've lost a man I've only just realised I actually like, I'm jobless, and I've just been kicked out of my flat by a landlord who definitely doesn't deserve his rent money as much as Alfie deserves Mr Fluffy's All-Organic Dog Delight for dinner. I know I like life to be exciting, but this is more like a car-crash than the rollercoaster I ordered.'

'Oh, Jess. I don't want to be *that* guy, but I thought you set up a direct debit ages ago? You promised.'

'I know, I know. But then I had a credit card bill to pay off. Then Instagram tempted me with the most *amazing* dog bed – it's printed all over with little bones! And by the time I remembered to set up a payment for my rent, I didn't have enough money to cover it. I hoped Brian might be rich enough to forget about it. You know, like the way we might forget about a fiver in our jeans' pocket, only a bit bigger.'

'Well, that worked fantastically, didn't it?' Mel said gently, putting her hand on Jess's arm as she lifted her head. 'I'll get more drinks in, shall I?' Standing up, she winced as she drew her bad leg out from underneath the table.

Jess thought she couldn't possibly feel any worse, but as the memory of Mel's accident suddenly slammed into her chest, she felt sick. 'Over my dead body,' she said, forcing herself to sound upbeat. 'You've listened to me wanging on about myself for ages. This is my round. And then you can tell me all about your day. I haven't even asked how that meeting went yet.'

'There's not much to tell,' Mel said quickly. 'We got a bol-locking over talent contracts. Apparently we mucked a few of them up. Nothing massive, but it wasn't great, to be honest. I might have to go home after these, if that's OK, and leave you to your leaving do – I'm exhausted.'

'I thought the meeting was about budgets? Bit harsh to spring stuff about contracts on you too, isn't it?'

'They did mention budgets as well,' Mel said vaguely.

Jess frowned, but decided not to push it. Now she mentioned it, Mel did look pretty tired.

At the bar, Jess ordered a shot of tequila – which she quickly downed while Mark poured two new glasses of wine – and wiped away the tear that was suddenly sliding down her face.

All the tiny cracks in her life that, until today, she'd happily papered over, had started yawning wide open – too wide for her to fix in her usual slapdash fashion. After years of doing whatever she wanted, she'd found herself broken at the bottom of a dark pit, with no idea how to get out of it.

There was no doubt that Friday the thirteenth had been the worst day of her life – the worse one since Mel's accident, at least – and she couldn't wait to wake up on Saturday morning and put it all behind her.

Chapter 9

'No, no, no, no *no!*' Jess yelled, grabbing her phone from her bedside table and turning off the alarm. 'It's *Saturday*! And it's seven-bloody-forty-five! Why are you waking me up on a Saturday, you terrible piece of garbage?' From his spot beside her bed, Alfie let out a sleepy 'woof' of solidarity.

Laying back down, Jess pressed her pillow over her face. She'd been looking forward to as long a lie-in as was humanly possible this morning, to delay the moment when she'd have to face up to the collapse of her life the day before.

But, instead, her phone had treacherously chosen to add insult to injury by letting out a chirpy tune like a psychotic ice-cream van at 7.45 a.m., when she always had her alarm switched off at weekends. She wasn't even hungover enough to drop back to sleep, which was pretty miraculous in itself, considering the amount of wine she'd drunk the night before.

'Urgh,' Jess said from under her pillow, as she started remembering what had happened.

Mel had waited for Jasmit, Rachel, Terrence and Ian to arrive for Jess's impromptu leaving-slash-YOU'RE-FIRED!

do before hugging her tight and heading home. After a couple more drinks, Jess had started complaining swearily about the Bush's lack of lifts, Brian's meanness, Tom's unreasonableness, the Bush's lack of lifts again, and Maggie being a 'big horrible mean bitchy bitch'.

In between rants, she was also fairly sure she'd sent some inadvisable texts to both Brian and Maggie. Reluctantly emerging from underneath her pillow, she picked up her phone and expertly slid the charger out of the bottom with one hand, congratulating herself on actually remembering to plug it in before she fell asleep. Then she made a cave out of her duvet, ducked inside it, and opened her apps to see how bad the damage was.

Except her phone appeared to be totally banjaxed.

The most recent text on her phone was Mel's message from yesterday morning showing up as unread again.

Mel: What's new, Pussycat?

The rest of her message apps had deleted everything from the past twenty-four hours.

'Where are my texts? You have got to be kidding me? Give them up, you pathetic piece of crap,' Jess said, reaching out a hand and banging the back of her phone against the bed frame. Opening her emails, she realised they'd been wiped too.

Perhaps it was fitting that Jess's phone had turned against her, seeing as the rest of her life had completely fallen apart, but it was seriously bad timing. She urgently needed to find out how much worse she'd made things while she was busy being drunk the night before. But the chance to sift through her texts looking for evidence of bad decisions, like a hungover Columbo in novelty slippers, had been taken away from her.

Why did technology always choose to let you down when it mattered the most, like a flaky friend you don't even like much? Like the time Jess printed off a job application at work, and the printer got jammed. The inky little snitch had chosen to spew the letter out an hour after she'd hit Print, just as her boss was passing, and she'd been caught red-handed.

Lifting the duvet off her head with a dramatic sigh, she decided to make the most of this temporary digital amnesia. Maybe it was better that she didn't know the level things had escalated to the night before so she could comfortably ignore her problems for a few moments more. If she tried hard enough, she could even pretend Friday had never happened at all.

Nudging her phone off the edge of the mattress, she let it slither onto the thinning carpet below with a hollow thunk, and was greeted by an outraged bark.

'Sorry, Alfie!' Jess said, leaning over the bed and letting him lick her face. He woofed, clearly hungry for his breakfast, and Jess decided she might as well get up, now she was already awake. With so much running through her brain, she had no chance of nodding off again.

Easing her legs off the edge of the bed, she concentrated hard on her head, waiting for it to explode. 'Easy, boy,' she muttered, as if her cranium were a jittery horse.

She felt surprisingly clear-headed so far, but the hangover she so richly deserved was definitely coming. She wondered if she was still drunk, which wouldn't be surprising after the number of shots she'd ploughed through last night, after deciding wine was an inferior alcohol-delivery system when it came to speed.

As she gently wiggled her head back and forth, testing its delicacy, her phone buzzed into life again.

Jess's stomach leapt – it was a text from Tom. Maybe he'd decided to give her a second chance after sleeping on it?

Opening the message, she frowned.

Tom: See you later. Looking forward to our date! xxx

'Oh, you have got to be kidding me,' Jess muttered. If her broken phone was going to drip-feed her yesterday's texts, forcing her to relive the worst day of her life in real time, it was going to find itself swiftly hoofed out of the window. Pushing her feet into her fluffy unicorn slippers, Jess shuffled into the kitchen, threw open the kitchen door, and filled Alfie's food bowl. Then she unwound the sock she kept wrapped round the tap to stop it dripping, filled and put the kettle on, and added two teaspoons of coffee and three of sugar to her Doug's Mug mug.

As the kettle boiled, she realised she'd have to pop to Borys's shop for breakfast later – or, even better, get Deliveroo to bring her a delicious sausage and egg McMuffin – because buying more Weetabix hadn't exactly been her top priority the day before. Sipping her coffee and wincing at its bitter sweetness, Jess shuffled into the living room and pulled the TV remote out from where it was jammed in between the sofa cushions. She'd never watched telly at the unholy hour of 8 a.m. on a Saturday before, but assumed they aired cartoons for parents to dump their kids in front of, and repeats of *Antiques Roadshow* to cater for people like her nan, who thought getting up after 5 a.m. was for 'lazy wankers'. (Pamela was from the East End, and what you might call 'salt of the earth'.)

But instead, Naga Munchetty appeared onscreen to read the news. 'Good morning. It's Friday the thirteenth at eight a.m.,' she said soberly. 'Welcome to *Breakfast* with me, Naga Munchetty.' Jess frowned. Had Naga just got the date wrong? Surely not, what with her having a brain the size of a planet?

'It's Saturday, Naga. SAT-UR-DAY,' Jess told the TV, waiting for the presenter to correct herself and apologise. But instead, she carried on talking, and gradually, Jess realised she was watching yesterday's news again. She'd always assumed *BBC Breakfast* was shown live, but perhaps they recorded it and had started playing the wrong tape?

'You're going *down*,' she told the TV, feeling oddly pleased that someone at the BBC had cocked things up, just like she'd done yesterday. She couldn't help but feel solidarity with this invisible stranger, who was definitely also getting fired this week.

Curious to see how long the mistake would last, she finished off her coffee while watching Naga end a lighthearted story about Morris dancers with a wink and a cheeky, 'And let's hope they don't get too much *stick* for it,' for the second day in a row.

'I wonder what today will bring,' Jess asked the TV out loud. 'Probably nothing exciting. I'm sure Friday thirteenth will be just fucking *wonderful*.'

Heading to Twitter, Jess scrolled through her timeline to see what everyone else was saying about the BBC's 'blunder', as the tabloid feeds would be calling it. But, like the rest of her apps, her Twitter feed was broken, still spewing out yesterday morning's posts.

Jess grabbed her laptop bag. Hopefully it was just her phone that was playing up rather than the entire internet and she could moan about it on Facebook. Because if something in your life goes wrong and you can't write a cryptic status update about it, has it even really happened?

She wasn't quite ready to tell the world about being fired, dumped and evicted all in one day, which at this stage was still a freshly wounding and hugely embarrassing car crash, rather than the hilarious story it would eventually become. But a bit of sympathy wouldn't go amiss, and these days a broken phone was greeted with more horror on social media than a broken leg.

As she took out her laptop and opened the lid, a bright-pink Post-it note fluttered off her keyboard and onto the floor. Bending down and snatching it up between her fingertips, she frowned as she read the message scrawled on the piece of paper in her hands.

Then she yelped like it was burning her fingers and dropped it on the floor.

Chapter 10

Ask Jas what to do re: Donna sitch.

The words were written in Jess's own handwriting, as clear as day. The note she'd screwed up and thrown away yesterday morning was, somehow, back inside her laptop again.

'I'm going mad,' Jess muttered, before remembering that talking to yourself is the first sign of madness. Taking a deep breath and shakily wiping her face with the hem of her T-shirt, Jess wracked her brain – something she was never usually required to do so early in the morning.

Nothing was making any sense. She stared at the note and then at the TV, willing an apologetic producer to make an announcement about running the wrong tape of the morning news. Jess felt a horrible prickling sensation at the back of her neck that ran all the way down her spine.

Powering up her laptop, she checked the BBC and Sky news, Facebook, Twitter, and dateandtime.com. And they all said the same thing: it was Friday 13th August.

This wasn't one of those moments where you wake up and

think it's Saturday for one brief moment before sulkily realising it's actually Monday. Yesterday had *definitely* been Friday, and although Jess wasn't sure if this was a time travel thing or a haywire-brain thing, something was definitely very wrong.

Taking a deep breath, she put her laptop down, walked into the kitchen and opened the cereal cupboard, sending a packet of butterscotch Angel Delight tumbling out onto the counter. She leapt away from it as if it might bite her.

Her heart pounding angrily in her chest, she stuffed it into the back of the cupboard and pulled out the Weetabix box, which had reappeared in the cupboard too. Inside were the last two biscuits she remembered eating yesterday.

'Fuck off! Just fuck off!' she yelled, throwing the box into the corner of the kitchen and slamming the cupboard door.

Suddenly feeling sick, she raced to the bathroom. Leaning over the toilet, her mouth filled with saliva, and she retched into the bowl. Rubbing her sweaty forehead with a shaky hand, she sat on the cool, tiled bathroom floor, her back against the bath. Alfie trotted in, gave a gentle whine, and curled up on the bathroom rug next to her. Stroking his head, Jess tried to concentrate.

She'd certainly experienced her fair share of weird hangover side effects in the past. One morning, her hangxiety kicked in so hard that she became convinced a dream she'd had about losing all her teeth was real, and she had to keep running to the mirror to check they were still in her head. But this ... This was something else entirely.

Had she somehow *dreamt* yesterday? Conjured up an entire day before it had even happened? And, if so, did this mean she hadn't actually been fired or dumped? Maybe it was some kind of warning, or premonition?

Urging herself to focus, she thought back to the day before. If today really was Friday 13th, yesterday must have been a dream. It was the only thing that made sense, but it had all been so vivid. She remembered tiny details no one would bother dreaming about, like forgetting to check there was enough loo roll when she went for a wee at work and having to use the cardboard tube, split in half lengthways, instead.

Then there were Tom and Mel's texts. They'd used the same words yesterday, and their messages had arrived at exactly the same time as yesterday, too. If it was all just a dream, how come the real Friday 13th was unfurling exactly the same way as she'd predicted?

She'd once seen a film about a man who was going through a very bad, slightly trippy day, and it turned out he was actually in a coma. Jess shivered at the thought that something like that might be happening to her, even though everything around her seemed totally real. Easing herself off the bathroom floor with shaky legs, Jess ran the cold tap and threw water in her face.

She jumped as her phone buzzed into life on the side of the sink with a text from The Devil Wears Primark WhatsApp group.

> **Jasmit: Jess, can you pick up a copy of the
> Sun and the Mail on your way in? I think
> the Bijou girls have nicked ours again.**

> **Jasmit: Oh, and chocolate. Maggie's already
> in a foul mood, and I need extra supplies.**

Jess read the text through twice, her hands shaking, before writing her reply.

Hurrying into the living room, she kicked off her unicorn slippers and stuffed her feet into the tatty flip-flops she left by the front door for the times she forgot to put the bins out until she heard the truck rolling onto her street. Grabbing her keys, she opened the front door, gently pushing Alfie back behind it as he tried to follow her outside.

'Not now, Alfie, walkies later, OK,' she promised, closing the door on his confused face and running down the steps from her flat towards the Polski Sklep.

As she pushed the shop door open, it let out its signature grating buzz, which was loud enough to make Jess jump whenever she stepped into the shop.

'Morning, Jess,' Borys beamed, not looking in the slightest bit perturbed that she was wearing checked pyjama bottoms and an old Belle and Sebastian T-shirt.

'Morning, Borys,' Jess muttered, heading for the stacks of newspapers piled along the bottom of the magazine rack. Picking them up one by one, she checked the date: Friday 13th August. When she got to the *Sun*, she recognised the front-page photo from yesterday of a footballer who'd been caught with his shorts down.

'Borys, have you got today's paper? Saturday? These are all from yesterday,' Jess said, plonking the *Sun* and *Mail* onto the counter and adding three grab bags of Maltesers.

'No, today's Friday. See? New papers. Not yesterday.' Borys stabbed his finger at the date at the top of the papers.

'No, today's Saturday, isn't it? Yesterday was Friday. Friday the thirteenth.' Jess wiped her top lip, which was beading with sweat. Borys took a step back from the counter, and she realised how she must look, trembling and sweating in her PJs, ranting about how it was definitely Saturday.

'Ah, I have done this,' Borys said, nodding, as if he'd solved a crossword clue. 'You get up and think it's the weekend, then heart sinks as you realise you have to go to work, yes? Sorry, Jess, today is working day. But weekend is tomorrow. Party time! Also, this is four pounds twenty-five, please.'

'Could you put it on my tab?' Jess said, pressing a hand to her forehead. She was burning up. Maybe she had a fever that was making her hallucinate. Maybe yesterday had really happened, and *this* was the dream?

'It is possible, but tabs are to be paid one day, yes?' Borys sighed, digging out a notebook from under the counter. 'Initial here, please. And don't forget to pay. My shop has bills too.'

'I promise, Borys,' Jess muttered, scribbling her initials on the pad again and gathering up the pile of newspapers and sweets in her arms.

Heading back outside and towards the flat, her phone started ringing in her pocket as she climbed her front steps. Unlocking the front door as fast as she could and stumbling inside, she dumped her bundle of stuff on the dresser by the door, patted Alfie consolingly on the head, and pulled out her phone.

'What do you mean, you've been fired?' Jasmit barked, as soon as Jess answered. 'I didn't know anything about this. What the fuck?'

'Please don't do this, Jas,' Jess said, her voice wavering through several octaves. 'Tell me you remember me being fired. Tell me you know about the whole Donna Wilson email thing. You have to stop this now. Like, haha, hilarious, but I'm honestly going nuts here.'

'What are you on about? Yesterday afternoon you went to Donna Wilson's place in Hackney to do her interview. We didn't see you after that. What's going on, Jess? You don't sound good, and you're scaring me a bit.'

Jess pressed the phone hard against her ear. She was starting to feel dizzy so, pushing the front door shut and kicking off her flip-flops, she crawled onto the sofa. 'What about the email I sent Donna?' Jess said, trying not to panic. 'You remember that? The one where I called her naïve and said her fiancé was a sleazebag?'

'You did what? Oh Jess, this is not good. Are you on your way in? Where are you? Come in and we'll sort this out together, OK?'

'I ... I'm running a bit late. I'm not feeling well,' Jess stuttered.

'What's going on? Are you in some kind of trouble?' Jasmit sounded genuinely worried. Although Jess wouldn't put it past Maggie to pull a stunt like this for the headline – 'PUNKED BY PREGNANT PAL'S MEMORY PRANK!' – she knew Jasmit wasn't faking her concern. Deep down, she also knew she'd never take Maggie's side if she concocted such an evil plan, even if her job was on the line.

'I'm not sure what kind of trouble I'm in,' Jess admitted. 'But I'm going to find out. I'll see you soon. And can I just check one thing? What day is it today?'

'Friday,' Jasmit said, sounding worried. 'Friday the thirteenth.'

Hanging up, Jess dug her cigarettes out of her handbag and lit one, taking a long, shaky drag. As confused thoughts whizzed around her head in all directions, smashing into each other and exploding into yet more confused thoughts, she felt like a human hadron collider.

There was only one person who could calm her down and make everything feel better.

Pulling out her phone and hitting speed-dial, she took another deep drag of her cigarette. Assuming it really was Friday again, Mel would be at work, running around shouting orders at runners on the breakfast show.

Sure enough, her phone went straight to voicemail.

'Mel, it's me. I need you, now. Call me, as soon as you can.'

Her cigarette still stuck in the corner of her mouth, she headed to her room and pulled her favourite vintage T-shirt from the bottom of the wardrobe. It should have stunk of boozy sweat and the half-packet of cigarettes she'd puffed her way through the night before, but, giving it a tentative sniff, she realised it was fresh and clean-smelling, like it had been worked on overnight by dry-cleaning elves.

Deciding that wearing the same outfit as she'd done yesterday – or in her dream, or whatever it was – was only tempting fate, she threw the T-shirt back into the wardrobe, and pulled a purple skater dress from behind the linen basket. Grateful that she'd had the foresight to have a shower before she went to bed, she tugged it over her head, deftly avoiding her cigarette, topping it off with the bee pendant she wore with everything.

Then, pushing her feet into her Converse, clipping Alfie's lead to his collar and grabbing her handbag, she headed outside.

'Time for Friday walkies, Alfie,' she muttered to herself. 'Again . . .'

Chapter 11

'Don't worry, we'll be at the office soon, and then we'll be able to work out what's going on. Don't panic, OK? It'll all be all right.'

Jess clutched Alfie to her chest like a good luck charm, rubbing his head with her thumb as she stepped onto the escalator. She realised she wasn't going to be late for work after all when she found herself standing behind the woman with a black spaniel puppy peering back over her shoulder.

Realising with a muttered, 'Balls,' that she'd forgotten to bring Jasmit's newspapers and chocolate with her, she chucked the puppy under the chin, and started talking to it in the International Language of Dog.

'WHO is a good girl then, WHO? Is it you? IS it?' she cooed, as the puppy stretched its chin towards her and closed its eyes in happiness.

'She's a he, actually,' the woman said, smiling over her shoulder. 'This is Inkblot, and I'm Beth.'

'I always think it's weird that people automatically go for "Who's a good boy?" so I like to err towards the other fifty per cent,' Jess said, as Inkblot licked the air with a tiny pink tongue. 'You know, #WoofToo.'

Beth laughed. 'Good point. I never thought of it like that.'

'I'm Jess, and this terrifying beast is Alfie,' Jess said, while Alfie woofed in greeting.

'Nice to meet you both. Come on, Inky,' Beth said brightly, patting the puppy's head as she stepped off the escalator and headed for the platform. As Jess stepped off herself, she held back for a moment, pretending to be fiddling with Archie's lead. She hated it when strangers started talking to her when she was still only one coffee into the day, and couldn't imagine Beth felt any differently.

So far, everything that had happened that morning had been exactly as she'd dreamt it. But it couldn't have been a premonition, or surely she wouldn't have been able to change what she was wearing? Wouldn't she have been compelled by a strange force, masquerading as free will, to wear her vintage T-shirt and baggy jeans again? Or had she just watched too many movies?

Emerging from the Tube, she took Alfie to Hoxton Square, then found her footsteps slowing as she got closer to Aevum House. What would she do if everything was the same as yesterday? What would that mean?

Taking a deep breath, she pushed her way past the revolving doors into Aevum House's reception area, hit the button for the fifth floor, and hoped that when she stepped out of it, everything would look different to yesterday.

A different maternity wrap dress would be stretched over Jasmit's bump, Rachel would be sitting at her desk bang on time for once, and Ian wouldn't be dressed like he was liable to Hulk out of his skin-tight outfit with a single misplaced sneeze.

Stepping out of the lift, Jess steadied herself against the wall as Terrence sloped past her clutching a cup of tea trilling, 'Morning!' before coughing, dropping his voice a couple of octaves, and trying again.

Jasmit was doing the splits, trying to rescue a load of spilled paper clips from the floor. As Jess stared at her, frozen to the spot, Ian hopped off his chair and took over, urging Jasmit back to her desk. Someone cheered, 'Eleven! Woop!' and a smattering of claps ran out as June on the ads desk finished her sneezing jag and blew her nose loudly into a tissue.

'There's a perfectly good explanation for this,' Jess muttered to herself, smiling a bit manically as she forced her feet to move and stalked to her desk.

Pulling open her laptop, she saw the note that she'd slid back onto her keyboard glowing pinkly at her.

Ask Jas what to do re: Donna sitch.

Shredding the Post-it into tiny strips and scattering them into the bin under her desk thinking, '*Take that, Friday!*' Jess fired up her emails and brought up the one she'd sent to Donna on Thursday afternoon.

'Hey, what's happening?' Jasmit hissed across the desk, before using her heels to scoot her chair around to Jess's side.

'You're getting good at that,' Jess said, barking out an unconvincing laugh. 'Next stop, the Olympics.'

'Do you want to tell me what's going on?' Jasmit whispered. 'Something about being fired? You can't be fired, I'm too pregnant.'

'Well, in about five minutes, Donna's going to arrive for her photo shoot,' Jess said calmly, feeling a hysterical laugh bubbling up inside her chest. 'Then five minutes after *that*, her fiancé is going to start greasing up to Maggie, who's going to put on one of the most disgusting shows of flirting you've ever seen, while looking simultaneously pissed off at me for dressing Donna as Elvira instead of an egg. And while all *that's* going on, Donna is going to check her emails to find out if she's won the lottery and see this.' Jess swung her laptop around to face Jasmit, and watched as her eyes gradually widened.

'Oh Jesus, Jess,' Jasmit said weakly, looking pale. 'Maybe IT can do something?'

'Nope. If I'm right about what's going on here, I'm going to get fired in about ... ohh, twenty minutes?'

'And what is it that you think's going on, exactly?' Jas frowned, shooting a look at Ian, who shrugged.

'I think I'm reliving Friday the thirteenth, which was the worst day of my life and has already happened once yesterday, all over again,' Jess said. Then giggled. It was all too much to take in.

'Sorry, you're doing what now?' Jasmit's eyebrows shot up into her fringe.

Before Jess could answer, the doors to the lift pinged open, and Ashleigh walked out, followed by a sullen-looking Alejandro and a beaming Donna.

'These two are yours, I presume? I found them in reception, completely failing to work out how to use the lifts,' Ashleigh said archly, glaring at Jess and stalking off.

'Thanks, love!' Donna smiled at Ashleigh's retreating back. 'What a lovely girl.'

Jess's stomach clenched. She knew what was about to happen, but felt as powerless as if she were strapped down and being forced to watch a car-crash in slow motion.

'How have you both been?' she stammered, trying to arrange her expression into one a not-panicking face might make. She was thinking so many thoughts at once, it was proving difficult. How did her eyes usually go? And how did her mouth sit?

'The interview yesterday had a bit of an aphrodisiac effect, actually,' Donna giggled. 'We spent most of the afternoon in ...'

'Terrence. Costumes,' Jess interrupted, and walk-ran to Terrence's desk, Donna looking confused as she followed behind.

While Terrence talked Donna and Alejandro through their costumes, Jess paced back and forth, pulling at the hairs on her arms. If this were a dream, maybe the tiny shot of adrenaline would be enough to wake her up. And she really *really* wanted this to be a dream, so she could wake up on Saturday, go to see her nan, watch this season's *Love or Dare* final with her, and pretend none of this had ever happened.

Back at the features desk, Alejandro gave Jasmit a muffled, '*Hola, señorita*,' through his fake pointy teeth.

'*Hola* yourself,' Jess said distractedly, as Maggie stepped out of her office right on cue, chirping, 'Ah, this must be our two lovebirds!' and shooting Jess a dirty look as she clocked Donna's wig.

Everything was unfolding far too quickly. Jess needed time to think. All she could come up with was the idea she'd rejected yesterday. The one that would only work if she was living in one of those romcoms where the heroine is hilariously ditzy.

As a muffled 'ping' came from the direction of Donna's bag and she announced, 'That'll be my reminder to check my lottery numbers.' Jess realised she didn't have time to come up with anything better – but maybe if she visualised herself pulling it off, it would work. She just had to want it enough.

Jess took a deep breath, closed her eyes and pictured herself seamlessly faking a fall in slo-mo, accidentally hitting Donna's hand in the process and sending her phone soaring through the air and into a desk, smashing it into several Gmail-destroying smithereens.

Come on, universe, you owe me this, Jess thought, as she opened her eyes and watched Donna starting to scroll through her emails.

Jess let out a half-hearted yelp. 'Oh no! Argh!' she said, suddenly pitching forward from where she was standing, windmilling her arms and slapping at Donna's hands like she was putting out a small fire.

'Oopsie-daisy!' Donna said, reaching out a hand to steady Jess as her phone fell gently to the floor and bounced safely onto the carpet. 'Are you OK?'

'Umm, yeah,' Jess said. 'Sorry. I . . . like, fell.' She glanced at Jasmit, who was clutching her forehead in embarrassment, while Ian shot her a bemused look that said, *Mate, that was terrible.*

'No harm done,' said Donna, picking up her phone, which was wrapped in a glittery orange case. 'Screen protector, see?' She held up her phone, which didn't have a scratch on it, and beamed.

'Are you OK, Jess? Feeling faint are we?' Maggie said through a rictus grin.

'Never mind,' Jess sighed. 'Never mind.'

She slumped into her office chair, which rolled a few inches backwards towards her desk.

'Oh! I never saw this email you sent me, love,' Donna said. 'What's it about? I wasn't supposed to bring anything with me, was I?'

Dropping her box of office gonks on the floor outside the building, Jess winced before she heard the muffled tinkle as the glass in her photo frame cracked.

'Oh, for the love of god,' she muttered, leaning against the NO SMOKING sign and lighting a cigarette. Something weird – something weird *and* horrible – was going on, but Jess was certain by now that she wasn't dreaming.

Instead, for reasons she couldn't begin to understand, she seemed to be living through the worst day of her life all over again. She couldn't quite decide whether to laugh, scream or cry, but settled on opening her phone to google 'reliving same day help'.

Before she had the chance to hit Enter, she saw she had two unread texts: the one from her nan she'd never replied to, asking if Monty Don was married, and one from Tom. Although she already knew what it was going to say, as she read his text, her skin prickled all over, like an army of tiny ants scurrying over her body.

> Tom: I know about the other guy. It's over. I thought we had something special, but I guess not

It had been sent just after 10.30 a.m., exactly the same time as yesterday. So now that was two things she'd hated about Friday that she'd known were coming, but failed to prevent. How *had* Tom found out about Nate? Even if she hadn't been able to stop it happening, she really wanted to know.

Mel hadn't called her back yet, and Jess remembered that she was probably on her way to her meeting.

> **Hey Melbert, I know you've just got out of your meeting and are a bit knackered, but you've GOT to meet me at the Bush**

Before adding a P.S., she hesitated just for a moment. Strictly speaking, it was against the rules to use the Emergency Pizza Slice Code of Calamity in quick succession – a rule put in place one afternoon when Jess was hungover and used it to make Mel bring her biscuits – but seeing as she was pretty sure Mel wouldn't remember the first time, Jess guessed it didn't count.

> **Jess: P.S. You're my perfect slice of pizza**

Chapter 12

August 2005, the roundabout

'Sorry, but you're still rubbish at that,' Mel said, as she walked across the springy tarmac towards the roundabout. Jess was spinning slowly around, her back pressed against the central pole, trying and failing to blow smoke rings into the still air.

'Look, it's windy, OK? Give me a break. Practise makes perfect, and at least I'm trying.'

'Yes, you're very trying,' Mel said, sitting on the quadrant next to Jess's and folding up her long legs, like origami. 'Badum-tish!'

Wordlessly, Jess handed Mel her packet of Marlboro Lights, and Mel nodded her thanks.

'So what's this crisis meeting in aid of?' Jess asked. 'You haven't invoked the Emergency Pizza Slice Code of Calamity for ages, so it must be pretty bad. Are you OK?'

Shifting round, Jess turned to sit facing Mel, who did the same. Without the need for any consultation on the matter, they each held their cigarette in the hand nearest the centre of the roundabout, and took it in turns to lean down and propel themselves around with the other.

'I've got something to tell you, actually,' Mel said. 'Something pretty big.'

'What, have you got cancer or something?' Jess laughed. Then pulled her face straight when Mel didn't crack a smile. 'Oh god, you haven't, have you?'

'No, nothing like that. Although when I told my parents this . . . thing, I got the impression they'd have thought having some terrible disease was preferable.'

'You're pregnant? Oh my god. I can't believe it. Who's the father? It had better not be Jason Phillips; your kid will come out walking backwards.'

Mel laughed, grimly. 'Nope, not that either. Can you, like, stop cracking jokes just for a second?'

Jess blushed. She'd never been good with Serious Chats. 'Sorry, sorry. I'm listening. No more jokes, I promise.'

'You know that first time we met last year? When you asked me if I fancied Craig, and we started talking about our perfect pizzas?'

Jess frowned. 'Of course I do.'

Mel started fiddling with the shoelaces on her left foot. 'It's just that . . . I didn't fancy Craig for a reason. And I don't fancy any other boys either, for that matter. Because . . . well, I'm gay.'

Jess laughed, then clamped her hands over her mouth. 'I'm sorry, I didn't mean to laugh. But is that it? Your big news?'

'What?' Mel looked up, startled. 'Yes, it is. Sorry, isn't an emotional reveal about my essential being big enough for you?'

'Of course it is. And that's great!' Jess said, sighing with relief. 'I mean, it's only great if you think it's great,' she added, anxiously. 'Do you think it's great?'

Mel frowned. 'I suppose. I haven't really thought about it. It's just . . . who I am.'

Jess leaned over and grabbed Mel's hand. 'I'm very relieved it's not something horrible, like being pregnant with Jason's weird baby. And as long as you're happy about it, I'm happy. Although I'm a bit annoyed you didn't tell me sooner, you daft bugger. I mean, it's up to you when you come out, and nobody should feel forced to do so when they don't feel ready, or due to peer pressure. And obviously how you go about it depends on you and your personal relationships. But I'm your best mate. I know I turn everything into a joke, but I'm here for you when it really matters.'

Mel cocked her head at Jess. 'Did you just quote our SRE textbook at me?'

'Pretty much, yeah. See, those lessons weren't a useless bag of shite purely designed to give idiots like Amy an extra qualification after all!'

Mel laughed and rubbed her face in her hands. 'That wasn't really the reaction I was expecting, to be honest. I was kind of worried you'd be all weird about the times we've shared a bed during sleepovers, or changed in front of each other and stuff.'

'Now you mention it, you are a *massive* pervert, and I feel *violated*. Now budge up,' Jess instructed, shuffling underneath the roundabout spoke to sit next to Mel. 'So what happened with your parents? Were they complete dicks?'

'Kind of, yeah. Mum started crying and said that she'd always wanted grandchildren.' Jess grimaced. 'She said I was her only child, so what was she going to do now?'

'Always nice for your parents to see you as a baby-making machine. Very *Handmaid's Tale*.'

'I pointed out that lesbians can have kids too, but she just snorted, like I'd told her unicorns exist and the earth is flat. And Dad just looked really uncomfortable. He patted the arm of the chair I was sitting in and said, "Well done," then buggered off to his shed. It was so awkward. When I left the house, mum was whispering furiously down the phone to my Auntie May, as if I didn't know what they were talking about.'

'You poor thing,' Jess said quietly, linking her arm through Mel's. 'That must have been awful.'

'It was horrible, actually. You know, I kind of hoped coming out would be like it is in the movies. "We love you whatever you do with your life, we can't wait to meet your first girlfriend, yadda yadda," followed by a group hug and a Chinese takeaway. But I guess Mum and Dad have always had a set vision for me when it comes to my career. They put loads of effort into getting up early to drive me to race meets and making sure I eat right – all that stuff. I guess they must have had my whole future mapped out in their heads, and it involved a husband and grandchildren rather than scissoring.'

Jess laughed so hard, her cigarette shot out of her mouth, landing on the asphalt next to the roundabout. Mel managed a tentative smile in return, her eyes shining.

'Apparently my parents didn't have any idea I'm gay. Did you know?'

'I mean you *are* very fond of these,' Jess said, tapping Mel's sparkly silver Dr Martens with her foot. 'And you have been known to favour a flamboyant shirt. But you never can tell, can you?'

'Oi!' Mel laughed, flicking Jess's arm.

'I'm kidding! I did have an inkling, actually. I've seen you looking at some of the girls in our year the same way I look at pizza, and you not fancying Craig was a bit of a clue, too. He is an absolute hottie.'

'I mean, yeah, I can see that. If I wasn't a massive lesbian, I totally would,' Mel said. 'Look, I don't want to go back home tonight, to be honest. Can I stay at your nan's? Do you think she'd mind?'

'Of course not!' Jess said, resting her head on Mel's shoulder. 'Nan loves you as much as she loves me, if not more. And she'd love to hear all about your adventures in lesbianism. She'll probably have some story about how she bumped into Cynthia Nixon at Beigel Bake back in the day and tried to persuade her to come out.'

'That sounds about right,' Mel grinned.

'Plus,' Jess said, sitting up, 'I can make us the new recipe I'm working on: sausage and egg sandwiches, but with potato waffles for the bread.'

'Sounds revolting. But thanks, that would be great,' Mel said, suddenly bursting into tears.

'Hey, are you OK?' Jess asked anxiously, grabbing her hand. 'Have I overstepped the mark? I just wanted to make you laugh, I didn't mean it. You're obviously not a pervert.'

'No, I'm just relieved,' Mel said, leaning over and hugging her. 'You might be a bit crazy, but I'm so lucky to have you as my best mate.'

'Will I still be your perfect slice of pizza, even when you find some hottie who's got toppings in all the right places and can make you scream like a banshee in bed?'

'There'll never be a pizza like you, I promise. And we're not just friends, are we? We're family.'

Taking her arms from around Jess's neck and swiping away her tears, Mel leaned over, pushed at the floor with the palm of her hand, and sent them spinning around again.

Chapter 13

'Twice in two days? And before lunchtime, too. To what do I owe the pleasure?' Mark said, raising his eyebrows as Jess pushed open the door to the Bush and slapped her cardboard box down onto the bar. 'Ah,' he said, peering into the box, and assessing the tell-tale signs of being unceremoniously fired. 'White wine?'

Even though Jess had known Mark would say that, she felt a sense of relief to have reached a place that felt so much like home. It was her and Mel's safe haven, and the pub so rarely changed that Mark ordering a fresh set of cardboard beer mats was enough to make Arthur complain about 'the creeping advance of the PC Brigade'. Which meant it might be a bit samey, but was also the perfect place for Jess to forget she might be trapped in a time loop.

'Not today, Mark,' Jess said, climbing onto the seat at the bar, hanging her handbag strap and Alfie's lead over a bag hook and waving at Arthur, who grunted and raised his glass at her. 'I need something a lot stronger than that. Whisky?'

'Whisky?' He looked dubious. 'Are you sure?'

Jess had seen enough films to know that the correct response to a crisis is to order a shot of whisky. Then, when the barman asks what's wrong, you take a gulp, look into the distance and say something mysterious like, 'You wouldn't believe me even if I told you,' or, 'Trust me, you don't want to know.'

'Yes, please. A double. On the rocks,' Jess said, confidently, adding, 'And some doggy treats, please,' even though the request didn't quite gel with her attempt to look cool.

Mark shrugged and reached up to take a glass from the shelf above the bar, exposing an inch of pale hairy stomach below his *Pulp Fiction* T-shirt, which told the world he was 'One Charming Motherf*ckin' Pig'.

He started polishing Jess's glass with a tea towel – something he always did, even though he had a dishwasher, to make the tourists happy.

'See, in British romcoms, you never see barmen fishing huge unflushable turds out of the toilet, or arguing with the brewery over the latest rent hike,' he'd once explained to a wide-eyed Jess and Mel. 'They're always just serenely polishing glasses behind the bar with a tea towel. It's what the tourists expect to see, and I like to give my audience what they came here for.'

Jess had to concede it was a shrewd marketing move. He looked like he'd stepped straight out of *Corrie*.

Mark handed Jess the glass of whisky she'd ordered, and she knocked back half. Then immediately slammed down the glass and was nearly sick on the bar.

'What the hell? This is disgusting,' she spluttered.

'Yeah, I thought that might happen.' Mark shrugged, folding his arms and leaning against the till. 'Not quite the same as a nice glass of Pinot, is it?'

'No. It is not,' Jess said, wiping her mouth and sticking her tongue out. 'Can I get some coke in this please? And, um, a glass of house white.'

Mark laughed, topped up the whisky with a jet of frothy cola from the pump, and grabbed a bottle of wine from the fridge.

Taking a swig of wine to help get rid of the taste of peat, smoke and old boots that lingered on her tongue, and dropping the dog treats down to Alfie, Jess pulled out her laptop. There was no point wasting time while she waited for Mel to arrive, and maybe someone online would know what was happening to her. She'd once heard the internet described as an 'everything machine' – so surely it would have some answers, if they existed?

Hitting Google, Jess typed 'reliving same day possible?' and immediately got sucked into an internet vortex. She found some unintelligible diagrams explaining how time loops could theoretically work, some *very* disturbing Marvel fanfic, and a thread on Reddit called r/Timetravel that urged 'Time travelers click here!'

> Are you a time traveler who came here to talk
> about your travels? Great! We welcome you
> with open arms!

At the top, a man claimed to have re-lived one of his school days over and over again when he was seven. Jess felt a swoop of nausea. What if this wasn't just a one-off? What if she was going to wake up on Friday again tomorrow? She shook her head, hard. This was just a blip. A glitch in the matrix. Not a time loop. She'd wake up tomorrow and it would be Saturday, because the alternative didn't bear thinking about.

She read the man's story all the way through, but he didn't explain how he'd eventually broken out of the time loop.

'Helpful,' Jess muttered, scrolling down the comments. There was nothing of any use there, either – it was full of smart-arses trying to out-geek each other.

u/physicsmajor5678: Even those who believe in time travel understand that the chance of temporal loops being real are infinitesimal. A closed, time-like curve is similar to a time loop, but would require you to travel faster than the speed of light, and possibly the help of a wormhole, to actually leap in time.

u/mulder_and_scully2000: Although it's a non-zero probability, time loops are generally used as a science fiction trope, used to teach the looper a lesson about themselves. It's not a concept physicists believe could ever actually happen, even if you stretch what we already know about quantum physics to its limits.

u/dangerzoner555: GROUNDHOG DAY FTW!!

Jess sighed and carried on looking for more stories like hers. She leaned in as she read about a thirty-eight-year-old man whose memory shrank to just ninety minutes after he woke up from a root canal treatment. He thought every day was 14 March 2005, and that he had a dentist appointment that afternoon. Jess hated the dentist, and decided the poor guy was much worse off than her.

Shutting the lid of her laptop, she wondered if something similar had happened to her. Something on Friday that had affected her brain. Possibly, it was thanks to the Malibu and tomato juice cocktail, topped with squirty cream and prawn cocktail crisps, which she'd forced Mark to make her at her leaving do. If anything could send someone's brain a bit funny, one of her home-made cocktails could probably do it.

'Oh my god. The moped!' Jess said suddenly, slapping the bar. From under her chair, Alfie woofed in surprise.

She'd somehow forgotten all about the final, terrible thing that had happened to her on Friday 13th. After waving good-bye to her friends at the pub, she'd decided she'd rather get home under her own steam than call an Uber. More than once when she'd been that drunk, she'd been flipped onto the street by a disgruntled driver like a floppy fried egg, so she'd decided to take the Tube home instead.

Navigating her way through the underground using an impressive homing-pigeon instinct, she and Alfie had been just five minutes from their front door when a moped had driven up behind them.

Bumping up onto the pavement, the rider had grabbed the strap of Jess's favourite bag – the dark blue one with the gold embroidered stars – and pulled it off her shoulder. In the process, the front wheel of the moped had hit her right leg, sending her flying into the air and thudding onto the pavement.

She couldn't remember anything else after that. Goosebumps tingled up her arms as she wondered if she'd banged her head, and it had caused some kind of brain trauma. Maybe she really *was* in a coma like the guy in the film she'd seen, and this was all a twisted dream? Maybe she was processing the conversations of the doctors and nurses around her bed, and turning them into Mark talking about whisky?

Lifting her handbag from the hook under the bar, she stroked the 'Pugs Not Drugs' badge she'd pinned to the strap. Just like the Post-it note she'd screwed up and tossed towards the recycling bin, her stolen bag had been resurrected – perhaps by her own mind, as she lay in a hospital bed somewhere, her damaged brain creating a glitch in time to protect her from the truth.

Taking a gulp of wine, she swiped away a tear, then jumped as the door banged open behind her. Twisting round in her seat, Jess slumped into it with relief.

Mel – beautiful, reliable Mel! – was wearing the same floaty, calf-length summer dress as yesterday, matched with a denim jacket, biker boots, and a purple cane, which she waved at Mark in greeting.

Despite the cane, and the fact that it seemed as if a stiff wind might blow her over, Mel was a lot stronger than she looked. Her muscles seemed to have retained the memory of all the running she'd done before her accident. She'd even beaten Mark in an arm wrestle not so long ago. Meanwhile, Jess's ten-a-day fag habit and fondness for cheese meant she couldn't walk up more than a couple of flights of stairs without wheezing. Appearances could be deceptive.

'Good, you're here,' Mel said, her face brightening as she saw Jess, who hopped off her stool. 'What on earth's going on?'

Mel grabbed Jess in a massive hug. She wasn't a prolific hugger, due to other people's tendency to accidentally kick her bad leg on their approach, but on the rare times she dished them out, she was very good at them. Although she was slender, she had dips in all the right places for Jess to nestle her arms and chin into.

'Sorry,' she said, as tears dripped from her nose onto Mel's shoulder, quickly soaking through her dress.

'Another large house white?' Mark asked behind her.

'Make it a bottle of Sauvignon,' Mel told him over her shoulder, pushing her glasses back up her nose. 'Come on,' she said, gently unclasping Jess's arms from around her neck and handing Mark her credit card. As Jess grabbed the glasses and wine bucket, Mel ordered a packet of pickled onion Monster Munch, exactly as Jess had known she would.

Then, crisps dangling from her teeth, Mel led the way upstairs. Finding their usual spot by the window empty, they wordlessly dumped their bags and jackets under the windowsill. Mel leaned her cane against it, then they sat down, grabbed some beer mats, and set about folding them into squares and pushing them under the table legs. Alfie licked one, then shook his head, hard.

When the table had stopped wobbling and the pair were settled, Mel poured out two large glasses of wine. Jess and Mel had always been there for each other, through thick and thin. They'd shared all their secrets, ever since that very first day on the roundabout. But this was different. This sounded *mad*.

And now, as Mel looked at her expectantly, waiting to hear why she'd been dragged to the pub, words failed Jess for the first time. She so badly needed her best friend to believe her, but what she was about to tell her was clearly nuts. So she decided to start with the bits that were easier to believe: getting fired and dumped, all because she was a complete fuck-up.

When she'd finished, Mel sighed. 'Before I say this, I want you to know I totally love you, OK? But you do also know you're an absolutely enormous idiot, right?'

'Yes, I do know. I am totally an idiot,' Jess said, 'but getting fired, and dumped ... Believe it or not, they're not even the worst things to happen to me today.'

Jess flinched as a balled-up paper napkin flew past her face and landed in Mel's drink, then cursed herself for not remembering it was coming.

She plucked it out of Mel's glass, ignoring the snickering group of boys in the corner shouting, 'Shit, sorry girls!' in their direction.

'So somehow this story gets *worse*?' Mel said, raising her eyebrows. 'Do I even want to hear this?'

'Probably not. It feels a bit like I've been worrying about a pimple, then stopped to look at it in a car window and have been hit by a truck ...'

Quickly, Jess explained about being evicted, then mugged.

'Hang on, you say, you're *going* to get evicted? As in, in the future? So it hasn't happened yet? And how can you know you're going to get mugged? I'm really confused, Jess.'

Jess took a deep breath. How could she say what she needed to without sounding totally crazy? Reaching out and holding Mel's hands, she looked her straight in the eye.

'Because what I'm about to tell you is the real reason I'm here. Because I've done all this before. Friday the thirteenth, that is. I did all this *yesterday*, and when I woke up this morning everything had just ... reset. You'd texted me the same message as yesterday, Borys complained about my bloody tab again, the same puppy was in front of me on the escalator.

'Then I got fired, then dumped by Tom. *Again*. We came

113

and sat here, and you called me an idiot, exactly like you did just now. Which is how I know that in about ten minutes, Brian is going to call and evict me. Then, unless we do things differently this time, the guys from work will come and take over from you, and I'll get mugged on the way home. I don't remember anything after that, which is why I'm wondering if I banged my head or something, which might explain—' Jess waggled her arms around '—all this.'

'So you're saying we've already had this conversation?' Mel frowned, gently drawing her hands out from underneath Jess's. She clenched her empty hands into fists.

'Well, not this exact one,' Jess said quickly. 'We talked about me realising I might like Tom – like *like* him – and you said something about me being "so Jess about everything", which turned out not to be the compliment I was hoping it might be. And we discussed your meeting, which didn't go so well.' At this, Mel looked surprised. 'Well, it didn't, did it?'

'How do you know that?'

'Because you told me yesterday. And everything else has happened the same today, which means that must have too. Which I'm sorry about, by the way. I know you're tired. But you have to admit this is a pretty big emergency.'

'I mean, yes, if you were living through an *actual time loop*, it would be a huge emergency. But come on, Jess. It must have just been a vivid dream. You're not reliving the same day all over again. It's not possible.'

'I know that. Which is why I wondered if maybe I'd hit my head or something – when I got mugged, you know? – and this whole thing is just me in a coma. You might not be Mel at all. You could just be a nurse changing my drip, and I'm interpreting what she's saying as you and me, chatting down the pub.'

Jess tailed off, leaving an awkward silence behind her.

'Does it feel like you're asleep?' Mel said. Suddenly, she looked exhausted and worried all at once. 'I'm not sure I like the idea of being dismissed as a figment of your imagination. And I don't want to throw around accusations, but this isn't like the time you pretended you'd broken your arm to get out of forgetting my birthday, is it?'

'No!' Jess blushed. 'I learned my lesson, didn't I?'

'Only after you tried to open a bottle of wine with your "broken" arm and got rumbled. Look, it sounds like you've had a really tough day, so I wouldn't blame you for making this up to distract yourself from losing Tom and your job. But if this *is* a lie, it's a pretty big one. I won't mind if you're messing about, but I'd rather know now. We can forget all about it, have a drink, and work out what to do next.'

Mel looked at Jess expectantly, apparently hoping she'd suddenly say, 'Ha! Gotcha. Yeah, I made it all up. Your face, though!'

But instead, Jess rubbed her face with her hands. She had a habit of messing up, then trying her best to cover her tracks by whatever means necessary. Like telling Brian her auntie had died to avoid paying her rent, which she'd done more times than could reasonably be expected to correspond to real aunties.

As soon as any problem in her life was no longer screaming for her attention, she had an uncanny knack of forgetting all about it, until the plaster she'd patched up the problem with inevitably fell off.

It had always been Jess's secret superpower – being able to live life in a state of chaotic fun, without thinking too hard about the consequences. But that also meant she could hardly be offended if Mel didn't believe her now. As they endured one of the only uncomfortable silences that had ever sat between them, Jess's phone lit up on the table with an 0208 number.

'Brian!' Jess said, grabbing her phone. 'This is Brian. Calling to evict me.' She thought as quickly as she could. 'I'll pinky promise to pay my rent . . . and then he'll say something about not being an eight-year-old girl. Just listen, please, and I can prove to you I'm telling the truth.'

Putting her phone on speaker, Jess nervously hit the answer button and rested it in the centre of the table, like she was activating a bomb.

'Hello?' she said, pointing at her phone and checking Mel was listening. Which she was, intently.

As the conversation unfurled exactly as it had the first time, Jess punched the air and silently mimed, *Mind blown!* before hanging up and yelling, 'SEE? I told you!'

'OK, that was weird,' Mel said carefully, sipping her wine.

'So do you believe me now? Please say you believe me.' Jess suddenly felt tears pricking her eyes. 'This is all really scary and I need your help. Even if that's just by distracting me with cheese.' At the mention of his favourite treat, Alfie's ears pricked up, and he let out some gentle woofs. 'Me and Alfie, obviously.'

'OK. I believe you're going through something, although I can't say what,' Mel said carefully. 'But for now, let's assume you're not in a coma, nor have you punctured a hole in the space-time continuum, even if you are pretty accident-prone.

'Whatever you feel is going on, you can't possibly be physically reliving Friday. Maybe it's something like severe déjà vu. For all we know, this could be an actual thing – like a reaction to stress.'

Jess looked excited. 'I remember interviewing a woman for the magazine once who suffered from . . . Alice in Wonderland Syndrome, I think it was called. She felt like she was looking down the wrong end of a telescope, or that time was slowing down or speeding up, for a few minutes at a time. It drove her nuts. It was pretty mild compared to this. But maybe I'm going through something similar. Do you think Aya might know what's happening to me?'

Although she was a paediatrician, Mel's girlfriend had an uncanny ability to work out what was wrong with the patients in any medical drama, long before the fictional doctors twigged.

'That'll be an Intracranial Berry Aneurysm,' she'd say sagely, during the first five minutes of an episode of *House*, while it took Hugh Laurie a whole episode to work out what was going on. Although that was exactly the kind of thing that annoyed Jess about Aya, she had to admit she was always right. If the time loop was caused by something medical, Aya would know what it was.

Mel nodded. 'She's probably your best bet, if you don't want to go to your own doctor and risk being carted off.'

'Maybe I'll tell Aya what's going on and she'll be all, "Ah yes, that'll be *Groundhog Day* Syndrome. Nothing to worry about; just take some pills and you'll be fine".'

Mel snorted, then glanced at her Fitbit. 'I tell you what. Why don't you tell Jas you want to postpone your leaving do, and come back to ours for dinner? We were going to have salad—'

'Of course you were.'

'—but seeing as we're in crisis mode, I can make you mac and cheese if you like. You can ask Aya what she thinks while

117

eating a proper dinner, in lieu of whatever you reckon you had yesterday.'

'I think if you could call anything I ate last night – or tonight, or whatever – dinner, it was the Malibu and tomato juice cocktail topped with squirty cream and prawn cocktail crisps I made,' Jess said. 'It was awful, actually. Like drinking liquid despair. Can we have bacon in this macaroni cheese, or are you being a vegetarian this week?'

'Aya reckons the nitrates in bacon are eventually going to kill everyone off, but I'm sure she won't mind this once, Phil Connors,' Mel said, shaking her head.

'Who's Phil Connors?'

'The guy in *Groundhog Day*. Have you never actually seen it?'

'Well, I've heard of it, obviously. But no.' Jess shrugged.

'Why not? It's a classic.'

'Would you laugh if I told you I always thought it was a bit far-fetched?'

Chapter 14

'No cheese, you'll spoil your appetite,' Mel said sternly, rapping Jess's hand with a wooden spoon as it inched towards a pile of grated mozzarella. She'd propped herself on a stool at Mel's posh marble-topped kitchen counter to watch her making dinner.

'It's not for me, it's for Alfie,' Jess argued, looking down at the ball of fur that followed her like a fluffy ghost wherever she went and pressing a finger to her lips. Mel laughed, and Alfie woofed.

Although Mel claimed to genuinely enjoy salads, which Jess had never quite believed, she was also an expert at creating delicious, junk-food masterpieces. Jess, who couldn't cook anything more complicated than pasta and Dolmio, despaired at her wasted genius.

'All that talent, and you use it to make bloody poached eggs.'

Dropping some cheese onto the floor for Alfie to nibble, Jess took a tentative sip of the posh wine Mel had poured her. She had no qualms about downing the vinegary corner-shop stuff she bought for herself, but she didn't feel comfortable doing that when it was a Chablis that cost about three quid a gulp, even if she wasn't paying for it.

'Here, give me a hand grating these,' Mel said, waving two blocks of Cheddar. 'And try not to eat . . . I mean "give Alfie" half of it along the way. Are you feeling any better yet?'

'I guess so.' Jess shrugged, peeling the wrappers off the cheese and getting to work. 'It feels less weird now I'm not watching the same things unfolding at the same time as yesterday. It was starting to creep me out.'

'Good, I'm glad,' Mel said, gently stroking Jess's face and leaving a trail of ketchup behind.

'Oh, you cow!' Jess laughed, grabbing a piece of kitchen roll and scrubbing at her face with it. 'Here, I've got a joke for you,' she said, raising her eyebrows at the ridiculously small TV perched on one of Mel's bookshelves. 'How do vegans who don't have a TV know which one to tell you about first?'

'Ha bloody ha. Except I'm not even vegetarian, as the criminal amounts of bacon I'm forcing into this macaroni cheese just to cheer you up will prove.'

Hopping off her stool, Jess wandered over to examine a new framed photo collage on the shelf beside Mel's tiny TV. Around half the photos were of Mel and Jess, while the rest were of Mel and Aya, including their recent visit to Japan to see Aya's family.

'Hey, do you remember this?' Jess said, picking up a framed photograph of her and Mel squashed side-by-side on her nan's tatty sofa. Which reminded her, with a stab of guilt, that she hadn't replied to Pamela's random text about Monty Don, for the second day in a row. In the photo, Mel and Jess were both laughing, their arms linked, and they were sitting in a man-made nest of blankets, DVDs, magazines, bags of sweets and crisp packets.

The photo had been taken just a few months after Mel's accident. That summer, she'd been driven nuts by her mum fussing around her as she recovered, so she'd spent a lot of time in Pamela's musty old house, enjoying the kinds of meals that were banned by her parents.

Jess had been more than happy to play chef for Mel that summer, despite the guilt that played havoc with her stomach whenever she looked at her friend's leg. It was ringed with hoops of metal, with angry-looking rods protruding from them into her bones, hurting and healing her at the same time.

Although, really, Jess told herself for the thousandth time, the accident had been a blessing in disguise for Mel. She'd been forced to ditch the idea of pursuing a running career and had been offered an entry-level job in TV after an introduction made by her physio.

From there, she'd worked her way up the ladder until she'd landed a producer role on *Wakey, Wakey, Britain!*. Hardly anyone makes serious money through running, but Mel was doing brilliantly for herself now. She was made for her career and had a bright future ahead of her – and her leg injury had serendipitously put it right in her path.

At least, thought Jess, she wasn't having to relive *that* day all over again. She shivered, then jumped as the front door cracked open, nearly dropping the picture.

'Careful,' Mel warned, plucking it from her fingers.

'I wasn't going to drop it,' Jess grumbled.

'Isn't that what you said just before smashing Aya's Excellence in Paediatrics award? And my favourite mug?'

'You were a grown woman with a Care Bears mug. I did you a favour, if anything.'

'Hey sweetheart, I managed to get home early. You OK?' Aya called from behind the huge bunch of lilies she was man-handling through the door.

'I'm fine, thank you, honeybun,' Jess replied. 'How are you?'

'Oh, hi, Jess.' Aya grinned as she poked her head around the bouquet. 'I didn't see you there.'

'Hey gorgeous,' Mel said, kissing Aya on the cheek. 'Are these for me?'

'Who else?' Aya said, wrapping her arms around Mel's neck. Although Jess felt her usual pang of jealousy, she had to hand it to Aya – at least she seemed to appreciate that she'd landed the best girlfriend ever.

Jess had pretended to be happy for Mel when she'd started describing Aya as her ideal pizza – 'Funny, kind and intelligent, with all the best toppings. Not a mushroom to be seen.' – and tried to ignore the dark puddle of jealousy that welled up inside her.

Scooping Alfie up from the floor, Jess buried her head in his fur, letting him lick her face, then fed him some of the scraps of cheese Mel had left on the kitchen counter.

'How did the appointment go?' Aya asked, kissing Mel's nose.

Jess frowned. Mel had mentioned that she'd had a meeting today, not an appointment. Had Mel got it wrong, or had Aya?

Mel glanced at Jess, who pretended to be too busy feeding Alfie to notice, then quickly whispered something into Aya's ear, which made Jess's cheeks turn pink. She hated feeling excluded more than anything. It took her right back to her schooldays.

'Jess is having a bit of a crisis. And not even the usual sort – this is a brand-new one,' Mel said, taking the flowers from Aya's hands and putting them in the sink. 'We wondered if you might be able to help, actually.'

Jess felt a mean stab of pleasure as she realised Aya either didn't know that Mel hated lilies, or had forgotten. Jess might only have a two-year head start on her, but she was certain Aya would never really know Mel as well as she did. After all, she'd only known her after the accident, not before.

'I'd love to, if I can.' Aya smiled. 'Shall we thrash it out over dinner? I'm absolutely starving.'

'Blimey. Mel was right when she said you were having a bit of a crisis, wasn't she?'

Jess nodded, expertly threading three pieces of macaroni onto the tines of her fork. 'You could say that.'

'Jess was wondering if she might be in a coma after getting mugged, and imagining this whole thing, but I'm pretty certain we're not a figment of her imagination,' Mel said. Aya nodded. 'So could it be stress-related? Something like that?'

'It's not something I've heard of, I'm afraid. The classic symptoms of stress are things like insomnia and high blood pressure, rather than creating a wormhole through time and space. Sorry.'

Jess laughed ruefully. 'I'm really hoping this is a one-off – a temporary glitch that will resolve itself tomorrow. That would be a lot easier to handle than being stuck in an actual time loop. Apart from anything else, I'm due to see my nan on Saturday, and the *Love or Dare* final is on. I really want Ryan and Clare to win, but Nan fancies Jez and Ramona. We've got five quid riding on it.'

Aya smiled reassuringly. 'Then I guess all you can do is wait for tomorrow to come,' she said. 'But I'm afraid I can't give you a medical explanation – at least nothing that's in any textbook I've ever read. Unless you're Patient Zero of a brand-new illness that will make me famous. I wouldn't mind that, actually. I might even get another award to replace the one you smashed to smithereens.'

After dinner, as Jess helped to pile up the plates and line them up on the kitchen counter, Mel squeezed her arm.

'Listen, Jess,' she said, glancing at Aya, who nodded, 'I've been thinking. Why don't you move in here for a bit? Just until you get back on your feet. Your place is falling to pieces, anyway. I promise not to make you eat salad every day.'

'That's a lovely offer, but there's no way I'm leaving my flat,' Jess said, plucking an uneaten piece of macaroni off someone's plate and popping it in her mouth. 'I'll win Brian round somehow – he's always let me off before. I'll just have to think of a fake relative I haven't killed off yet. And I'm sure I can get my job back if I wheedle at Maggie hard enough – I'm their best writer by miles, and it's not like they've never been threatened with libel before.'

'What I love most about your fix-its is how absolutely water-tight they are,' Mel said, patting Jess on the back.

'I reckon I can even get Tom back onside now I've real-ised I actually like him,' Jess continued, ignoring her. 'There must be a way of persuading him that Nate doesn't exist – all I have to do is figure out how I got rumbled and make up a believable excuse.'

'Or – and hear me out here – maybe this time you just accept that you fucked up, apologise if you need to, and try to move on,' Mel said, raising an eyebrow. 'Whenever you try to shove a sticking plaster over your problems, it never works for long. You've claimed so many dead relatives, Brian must think you're cursed. But you've never managed to just set up a direct debit, or put aside the money each month, like a normal person.'

Jess scowled. 'But that's *boring*,' she said. 'And weren't you listening? The dog basket I bought for Alfie has *bones* printed on it.'

'The what?'

Jess remembered Mel wouldn't remember their conversation from yesterday and shook her head.

'OK, maybe it is boring,' Mel said. 'But your kamikaze tactics have only just saved you by the skin of your teeth in the past. So why not try something different this time? Something a grown-up might actually do? And in the meantime, please at least think about our offer. We could hang out all the time, like the olden days. We've always got plenty of Alfie's favourite food in stock, plus our spare room is nice. You can even open the bedside table drawers without pulling the whole bloody thing over.'

'OK, I promise to think about thinking about it. Will that do?'

'I guess that's the best I'm going to get, isn't it?' Mel sighed. 'Anyway, isn't it about time you suddenly needed a wee?' she added, glancing at the dishwasher.

'Do you know what? I think you're right,' Jess said. Ducking out of helping under the guise of a weak bladder had become something of an in-joke.

Like the rest of Mel's flat, the bathroom was pristine, with 'hers and hers' sinks, a claw-foot bathtub, and dressing-room lights set around the mirrors that gave Jess's skin a perky glow. She tried to ignore the shower in the corner of the room, which had been adapted with a seat and grab handle, its toiletries laid out along low shelves Mel could reach while she was sitting down. She never got to use her beloved claw-foot bathtub unless Aya helped her in and out of it, which Jess knew she hated.

Walking back to the front room, she heard Mel and Aya talking together in low voices in the kitchen. She didn't like to eavesdrop, especially on her best friend, but when she heard her name being muttered, she froze. 'And you're *sure* it's not a medical thing?'

'The brain can do some weird stuff under stress, but reliving a whole day, down to the last detail? That doesn't seem likely, I'm afraid.'

'It was weird the way Brian called when Jess said he would, but I assume he'd just told her he was going to phone at 1.30 p.m., and she wove that into her story. Or her subconscious did.'

'Perhaps it's a form of avoidance? She does have a habit of making mad stuff up to get out of trouble, doesn't she?'

'I don't know. It's a pretty big thing to make up,' Mel said, sounding troubled. 'Although she had drunk quite a lot of wine by the time I got to the pub. Something's clearly going on, but I don't want to press her too hard. She'll do anything to avoid having a serious conversation about her problems.'

'That makes two of you, doesn't it?'

'Let's not discuss that now,' Mel said. 'I'll talk to her when the time's right. Which obviously isn't tonight.'

Jess frowned. *What the hell did that mean?*

'Well, hopefully she'll take up your offer and stay with us for a bit. We'd be able to keep an eye on her and make sure she's OK. And Alfie, of course.'

'It would be nice to have her around and get that closeness back,' Mel agreed. Jess imagined her leaning against the dishwasher, her arms folded. 'Sometimes it feels like we're two different trains on two different tracks, and the tracks are gradually getting further and further apart. And now she's making up a time loop of all things to avoid her problems – it's totally mad.'

Jess felt a tear sliding down her cheek. She wiped it angrily away. Mel had always been the one person she could really rely on. She could tell her anything, and Jess knew she would always be in her corner.

OK, so she'd told the occasional white lie in the past, but this time she was telling the truth. Yet Mel didn't believe her – and was prepared to talk to Aya about her suspicions instead of telling Jess to her face.

Jess crept back to the bathroom and sat on the loo, trying to calm down. She should probably challenge Mel and make her admit that she thought Jess had made this whole thing up. But suddenly, she felt too exhausted. She'd been through more than enough emotions for one day. Speaking to Mel would have to wait for tomorrow – if that day ever came.

Lifting her head towards the ceiling, she blinked her eyes furiously, silently ordering herself not to cry, then headed back to the living room.

Aya and Mel had put their favourite Hits of the Noughties playlist on Spotify, lit some candles, and decamped to the sofa. Although Mel's armchair looked cosy and welcoming, Jess didn't want to feel like a spare part, and she wasn't sure she could last a whole evening without blowing up at Mel before the end of it.

'I think I'm going to turn in, guys,' Jess said, faking a yawn.

'It's been a very long day, and I could do with an early night, if that's OK with you? Come on, Alfie.' His ears pricked up from his spot next to the sofa, and he trotted to Jess's side.

'Of course, if you're sure,' Mel said, easing herself off the sofa and limping towards her, wrapping her in a hug. 'The spare room's all made up for you, and there are towels at the end of the bed. Let us know if you need anything. And do think about our offer, OK? I love you, you idiot, and I just want you to be happy.'

Do you? Jess thought, bitterly.

'Night then, Jess,' Aya waved from her spot on the sofa. 'See you tomorrow.'

'I guess we'll see, won't we?' Jess murmured, and headed for her room.

Chapter 15

Jolted awake by her alarm, Jess stared at the ceiling – which she couldn't help noticing was the colour of five years'-worth of nicotine stains, rather than Elephant Breath, Mel's favourite Farrow and Ball paint shade.

'Not again. *Please* not again,' she pleaded without much hope. Then plucked her mobile from the bedside table.

7.45 a.m. Friday 13th August

Mel: What's new, Pussycat?

She hadn't dreamt it. Any of it. Not the first Friday, not yesterday. And it wasn't a one-off glitch, either. She was trapped in a time loop, and about to live through Friday 13th all over again.

Taking a deep breath to stop herself bursting into tears, Jess stared numbly at the ceiling, trying to make sense of what was going on. Then, just like yesterday, she checked all her apps – messages, Twitter, email – to make absolutely sure it really was Friday 13th, her lower lip trembling as she saw that everything had been reset again.

Throwing her phone onto the duvet and reaching down the side of her bed, she scooped Alfie onto the pillow beside hers. Jess needed a cuddle, and he wouldn't start thinking climbing on the bed was OK if he'd simply forget about it tomorrow, would he?

Alfie barked contentedly, while Jess's phone sprang into life with a new text.

Tom: See you later. Looking forward to our date! xxx

Jess covered her eyes with her arm. She was desperate to tell Mel that what she'd told her yesterday was all true, and that it was all happening again, but how could she? Mel wouldn't remember their conversation, and wouldn't believe she was telling the truth even if she did. The memory of Mel and Aya talking about her still stung.

And there was another thing, too. Something Mel needed to talk to Jess about, but couldn't, which was so unlike her. They told each other everything, and the thought that her best friend was hiding something gnawed at her.

'She'll do anything to avoid having a serious conversation about her problems.'

'That makes two of you, doesn't it?'

'I'll talk to her when the time's right.'

Jess's first Friday had been terrible, the worst day ever. But her second Friday 13th had somehow managed to be even worse.

Why did she have to be reliving *this* day? Why not Christmas Day, which she looked forward to each year, even though she always spent it in her nan's tiny house, promising herself that this year she wouldn't burn the turkey. Or the sprouts, or potatoes. Why couldn't she have re-lived one of the long, happy days in the summer holidays before Mel's accident? Jess hadn't wanted those to end even then.

With a sigh, Jess swung her feet over the edge of the bed, wedged them into her unicorn slippers and padded into the bathroom. Pulling down her lower eyelids and marvelling that they weren't more bloodshot, considering everything she'd been through lately, she wondered if her body was resetting each morning as well as her brain.

Ruffling her fingers through her fringe, she grabbed her nail scissors from the bathroom cabinet, and cut a hunk of hair off at the front. She looked ridiculous, but if it turned out that her body was resetting each morning along with everything else, she could at least enjoy being able to eat as much as she wanted without gaining weight.

Taking a photo of her reflection, she sent it to Mel by way of reply to her morning text. There was no point holding a grudge against her when she wouldn't remember the night before.

> **Mel: What on earth are you doing?**
> **You look like Emo Philips**

Who's Emo Philips?

Jess's phone made a swooping sound as Mel sent her a photo of a gangly man in a pair of white dungarees, whose hair looked like he'd let a toddler have a go at it with a pair of Fisher Price scissors. She had to concede that Mel had a point.

'Good morning. It's Friday the thirteenth at eight a.m. Welcome to *Breakfast* with me, Naga Munchetty,' Jess murmured along with the presenter as she scooped spoonfuls of marshmallow-topped Weetabix into her mouth. Alfie had already finished his breakfast, and was chasing something invisible along her laminate floor, making soft snuffling noises.

'HAHA, NAGA, GREAT JOKE,' Jess shouted at the TV as she made her usual joke about Morris dancers, plucking a tiny pink marshmallow from the top of her breakfast and throwing it at the screen. She was starting to feel slightly hysterical. Everything felt so completely surreal.

Unwilling to peel herself from the sofa for long enough to face what was happening to her, after taking Alfie for his walk, Jess slumped back down on it to watch something called *The Planet's Funniest Animals* (in order to qualify as a Funniest Animal, you had to fall off something or knock a toddler over, which didn't seem all that hilarious to Jess).

Next, she started watching *Wakey, Wakey, Britain!*. She knew Mel would be watching too, giving instructions to the presenters through their earpieces. Usually, it would be comforting to know they were watching the same thing, even if they weren't together. But instead, it was a painful reminder of the conversation she'd overheard Mel and Aya having in the kitchen.

Thinking about that made her stomach do unpleasant loop-the-loops, so she flicked past *Wakey, Wakey, Britain!* onto an old episode of *Friends*. Watching Joey doing lunges wearing all of Chandler's clothes, Jess felt herself relaxing. She'd seen every episode of this show so many times already, she could happily watch it every day and still not get bored. Except for the Emily episodes, obviously.

'What shall we do now, boy?' Jess said, leaning down and rubbing Alfie's head. 'Should I order a massive McDonald's? Yes, I *should*. Yes, I *should*.' Taking Alfie's tiny paw in her hand, she gave herself a high five. Alfie looked confused.

'You know, it would be really cool if you could just learn how to do that, like a normal dog. I'd give teaching you how to do it a go, now it looks like I've got eternity to try it, if your fuzzy little brain wouldn't forget everything the next day.'

As the morning wore on, Jess munched through her second breakfast and half-watched the TV, which wasn't quite as interesting as the drama unfolding on her phone. Watching her job imploding from afar was certainly more fun than being there in person to receive a massive bollocking then get fired.

8.10 a.m.

> Jasmit: Jess, can you pick up a copy of the Sun and the Mail on your way in? I think the Bijou girls have nicked ours again

> Jasmit: Oh, and chocolate. Maggie's already in a foul mood, and I need extra supplies

9.40 a.m

> Jasmit: Earth calling Jess? Where are you? I need those papers, and Donna and Alejandro's shoot is in five minutes. I'm sharpening my knives ready to kill you . . .

> Jasmit: Hope you're OK, though!

133

Ian: Translation: 'If you've been
murdered I don't want my last text
to you to be a death threat'

Jasmit: Fuck off, Ian.

Jasmit: But yes. I don't really want
to murder you #Disclaimer

9.45 a.m

Jasmit: Oh Christ, Donna and Alejandro
are here. WHERE ARE YOU, JESS??

Jasmit: (Hope ur not dead)

9.57 a.m. Missed call: Jasmit

9.58 am Missed call: Jasmit

9.59 a.m. Missed call: Jasmit

10 a.m. Missed call: Jasmit

10.05 a.m

Jasmit: Jesus, Jess. Maggie just FIRED
YOU!!! Why the hell did you send Donna
an email about Alejandro being a sleaze?!
She read it out to the entire office. What
were you thinking? CALL ME!!!

Jasmit: Maggie is going ballistic.
Please answer your phone

Ian: (Not an exaggeration. Maggie is currently
the colour of a strangulated ballbag. And
unfortunately, I know exactly what that
looks like, thanks to editing 'My Hubby's
Terrifying Tackle' in the Summer Special)

Jess had decided to ignore her work texts, but now she started worrying that Jasmit might go into early labour if she didn't prove she was at least alive.

I'm not dead, although thank you for your definitely
genuine concern on that score. I also know about
being fired. Don't worry about it – I'm fine, and I'll
sort it out. Over and out!

As she sent her last text, her phone lit up with the text from her nan, which she still hadn't replied to yet. Googling 'Monty Don married?' Jess tapped out her reply.

I'm afraid he is, Nan, sorry. Xxx

Nan: Oh hello love, I meant to type that into
Google! Bloody phones. Made by arseholes.
Shame about Monty. Lovely bum on him.

Rolling her eyes at her nan's delightful language, she threw her phone onto the coffee table. At the same time, Alfie cocked his head, then started yelping as a key rattled in the door. No one but Mel had a key to the flat, and Jess knew it couldn't be her. She'd be busy with work or at her meeting – or was it actually an appointment? Jess would have to find out.

Grabbing a cushion from the sofa, Jess held it in front of her like a shield, as if it would do her any good against a gang of burglars with knives, which is what she imagined was about to burst into her flat.

'Who is it? What do you want?' she asked, trying to sound brave as she scrunched herself into the sofa and the front door swung open. Behind it, looking at her in confusion, was Tom.

Chapter 16

'Thank fuck for that,' Jess breathed, uncrunching herself and throwing the cushion back into the corner of the sofa. 'I thought you were a knife-wielding rapist.'

'Umm, no. Just Tom, the devilishly handsome guy you're dating,' he said, coming into the front room and shutting the door behind him. He was clutching a bunch of red roses in one hand, and a small bunch of keys in the other. Alfie kamakazed off the sofa like he was doing a parachute jump and started leaping up at his shins.

'Hey, Alfie! Nice to see you, buddy,' he said, leaning down and chucking him under the chin. Alfie wagged his tail excitedly.

'Come back here, you traitor,' Jess said, patting the sofa to summon Alfie back. 'Some guard dog you are. What on earth are you doing here, Tom? And who gave you my keys?'

Tom's face turned pink. Despite having an oddly youthful-looking face, he dressed more like a middle-aged man than someone who'd waved goodbye to his twenties not that long ago. The morning was already warm, but he was wearing brown corduroy trousers and a dark-green V-neck jumper over a checked shirt, and his short brown hair was sticking up at the back even though he'd amazed Jess when they'd first met by revealing that he always used an *actual comb* on it, instead of just using his fingers like a normal person.

'I could ask you the same thing,' he stuttered. 'Apart from the keys thing, obviously. I thought you weren't supposed to be at home?'

'According to who?' Jess challenged, which caused Tom to look even more flustered. He looked like a professor trying to unlock a cipher in a BBC drama about the Enigma code. But despite her ideal man being Hugh Jackman circa 2005, Jess realised she found his confused-geography-teacher look quite adorable.

She folded her arms and waited for Tom to come up with an excuse. She could think of a handful he could use right off the top of her head:

I'm fixing your leaky tap as a surprise.

I've come to read your gas meter, seeing as you've ignored the last dozen reminders.

I'm here to set a booby trap to pay Brian back for evicting you.

Although technically, she hadn't been evicted yet, so maybe not that last one. But Tom was completely guileless, and incapable of lying on his feet.

'OK—' he sighed, giving up his attempts to think of something '—Mel gave me your keys. We were in cahoots.' *Cahoots!* Jess stifled a smile. 'I was going to scatter these rose petals on your bed, and . . . Oh god, this sounds awful when you say it out loud. What was I thinking? I'm not thirteen.' Tom ruffled the back of his hair with one hand.

'Go on,' Jess said. She was starting to enjoy herself.

'Well . . . I was going to spell "Will you be my girlfriend?" in petals on your bed for you to see when we came home after our date tonight,' he stuttered. 'Then you were going to start crying *maybe*, and say yes, and we were going to be a couple. You know. Violins swell, we live happily ever after, the end.'

'Wow. That is a really terrible plan. Didn't Mel tell you how much I hate all that corny crap?' So this was how Mel had known Tom was really into her.

'Oh, she did. An embarrassing number of times, actually. She even shouted it out of the window after I'd left her flat. But I know you really love movies, especially the stuff with grand gestures. And they're always doing this kind of thing on *Love or Dare*. I looked it up. So I thought you might come round to the idea of being my girlfriend if I really went for it. You know, like Julia Roberts in *Pretty Woman* rescuing Richard Gere right back.'

'You thought you might melt my stony, sex-worker's heart with roses? I mean, you might have pulled it off if you'd also bought me a huge diamond necklace. Did you?'

Tom shook his head. 'I've got some Skittles if you want some?' he added, hopefully.

Jess shrugged. 'I could do Skittles. Sit down.' She nodded at the sofa for Tom to sit and headed into the kitchen, before returning a few moments later clutching the bag of mini marshmallows, which, along with Weetabix and booze, seemed to be the only edible item in the flat she could be reliably expected to keep topped up.

'Skittle sandwich?' she suggested, sitting next to Tom. He handed her the bag. Pressing a red Skittle into a pink marshmallow, she topped it with a white one, and popped it into her mouth.

'What's it like?' Tom asked, studying her face.

'Squashy,' she said. 'You try.'

Tom pressed a green Skittle between two marshmallows – which was classic Tom, when everyone knows green are the worst ones – and chewed on it thoughtfully.

'I'm not sure I can improve on your review, really,' he said. 'What *are* you doing at home, anyway? Are you feeling OK? I was looking forward to taking you out for dinner tonight.'

'No, I'm not ill.' Jess sighed, plucking absent-mindedly at a bit of foam stuffing that was poking out of the arm of her sofa. 'I was kind of about to get fired, is all, and I couldn't face it.'

'Fired? You're joking?'

'It's no big deal, really,' Jess said. 'I'm not exactly cracking major stories for the *New York Times*, am I? The world won't crumble to dust if it doesn't get another one of my articles about a hamster foiling a burglary.'

'Maybe not, but you're amazing at what you do. I mean, "HOME-ALONE HAMSTER" was a stone-cold classic. And who can forget such gripping tales as "HELP! MY BABY BLEW ME UP!" AND "BUSTED BY MY BUNIONS"?'

Jess raised her eyebrows. 'Don't tell me you've actually read *Real Talk!*?'

'I might have picked up a copy or two. Come on, the girl I'm dating is the editor of Jess's Totally Hot Top Tips!, the most cunning tips page on the market. You're practically a celebrity. And how else would I find out that the best way to boil a cracked egg is in vinegar? That one went straight into my facts vault.' Tom tapped his temple, and Jess grinned.

'And you might poke fun at yourself, but your stories

entertain people, which is what they're supposed to do, right? It's obvious how much effort you put into them. They're like mini sagas all in one, with a story arc and everything.'

Jess felt a warm feeling flooding through her. She always pretended to laugh along when her friends posted memes on Facebook that made fun of the kinds of stories she wrote, or mocked up weekly magazine front covers that were even more sensational than the real thing. But really, she was proud of her job and how far she'd come.

She might not get to write reports on the gender pay gap, or interview up-and-coming female politicians like the *Bijou* girls did, but she loved hearing people's stories – all the twists and turns of their lives, and the highs and lows that went hand in hand with them. She got emotionally invested every single time and felt a burst of pride when they thanked her for putting into words what they were unable to articulate themselves.

'That's exactly how it happened. It's like you were there with me!' they told her, time and time again. And in her own small way, she knew she was making a difference by showing people that whatever challenges life threw at them, they were not alone.

'I can't believe you can see that about my writing,' Jess said. 'I assumed you'd think it was rubbish. And actually, I'm not really that blasé about losing my job. I don't know what I'd do without Jas and Ian and Rachel. And even Maggie. Kind of. So I'm hoping to fix things somehow.'

'If there's anything I can do, let me know. I could always karate chop your boss for you, if you like. I've seen every single *Karate Kid* movie. Even the stinkers.'

Jess was shocked to feel her eyes filling with tears. Mel,

Alfie and her nan had always been her whole world. But now Mel felt they were drifting apart, her nan wasn't always quite there, and Alfie ... well, he was a dog. Although she'd always resisted having a boyfriend, she could see how this part of a relationship could be appealing. It was nice feeling like she had someone else on her team. Someone like Mel, who was kind and could make her laugh.

'Hey, it's all right if you don't want to talk about it,' Tom said, looking at her with concern and winding his arm around her waist. 'But I think you're being brave. I mean, you're pretty calm for someone whose life's just kind of ... imploded.' Tom mimed explosions going off and people screaming.

'Oh, thanks a lot.' Jess laughed, thumping his arm, then leaned over to kiss him. He was a very good kisser.

When they pulled apart, Tom grinned back at her. 'I don't know what I'd do if I got fired. Probably cry. Then beg for my job back. Lie on the floor blubbing. Something pretty sexy along those lines, anyway.'

'OK, so I've got a question for you,' Jess said, offering Tom some more marshmallows. 'What would you do if you got fired, but then you got stuck in a time loop, and had to live that same day over and over again?'

'Like in *Groundhog Day*?'

'Yes, like in *Groundhog Day*.'

'What's turned you so philosophical all of a sudden? That's not a Jess kind of question. Yours are usually a lot more cheese-based.'

'Isn't this the kind of conundrum your people like?'

'Your people?'

'You know. With your elbow patches and Warhammer figurines and jelly-like muscles from staying indoors all day.'

142

'Ah. The super-cool lot, you mean?'

'Yes, those ones. You love questions about stuff like time loops, or which superpower you'd choose, or "would you rather fight fifty tiny geese or one giant cricket".'

'In terms of your other excellent questions, I'd go for flying, *obviously*, and I'd fight the geese, please. Unleash some of those *Karate Kid* moves on them.'

'Aww, you're so nerdy. It's kind of adorable.'

'I'm not nerdy, I'm a geek. There's a huge difference. You've got your superhero geeks, who might watch all the Marvel films, but they're different to comic-book nerds, who'll go mad if someone's origin story isn't completely accurate. Then there are computer geeks, and your tech nerds, and your LARP-ers and your D&D-ers . . .' Jess shook her head disbelievingly, and Tom blushed. 'But maybe that's a conversation for another time.'

Jess laughed, leaned forward, and kissed Tom on the nose. Now she'd realised that she liked him at all, she was starting to realise she actually liked him quite a lot.

'Anyway, back to my *actual* question . . . ?'

'OK, I've got this,' Tom said, rubbing his hands together. 'First, I'd have a nervous breakdown, obviously. That would probably last at least a week before I got used to the idea that time travel was real. But after that I guess it would depend which day I was reliving. If it was the day I'd got fired, I'd probably try to fix that first.'

'You and me both.'

'Then I guess I'd just try to make the most of not having to deal with any consequences of my actions, and the money in my bank account reappearing each day. I'd try to travel a bit, too. Depending on what triggers the time loop to reset itself,

I guess I'd spend some time as far away as possible – maybe at Loch Ness and by the sea. I'd read all the books I wouldn't get round to otherwise, and not feel guilty for ditching the boring ones halfway through, and I'd watch *loads* of films. I'd swot up on all the time travel stuff, like *About Time* and *Hot Tub Time Machine* to find out how to escape, when I was ready to.'

'Ohh, eternal homework. That sounds fun,' Jess said, giving a thumbs up – although behind her sarcasm, she was starting to see that the time loop might actually have some positives. She half-wished she could take notes – especially ones that wouldn't disappear overnight.

'Then in the evening, I'd look out for people who'd had a really bad day, and try to make things better for them the next one. Like I'd call them up and say, "You know there's that big circular saw you use at work, and that you're really fond of both your arms? Why not take the day off?" Stuff like that.'

Jess felt sheepish. It hadn't crossed her mind for a millisecond that the time loop might be a way of trying to help other people. She'd mainly just wondered if she'd get fatter if she ate pizza every day.

'You're so noble,' she said, leaning forward and kissing him again. Then leaned back and raised her eyebrows at Tom's suddenly bulging crotch. 'What's that you've got there, young Thomas?'

Tom looked down and turned pink. 'It's not mine, Miss. One of the bigger boys must have put it there to get me into trouble.'

Jess laughed, and felt a familiar warmth creeping through her body. Tom might be bookish, but that meant he was very thorough in his research in all areas of life – including knowing

full well how to help Jess achieve her 'WOOOOAH!', sometimes more than once in one session.

As Jess grabbed his hand and led him towards the bedroom,
Tom pulled her towards him, kissed her again hard, then
gazed at her face.

'Before we . . . you know, can I ask you just one thing?' Tom
said softly. Jess nodded, breaking into a smile. 'What on earth
have you done to your hair? You look like Emo Philips.'

An hour later, Jess was busy failing to blow post-coital smoke
rings at the ceiling as usual, her ashtray balanced on her chest.
'Hey, look! That was almost a smoke ring.'

'No, it absolutely wasn't. Here, give me that.' Tom frowned,
pinching his fingers together and gesturing at her cigarette.
'It's torture watching you be so bad at this, despite so much
effort. Can it possibly be as difficult as you make it look?'

'It's so hard!' Jess wailed, propping herself on one elbow
and nestling the ashtray in the sheets between them. 'Here.'

Taking the cigarette, Tom took a deep drag, blowing a
perfect circle into the air with one smack of his lips before
breaking into a coughing fit that lasted a full minute.

'OK, so smoke rings might be easy. But smoking with
panache is hard,' Jess muttered, taking the cigarette back and
stubbing it out.

'With just a few more years' practise, you'll be able to make
ships out of smoke, like Gandalf,' Tom said.

'I refuse to know what a Gandalf is, because it sounds mega
nerdy. Sorry, *geeky*.'

'Come on, everyone knows who Gandalf is. He's from *The
Lord of the Rings*. Grey cloak, big beard, hangs out with hob-
bits. I still can't believe you haven't seen the films.'

'Of course I haven't, in the same way that I don't own a Magic The Gathering T-shirt, or know the Klingon for "Hello". As you so rightly pointed out, I'm more of a cheesy romcom kinda girl. If Gandalf doesn't spend the films spilling coffee down hot men's shirts or changing his mind at the altar, I'm not interested.'

'*The Lord of the Rings* isn't *niche* nerd, it's *mainstream* nerd. Did you know it made almost three billion dollars at the box office? That many nerds can't be wrong. Oh, and Klingons don't say "Hello"; they say, "What do you want?".'

'Go on. I know you're dying to tell me.'

'*nuqneH*,' Tom said, primly.

Jess buried her head in his surprisingly toned chest – she assumed from carrying all those extra-heavy books around at the bookbinders – and laughed.

'How about we start watching the films this afternoon?' Tom suggested, kissing the top of her head. 'We can ease you in gently, and only watch the first one.'

'Oh, we only have to watch one three-hour-long film about elves, do we? Fantastic,' Jess said, propping herself on her elbows. 'If you're dead set on torturing me, can we at least make our own toffee vodka to help ease the pain? I read somewhere that you can make it in a dishwasher using Werther's Originals, and I've always wanted to try it.'

'You don't have a dishwasher.'

'Dishwasher smishwasher. We'll just put it in a bucket of hot water for a bit.'

'Great idea,' Tom said, leaping out of bed. Throwing on his corduroy trousers and shirt, he started straightening out the bedsheets and fluffing the pillows, before suddenly stopping in his tracks. 'What are these?' he asked, plucking a tiny blue pair of Hollister trunks with palm trees dotted across the waistband from underneath Jess's pillow.

'What, those? Oh, they're nothing,' Jess blushed, snatching them from his hands. Her heart pounded. So was this how Tom had found out about Nate? Had he found the pants under her pillow when he was preparing his rose-petal proposal?

Nate had probably expected Jess chancing upon his musty pants would be a lovely surprise, the way some men think their dick pics are – when they actually inspire women to forward them to their friends saying, 'THIS PENIS LOOKS LIKE DOMINIC CUMMINGS.'

'I . . . I just like wearing men's pants sometimes, that's all,' Jess muttered, throwing them into the corner of the room. 'More comfy, you know?'

'While that might be true, I'm pretty sure I've never seen you wearing anything other than M&S stuff or those days-of-the-week underpants you like so much,' Tom said slowly, sitting on the edge of the bed. 'Plus – no offence, because it's a great bum – you couldn't get a single one of your cheeks into those tiny things. So whose are they, Jess? Are you seeing someone else?'

'It's just . . . just some guy, OK?' Jess stuttered. 'Look, it's no big deal. We're not exclusive or anything, are we? We're just having fun. And I thought – quite reasonably, actually – that it would be OK for me to have fun with someone else too. Think of it like . . . sharing your paint pot with the other kids at school.' She nudged Tom, hoping he would laugh. But instead, he looked distraught.

'Right,' he said, shaking his head. 'So you're a paint pot I should be happy to share with other guys? I guess I'd never thought of cheating like that before.'

'It's not *cheating* cheating,' Jess said, trying to sound breezy. 'We're not boyfriend and girlfriend, are we? I was just trying a few guys on and seeing how they fit. I can get rid of Nate if it bothers you that much. Honestly, it's no big deal.'

Jess swallowed. She really needed Tom to see this the same way as her.

'Nate? What kind of name is Nate? Now I'm just imagining some *Love or Dare*-style hunk impressing you with his bouncy pecs. Which is great. And being just one of a few guys you're trying on, like I'm a ... dressing gown or something makes me feel so special. It really does.'

Tom looked genuinely upset, and Jess felt a wave of guilt crashing over her.

'To be honest, I'm not up for this, Jess. I thought we had something special here. I know I'm a bit of a geek, and you're just this ... ball of energy. But we have so much fun together. You're beautiful, and bright, and funny, and I really like you. Whatever you think about yourself, I think you're brilliant. And I was kind of hoping that if I liked you enough, you'd start to like yourself, too.'

'What do you mean, "Whatever you think about yourself"? I like myself just fine, thank you,' Jess said, getting angry.

'Sure, OK. But that's not how it seems from the outside, Jess.' Tom started blinking hard. 'Although maybe I got you all wrong. And maybe there's a reason you don't like yourself so much after all. We're obviously on completely different pages when it comes to whatever this is. *Was*. I guess I'll see you around.'

Taking a deep breath, he stood up, plucked his green jumper from the floor, and headed for the door.

'Wait,' Jess said weakly, but didn't bother standing up

as Tom stalked stiffly out of the room. Slamming the front door behind him, Jess slumped backwards onto the bed. If she was lucky, she could nap her way through the afternoon – because after a promising start to the first Friday she'd actually been starting to enjoy, suddenly tomorrow couldn't come soon enough.

Chapter 17

Waking up with a start, Jess slapped off her alarm and plucked her phone from the bedside table. She stared at it, confused.

Mel: What's new, Pussycat?

By concentrating very hard on not thinking about it, after her argument with Tom she'd somehow managed to drift off to sleep on top of her bed. But now, she was lying under her light summer duvet, and her thin curtains were drawn, soft morning light casting a shadow of the lamp post outside her window against them.

She'd assumed that each new Friday reset at 7.45 a.m., when her alarm went off. But there was no way she'd slept all the way through the afternoon – especially not with Alfie's rumbling tummy and his attendant face-licking to deal with. Apparently falling asleep had reset the day.

'Amazing. I've invented a nap-triggered teleportation service. Not bad, eh?' Jess said, throwing her phone on the duvet. 'Especially as I'm absolutely amazing at naps.' Alfie woofed as he jumped onto the bed and curled himself on the pillow beside hers.

'Hang on, cheeky chops. What are you doing up here?' Jess said, narrowing her eyes at Alfie, who woofed innocently. 'You know you're not allowed on the bed. You're too furry and stinky.'

Grabbing her phone, she took a selfie of her and Alfie and sent it to Mel. Her fringe was back to its former, non-Emo glory, which meant she could eat, drink and smoke to her heart's content, without worrying about the effects on her body.

She might even abandon her regular vow that today would be the day she'd discover yoga (it seemed one didn't 'try' yoga, one 'discovered' it), because there was no point in exercising if the results weren't going to stick, was there?

'Well, I guess this time loop has its plus sides,' she told Alfie, holding his paw and rubbing it with her thumb. 'At least I can avoid upsetting Tom today. All I've got to do is hide Nate's stupid, doll-sized pants, and he'll be none the wiser.'

From her duvet, Jess's phone buzzed.

Tom: See you later. Looking forward to our date! xxx

Jess hesitated before replying. Was an exclamation mark too racy? Did a kiss suggest she suddenly wanted a boyfriend? Deciding it probably didn't matter today, she hit Send before she could change her mind.

Can't wait! See you outside the Tube xx

Jess felt a swoop of guilt as she remembered how sad Tom had looked the day before, and his bewildered face when he explained that he wanted Jess to like herself as much as he liked her.

The time loop had given her a gift, in a way. If she upset anyone, she didn't need to feel guilty, because they simply wouldn't remember – although, of course, the memory of whatever she'd done would stay with her, and was likely to creep out of the corners of her brain as soon as she tried to get to sleep.

Here, let's take a look at this memory of the terrible thing that happened to Mel. Now think about how sad Tom looked when he found Nate's pants. Hey, why don't we go on a guilt trip about Donna's reaction to your email? That'll help you get to sleep, right? Lol.

Still, she was grateful that Tom wouldn't remember a thing about it, even if she still had to live with the memory.

Swinging her legs off the bed with a sigh, Jess grabbed Alfie and squeezed him to her chest. He snuffled at her neck, then licked it. So far, Jess thought, every day of the time loop had been a bit rubbish. Yesterday had been fun, until its disastrous conclusion – but surely there was a way of making more of the time loop than she'd managed so far?

When they'd discussed what Tom would do if *he* was stuck in a time loop, he'd said something about the money reappearing in his bank account each morning. Jess had hardly anything in her bank account as it was, and her credit cards were rinsed. But she had all the time in the world to work out how to change that, didn't she? As she ruffled Alfie's fur, Jess pondered, then pondered some more. Then she broke into a grin.

'You know what?' she told Alfie. 'I think I've got a cunning plan . . .'

*

'What I don't get is why Benjamin keeps trying it on with Hazel,' Tom said, waving his glass of whisky in the air, spilling about £50-worth onto his kilt and narrowly missing Jess's head, which was nestled in his lap. 'I mean, it's so obvious she's not into him, and he's just being creepy. And Lesley should be nicer to Philip. She's a Botoxed she-devil. Can we watch another one? *Pleeease?*'

'Is this the same man who thinks all reality TV is rubbish?' Jess asked, hiccupping delicately and pulling up the bodice of her Vera Wang wedding dress. 'And yet here you are, looking quite a lot like someone who's incredibly invested in *Love or Dare*. You'll be begging me to come over to Nan's and watch the final with us tomorrow at this rate. BEGGING ME.'

'The thing I still don't understand is how you suddenly became this ... poker genius overnight?' Mel said from the other end of the sofa, sleepily brushing crumbs off her own designer wedding dress.

'Victoria Coren-Mitchell started playing when she was just a kid, and she was forty ... forty-one when she won at San Remo for the second time,' Tom said, squinting at the telly with one eye closed.

'Beginner's luck, I guess,' Jess said, drowsily. 'Or I'm just a natural poker genius. Actually, let's go with the genius thing. Is there any champers left?'

After a day of shopping, eating and more shopping, Jess's living room looked even more like it had been burgled than usual. Cardboard bags from Chanel, Vivienne Westwood and Selfridges surrounded the sofa like an expensive moat, spilling out tissue paper, shoes and the taffeta hems of brightly coloured dresses.

A designer cane embellished with brilliant white Swarovski

crystals lay on the floor next to Mel's end of the sofa, and Tom was sipping a £1,500 bottle of twenty-five-year-aged single-malt whisky from Harvey Nichols that Jess had treated him to, despite his protests. To 'honour the malt', Tom had also bought himself a kilt, sporran and those knee-length socks with bows that only five-year-old girls and burly Scotsmen at weddings can get away with wearing.

A whole leg of serrano ham was propped in a stand on the coffee table, looking slightly mangled from Jess's attempts to get the hang of carving wafer-thin slices from it. The man in Harrods Food Halls had nervously explained that correct slicing was essential to achieve the desired flavour, but stuffing thick, wonky chunks into buttered rolls also seemed to taste just fine.

In the kitchen, the Bush's quiz machine flashed merrily, its bleeping noises enticing Tom to play *Who Wants to Be a Millionaire?*. It was his favourite quiz game, so Jess had persuaded Mark to part with it in exchange for £2,000 cash. It was the best present she'd ever bought anybody, and Tom was delighted with it. It seemed he was one of those people who are lovely to buy presents for, because they get so lavishly excited. Jess loved buying people presents, so she took this as a good omen.

Three empty bottles of champagne lay on the floor by the sofa, and Jess's feet, which were nestled in Mel's lap, glinted with a pair of red high-heeled shoes that she'd decided she might buy again tomorrow. She was hopeless at walking in heels, but they were so beautiful.

The best thing was that she hadn't even had to extend her overdraft again in order to afford all this stuff. Yesterday morning, she'd known absolutely nothing about poker. But then she'd downloaded a casino app, put the chain across the front door to keep Tom out, and at 8 a.m. on the dot had started a game against some players in Australia. She wrote down every hand dealt, and every move made.

After she'd spent three hours on various poker sites working out how to use the information to make sure she'd win next time, and was sure she knew what to do, she'd willed herself asleep, wondering whether to hit Bond Street or Harrods first as she drifted off.

Luckily, her plan had worked – and by the time Tom had wandered into her flat just after 10.30 a.m. that morning, she was almost £52,000 better off than she had been when she'd woken up. It didn't take much to persuade him to go shopping with her, or for Mel to join them after her meeting – or appointment, if that's what it really was.

Jess still felt hurt by what she'd overheard in Mel's kitchen, but not enough to let her miss out on the shopping spree to end all shopping sprees – and it turned out that spending tens of thousands of pounds on ridiculously expensive crap nobody needed was exactly as much fun as it had been in Jess's wildest, Lottery-winning fantasies.

'It's weird how you can buy a really really *really* expensive version of pretty much anything, even if the version that costs a quid does exactly the same thing,' Jess said now, holding her Murano glass wine goblet up to the light with a swaying hand. 'This cost a hundred and thirty-five quid! And it just holds wine! Rich people be crazy.'

'You're still taking some of this stuff back tomorrow though, right?' Mel said, sipping a Bellini. 'I know you won a lot of money, but you really don't need a Smeg fridge to hold your mouldy, leftover baked beans collection. Or a drone. Or this.

What even is this?' she asked, plucking a bright-pink sculpture from the coffee table. It looked like a cross between the Michelin Man and a trunkless elephant.

'That is *art*, and cost me twelve hundred pounds,' Jess said, snatching it from Mel's hand. 'And yes, it is horrible, and will be going back to the shop.'

'Maybe you should just keep the unbreakable things. Like this dress. Can I keep this, please please please?' Mel asked, plucking at her tulle skirt.

Jess nodded. 'Of course; I can always win more money tomorrow, what with being a bona fide poker champ. Plus nice things are nice. And you're nice, too, Mel,' Jess added, propping herself up on her elbows and waving her glass in her direction. 'In fact, you're the smashingest one ever. Is that a word?'

Mel shrugged. 'I guess it is now. You're loaded, you get to do whatever you like.'

'Listen,' she said, earnestly, putting her glass on the floor and sitting up to clutch Mel's hands. 'I know there's something you want to talk to me about. Something you need to tell me. Something serious. Maybe ... maybe something to do with your appointment today?'

Mel blushed bright red, but Jess ploughed on. This was a lot easier to say when she was drunk. 'I just want you to know that whatever it is, you can trust me, OK? I promise. Promise promise. Because it makes me sad to think you feel like you can't tell me everything.'

Mel swallowed and looked flustered. 'Let's not talk about it today. We can talk about it tomorrow when we're soberer. But I'm sorry if I've upset you. I never meant to do that. You know I love you, right?' she said, leaning over and hugging Jess tightly.

'I love you too,' Jess said, squeezing back.

'Today has been amazing. Thank you so much, Jess,' Tom yawned from his end of the sofa, failing entirely to read the room through his whisky fog. 'I wish we could do this every day. This must be what it's like to be super-rich.'

'Or living in a time loop.'

'Aww, that's the geekiest thing you've ever said. I'm so proud,' Tom grinned. 'I think you're the smashingest too, Jess Janus. In fact . . . I think I might be falling for you.'

Mel grimaced. Then looked shocked as Jess replied, 'Thank you, Tom. That's a lovely thing to hear,' and turned around to kiss him.

She paused, waiting for panic to set in. What Tom had just said was pretty huge, after all. So she was surprised when the panic never came. She still wasn't ready for a boyfriend, but hearing that Tom was falling for her wasn't as terrifying as she'd expected. After all, he'd forget all about it tomorrow – and Jess had all the time she needed to get used to the idea. Mel raised her eyebrows. 'What's happened to my cynical, relationship-dodging mate Jess Janus?'

Jess took a sip of her drink, and swallowed it past the lump that had formed in her throat. 'You wouldn't believe me even if I told you.'

Chapter 18

After her Fabulous, Expensive Day Of Fun with Mel and Tom, Jess had expected to feel full of beans when she was jolted awake by her alarm as usual the next morning. But instead, she felt oddly deflated.

Mel: What's new, Pussycat?

'Absofuckinglutelynothing,' she said, sighing so deeply it felt like it came from the very depths of her soul. Then she tried sticking her tongue as far up her nose as it would go, took a photo, and sent it to Mel.

She'd had such a brilliant day yesterday, but without even having to check, she knew everything they'd bought the day before – the quiz machine, the ridiculous dresses – had disappeared like Cinderella's pumpkin carriage as soon as she'd fallen asleep, like a horrible reverse Christmas. The thought that while she was stuck in the time loop she could make new memories, but nobody would be able to share them with her, made her feel horribly sad. What she really needed right now was to see her nan. She usually saw her on Saturdays and Wednesdays like clockwork, and before the time loop had thrown a spanner in the works, watching the *Love or Dare* final together had promised to be one of the highlights of her week.

Pamela didn't pull any punches when it came to calling the male contestants 'sleazy, no-dick wankers', which Jess always found hilarious, coming from her tiny nan. Despite her love of using language that would make Shaun Ryder blush, she looked like a light breeze might knock her over.

But it was starting to feel like she might never reach Saturday, and although they'd exchanged texts – mainly about Monty Don's marital status – Jess was starting to miss her. She'd make her feel safe and loved, even if Jess might not find the courage to tell her what was going on.

'Shall we visit Nan?' she asked Alfie, ruffling his ears. They pricked up and his tail started wagging wildly at the mention of his second-favourite person in the world. Pamela was besotted with Alfie, and, despite Jess's constant protests, she'd cook him entire steaks, or give him a whole jar of peanut butter to lick his way through, whenever they visited.

Alfie barked excitedly.

'Yeah, I thought you'd like that, you big fatty.'

Plucking Nate's pants from under her pillow, Jess stuffed them in the linen basket, then pulled on her jeans and vintage T-shirt, topped by her bee pendant. She stroked it thoughtfully as she tucked it into her T-shirt, then looked in the mirror and sighed. Because she'd been planning on doing a big wash on Saturday (and had left it until the last minute, as usual), she only had a couple of clean outfits to choose from each Friday morning. But, of course, she knew now that there was an easy way of fixing that.

'We might have to go shopping first, Alfie. Is that OK with you?'

'I'm afraid Monty Don is married, Nan,' Jess called as she slotted her key into her nan's front door and pushed it open.

'Jess, is that you?' Pamela called back, waddling out of the kitchen. She listed alarmingly to the left, like the figurehead on the bow of an abandoned ship, thanks to her dodgy hip. 'Did I text that to you? I thought I'd googled it. Bloody mobile phones. I might just throw mine in the bin, the good it does me.'

Jess kissed her powdery cheek. 'You know you need to keep your mobile so I can get hold of you, now you don't have a landline.' Pamela had unplugged her phone after a scammer had managed to wangle £1,000 out of her already-bare bank account. Jess's nan might be as lively and as rude as ever, but her mind wasn't as sharp as it had been, which made her easy prey when she was having a bad day. She hadn't even remembered to tell Jess what had happened until it was too late to get the money back.

'Look who it is!' Pamela said suddenly, spying Alfie wriggling on the floor, eager for a cuddle. 'You bought Reggie to see me,' she said, scooping Alfie into her arms.

Jess stroked his nose as he licked her nan's face. 'Can't you just call him Alfie, like a normal person? That is his name, you know.'

'And a bloody silly one, if you ask me. Reggie's much better.'

'He looks like a fluffy marshmallow, and you want to name him after one of the Krays? It doesn't make sense.'

Pamela tapped her nose and chuckled knowingly, and Jess decided she didn't want to know any more. Even after all these years, her nan was always coming out with new revelations about her past, surprising Jess with an out-of-the-blue, 'You wouldn't think to look at him, but Jimi Hendrix loved *Coronation Street*. Big fan of Hilda Ogden.'

It was weird how she had pin-sharp memory when it came to things that had happened fifty years ago, but couldn't tell Jess what she'd had for breakfast. She supposed watching Jimi Hendrix put his feet up in front of ITV was a bit more memorable than chowing down on a bowl of soggy cornflakes.

Jess followed her nan into the kitchen, who reluctantly handed Alfie over to Jess so she could pour some tea from a ready-made pot, arrange some Garibaldis on a plate, and give Alfie a cooked chicken breast the size of his head to gnaw through. Jess rolled her eyes.

'What are you doing here, anyway? Why aren't you at work writing my magazine?' Pamela said, plucking her copy of *Real Talk!* off the counter and waving it in Jess's direction. 'I did like your story about that couple who got caught shagging at Knutsford services. The dirty buggers. Serves them right.'

'Actually, Nan, I'm having a day off,' Jess said. 'I'm not having the best day, to be honest. Although I went shopping, which was fun. What do you think of my new outfit?'

'Stand over there and let me look at you,' Pamela said, pointing at the kitchen window and squinting at Jess. 'Blimey, that's all right, innit? Give us a twirl.' Jess spun around, her expertly cut dress gently skimming her thighs.

Before heading to her nan's, she'd played a quick hand of poker, winning enough money to buy some new clothes, then stopped off at Covent Garden. As much fun as her last shopping spree had been, she wasn't sure how her nan would react if she turned up at her house in an £8,000 wedding dress.

So instead, she'd made for one of the high-end high-street shops she sometimes went to with Mel to help her choose work outfits.

Plucking a slouchy olive-green mini dress and a quirky black-wool biker jacket from the racks, she'd chosen a long gold necklace with asymmetric black and gold shapes hanging from it and a chunky gold ring to go with it. Spinning around in the mirror, she'd smoothed the clothes down over her curves. They fit like a dream, and seemed to smell faintly of perfume.

She felt put together, but not too polished, and wondered if this was how Mel felt all the time. She quite liked it. In fact, she almost felt like a grown-up.

'You look stunning, love,' Pamela said now, as Jess did 'ta-da!' hands at herself.

'Thanks, Nan,' Jess said. 'I might make this my new look.'

'You do sometimes look like you should be pushing a shopping trolley full of carrier bags, but I didn't like to say,' Pamela said, leading the way into the living room.

'Thanks, Nan. That's . . . helpful,' Jess replied, settling into her usual spot on the sofa. It was the same one she'd watched *Blue Peter* from when she was a kid – when it came to wringing the most possible wear out of soft furnishings, her nan could rival Brian.

'Ohh, that's lovely,' her nan sighed happily, nibbling the edge of her first biscuit. 'Go on then, why have you had a bad day, love? Tell me all your troubles, starting with A and ending with Z.'

Jess's throat constricted at the memory of her nan asking her that question as a child, stroking her hair as she tried to hide how lonely she'd felt after falling out with Amy.

Jess's nan had been her everything, ever since her mum and dad – Pamela's son – had fallen pregnant young and, unable to cope, had left Jess on her nan's doorstep with a note that simply said, 'Sorry, Mum,' before scarpering, like a rubbish Bonnie and Clyde. They'd since kept in touch through the occasional postcard, but had left Pamela to raise their daughter.

Although being brought up by a woman who thought any pair of shoes costing over five pounds was 'a fucking rip-off' had sometimes been difficult, it had also taught Jess that there was nothing more important than the few people in life who you could truly rely on and would stick by you through thick and thin.

'It's Mel, Nan,' Jess sighed. 'We've had a fall out. Kind of, anyway. She didn't believe me when I told her about something big. And I found out that she's hiding something from me, which really isn't like her. I'm worried we're not as close as we used to be.'

'Well, people grow at different rates, don't they, love?' Pamela said, patting Jess's hand. 'You can't expect to be glued to the hip now you're not at school any more, but you'll always end up patching things up, even if you have a falling out. She's not like that bloody Amy.' Jess smiled. Her nan remembered pretty much every detail about Jess's life, even though her own was fading around the edges.

'The two of you have been thick as thieves since the day you met,' her nan continued. 'What is it they say on *Friends*? That you've got crabs?'

'You mean we're lobsters? I suppose you're right,' Jess said. 'But along with you and Alfie, she's my only family. I don't want to lose her.'

'You won't,' Pamela said firmly. 'Everyone says blood's thicker than water, but that's bollocks. Look at my Bill, and your useless dad. No offence, love.'

'None taken. He's crap.'

'My own husband and son both ran off in their time, the bloody buggers. The two people I was supposed to be able to rely on the most. And your mum, an' all! It makes me furious just thinking about them. But your Mel's been around longer than any of them. She's going nowhere, pet.'

Jess felt a pulse of hope in her chest. Her nan was right: she'd never been let down by Mel before. 'The problem is, I'm not even sure how to talk about it with her,' Jess said, rubbing the back of her nan's hand with her thumb. The skin there was paper-thin. 'And I don't want to find out anything I don't want to know.'

'Do you want me to have a word with her? I'm still handy with a frying pan. I reckon I could get it out of her in five minutes.'

Jess laughed 'No, thanks. I'm sure it'll sort itself out. Somehow.'

'And what's this about her not believing you? As if you'd tell porkies. What was that about?'

Jess was glad her nan couldn't see her blushing. 'I'm worried you'll think I'm daft.'

'I already know you're daft, love. Have done ever since you were a baby. Doesn't stop me loving you, does it?'

Jess smiled, her eyes filling with tears. As long as she didn't give her nan a stroke in the process, it would feel good to unburden herself to someone who might actually believe her, and wouldn't just laugh at the thought of Jess living through a time loop.

'Well, the thing is, Nan ... I'm kind of living Friday the thirteenth over and over again. This is, like, the sixth time I've been through it. I think. I'm already losing count.'

'Like in that film? What's it called? The one with that fella who catches ghosts. Hair like a tramp's fanny, face like Deputy Dawg.'

'You mean *Groundhog Day*?'

'That's the one.'

'Yes, just like that, Nan. Except it's today I'm living over and over. I kind of got fired from my job, and got dumped by a guy I was seeing. And evicted. Then I woke up the next day and it happened all over again. But nobody believes me.'

'I believe you, pet,' Nan said, pulling a cushion onto her lap and patting it. 'When you get to my age you'll know that stranger things have happened, believe you me.'

Curling her legs up, Jess lay down and let her nan stroke her hair, sighing with relief. From where she lay, she had a cosily familiar view of the front room, which hadn't changed since she'd left home. If she tried hard enough, she could imagine her nan was twenty years younger, she was a teenager again, and Friday 13th had never happened.

'You're not on drugs, though, are you?' Nan added. 'Remember that time Keith Richards was on MDMA and he thought he worked the Tubes? We were pissing ourselves. Although the driver wasn't amused when Keith tried to hijack his train.'

'I remember you telling me, yes, Nan. But no, I'm not on drugs. Pinky promise.'

'Good girl. That chipmunk man used the day he was stuck in to get the girl he had a fancy for. So maybe this is a way of getting your fella and your job back, eh? I do like those stories,

165

and it would be a shame if you can't bring me my magazine for free any more. It's ninety bloody pence!'

'Do you think so, Nan?' Jess asked, sitting up. She felt a prickle at the back of her neck. Was her nan right – was the time loop giving her a second chance to fix her terrible day? Maybe that was why she was reliving Friday 13th, instead of a day that would have been a lot more fun.

Grabbing her phone, she checked to see if she'd had a text from Tom. It was just after 11 a.m., so if she was wrong about Nate's pants being a pair of palm-tree-bedecked snitches, she should have been dumped by now. But instead, his last text to her was still the one about their date.

There was nothing particularly special about that first Friday, as far as she could tell, apart from all the awful things that had happened. So perhaps this was the cosmos offering her a way to patch things up.

'Nan, have you got a pen and paper to hand? I've got an idea.'

'In the dresser, love. My crossword notebook's in there.'

Grabbing the small, lined notebook from the drawer, which had a biro neatly attached to the spiral binding, Jess brushed the crumbs off her sofa seat and settled back down next to her nan.

Then, she started writing out a list.

1.   Stop Tom from dumping me.
2.   Stop Donna seeing that email.
3.   Stop Brian evicting me.
4.   Don't get mugged, idiot!

Jess felt a tingle as she read through it. It seemed so obvious now, but she was certain her nan was right. The time loop was simply the universe's way of giving her the opportunity to fix everything that had gone wrong on her worst day ever. And if she was careful enough, she might even be able to do it all in one go.

Grinning to herself, she drew a line through the first point.

1. Stop Tom from dumping me.

She'd hidden Nate's pants, and Tom hadn't dumped her, which meant she was already one step closer to breaking free of the time loop. She had an infinite number of chances to work out how to stop Donna seeing the horrible email she'd sent, and, as for her flat ... well, it was hardly Buckingham Palace, but she'd spent weeks trawling the stabbier parts of London with Mel to find her tiny, tatty home, and there had to be a way of persuading Brian to let her stay in it. Maybe by winning more poker money and paying him her year's rent in advance.

'I think you might have cracked it. You're amazing!' Jess said, grabbing her nan in a hug.

'Careful! I nearly dropped me Garibaldi,' Pamela scolded.

Smiling to herself, Jess lay back down and nestled her head back into the cushion on her nan's lap. She knew coming here would be a good idea. Her nan always knew the right thing to say.

'Will you tell me another one of your stories?' Jess asked, stifling a yawn. After reading about old people freezing to death over winter, Pamela kept the house boiling hot, and it was making Jess sleepy. 'What about the one where you went to Liverpool and met Cilla Black? I like that one.'

'Ohh yes. She introduced me to Ringo Starr. What a dark horse that one was. Thomas the Tank Engine, my arse.'

As her nan started talking, Jess closed her eyes and let her mind drift towards how she might try to fix all her problems once and for all.

Chapter 19

Jess already had a grin on her face as she slapped her alarm off with more vigour than usual.

'Project Get The Fuck Out Of This Time Loop, that's what's up,' Jess told Mel's morning text brightly, as Alfie leapt up onto the pillow beside hers. Jess tutted at him gently as she took a photo of his friendly face, which somehow always looked like it was smiling, and sent it to Mel. Then she leant forward, tugged Nate's pants from underneath her pillow and tossed them expertly into her open washing basket.

'Gone in sixty seconds,' she said, holding up her hand to Alfie's paw for a high five. 'Absolutely bloody useless,' she added, when he looked at it quizzically, before licking it.

Swinging her feet out of bed, she kicked away her unicorn slippers and, after letting Alfie out and filling his bowl, quickly got dressed in her Friday outfit of jeans, T-shirt and slouchy cardi. Before she'd drifted off to sleep on her nan's sofa, Jess had been wondering about the best way to stop Donna from seeing the email she'd sent. And now, she knew exactly what she should do.

Donna hadn't looked at her emails until she'd arrived at the *Real Talk!* offices, *so*, Jess decided, the best place to intercept it was at her flat, before she left for the photo shoot.

When Jess had interviewed her, Donna had left her phone on the little coffee table in the front room. Which meant if Jess could persuade her to have another chat – maybe disguised as a top-up interview – she might have a chance to delete it.

Although, if she was going to catch Donna in time this morning, Jess had none to lose.

Nipping into the kitchen, she put the kettle on and stuffed a handful of doggy treats into her handbag, and one of the mini marshmallows into her mouth. Then she drank a quick cup of coffee while Alfie finished his breakfast, grabbed his lead, and texted Jasmit as they trotted to the Tube.

> I might have made a tiny mistake – miniscule, really, and definitely NOT anything libellous – so I need to go to Donna Wilson's house to straighten things out. I'll bring her and Alejandro in for the photo shoot a bit later, if that's OK?

Jasmit: Oh Christ, what the bloody balls have you done now?

> Don't you worry your pretty little head about it

Jasmit: The fact that you can even be arsed to tell me you've done something wrong means this is huge, doesn't it?

But I'm too pregnant to come and kick
your arse right now. Just sort it out

Thanks, Jas. Cross everything for me!

Jasmit: Even my legs? You could have
told me to do that a bit sooner. Like, just
before I got knocked up with twins

Jasmit: Jokes. Obvs over the moon
about the miracle of birth etc

By the time she and Alfie arrived at Donna's flat, it was just before 9 a.m., which, if Jess's maths were correct, meant she and Alejandro wouldn't have left yet. Taking a deep breath and pressing a finger on the doorbell, she heard a tinny rendition of 'Hit Me Baby One More Time' playing through the door. Jess grinned, despite her nerves.

Once again, Donna peered cautiously through the net curtains. Then, seeing Jess on the doorstep, her face lit up.

'What a lovely surprise,' Donna beamed, opening the door.

'Sorry to spring a visit on you, but I had a few extra questions and thought I might pop in to see you both on the way to the shoot,' Jess said, smiling back, as Alfie jumped up at Donna's shins. 'It's a lot quieter here than in the office. Then I'll treat us to an Uber and we can travel in together. Does that sound good to you?'

'Of course! Whatever's best for you,' Donna said, ushering her inside. Bending down, she stroked Alfie and chucked him under the chin.

Stepping into the living room, Jess nodded primly at

Alejandro, who was slouched on the sofa, looking like a sulky teenager. Then her eyes were drawn to Donna's phone, which was perched on the coffee table in front of him.

'Do you fancy a cuppa, love?' Donna asked. 'I might still have some of those Party Rings left, too, if you're peckish.' Jess nodded brightly – 'Milk, three sugars, please' – then sagged as Donna scooped her phone off the table and took it with her into the kitchen.

Suddenly alert, Alejandro leaned forward in his seat.

'It is so good to see you again, Jess,' he said, shooting her a creepy smile that she could only assume he thought looked sexy. He appeared to have based his flirting style on Paolo from *Friends*, including the greasy hair and being a complete crap-weasel. 'I would like us to get to know each other better, no?'

'Yeah, no,' Jess said firmly, standing up and heading for the kitchen, hoping Donna wouldn't mind. In her years of interviewing, Jess had noticed a lot of people were quite protective over their kitchens. She supposed you could tell a lot about a person from the food in their fridge and the items in their cupboards.

In Jess's case, for example, nosy guests would find some out-of-date ham, half a jar of Dolmio, a block of Cheddar with bits hacked off it, and a loaf of bread she kept chilled after one of the readers of Jess's Totally Hot Top Tips! had suggested it makes it last longer.

They'd also see she only kept one set of cutlery alongside her plastic spork collection, but had three teaspoons, which could potentially be incriminating. Perhaps she was the reason there were so many STOP NICKING THE TEASPOONS! signs stuck to the cupboards at work, although she couldn't actually remember stealing them.

Jess poked her head into Donna's kitchen – which was a small, immaculately tidy space with bright-yellow walls and so many magnets on the fridge its door must have been at risk of falling off – and saw her looking at her phone as she waited for the kettle to boil. 'Can I help?' she yelped, a bit too loudly.

'Oh no, it's OK, love,' Donna said, quickly putting her phone down. 'But I wouldn't mind a natter while the kettle boils. It seems to take longer and longer every time. Biscuit while you wait?'

Jess took a yellow Party Ring with pink swirls from the plate. As she munched, she spotted a photo framed on the wall just outside the kitchen, which she hadn't noticed before. Apart from the picture of Donna and Alejandro on holiday, which was still in Jess's bag, it was the only one in the flat.

A much-younger Donna had her arm wrapped around the neck of a girl around the same age. Both were grinning so hard, Jess could imagine the ache in their cheeks, and they were wearing matching glittery blue eyeshadow.

'Who's this?' Jess couldn't help asking, as Donna shuffled around the kitchen. After she'd plopped teabags into the mugs, Donna came over to look at the picture. Her face softened. 'It's funny, I barely notice that photo any more. That's my best mate, Jane Doe. Or rather, she was. Odd name, isn't it, Jane Doe? Like the one they give dead bodies.'

'Was, you say? I'm so sorry. Did she pass away?' Jess asked, pressing a gentle hand on Donna's arm.

'Oh no, love!' Donna laughed, patting Jess's hand. 'We drifted apart, that's all. She got a job in the city and our lives went different ways. You know how it goes – she had the nice apartment and the smart boyfriend, all that, while I was perfectly happy being a temp. I wasn't ready to be tied down

173

and just wanted to have fun. Like the Cyndi Lauper song. Everyone settled down in their twenties in those days, but that seemed terribly young to me.

'So I made some new, younger friends who were still on my level when it came to going out and drinking. Although we weren't as close as before, I was still friends with Jane, and we still hung out. But then we had a huge argument, and that was that. Sad, really.'

'It is sad. You look so happy here,' Jess said, gently touching the glass with one finger, as Donna nipped back into the kitchen to pour the tea.

'We were thick as thieves back in the day,' she called over her shoulder into the hallway. 'Come to think of it, we were actual thieves a lot of the time, too. Forever nicking make-up from Superdrug and stuffing Woolies' pick 'n' mix into our pockets. It's strange how things turn out – I never would have dreamt that one day we wouldn't be friends.

'But I've had my fair share of fun since we fell out, too. And now I've got Alejandro and, well . . . I know I'm a bit old, but maybe it's not too late for me to have a family. I mean, you read about older women having kids all the time, don't you? Like Madonna. She's trying way too hard to look young – looks a bit like Gollum, if you ask me – but she had a kid at forty-two, didn't she?'

'She did,' Jess said, wondering what a Gollum was and feeling another pang of sympathy for Donna as she squeezed the tea bags against the sides of the mugs and dropped them into the bin. In her early 50s, she was unlikely to get that longed-for family now, but she deserved so much more than the hand she'd been dealt in life. And all because, as a daft twenty-something, she'd wanted a bit of fun.

'Come on then, what did you want to ask me about?' She smiled, as Jess led the way back into the living room, Alfie trotting at her heels.

'I will leave you to talk,' Alejandro drawled, standing up. 'Women and their talking are the same all around the world. It is like they're worried their mouths will fall off if they stop.' As he slunk off into the bedroom, Donna let out a peal of laughter.

'He's so funny. Always saying hilarious stuff like that.'

'Yep, he's a total sweetheart,' Jess said through gritted teeth.

Sitting together on the sofa, Jess watched as Donna put her phone on the coffee table. She'd have to make sure Donna didn't leave the room with it again, and racked her brain thinking of ways she could prise it off her, even if only for a few moments, just long enough to delete the email.

As she was busy staring at the phone, Jess realised Donna was sipping her tea and looking at her expectantly. In her haste to get to the flat, she'd forgotten to come up with some new questions to ask. They'd spent a couple of hours together talking during their interview – Jess even knew the colour of the beach towel Donna had been sitting on when Alejandro hove smoothly into view (green and from Debenhams). What else was there to ask?

'Right, questions,' Jess said, a bit too brightly. 'Questions, questions, questions. I actually needed to get a bit of extra background from you, Donna, if that's OK? Bits about your past relationships. Boyfriends and stuff.'

'What's that got to do with Alejandro?' Donna frowned.

'Sorry, boss's orders. She's, er, keen to get a real picture of your past. Draw the readers in. We don't have to go into too much detail if you're not comfortable, though. So let's start with your first boyfriend. When was that?'

'Umm … I was twenty-one, I guess? I've always been a bit shy around boys, you know. Bit of an outsider at school. It wasn't until I met Jane that I came out of my shell a bit and got more confident.'

Jess felt her arms prickling with goosebumps. 'What was the argument with Jane about, if you don't mind me asking?' she blurted. 'Sorry, I know this question isn't about Alejandro and you, but I'm a journalist. And just a bit nosy, really.'

Donna laughed. 'At least you're honest. It was silly, really. I always pretended not to care that her life was so much more together than mine. She had the house, the boyfriend, everything I pretended not to want because I was scared about what might happen if I actually got all that too. What if I ruined everything? I didn't think I deserved it, you see.

'Anyway, one evening Jane invited me over to meet some of her new workmates, and I was really nervous. I got far too drunk and decided they thought I was an idiot. Then I decided her boyfriend thought so too, and that she must agree with them. I didn't see why they'd want me to be part of their gang, so I made damn sure they had a reason not to. Of course, I didn't see that back then. I started flinging insults at them, calling them boring and all sorts. I thought I was just being honest, but it makes me cringe just to think about it now.'

'You must have had the hangover from hell the next day,' Jess said, blowing into her mug and taking a sip of tea.

'I felt awful the next morning and wanted to apologise, but I just couldn't. This will sound ridiculous, but facing up to it felt even harder than just blocking it all out and losing Jane.'

'It doesn't sound so silly to me,' Jess said, swallowing down the lump that had formed in her throat. 'Couldn't you have talked to her and told her how you felt? Just explained that you'd felt out of your depth?'

Donna shook her head. 'It sounds easy, doesn't it? And Jane was lovely, too. If I'd just told her my nerves had simply got the better of me and that I was sorry, she'd have forgiven me in a flash, but I just carried on as if nothing had happened. I thought it would eventually blow over. We could never stay mad at each other for long. But it was obvious to everyone but me that I needed to apologise, and I think that was the final straw for Jane.

'When she stopped getting in touch, I decided it was for the best that we parted ways, and I'd be better off without her. Which was ridiculous, of course. I can't say I blame her for avoiding me, but I still miss her.' Donna looked at her hands, massaging her left palm with her thumb, then shook her head, and smiled brightly.

'All's well that ends well though, eh? She's doing really well for herself now. She married the boring boyfriend, had a couple of gorgeous kiddies and lives in a lovely house in Brighton. She set up a PR business, not that I know much about that kind of thing. And now I've got Alejandro, I'm finally catching up. Maybe it's my turn for some happiness, eh?'

Jess swallowed hard. Donna's past felt a bit too close to her present. The only difference was that Mel had always forgiven her for putting her foot in it – so far, at least. But now, she wasn't sure how long her patience would last, based on the conversation she'd overheard her and Aya having.

And here Donna was, years after losing her best mate, thinking she'd found her salvation in Alejandro, when Jess knew he was going to break her heart. It was clear that Donna deserved to know what he was like, even if it meant wrecking the Halloween Hunk story.

'Listen, Donna,' Jess said, taking a deep breath. 'I need to tell you something.'

'What is it, love?' Donna frowned. 'Another Party Ring?' Jess shook her head and opened her mouth at the same time as the doorbell rang.

'I'd better get that. Alejandro isn't keen on opening the door. He's like a stroppy teenager sometimes,' Donna said, laughing. 'Excuse me for a sec, love.'

As Donna headed into the hall to get the door, Jess took her chance to scoop up Donna's phone. Thankfully, she hadn't bothered setting a password and it opened immediately. Keeping her ears open for Donna or Alejandro coming back into the room, and with half an eye on the door, she quickly opened Donna's email app, scrolling to the top with shaking hands and finding hers unopened at the top.

Subject: 'Halloween Heifer'
To: Donna Wilson
From: Jess Janus

Deleting the email, she closed the app and set the phone back on the table before Donna had finished chatting to the postman.

In her mind, she scored a line through the second problem on her list.

2.   Stop Donna seeing that email.

Flooded with relief, Jess wondered now whether she'd been

too hasty in considering telling Donna the truth. She'd never see the email now, which meant Jess had saved her job and avoided the magazine getting sued for libel. If she told Donna about Alejandro, she'd just be causing unnecessary problems. And of course, that would stress Jasmit out, too, which probably wouldn't be good for the babies.

Maybe she should just get the shoot over with and tell Donna the truth about Alejandro when she finally reached Saturday? After all, Donna had been really looking forward to being photographed. It would be a shame if she didn't get to dress up as Elvira, wouldn't it?

Or maybe ... maybe Jess could wait a little while longer, until after the article was printed? Maggie couldn't get annoyed at her at all then, and Donna would have a few more weeks of living in blissful ignorance. She deserved a bit more happiness, didn't she? Yes, Jess told herself firmly, keeping quiet was a much better idea all round. She'd solved her biggest problem, which was getting fired, and that meant she was halfway through escaping the time loop. There was no need to jeopardise that now.

'I'll call an Uber, shall I?' Jess said brightly as Donna returned. 'We've nattered our time away. Come on, I can ask you the extra questions in the cab. I can't wait for you to see your outfit ...'

Chapter 20

When Brian's call came that afternoon, Jess was lying propped up next to Nate on top of the lumpy futon that passed for a bed in the house he shared with three other twenty-somethings. Alfie was snuffling his way around it, searching for treats, even though he'd only just finished the handful Jess had given him when they'd arrived. When she'd left the office after Donna's photo shoot, faking a headache so half-heartedly that Jasmit had told her to 'Enjoy the pub!' on her way out, she'd decided to make sure there would be no loose ends once she'd got out of the time loop by telling Nate to his face that it was over. He'd taken the break-up almost insult-ingly well. 'No problem, babe. If you've got any single mates you think might want some fun, let them know I'm woke, broke, and ready for a poke.'

Then, when he'd suggested she stay for lunch – one last takeaway, for old times' sake – she'd nodded eagerly. Having skipped breakfast, she was absolutely ravenous, and she didn't want to feel faint from hunger when it came to tackling Brian. Because she'd had to get to Donna's flat in time to intecept her email, she hadn't had time to win the money to pay him off. She'd just have to use her powers of persuasion instead.

'Hold on, I have to take this,' Jess said now as her phone rang, throwing the remains of her last slice of pizza back into the box. Her palms felt clammy. Although she knew that, technically, she had as many attempts to get this conversation right as she needed, the end of the time loop felt so close she could taste it. She had to do it today.

'Don't touch my pizza, I still want it,' she warned Nate, as she answered the phone.

'Hi, Jess, it's Brian. Glad I've caught you. You've been avoiding my calls, haven't you?'

Jess took a deep breath, plucked a tissue from the box on Nate's bedside table, and screwed up her face. 'I'm so sorry, Brian,' she said, making her voice wobble up and down. 'I know I owe you two months' rent, but you see ... I lost my favourite uncle. We were really close. He was like my dad, really. I told you that my real dad abandoned me when I was a baby, right? And I haven't been avoiding you, I promise. I just haven't had the emotional energy to take any calls. Except for the ones from, like ... undertakers and things.'

Jess blew her nose loudly down the phone, while Nate rolled his eyes and took the opportunity to snaffle another one of her cigarettes.

'Oh, Jess. Oh god, I'm so sorry,' Brian said, his voice cracking with sympathy. 'I didn't know about your dad, or your uncle. And I really don't mean to hassle you, it's just that—'

'Oh. Do you need the money really urgently?' Jess said quickly. 'I could always tell the undertaker to swap Uncle Monty's coffin for something cheaper, I suppose. Get him a balsa wood one.'

Jess winced, worried she'd gone too far. She wished she could think of an easier way out of her predicament than telling such bald-faced lies, because surely Brian wouldn't believe this act?

'No, no, of course not. Sorry, I was just thinking aloud,' Brian stuttered, to Jess's amazement. 'Is there anything I can do? Anything at all?'

'No, it's OK. It's just ... my money's a bit tied up at the moment, that's all. You know, flowers and stuff. If I could have a bit more time for the rent? It would be such a help.' Beside her, Nate lay back on the futon and covered his face with his hands.

'Of course, Jess,' Brian said kindly. 'And I'm sorry for bothering you, I really am. You take all the time you need. Take care, love.'

'Thank you, Brian,' Jess said, feeling a familiar knot of guilt setting up home in her stomach. 'I appreciate it.'

Hanging up, Jess double-checked the call had been cancelled before deciding to ignore her conscience nagging at her, and allow herself a moment of triumph.

'I did it!' she whooped. 'I'm almost free!'

'Free of what? Sound morals?' Nate said, sitting up on one elbow and shaking his head. 'I'm all for sticking it to the man, but that was pretty harsh. You can't kill off a relative and make up a missing father to get out of paying rent.'

'He's not a real relative, and I didn't make up the missing dad bit. That really happened. I'm practically an *orphan*. And, anyway, I'll work out how to pay him properly later; I just need a bit more time.

'Speaking of which ... I've got a question for you. Just a hypothetical one, obviously.' Sitting back next to Nate, she gestured for him to hand her the cigarette, and blew a smoke blob into the air. 'What would you do if you were living the same day over and over again? Like, if you could do whatever you wanted without any consequences and predict what was going to happen and stuff?'

'You mean like in *Groundhog Day*?'

'Yes, like in *Groundhog Day*. Why has everyone seen that stupid film except me?'

'That would be pretty amazing, I reckon,' Nate said. 'Imagine being able to just chill all day without worrying about money? I'd practise my meditation and yoga, listen to music, get high. Experiment with stuff like snorting nutmeg. I've always wanted to see if that works. Apparently, it can make your eyeballs pop out if you do it wrong. But it's also hallucinogenic and makes you see God. Or Jimi Hendrix ... I can't remember which.'

'Apparently Jimi was a big fan of *Corrie*. According to my nan, anyway.'

'See, with unlimited time you could find out all sorts of cool stuff like that. Stalk celebrities, get arrested, do a parachute jump. Go anywhere and do anything without worrying about the consequences.'

Jess nodded. Nate's Big Fat Groundhog Day of Fun sounded like her cup of tea. She felt a slight pang that she'd cracked the time loop so easily and wouldn't be able to make more of its plus sides. It had to be a good way of finding out what kind of person you really were, too. Would you spend eternity learning a language, meeting as many new people as possible, doing good deeds like Tom, or loads and loads of drugs like Nate?

Jess would quite like the chance to find that out about

herself, but she simply couldn't risk missing her opportunity to get out as quickly as possible. She wanted to reach Saturday even more than she wanted to snort nutmeg and find out if her eyeballs flopped out on little stalks. She wanted to watch the *Love or Dare* final with her nan, and she wanted to teach Alfie how to give fluffy-pawed high fives. She wanted to be able to make an impact, because nothing she did while she was in the time loop would stick. And once she reached tomorrow, she vowed, she'd start pulling herself together. After going through the worst day of her life more than once, and having to suffer the consequences, she'd well and truly learned her lesson.

Chapter 21

'Oh my god. I think my dinner baby might be twins,' Jess groaned that evening, rubbing her stomach as she and Tom emerged from the Tube.

'I can't wait to meet you, kids,' Tom said, leaning over and kissing the bulge of her tummy.

Jess let out a laugh. Despite all the Fridays she'd lived through, this was the first time she'd actually reached her date with Tom, and it had been much more enjoyable than she'd expected on Friday the First.

Ever since Tom had promised he was taking her to 'the hottest place in town', she'd felt a bit nervous. She hated posh restaurants, and always worried the waiters were sending 'You shouldn't be here, commoner wench!' vibes in the direction of her carefully curated collection of New Look dresses and Converse shoes complete with wonky Sharpie hearts.

Jess's worst-ever date had been a night at an eye-wateringly expensive place, where her date had ordered the eight-course tasting menu without even blinking. Although it was the nicest meal she'd ever eaten, she hadn't been able to enjoy it, feeling uncomfortably out of place with her Superdrug eyeliner and cheap bag. Some of the women there actually had a special table to rest their Louis Vuittons on.

It didn't help that Jess could practically see her date mentally equating each course with the sex act he expected to get in return. *Amuse-bouches: kissing with tongues. Second main course: blow job.*

He was so creepy he hadn't even got a snog, and, to add insult to injury, Jess had had to stop off at McDonald's on the way home because half the courses featured foam instead of solid food and she was still starving.

So, she'd been delighted when Tom's 'hottest place in town' had turned out to be Hot Stuff, a chilli-heavy junk-food restaurant that had just opened in Soho. They'd had an amazing meal of fried chicken burgers, chilli-cheese hotdogs and giant ribs slathered with hot sauce, which was much more Jess's kind of thing than half a carrot decorated with a 'molasses and paprika jus' that tasted like bog-standard barbecue sauce.

The waiters had even given Alfie a little bowl of sauce-free chicken to nibble on under the table, so it got a big paws-up from him, too.

Over the meal, Jess had felt so sleepy-full, and happy that this was her last Friday 13th, she'd found herself opening up about her past to Tom for the first time.

She'd told him all about her parents leaving when she was a baby, and being brought up by her nan, while he'd told her about his dad's terrible sense of humour and his mum's love of porcelain ornaments and antimacassars. Jess didn't know what one of those was, but she was sure Tom had a fact about them tucked away somewhere.

Now, as they walked towards Jess's flat, Tom took her hand and curled it around his arm. He turned to her and grinned, reminding Jess that when they got home she'd be faced with his rose-petal message, and she'd have to decide what to say in return. She liked Tom, that much was clear. But was she really ready to be someone's girlfriend?

'Look out!' she shouted, as a moped raced past him, dangerously close to the kerb. Up ahead, it bumped onto the pavement behind a woman who was walking a small black dog.

'Hey!' Tom shouted, as the rider stuck out an arm and grabbed the handbag from the woman's shoulder, spinning her around and sending her crashing painfully to the ground. At the same time, she let go of her dog's lead and he sprinted up the pavement, delighted at his new-found freedom. Alfie barked and strained at his lead, trying to run after him.

Jess ran with Tom towards the moped-rider's victim, who was leaning up on one elbow, looking dazed. Jess recognised her as the friendly woman she'd met on the Tube escalator on the first day of the time loop.

'Oh my god, Beth, are you OK?' Jess asked. Crouching down, she helped her into a sitting position.

'I'm OK, I think. But my dog . . . ' She looked in panic past Jess in the direction Inkblot had run.

'Don't worry, I'll catch him,' Jess said, tossing Alfie's lead to Tom and sprinting down the road calling Inkblot's name. It wasn't long before she found him snuffling his way around the base of a lamp post, nose pressed to the ground, seemingly deciding whether or not to have a wee.

'Come on, boy. Here, Inky,' Jess coaxed, crouching down on the ground. Inkblot's ears pricked up, but he stayed behind the lamp post, peering at her from behind it, looking slightly nervous. He was clearly about as keen on strangers as Jess was.

Pulling a foil package out of her handbag, Jess unwrapped it to reveal a pile of leftover chilli and burnt barbecue ends, which she'd brought home from the restaurant.

With a delighted woof, Inkblot started attacking the pile of food, which was almost bigger than him.

'Good boy, Inky,' she said, chucking him gently behind the ear. He let out a soft growl in defence of his food, and Jess wondered if he might be her spirit animal.

After Inkblot had finished eating, Jess carried him back to Beth who, with Tom's help, had managed to get shakily to her feet. Crouching down, Beth held out her arms, beaming widely as Jess deposited Inkblot on the floor and he ran into them.

Immediately, he started transferring bits of meat to Beth's face with his tongue, but she didn't seem to care.

Beth looked up at Jess. 'You knew our names already – how?' she said, pulling her face away from Inkblot's tongue in a futile attempt to escape his happy licks.

'Do you live nearby?' Jess asked, innocently, cursing herself for forgetting that, as far as Beth was concerned, they'd never met before. 'Maybe I've heard it somewhere and stored it in my subconscious.'

'I do, actually, just around the corner,' Beth said, as Jess pulled an 'Oh, really?' face.

'Then let's get you home safe and call the police,' Tom said. 'I caught a glimpse of his number plate, and I think I've remembered it correctly.'

'You've got a good one there,' Beth said to Jess, hugging

Inkblot tightly. 'This isn't the first time I've been mugged. Last time – and I swear this is true – someone walking past asked me for directions to the Tube while I was lying on the floor. I enjoy living in a buzzing city, but honestly . . .'

Jess squeezed Tom's arm, then realised, with a jolt, that this moped mugger was *her* moped mugger – the one who had run her down on what she now called Friday the First.

It had happened at around this time of night, when she was on her way home from her leaving do. This time, though, Beth had suffered instead, which definitely wasn't how Jess had planned to escape the time loop. She hadn't walked down her street at this exact time since, but did that mean that Beth had been the one getting mugged in her absence?

'Is your head OK?' Jess asked anxiously as they walked towards Beth's flat.

'I think so,' Beth said. 'Luckily I fell on my knees, although they really sting.' With Beth limping, they walked slowly to her front door. Before they left, Tom wrote down the mugger's number plate on a pink Post-it note and handed it to Beth.

'That was pretty quick thinking,' Jess told Tom as they walked back to her flat. 'It's quite sexy, watching you fight crime.'

'Oh really? How sexy are we talking, exactly?' Tom asked, waggling his eyebrows.

'Don't even think about it, hero,' Jess said, as she opened her front door. 'I'm cream-crackered after all that drama.' Throwing her keys onto the table in front of the door, she realised Tom had gone quiet behind her.

She'd almost forgotten the message that must be waiting for her in her bedroom. But she was fairly certain what she needed to do.

Just a few days ago, she didn't want a boyfriend, and didn't want to date Nate or Tom long-term. But the time loop had shown her that she liked Tom more than she realised. Although she still equated being someone's girlfriend with the end of freedom and fun, she had to admit she'd enjoyed hanging out with him. And it looked like saying 'yes' was one of the changes the universe was urging her to make.

Jess headed into her bedroom, feeling Tom following quietly behind. Summoning up her best acting talents, she pretended to be both surprised and delighted when she saw WILL YOU BE MY GIRLFRIEND? spelled out in petals on the bed.

'Oh, Tom, this is the cheesiest bloody thing I've ever seen,' she said.

'So how about it?' Tom said, hopefully, hovering behind her. 'We've already found our ideal restaurant. And let's face it, you're not going to find anyone better than someone who can remember a number plate at first glimpse. Which, if you recall, you find devastatingly sexy.'

Tom gestured lavishly at himself, as if he were a prize on a quiz show. Turning around, Jess wound her arms around Tom's neck, her head resting on his shoulder so he couldn't see her face. 'You're probably right. So it's a yes from me. Let's do this thing.'

As the words left her lips, Jess felt a rush of triumph.

She'd won. She'd solved the puzzle and beat the universe.

Tomorrow was going to be Saturday. She'd get to watch the final of *Love or Dare* with her nan. And she'd have the chance to finally find out what Mel was hiding from her.

It had been a weird few days, but she'd learned some very valuable lessons about being more careful in the future and covering her back. And she guessed she was going to have to learn how to be a girlfriend now, too. *The cosmos wants what the cosmos wants*, she thought.

'So now you're my girlfriend, are you going to give up smoking and start eating vegetables?' Tom asked, pulling away from Jess and beaming at her. 'I'm not sure I want to spend our future together wheeling you around attached to an iron lung, while your teeth fall out from scurvy.'

'Not a chance,' Jess said, curtly. Perhaps being a girlfriend was going to be harder than she thought. But she could always work on it tomorrow.

Chapter 22

Jerked awake by her alarm, Jess gasped like she was coming out of a terrible nightmare. Her heart pounded as she picked up her phone and stared at the message on it, her hands shaking.

Mel: What's new, Pussycat?

'It can't be,' she whispered. Then shouted at the ceiling, 'No! It can't be happening again! I fixed it!' Flinging her phone at the wall, it made a crunching sound as the screen shattered, before bouncing onto the carpet and landing next to Alfie. Whimpering, he backed himself under the bed.

Jess had fallen asleep holding hands with Tom, feeling oddly excited about what they'd do together on Saturday. But now, his side of the bed was cold and empty, and she couldn't do anything to stop the tears falling down her cheeks.

She'd ticked everything off her list. She'd saved her job, stopped Brian from evicting her, and avoided being mugged. She even had a *boyfriend*, for Christ's sake. If that wasn't a sign that she'd learned her lesson and grown as a person, she didn't know what was.

So how could it still be Friday? *How*? And if fixing all the disasters that had occurred on Friday the First hadn't worked, how was she supposed to escape the time loop – if it was even possible?

With shaking hands, she checked the apps on her phone – Twitter, email, WhatsApp – before leaping out of bed, running into the living room and digging the remote out from between her sofa cushions. Switching on BBC1, Naga Munchetty appeared, smiling cheerfully.

Jess flung the remote as hard as she could at the TV. The screen flickered, a thin crack zig-zagging across Naga's face like a scar, before sputtering out. Her legs shaking, Jess sank onto the sofa and started to sob helplessly.

'What do you want from me?' she screamed into the air. 'I did everything you wanted me to, didn't I? What more could you possibly want?'

Her heart was thumping so hard it felt like it would beat its way out of her chest. Maybe, she thought with a shudder, there was no reason for the time loop after all. It wasn't the universe's way of giving her a second chance to patch things up. It was just a glitch in time, and she was doomed to relive the day over and over again, no matter what she did differently.

Standing up, she paced the living room, her mind racing, pushed forward by adrenaline. There had to be an answer. There just had to be.

But she couldn't snag any of the thoughts speeding past and hold onto them long enough for them to make sense.

She was terrified and had never felt more alone in her life.

She couldn't even phone Mel and tell her what was happening because she simply wouldn't believe her.

What she really needed right now was oblivion, plain and simple. Usually, when she was having a crisis, she would sleep her way through it and would wake up the next day and start afresh. But this time she'd just wake up right back where she started.

Heading into the kitchen, she opened the cupboard and caught the packet of Angel Delight as it fell out. Pulling a half-empty bottle of milk from the fridge, she opened the lid, tipped in the powder, gave it a shake, and shoved it in the fridge.

That would do for lunch.

Then she grabbed her Doug's Mug mug, drew her emergency bottle of vodka from the back of the cupboard and set out to get completely and utterly wasted.

Chapter 23

September 2006, The Roundabout

Jess watched the tops of the trees spinning slowly above her as Mel rummaged in her rucksack.

'Close your eyes,' she said. Jess squeezed her eyes shut and sat up, leaning her back against the central column of the roundabout.

'Happy birthday!' Mel said. 'Keep your fingers on your present; it keeps popping open. Stupid glittery glitter is stupid. What's the point of wrapping paper that Sellotape won't stick to?'

Jess opened her eyes to see a pink envelope and a small square parcel nestled in her hands. It was wrapped in pink paper decorated with glittery hearts, and the Sellotape holding it together had long ago given up trying to do its job.

'If it's any consolation, my bedroom is absolutely covered in glitter now, and Mum's probably going spare trying to hoover it out of the carpet as we speak,' Mel said. 'Here, let me take it while you open your card.'

Ripping open the envelope, Jess pulled out a Tweenies card that said YOU ARE 8! The number 8 was printed on the yellow badge, and Mel had added a 1 in front of it using a black Sharpie.

'Woo hoo! You are the Legally Adult, Special Magical Princess Birthday Girl!' she yelled, more loudly than strictly necessary, yanking the badge off its little square of sticky polystyrene and attaching it to the front of Jess's cardigan.

Jess opened the card and laughed.

Happy birthday, knobhead.
    Nobody's perfect, but you come close. Never change, OK?
    Lots and lots of love (no tongues),
    Mel.

P.S. Do you think Mark will go nuts when he finds out we've been underage all this time . . . ?

'I've only got one card, and you've made sure I can't even show it to my nan,' Jess laughed.

'Ahh, that's where this comes in.' Mel rummaged in her bag again and produced a plain white envelope with 'Jessica' written on the front. Inside was a card with a watercolour painting of a cottage by a river on the front. Jess opened it and read out the message.

Dear Jess.
    Fondest regards on your 18th birthday. I can't wait to see what you do next. You are my hero and an icon.
    Best wishes, Melanie.

P.S. I know you'll disapprove, but, now we're 18, can we please stay up past 11 p.m. when you stay at mine?

Jess burst out laughing, before reading the card out again in a faux-posh voice.

'Oh my god, I think you might be a genius!' she said, wiping tears from her eyes. 'My nan will actually fall for this, god love her. And she'll probably have a go at me for being boring, too.'

A lot had changed in the years since Jess and Mel had met. Like trees planted side by side, they'd grown closer and closer, their roots and branches entwining until they were so solidly knotted together they blocked out the sky. There was no room for anyone else.

Without having to worry about finding new friends, Mel had the chance to focus on her training. She was getting really good at sprinting – maybe even national-level good, her coach said. Jess, meanwhile, had used their solid friend-ship as a springboard to start exploring who she was. Her clothes changed constantly, from all-black one week to crop tops and platform trainers the next, including an eighties throwback look that had included the inadvisable addition of leg warmers.

Already, they'd set the pattern for their friendship, Mel single-mindedly aiming for the goal she'd set herself, while Jess approached life like a dropped machine gun, wildly firing bullets in every direction. With the confidence her new-found friendship had given her, she was busy trying everything she could get her hands on, and not caring much whether she succeeded or failed, or noticing the times Mel gently steered her in the right direction.

When you looked at the broad strokes of their lives, Mel and Jess were already very different. But Jess's wildness, sense of fun and freedom relieved Mel of the pressure she felt in a rigid family home where every moment was regimented. And in the ways that really mattered to them – their loyalty, their sense of humour, the way they could take any subject and dissect it between them down to its tiniest parts, until they were exhausted but never bored – they'd found their perfect slice of pizza in each other.

After opening her birthday cards, Mel pressed the badly wrapped present back into her hands. Jess allowed the Sellotape to spring open. It revealed a small black cardboard box, dusted with red glitter. Pulling the lid off, there was a small rectangle of card on top that said, 'Could you BEE any more perfect? (Sorry)'. Next, Jess slid her fingers underneath the folds of a piece of pink tissue paper and revealed a beautiful pendant, shaped like a bee.

Its body was gold and silver stripes, ridged with metal fur, and its slender silver wings were faintly veined. She held it up to the light by its chain, where it spun slowly, glinting in the afternoon sunshine.

'Oh, Mel. It's so beautiful. I can't even think of anything sarcastic to say.'

'Wow. You must really like it. I saved up for it myself, from my shop money,' Mel said proudly, as Jess slipped it round her neck and adjusted the chain.

Rubbing the pendant between her fingers, Jess felt her eyes stinging with tears. Mel gave up every spare hour to training, which her parents made sure she never missed, even when she had a snotty cold. Yet they still wouldn't give her pocket money, insisting that learning a strong work ethic now was more important than silly things like having fun, or hanging out with friends.

Along with homework, it meant every hour of Mel's day was accounted for, including somehow squeezing in shifts at her local corner shop so she could earn a little bit of cash. She'd only been allowed this Sunday afternoon off by reminding her parents of her coach's oft-repeated mantra, 'Before race day, take a rest day'.

She was competing the next morning and UK Sport talent scouts were rumoured to be attending.

'But no birthday cake,' her mum had warned, darkly. 'And bed by nine p.m.'

Mel had agreed to everything immediately, delighted that she'd get to spend at least some of Jess's eighteenth birthday with her. That evening, Jess had promised to go home and celebrate with her nan and a Chinese takeaway, but, until then, they had a whole afternoon ahead of them.

'So what do you want to do next?' Mel asked, tucking the discarded wrapping paper back into her rucksack.

'How about this?' Jess grinned, pulling a small bottle of vodka from her bag.

'Ohhh, now you're talking,' Mel said, grabbing it from her hands. 'But make sure I've stopped drinking by five, otherwise I'll still be pissed when I get home. And I'm not keen on having both my legs broken by my mum before the qualifier. It might slow me down a bit.'

'You're kidding, right?' Jess laughed. 'You'd just use your elbows to drag yourself along, like the Terminator.'

By the time the sun was low in the sky, Jess and Mel had finished off the vodka and were tipsy-drunk – that sweet spot where everything was funny and Jess felt invincible.

Walking down the high street, they watched as the shops started putting up their shutters, which gave Jess an odd, empty feeling in her chest. Then they headed past the park and found themselves wandering towards the edge of town, the streets lined with houses on one side and trees and scrubland on the other.

'I'll have to go home soon,' Mel said, frowning at her phone. 'Mum will go spare if I miss dinner.'

'Turkey and boiled eggs?'

'Something like that.'

Jess had picked up a branch from the side of the pathway and was thrashing at the nettles that grew alongside the road, pretending to be Inigo Montoya in *The Princess Bride*.

'You killed my father. Prepare to die!' she yelled.

'You know that stick is probably covered in dog saliva and fox wee?' Mel asked.

Jess pouted. 'Have you got time for us to do one more thing? Seeing as it's my birthday?'

'Oh no. You're kidding,' Mel said, stopping abruptly in her tracks as she realised where Jess had led her.

'Come on! Please? Turning eighteen is like having an all-day hall pass. You have to do whatever I want. We can do the same on your birthday. We can even eat lettuce all day if you like.'

Grabbing her arm, Jess dragged Mel towards the bungalow at the end of the row of houses, beyond which was a narrow path leading into the woods.

The building stood in stark contrast to the rest of the houses on the road, which had been gradually bought up by developers and smartly renovated, with white wooden gates, tiled footpaths and doors decorated with small stained-glass windows. Like a rotten tooth in a row of veneers, the bungalow was a dirty shade of brown, its small front lawn filled with dead plants in terracotta pots.

A broken gutter filled with brown leaves sagged in front of a window boarded up with plywood, and the rest of the windows were cracked and hung with filthy net curtains. Against the other houses, it looked like a sepia photograph, everything about the place brown with death and neglect.

Rumour had it that the family who'd lived there had all been killed in a car crash – wiped out all at once, just like that – and that it was now haunted by their ghosts. Nobody had wanted to buy a house cursed with so much sadness, so it had been allowed to rot away, waiting for someone to raze it to the ground, or for an optimistic developer to buy it and hope the new owners wouldn't look into its history.

Either way, Jess had always been desperate to see inside to find out if the rumours were true. And this was the one day of the year – perhaps even of her life – that Mel couldn't refuse her.

As they stared at the house, Mel shivered. It was a warm evening, but the house had always given her the creeps. She knew what she was about to be roped into and hoped that Jess's apparently unbreakable good luck would protect her too.

No matter how far Jess pushed her boundaries, she never seemed to get found out. It was like there was an invisible force field around her that trouble just pinged off. Meanwhile, Mel couldn't even get away with sneaking a packet of Maltesers into the cinema – which was about as daring as she ever got – without getting told off by an usher the moment she quietly opened them under her coat.

'Jess, please, my mum will kill me if she knows I've been

in there,' Mel groaned now. 'It could be dangerous. And there will definitely be rats. And spiders! You hate spiders.'

'Admittedly, spiders and I have had a bit of a rocky relationship up until now,' Jess conceded, 'but imagine being able to tell everyone at school that we've been in there? We might even find proof that it's haunted. We'd be *heroes*. And get to be on telly.'

'Why can't you be the kind of drinker who just gets depressed and wants to go to bed? How can this possibly be your idea of fun?' Mel asked, as Jess looked down the row of houses and into the forest to check no one was watching, before kicking open the mouldering front gate.

'Because it *is* fun!' She grinned, tugging Mel behind her. Moving a fly-covered bin away from the path that led down the side of the house, they headed towards the back garden, which was every bit as depressing as the front.

Weeds poked through a hole that had rusted through the bottom of an overturned wheelbarrow. The grass had grown to waist height, and the short path to the back door was covered with piles of rotting newspapers that had once been tied together with string.

Every window in the back of the building was cracked or broken, where kids on a dare had snuck into the garden and flung stones at them. A small set of steps led down to a basement door that was in a similarly rotten state, and the main back door had six empty squares where the glass had once been, now covered up from the inside with brown paper.

'Could this place look any more murdery?' Mel shuddered. 'Can we just go home? This isn't fun. We're trespassing; we could get arrested.'

'Don't be daft, who exactly is going to call the fuzz on us?'

Jess shrugged, gesturing at the fence around the garden. It was made of solid planks of wood and six feet high, making them feel completely shut off from the rest of the world.

'Come on, let's go inside,' she added, rattling the back door handle. It was locked, but she could feel the softness of the wooden door frame, weakened by years of rain and neglect, as she pulled. By yanking with all her strength, the frame splintered and cracked, sending the door flying open and Jess staggering backwards.

'Your palace awaits, madam,' she said, gesturing for Mel to go inside first.

'Absolutely no way,' Mel said firmly, and watched with pursed lips as Jess stepped across the threshold. Knowing there was no point resisting Jess once she'd got a bad idea in her head, Mel followed her inside with a sigh, muttering about her human rights.

The air inside the bungalow reminded Mel of something. Sniffing tentatively, she realised it was the exact same smell as the one they pumped into the London Dungeon; that musty, mouldering-cave tang that apparently made it smell more like a torture chamber. She shivered as she thought about the ghosts said to haunt the bungalow.

'Right, we're in now. Can we go, please?' Mel pleaded.

'Not a hope in hell,' Jess said with a wink, and then she bounded ahead through a door that led to the hallway.

Mel held back and looked tentatively around the kitchen, rubbing her arms for warmth. The damp added a creepy chill to the air that really wasn't necessary in such an already spooky house.

The counters were rotting and covered in mud and leaves that had blown in through the broken windows, and an ancient, doorless gas oven sat in one corner. She could hear a rustling coming from inside that she wasn't tempted to investigate.

Next, she wandered into the hallway. 'Come and look at this,' Jess called, and Mel followed the sound to where she was looking at a photograph in a picture frame on the wall. It was one of those studio family photographs, where everyone dresses in their Sunday best, grins unconvincingly, and has their picture taken in soft focus.

Judging by the shoulder pads and epic hairstyles on display, this one had been taken back in the 1980s: a mum, dad, and two children, a girl and a boy.

'They must have lived here once,' Mel said softly, using a finger to straighten the picture.

Turning to look at the front door, she saw a mountain of unclaimed junk mail; yellowing envelopes at the bottom, and pristine takeaway menus at the top. The fact that businesses had continued to try to sell pizza and chow mein to the probably dead occupants of the house made her feel suddenly sad.

'Those hairstyles,' Jess snorted. 'Maybe they died of embarrassment rather than a car crash.' As Jess headed into what looked like one of the bedrooms, Mel made her way to the edge of the front room, which looked like it had been used as a dumping ground for furniture from across the house: as well as a sofa covered in faded yellow and brown floral fabric, there was an old mattress, its cover torn by hundreds of claws over the years, and a chair with three legs.

The carpet had been half rolled-up from the door towards the fireplace, and the floorboards underneath were black with damp and rot.

'Boo!' Jess yelled behind her, grabbing Mel's shoulders and laughing as she nearly jumped out of her skin.

Squeezing past Mel, she hopped nimbly from the hallway into the room, landing on the carpet. 'Shall we take a souvenir?' she said, plucking a broken ornament from the mantlepiece above the fireplace. It was the top half of a china clown clutching a bunch of balloons, a couple of which looked like they'd burst. 'Could this place tick any more creepy-cliché boxes?' she said, stuffing the ornament in the waistband of her jeans.

'You've got your horrible clown ornament. Time to go now,' Mel said, trying to sound stern as she stepped into the room.

Then she let out a panicked scream as, to the sound of rotten wood sagging and splintering, she disappeared.

'Mel!' Jess screamed, running towards the jagged hole in the living room floor that had suddenly appeared. Kneeling next to it, she peered in to see Mel sprawled on the ground beneath, surrounded by shattered pieces of wood.

'Mel, are you alive?' Jess screamed, tears already streaming down her face, her cockiness completely evaporated. 'Oh, please be OK!'

Mel groaned and tried to sit up, and Jess sobbed even harder with relief.

'I'm going to go and get an ambulance, OK? I'll be five minutes, stay there.'

As Jess's panic-stricken, tear-streaked face disappeared from the patch of light above her head, Mel carefully sat up and let out a scream, clamping her hands over her mouth. Even in agony, she was worried about getting in trouble.

Her legs were sprawled in front of her, the right one bent at the shin at a sickeningly unnatural angle. It reminded her of a scene in *Misery*, which she and Jess had secretly watched one night, despite horror films being strictly banned by her parents. It had given her nightmares for a week.

Feeling woozy, she closed her eyes tightly shut, then leaned over and retched onto the floor.

The basement was cold and damp, and Mel was shivering uncontrollably. She felt dizzy, the pain in her leg fading into the background as her head, stomach and pounding heart sent alarm signals over her whole body. The fight between morbid curiosity and not wanting to be sick again was won by an irresistible urge to see what had happened when she fell. Taking a few deep breaths, she leaned over to look at her leg.

She was wearing a light summer dress, and the damage that had been done was clear to see, even by the small amount of light coming through the hole above her. The shock of falling through the floor hadn't given her time to bend her knees to absorb the impact, and the full weight of the fall had been taken on her right leg. A shard of bone protruded from a hole of ragged skin torn in her shin, blood pooling underneath it.

Reaching forward, she touched the edge of the bone with the tip of her finger. It felt cold and sharp, and it seemed weird that she couldn't feel anything as she touched it, when it was still part of her body. It reminded her of a video she'd once seen of a patient having her brain operated on while she lay awake, playing the violin, seemingly oblivious to the surgeons working away inside her head.

Staring at the bone, bright white against red blood, she started to feel woozy again. She heard a faint call in the background, which got louder as Jess ran towards the hole in the floor. 'I'm here, I'm back!' she panted, her tear-streaked face suddenly appearing above Mel's head. 'Are you OK?'

'I'm not sure I'm going to make the race tomorrow,' Mel said, thickly. Looking up at Jess, her face looked like a full moon in the darkness. She was deathly pale, her lips a faint blue.

'They're coming, they're all coming, hang on! Don't die or anything,' Jess said. Laying on her stomach, she reached down and tried to touch Mel. 'Reach up to me, hold my hand,' she begged.

But no matter how far she stretched, Mel's fingertips never quite reached hers.

Chapter 24

Nan: Is Monty Don married?

Jess: This isn't Google, Nan.
But yes, he is. Sorry

Nan: Shame. He's got a smashing arse for a
man of his age. Mine looks like a sad pancake.

'Jess? Are you in there? It's me, Tom.'

Jess sighed and waited for Tom to get bored of pushing against the chain she'd put on her front door, and for Alfie to stop trying to squeeze through the gap to lick his ankles. It would take him precisely four minutes and forty-eight seconds, but he'd only been trying for sixty seconds so far.

Having failed to escape the time loop, Jess had let herself get drunker than she'd ever got in her life before. When she'd fallen asleep on the sofa, waking up back in bed on Friday morning, she'd lost the will to get up that day too. And the next. And the next.

After an early awkward encounter with Tom, who'd come into her room to scatter petals on her bed and been extremely confused to find her lying in it, chain-smoking, she'd learned to put the chain on the door after feeding Alfie, before going back to bed. From then on, every morning he'd send her the same, worried texts from her doorstep.

> Tom: I came to your flat earlier today, but the chain was on and you weren't answering.
> I don't mind if you don't want to see me, but just let me know you're OK, OK?

> I know you will completely ignore this text, but I AM FINE and you DO NOT need to order me Domino's pizza in a pathetic attempt to lure me out

> Or get Mel to wheedle at me through the gap in the door

By Jess's calculation, that was almost three weeks ago – although without time moving forwards, or a calendar to check, time was hard to grasp, like melting butter slipping through her fingers. Even cavemen were able to carve dates on their cave walls, but all Jess had was her own, flawed memory.

'Are you OK, Jess? I just want to know you're all right.'

One minute, thirty-two seconds.

Put off by how painful failure had been, she hadn't tried to work out a new way of getting out of the time loop. That hopeful certainty, followed by crushing disappointment, was exactly the kind of experience she spent her whole life dodging commitment and responsibility to avoid. And besides, she'd kind of got used to the fact that every day was Friday 13th by now.

Perhaps she should be waking up every morning and running down the street screaming. But the fact that she seemed to have reached an uneasy peace with her situation almost made sense, when she thought about the stories she wrote for *Real Talk!*.

Years of interviewing people who had been through some of the worst days of their lives had taught her that humans usually cope with the events they expect will destroy them much better than they think they will.

Whenever Rachel was allowed to interview a reader with an emotional story to tell – which wasn't often, as Maggie thought crying was a sign of someone's brain cells leaving their body – she'd end up sobbing in sympathy, while the interviewee sat patiently at the other end of the phone waiting for her to pull herself together.

'If anything like that happened to me, I wouldn't be able to handle it,' she'd declare when she came off the phone, her desk covered in snotty tissues. 'How can they talk about stuff like that without crying? I simply couldn't do it.'

But Jess understood exactly why her interviewees could talk about the worst thing that had ever happened to them without crying. She knew that once you've gone through something terrible, you can't help reliving that moment of grief or fear or anger over and over again – until eventually, it loses its power.

In the months after Mel's accident, she'd seen her best friend plummeting through the floors of that old bungalow again and again, an action replay that was always with her, lying in wait, ready to pounce at unexpected moments. She'd catch a hint of that musty, old-cellar smell, or hear a tree branch cracking, and be taken straight back to that terrible day.

But after a few weeks, she no longer flinched when the memory hit her. It was just another part of her day. She'd learned that you could get used to anything eventually, like a crack in the ceiling that worries you incessantly until you somehow stop noticing it.

Eventually, the awful something you've been through becomes a story you can tell as if it had happened to someone else. It didn't mean you no longer cared that it had happened – it just meant you couldn't keep up that level of grief or fear or anger for ever, or you'd simply burn out in a puff of smoke.

'Please let me in. I just want to check you're not dead.'

Two minutes twenty-three seconds.

The ashtray balanced on her chest rose and fell as Jess sighed heavily. She knew she couldn't stay in bed for ever. But she also knew that once you started wallowing, it was very hard to stop. Falling into quicksand was a lot easier than climbing out again. And besides, lying in bed, practising smoke rings and ordering Dominos or McDonald's for every meal wasn't a bad life, really.

At one point, she'd tried staying awake as long as she could, to see what would happen. If she could drink a ton of coffee and stay up for two days' straight, she'd at least get to enjoy the *Love or Dare* final with her nan, even if she pinged right back to Friday morning when she eventually fell asleep.

Instead, she was in the middle of an argument about baked beans on toast with some Americans on Twitter when she'd reached 6.45 a.m. and suddenly found herself waking up to the sound of her alarm on Friday morning, feeling as refreshed as if she'd just had seven hours' sleep.

'Come on, I know you must be in there. Jess!'

Three minutes, fifteen seconds.

But then again, apart from taking Alfie for walks in her pyjamas she'd barely seen daylight for three weeks. Or spoken to anyone. Or eaten a vegetable. Technically, she supposed, she'd only been languishing for a single day, and it wasn't like her muscles were going to atrophy after twenty-four hours of lounging. But her brain was on a different timeline to the rest of her body, and it felt like she was slipping into a mental fog.

'OK, I'm going now. Bye!' Tom yelled from the front door.

No you're not. Not for another thirty-three seconds.

Outside Jess's front door, Tom fell silent, trying to trap her into going into the front room. Which had worked three weeks ago – although only once.

Opening her phone, Jess reread Mel's morning text, which she'd replied to by sending her a close-up picture of her cleavage with the caption, *boobs or butt?* Jess was really starting to miss her. Since the day they'd first met, they'd never spent this long apart.

'Oh, for goodness' sake,' Jess muttered, stubbing out her cigarette, throwing the ashtray onto her bedside table, swinging her legs out of bed and stuffing her feet into her unicorn slippers.

Shuffling to the front door, Alfie following at her heels in the hope that she was heading for the treats cupboard, she saw Tom peering through the gap and was surprised to find herself breaking into a smile at the sight of him – her first proper smile since Alfie had accidentally flung himself off the edge of the bed chasing a doggy treat, about two weeks ago.

Tom's hair was sticking up at the back, the same way it had done every Friday since the first one, and he was still wearing that same old-fashioned jumper-and-shirt combo, even though the sun outside was shining brightly.

'Hold on,' she said, sticking her hand through the gap and poking Tom away from the door. Closing it, she undid the chain, and pulled him inside. Alfie immediately started jumping up at his legs, woofing happily.

'Hi,' Tom said uncertainly, looking a bit blindsided. He looked around the room as if he half expected someone else to be there. 'Sorry if you thought I was a burglar,' he stuttered. 'Did you know most burglaries happen in daylight, and thirty-four per cent come in through the front door? Isn't that weird?'

Jess rolled her eyes. 'And what percentage of burglars shout their own name while they're breaking in, use a front door key, and make as much racket as you just did?'

'Good point,' Tom said, blushing. 'I thought you weren't supposed to be at home?'

Jess couldn't help herself and folded her arms. 'According to who?' Tom went even pinker as he tried to think of an excuse again, until Jess took pity on him.

'According to Mel, perhaps? Well, Mel was wrong, I'm afraid.'

'Umm . . . yes, actually. She, er, gave me your keys . . . '

'Because you were in cahoots? And you were going to scatter those rose petals over my bed in the hope that I'd fall helplessly into your arms like Julia Roberts in *Pretty Woman*, correct?'

'Well . . . yes. Exactly that, in fact. But how do you know all that?' Tom said, looking bewildered.

Jess paused for a moment. There was no reason not to try it, even if he ran away screaming. It would almost be worth it just to see the look on his face.

'Well, the thing is, Tom, I'm living through a time loop.

That's how I know about the roses.' She gestured at the flowers Tom held in his hands. Wordlessly, he handed them over. 'Every day is Friday the thirteenth of August, and has been for almost five weeks now.'

'Like in *Groundhog Day*?'

'Yes, like in *Groundhog Day*. Jesus.'

'OK,' Tom said, slowly. 'I might need to sit down for this.' Walking around Jess to the sofa – was it her imagination or was he giving her a wide berth? – he perched on the edge of the corduroy marshmallow. 'Go on.'

'The first Friday was terrible. You dumped me, for reasons we really don't need to go into right now. I also got fired, and evicted from the flat by Brian for what are *extremely* unfair reasons, if you look at them the right way. Then to top it all off, I got hit by a moped and possibly smashed my face in. Although I don't actually know whether I did or not, because I don't remember much about that, and, when I woke up, it was Friday the thirteenth of August again, and my face was as completely gorgeous as ever. And now every morning when I wake up, it's the same old Friday.'

Tom opened his mouth, closed it again, then settled on looking completely perplexed.

'I've spent the last few weeks sulking about it, to be honest. I thought I'd figured out how to leave, but I hadn't, and being stuck in a time loop sucks. Would not recommend. One star out of ten. But I'm starting to think maybe it's time I started trying to find another way out of it. So, there you have it. That's my day. Cup of tea?'

Looking shell-shocked, Tom nodded mutely.

'Cool bananas,' Jess said, clapping her hands and shuffling into the kitchen.

Moments later, she heard muted footsteps and Alfie barking his head off, followed by the front door slamming.

Alfie trotted into the kitchen and looked up at her.

'Well, that was rude, wasn't it, Alfie?' she asked, scooping him up and kissing his fluffy head. 'Maybe we'll try again tomorrow.'

Chapter 25

Nan: Is Monty Don married?

Afraid so, Nan. I've heard Brad Pitt's currently available though?

Hearing footsteps, Jess leapt up from the sofa and opened the front door, just as Tom was searching through his bundle of keys looking for the right one. As Alfie pounced on his feet, he looked up at her in confusion.

'Oh, er, hello. I thought you weren't—'

'—supposed to be at home? Yes, I know, sorry. Mel was wrong, I'm afraid. But it's fine, come in. I'll take those flowers if you're offering?'

Jess held the door open and Tom stepped into the flat. Holding out the flowers, he looked confused, like an actor who'd forgotten his script mid-scene.

'Me and Mel ... We, um ...'

'Were in cahoots and she gave you my key? I know, don't

worry. Sit down, and I'll make us some tea. You can change the music if you like.'

'No, this is fine,' Tom said. 'I like eighties stuff. Without wanting to sound like an old fogey, I don't understand kids' music these days.'

'You totally sound like an old fogey, but I'm inclined to agree with you. Modern lyrics are all about lady flaps and huge dicks, and I really don't get the appeal.'

Hovering in the kitchen doorway for a moment to make sure Tom wasn't planning an escape, Jess watched him sit on the sofa and pull Alfie onto his lap. He started singing along to 'True' by Spandau Ballet, gently flapping Alfie's ears in time to the music.

Jess relaxed enough to unwind the sock from her leaking tap and fill the kettle.

'Sorry for barging in,' Tom said, as she handed him his cup of tea. 'I just . . .'

'Don't worry, it's fine. Mel told me about your plan with the roses and whatnot. She was worried I'd think it was too cheesy, so she wanted to warn me, and I decided to take the day off. I think Mel likes you. She didn't want you to be upset if I didn't react the right way.'

Tom smiled. 'That was kind of her. I like Mel too. I mean, I'm definitely going to give her a piece of my mind for ruining my amazing surprise. Which, now I'm here, seems a bit . . .'

'Stupid?'

'Yes, that. But you haven't run away screaming, have you? And I'm flattered that you took the day off to spend it with me. Haven't you got to write up that big interview with – Donna, was it? – you did yesterday?'

'Wow, you really do listen, don't you?' Jess said, impressed.

'Nate always just nods and smiles, then when I ask him about what I've told him later he hasn't got a scooby.' Suddenly, she realised she hadn't thought about Nate in weeks.

'Who's Nate?'

'Just . . . some guy at work. Don't worry about it.' Jess took a swig of tea and tried not to blush.

'So what will we do with our day then? Rob a bank, go skydiving, try and crash a film premiere?'

'Do you know what? I actually fancy just ordering takeaway and watching a film, if that's OK with you.'

'Thank god.'

Jess laughed. 'How about *Groundhog Day*? I've never actually seen it.'

'You've never seen the greatest time-loop film of the genre and the greatest Bill Murray film full stop?' Tom said, pretending to look aghast. 'Let's do it! It must be showing on one of the billion channels you spend all your rent money on.'

'Look, some people spend their money on crap like running shoes; I spend mine on making Alfie the luckiest dog in the world, and movie channels. And you get the benefit too, Mr "All I Need is Freeview". So shush.'

'We could make a day of it if you like,' Tom said. 'We could find some more time travel classics. You know, *Hot Tub Time Machine*, *Palm Springs*, *Back to the Future* . . .'

'We could even try making our own toffee vodka,' Jess said, hoping that she might actually get to drink it this time. In fact, she was starting to feel excited about the day ahead for the first time in three weeks. Even if it did technically involve homework. 'I read somewhere that you can make it in your dishwasher using Werther's Originals.'

'You don't have a dishwasher.'

'Dishwasher smishwasher. We'll just put it in a bucket of hot water for a bit.'

'OK. You're not allowed to tut if I have some very interesting facts about time travel to share with you along the way, though. Or dishwashers, for that matter. Did you hear about that kid who died after a knife was left pointing upwards in the cutlery drawer and he tripped over? True story.'

'Well, that's heart-warming. You're only allowed two facts per movie, tops,' Jess warned. 'And that counts as one. I'll pop to the shops while you stay here; keep an eye on Alfie and look pretty.'

'Easy. Got it nailed, haven't we, Alf?' Tom said, stretching himself across the sofa like Kate Winslet in *Titanic* and batting his eyelids.

Skipping down the steps and to the corner shop, Jess filled a basket with a week's-worth of treats: booze and sweets, peanut butter and popcorn, frozen pizzas, and two tubs of Ben & Jerry's. All the stuff, in fact, that she usually tried to resist for the sake of her trousers, but could eat as much of as she liked as long as she was in the time loop.

'Thirty-nine pounds fifty, please,' Borys said, barely even glancing into the basket. Jess knew better than to question the price. She'd once tested Borys's supernatural totting-up abilities by grabbing an armful of the wildly random stuff the shop sold – from sheer nude stockings and a faded bag of rubber bands to ribbed condoms and Polish sausages – and adding up the price as she went along.

She'd expected Borys to have to sort through everything – how many baby-bottle teats could he realistically sell each week? – but instead, he'd barely glanced at the pile before telling her, 'Seventeen pounds and twenty-eight pence, please.' He was like a corner shop Rain Man.

'How come the only place in the world you ever see black carriers like these is in weird corner shops in London?' Jess asked, as Borys placed all the food in two flimsy plastic bags.

Borys shrugged. 'Good for early morning drinkers who don't like booze to be seen. Mums on way to school run. Underage drinkers we turn blind eye to. Police taking bribe for ignoring underage drinkers.'

'Ah. That makes sense,' Jess said, nodding. 'Who knew our road was so exciting?'

Half-trotting her way back to the flat, Jess opened the door and yelled, 'Hi, honey, I'm ho-oooome!' But Tom wasn't in the living room.

'I'm in here,' he called in a shaky voice from the bedroom.

'Oh shit,' Jess muttered, dropping the bags on the floor. Pushing her bedroom door open, Tom was sitting on the edge of the bed, surrounded by torn rose petals, holding a pair of tiny blue Hollister trunks with palm trees dotted across the waistband.

'Whose are these, Jess? Are you seeing someone else?'

Chapter 26

'Hi honey, I'm ho-oooome!' Jess called, pushing open the door, clutching two black plastic carrier bags. Seeing the sofa empty, she felt a cold prickle creeping up her back. She'd definitely remembered to throw Nate's pants into the washing basket this time. Or behind it, at least. She wasn't that great a shot.

'Hey, you're back,' Tom said with a grin, as he walked in from the kitchen. He was carrying an ice bucket that was steaming from the top. 'I got our fake dishwasher ready. Did you get the vodka and Werther's?'

'Roger that!' Jess smiled, holding up the bags like they were trophies. In the kitchen, she spread the sweets out on a tray like tooth-rotting tapas and brought them into the living room with a 'ta-da!'.

'I didn't think you had a sweet tooth,' Tom said, popping a chocolate button into his mouth.

'Don't worry, I bought pizza too. But first, I want us to play a game. It's like twenty questions, but instead of me thinking of something and you trying to guess, it's just you answering

221

some questions. Which might seem weird, but it's for a thing. Is that OK?'

Jess handed Tom the list of questions she'd written out while she'd been waiting for him to arrive that morning, and he began reading them out.

1. What's your current work password?
2. What's your earliest memory?
3. What's your favourite nerdy fact?

'Is the thing this is for ... you hacking into my bank account and stealing all my money?' Tom asked, raising one eyebrow.

'You can change your work password straight afterwards; I just need to know what it was this morning,' Jess said. 'Come on, humour me. I promise it's important and that I won't rob you.'

'Luckily for you, I can't resist a quiz,' Tom said, taking the pen Jess was offering him. It had a sparkly unicorn on top decorated with feathers, which wobbled back and forth on a spring.

'Unicorns probably wouldn't have pink feathers, even if they were real,' Tom tutted as he started scribbling down his answers. As he finished the last question, Jess plucked the list from his fingers and scanned through his answers.

'Why only forty-five minutes?' she asked as she read the third answer, but barely heard Tom's reply as she was gripped by a sneezing fit. As she frantically patted her pockets for a tissue, Alfie trotted into the living room, carrying what looked like a handkerchief in his mouth. Jumping up and resting his paws on Jess's knees, he let it go onto her lap.

'Hey, he brought you a hankie,' Tom said, picking it up. 'Could he be any cuter? Good boy, Alfie!'

Then Jess watched in horror as he unfolded the hanky to reveal a pair of tiny blue Hollister trunks, with palm trees dotted across the waistband.

Chapter 27

Nan: Is Monty Don married?

'Oh, Nan. Just give it up will you?' Jess sighed. 'He might be ancient as hell, but he's still far too young for you.' Throwing her phone on the sofa, Jess stood up and stretched.

She was determined to spend a whole day with Tom today if it killed her. Plus she had to watch *Groundhog Day* eventually. It might hold the secret of how to get out of the time loop, but she didn't want to watch it on her own in case all the meta made her brain explode.

She'd taken the precaution of putting Nate's pants in the washing basket, stuffing half her wardrobe on top and resting some thick hardbacks – all presents from Mel – on top of that, to foil Alfie's attempts to ruin her day.

'Don't go in there, OK?' she warned him, as she heard Tom's footsteps on the front steps. She opened the door just as he was searching through his bundle of keys looking for the right one. He looked up at her in confusion.

'Oh, er, hello. I thought you weren't—'

'—supposed to be at home? Yes, I know, sorry. Mel was wrong, I'm afraid. But it's fine, come in. I'll take those flowers if you're offering?'

Ten minutes later, Jess handed Tom a mug of coffee.

'So, Tom,' Jess said, 'before you take a sip of that, you should know that it's got rum in it. And the reason it's got rum in it is that we need to talk, and you might need a drink afterwards.'

'Oh god. You're not going to dump me, are you?' Tom said, as Jess sat beside him, her Doug's Mug mug clutched in her hands. She'd given herself a generous shot of rum too, because rum and coffee are delicious, even before 10.30 a.m., and she couldn't think of a single reason not to.

'No conversations that start, "So, Tom," and include the words, "We need to talk," have ever ended well for me,' he babbled. 'That's how my boss told me he was letting me go on Christmas Eve. And that time my best friend said he didn't want to play Call of Duty with me any more because I was scared of Zombies Mode. Although anyone will tell you Zombies Mode can be genuinely scary. Did you know, for example, that—'

'Bupupupup,' Jess said, holding up a finger. 'Stop stalling and listen to me for a moment. I'm not going to dump you, I just have something to tell you, and I need you to have an open mind about it. Rather than sneaking out when I go and make us a cup of tea, which is a very strong possibility. Will you hear me out?'

Tom nodded warily, so Jess told him all about her Worst Day Ever – skipping the bit where Tom dumped her because she was sleeping with Nate – about waking up trapped in a time loop, and about all the days she'd lived through up until today.

'And last time I told you all this, you legged it when I went into the kitchen. Which was very rude, by the way. But today I think I might be able to persuade you I'm telling the truth.'

As she finished, Tom wiped his forehead with a pale hand. 'If . . . *if* this time loop is real, you seem very calm about all this. Shouldn't you be running through the streets screaming?'

'I totally get your point. And at first I was very close to doing just that. But remember, this isn't my first rodeo. I've done this—' Jess tried to count on her fingers, then gave up '—lots of times. I can't exactly spend every morning having a meltdown, can I? It would be a total waste of time. Although, technically, I do have an infinite amount of it *to* waste. Anyway . . . '

'And does Mel know about all this?'

Jess's neck prickled. 'I did try to convince her once, but she thought I was either making it up for attention or having a nervous breakdown.' She shook her head at the memory. 'But that's not important right now. The important thing today is that you believe me.'

'Why's it so important? I'm not sure I want to believe that time loops exist, to be honest. It would be a bit of a head-fuck.'

'Because it's lonely being stuck here with no one to tell. And because if I'm telling the truth you won't remember tomorrow anyway, so I'm not worried about melting your brain. But most importantly, it's because we still haven't watched bloody *Groundhog Day* together and I want to take notes. A little bird tells me it's the greatest time-loop film of the genre, and the greatest Bill Murray film full stop.'

Tom frowned, as if he was trying to remember something, then shook his head.

'So how do you plan on proving this then? By telling me tonight's EuroMillions numbers?'

'No, because you wouldn't believe me until eight p.m., and I need you to believe me now. Although they're six, nine, twelve, fourteen and thirty-two. Lucky Stars five and eleven. FYI.'

Tom nodded. 'Good to know.'

'I'm going to start by telling you I know you had a sausage and egg McMuffin for breakfast on your way here, and you're wearing blue striped pants under those jeans.'

Tom peeked into his waistband and blushed.

'OK, but that doesn't really prove anything. You could have found out about my breakfast using Find My Phone or something. And guessing what pants I'm wearing is hardly Derren Brown territory, is it?'

'You do like a stripy pant,' Jess conceded. 'Which is why I came up with my masterplan.'

Jess handed Tom a piece of paper. He frowned as he read what she'd scribbled on it: a list of sentences, none of which seemed to be related to each other, or make any sense on their own, either.

I think it's about time for a Negroni, don't you?

Gif of Ron Swanson saying 'This is my hell'.

A video of an otter swimming on his back, holding a stick in his mouth (he looks a bit like you).

Happiness is scented candles.

I'm Crowdfunding for my attempt to holiday in a different country every fortnight for a year!

'What does all this mean?' Tom asked.

Jess checked the time and handed him her phone. 'Open Twitter. Quickly, it'll start in a bit. At exactly ten-fifty a.m., in fact.'

Taking Jess's phone from her hand, Tom opened the app and scrolled up.

'OK, the first one should come in right about . . . now,' Jess said, folding her arms and leaning back on the sofa.

Tom paused for a moment. Then, '@Biltawulf says, "I think it's about time for a Negroni, don't you?",' he muttered. 'And now @Dookie3000 has posted a Parks and Rec gif. What the . . . ?'

Tom looked flustered as he swiped at the screen to refresh it, his eyes widening as each of the tweets Jess had predicted came up on her feed, one by one.

'Wow. OK. That is weird. Although that otter does *not* look like me. Plus, I've got an Android phone. You could have some kind of . . . delay function on an iPhone for all I know.'

'OK, so what if I did the same trick, but with your brain? I mean, not *exactly* that trick. But what if I knew things about you I couldn't possibly know unless you'd told me on one of the other Fridays?'

'Like what?'

'Like that your password at the bookbinders is JackKirby1978!, after the year your favourite artist published his last Marvel comic. *The Silver Surfer*, wasn't it?'

'Graphic Novel,' Tom muttered.

'Or that your earliest memory is a conker falling into your pram after your mum parked you under a tree, and you scream-ing blue murder. You've been scared of conkers ever since, but you tell everyone it's because you're allergic to them.'

'OK, maybe you can stop now,' Tom said, looking slightly freaked out.

'Or that your favourite fact is that no one can sit in the quietest room in the world for more than forty-five minutes, partly because the sound of your own lungs and heart doing their thing sends you doolally.'

'I mean, it is a good fact,' Tom said weakly.

'And that ... and that you're falling for me,' Jess added, quietly.

Tom suddenly looked alarmed. 'When did I tell you that?'

'When you were sitting on my sofa wearing a kilt, drunk on the grand-and-a-half Scotch I'd bought you after winning a fortune in a poker game.'

'Wow. OK. Wow. OK,' Tom said, and Jess burst out laughing.

'I'm sorry, it's not funny,' she said, squeezing his thigh. 'I know it's a lot to take in. But this is a pretty good result from my perspective. I mean, judging by the look of horror on your face, you totally believe me.'

'I suppose so,' Tom said, shaking his head in wonder. 'I don't have much other choice, do I? Sherlock Holmes says when you have eliminated the impossible, what remains, however improbable, has to be the truth.'

'Exactly. And surely me knowing that you dreamt you were playing chess with The Rock last night, when you haven't told a soul about that since you woke up, is more impossible than a time loop.'

'Stop it!'

'Because time loops might be improbable, but they're *technically* possible, aren't they? Something, something, wormhole, something, something, quantum probability, I think Reddit said.'

'That's word for word, is it?'

'You know what I mean. And besides, I don't even need you to believe me, really. I just need you to stay.'

Chapter 28

Outside a cosy B&B in Punxsutawney, Pennsylvania, Bill Murray lifted Andie MacDowell over a wooden gate and into a snow-covered street, while on a battered corduroy sofa in a tiny flat in East London, Jess Janus burst into tears.

'Hey ... hey,' Tom said, squeezing her shoulder. 'What's the matter?'

'Sorry. It's just ... I've been trying not to think about it too hard, but this time-loop stuff is actually really scary,' Jess sniffed, swiping at her nose with the back of her hand. 'What if I never get to tomorrow the way Phil Connors does? What if I have to kill myself, but just end up waking up on the same day billions of times? Once you've eaten all the doughnuts you want, being stuck in a time loop feels pretty lonely.

'I've had some fun, but not being able to change anything in your life permanently, for better or worse, makes it feel so ... pointless. It's starting to feel like I'll never reach Saturday.'

'Well, let's have a look at your notes. What do they say?'

Tom asked, having seen Jess grab her glittery mermaid note-book and unicorn pen from under the bed halfway through *Groundhog Day* and start taking notes.

'Not much that's very useful,' she sniffed, reading aloud.

Groundhogs are cute! Search for memes.

Helping bratty kid and grateful old ladies = good.

Gets to know Andie MacDowell (she is an irritant). Fave flavour of ice cream, etc.

Eats cake whenever possible. Good idea.

'That's all I've got,' Jess said. 'He was basically just nicer to people and stopped trying to get into Andie McDowell's knickers to escape the time loop. But I'm already in your knickers, so that's not very helpful. Also, I thought he was a lot more interesting before he turned into a massive sap and started telling Andie she looked like an angel in the snow.'

'Maybe the time loop is telling you that you should defi-nitely be my girlfriend?' Tom said, hopefully.

'How about I give you an answer tomorrow?'

'Totally unfair.'

'I think I need to do a bit more homework. Maybe we could make watching time-loop films on a Friday our "thing"? We can do *Palm Springs* next. And we won't have long to wait for tomorrow if I go to bed early – the time loop resets when I fall asleep.'

'And what happens to me? Do I just ... disappear too?'

'I've got no idea,' Jess said with a shrug. 'Maybe there

are loads of parallel universes out there, where each of the days I've done so far has played out in full, and just carried on into Saturday. Or maybe everyone leaps back to Friday morning with me and starts afresh. Perhaps when I fall asleep you all just go, "poof!" and leap to seven forty-five a.m. Unfortunately, there's no way of asking you, is there?'

'Wow. So people who died would be resurrected, only to die over and over again? Presumably everyone does the same things every single day? Has anyone changed their routine?'

'Well, I let Alfie jump onto my bed one morning, assuming he'd forget all about it. But he seems to have remembered, which is really weird. And naughty.' On hearing his name, Alfie shuffled out from underneath the sofa on his stomach and peered up at them.

Tom looked thoughtful. 'Was he with you when you were hit by the moped that first time?' Jess nodded. 'And do you know what happened to him?'

'I don't, actually,' Jess said, slowly. 'He was on my right-hand side, and the moped hit my right leg. So maybe he got hurt too? I hadn't even thought of that before. Poor Alfie.'

Jess reached down and booped Alfie's nose.

'Well, in that case, maybe he's living through this time loop too. Maybe you're not as alone as you thought.'

'And maybe I can teach him how to high-five. That would be good, wouldn't it, Alfie? Wouldn't it?' Jess picked up Alfie's tiny paw and pressed it against her palm. Alfie cocked his head in confusion, then licked her hand.

'God, imagine dying over and over like that. I wouldn't be able to handle that. Poor Tom Cruise,' Jess shuddered as she switched off *Edge of Tomorrow*. Lifting her head from the spot where it was nestled in Tom's lap, she took a sip of toffee-flavoured vodka.

'I appreciate you're in a pickle, but I think it's a pretty safe bet that you're never going to find yourself joining the US space force and fighting aliens on an endless loop.'

'That's what you think,' Jess said, darkly, grabbing her notepad. 'Never say never.'

Each morning for the past three days, she'd managed to convince Tom to stay in her flat and watch movies with her. By now, she had her psychic demonstration pared down to just seven minutes before Tom turned a bit green and went quiet, which was the main sign that he believed her – as much as he ever would, anyway.

Proving her prowess every day was actually fun, and, in the process, she'd also become quite invested in her research, making careful notes during each film for her to read over and memorise before bed. The message of most of them – apart from *Back to the Future*, whose lesson, if any, was not to go back in time, try to shag your own mum and risk your very existence – seemed to be about being a good person and making the most of life.

'The main characters – that's me in this case, by the way – are all much nicer by the end of each film,' Jess said, squinting at the notepad she held above her face. 'It's all about doing good deeds and being nicer to their families and learning to appreciate the little things.'

'And stopping themselves from being murdered,' Tom added. 'If that doesn't count as making the most of life, I'm not sure what does.'

'Well, I'm pretty sure no one's trying to murder me à la

Happy Death Day,' Jess said, grabbing her phone from the coffee table and googling 'how to do good deeds'.

'I did get mugged on the first night, but that was just some robbing bastard rather than a murder attempt. I hope, anyway. So maybe I just have to appreciate the little things and be a bit nicer, rather than just trying to fix my own stuff.'

'You're already nice,' Tom said, ruffling Jess's fringe as if she were a friendly dog.

Jess's stomach swirled. Could she really be that nice when she'd cheated on Tom, and her best friend didn't trust her enough to tell her something important?

'I could be nicer. I mean, I buy my friends coffee and get the *Big Issue* every week. And Alfie eats better than me, don't you, boy? And if anyone upset Mel, I'd karate chop them right in the neck. But even if it was an accident, I still sent that horrible email to Donna, which a nicer person wouldn't have done in the first place. And I've probably caused Brian more stress than he deserves, too.

'Plus, I'm sure I could squeeze a few more random good deeds into my day. Like helping old ladies to cross the road and paying compliments to people in bad but hopeful outfits.'

'Are you planning on being nicer in an episode of *Hey Duggee*? I've never seen an old lady who needs help crossing the road in real life.'

'Maybe good deeds don't always have to involve actually helping people. Look at this,' Jess said, tapping her phone. 'It says here, "A smile is infectious! Share one with strangers in the street, and they'll pass it on, creating a chain of good vibes – starting with you!".'

The website Jess had found was a bit cringey and featured a startling number of moody sunset photos. But at the same time, she quite liked the idea of doing nice things for people that didn't involve anything too complicated. 'It sounds a lot easier than catching children stupid enough to climb trees, at least. If I'd been Phil Connors I'd have let the little brat in *Groundhog Day* break an ankle.'

'So you're not planning on being *that* nice, then,' Tom said, raising an eyebrow.

Jess shrugged. 'Baby steps. How about you start by nipping to the Tube and grabbing me a copy of today's *Evening Standard*? When I asked you what you'd do if you were trapped in a time loop, you said you'd look in the evening newspaper to find good deeds to do, so why not start there?'

'When did I say this exactly?'

'Ohh ... about thirty-five Fridays ago, give or take.'

'OK, well, you can stop saying stuff like that, because, brrrrr,' Tom said, stretching his long limbs as he gently lifted Jess's head off his lap and stood up. 'And anyway, aren't we supposed to be leaving for dinner soon?'

'We've already been to Hot Stuff twice this week. The chilli dogs are amazing, but I really fancy pizza tonight, do you mind?'

'How could I possibly?' Tom said, shaking his head as he headed for the front door.

Ten minutes later, the newspaper was spread across the coffee table, and two large pizzas were on their way. Jess wondered how long she'd have to be trapped in a time loop to get bored of pizza, then felt bad for even thinking such treacherous thoughts about her favourite foodstuff.

The front page of the paper featured stories about a crooked banker's conviction at Southwark Crown Court, a footballer's affair, and local protests over a new runway at Heathrow Airport. 'Not much I can do about any of those,' Jess said, flicking to the next pages.

Skimming stories about politicians breaking their promises, new restaurant openings, and how little Kim Kardashian had been wearing recently, Jess paused at an advert for a new immersive theatre experience. It was her idea of hell, but Mel had always wanted to try one. Perhaps she should treat her to a ticket – that would count as a good deed, right?

Next, she stopped at a piece headlined POLICE FRUS-TRATED BY MUGGING GANG.

'Ah, this looks more like it,' she said, and she and Tom pressed their heads together and read.

Police are on the hunt for an orchestrated gang of moped riders targeting women in East London. The gang is thought to be responsible for dozens of muggings in the area, includ-ing 'snatch and ride' attacks by moped riders. Handbags and mobile phones are particular targets, and in some instances the gang's actions have caused serious injury.

'Well yes, I know all about that one,' Jess said. 'One time, you got the guy's number plate, but I can't remember it now. I haven't got your massive brain.'

Tom shook his head as Jess flicked on, stopping again at another headline that said ACCESS ALL AREAS.

It was about a national campaign to improve disability access. The writer of the article had interviewed a handful of men and women who lived in London and were helping to kick off the campaign.

'Hang on, Brian Parker – isn't that your landlord?' Tom said, pointing to a picture caption. It read, 'Sarah Parker, daughter of local landlord Brian Parker, is joining the fight for improved access and benefits'. Above it was a picture of a young girl in a wheelchair, beaming at the camera. Jess picked up the paper and read the piece out loud.

'Sarah Parker, eighteen, has joined the fight to improve disability access across London, and to campaign for simplified Personal Independence Payments.

'The teenager, who will be taking up her place at City University London to study Journalism this September, says wide-ranging changes need to be made to the capital's infrastructure and benefits system if students like her are to have access to better choices after graduation.

'"I would love to have the full uni experience, but I am still living with my mum and dad," Sarah, who lives in Bethnal Green, says. "Getting an allowance is a struggle, and there is not enough accessible accommodation in London."

'Sarah's father, landlord Brian Parker, says, "Because I have seen first-hand how hard the benefits system in London can be to navigate, I try to give my tenants some leeway when it comes to paying their rent. But it does mean I often have to go without the money I am owed myself."'

Jess felt a jolt of guilt hitting her stomach.

'Hey, that's you!' Tom exclaimed. 'You're in the paper!'

'Oh shush,' Jess said, knocking her head gently against his. Tom read out the rest of the article.

'"The knock-on effect is that without help from the government, Sarah is stuck at home with us, when she just wants to spread her wings like any other young woman her age. I am hoping the Access All Areas campaign will help her do just that."'

Putting down the paper, Jess groaned, and rubbed her face with her hands.

'Oh god, this is terrible. I'm literally taking money off a girl in a wheelchair and forcing her to live with her old, boring dad. What would Mel say if she saw this? I know how hard her life can be sometimes, and here I am making Sarah's life even harder. I assumed Brian was loaded!'

'Assuming makes an ass out of u and Ming the Merciless,' Tom said, before adding a hasty, 'Sorry,' when he saw Jess's face.

But she wasn't listening anyway. Instead, it was slowly beginning to dawn on her that if she was going to start being a better person, she had an awful lot of work to do.

Chapter 29

Nan: Is Monty Don married?

No, Nan. Fill your boots

**P.S. Google is the one that
says 'Google' on it. Xxx**

So far that morning, Jess had already attempted to do at least ten nice things, all of which had resulted in absolutely massive failure.

After hiding Nate's pants in her washing basket – which surely counted as a kind of good deed, seeing as it would stop Tom having his heart crushed? – and leaving Alfie at home with a pile of his favourite dog biscuits to munch through, she'd walked to the Tube, beaming at everyone and offering the occasional, chirpy, 'Good morning!'

So far, just one person – a chubby toddler in a pram – had smiled back. He'd even waved his squeaky giraffe at her, which was nice. But everyone else had looked at Jess much the same as she'd react to a stranger grinning dementedly at her in the street: like she was a crazy bag lady to be avoided at all costs.

Jess wondered if people might be more receptive on the underground, and headed into its depths, smiling as forcefully as a woman in an advert for toothpaste. Her cheeks were already starting to hurt.

On her way down she'd tried to help a woman with her suitcase, before being accused of trying to steal it, at which point she'd hurriedly dropped it, causing it to fall all the way down the stairs. Followed by the woman's full-blooded curses, Jess had run onto the Tube to hide, bagging the priority seat on her carriage so she could give it up for anyone who needed it.

Offering her seat with a flourish to an elderly lady whose face had more lines than the overground, she'd thrown Jess a murderous look, and told her quite hissily that she was only fifty-five.

'This is what having three sodding kids will do to you,' she'd said, stabbing a thick, gnarly finger towards her face.

Sitting down with an embarrassed plop, Jess had stood up for a pregnant woman next, who'd looked quite tearful as she sat down, before Jess realised she was just wearing a really unflattering dress.

Hopping off the underground at Oxford Circus, she'd dipped into her overdraft by taking £200 of £10 notes out of a cash machine, stopped off at the big branch of New Look and, checking no one was looking, stuffed cash into random pockets in the loungewear section.

Being nice was way harder than Jess had imagined, unless it simply involved giving people cold, hard cash. Where was the warm glow of altruism she'd been promised by the website with all the sunsets?

The final straw happened when she'd given directions to a man who was blocking the barriers to the Tube with his enormous backpack. He was staring at a map, looking hopelessly confused, trying to find Kensington Palace.

'Just take this blue line down to Victoria, then hop on an eastbound train on the Circle Line,' she'd smiled. 'You can just get off at High Street Ken and walk from there.'

The tourist had looked grateful, and Jess felt smug until she realised she'd sent another tourist in the wrong direction. What made her think she was cut out to dole out advice when she had such an appalling sense of direction anyway? She hoped he wouldn't end up sitting on the Circle Line for hours.

By the time her nan's text arrived at half past ten, she'd already realised that trying to help people was doing her absolutely no good whatsoever.

'Fuck it,' she muttered to herself. It was time to change tactics. Rather than helping complete strangers, perhaps Jess needed to suck it up and pay Brian the money she owed him. It might mean Alfie would have to join her in eating budget food, but it would certainly be the best deed she'd done all day.

Plus, with the benefit of painful hindsight, Jess felt awful about making so many, mainly premature death-based excuses about missing her rent and making Brian's daughter's life that bit harder in the process.

While Jess had been busy picturing Brian lighting cigars with fifty pound notes, he'd been generously cutting her some slack at the expense of his daughter's freedom.

After a stop-off at the bank to have a chat with her bank manager – something she didn't realise actually happened in real life – and extend her overdraft and set up a direct debit, Jess headed for Bethnal Green and down Roman Road, trying to work out which way the blue dot on her phone was pointing to find the right turn off for Brian's flat.

Inside her handbag was an envelope with two months' rent inside it. Handing Brian a cool wad of cash had seemed like a good idea this morning. As well as making her feel a bit gangster-like, Nate always enthused about 'cash in hand' jobs, and she hoped Brian would appreciate the gesture, rather than be aghast at the suggestion that he was a tax-dodger.

But now, walking through a slightly dodgy bit of East London, she wondered if it had been such a great idea after all. Reaching a set of gates in front of a tatty-looking yard surrounded by flats, Jess peered through them. Although this wasn't the swanky penthouse she'd pictured Brian living in, it did seem to be the right place. Leaning on the buzzer, it was only a few moments before a woman's voice, sounding slightly irritated, crackled over the intercom.

'Hello? You can stop that now. It's really loud.'

'Oh shit, sorry,' Jess said, straightening up. 'I was miles away. I'm looking for Brian? Brian Parker?'

'Who is this, please?'

'It's Jess. Janus. I'm one of his tenants.'

The woman paused. 'I'll let you in, hold on,' she said, before a door in the gates buzzed loudly. Jess pushed it open and walked into the courtyard. A front door on the right-hand side of the space opened, and a small blonde woman, pale and tired-looking, came out onto the step, wrapped in a pink towelling dressing gown.

'Hi, Jess, I'm Laura,' the woman said, holding out her hand. Jess took it and noticed how tiny it felt and how cold it was. 'Brian's my husband.'

'I'm—'

'I know who you are. He's worried to death about your late rent payments.'

'I'm really sorry,' Jess began. But Laura was just getting warmed up.

'My husband is far too soft, you know,' she scolded. 'We've remortgaged our couple of tiny flats to pay for our daughter's treatments – she's got scoliosis, see – so he can't even sell the bloody things. He's got such a soft heart, but I swear he'll get an ulcer chasing you lot for your money. So please tell me you're here to pay your rent.'

'I am, actually,' Jess said. 'In cash. Two months' worth.'

'That's a big relief,' Laura said, smiling. She instantly looked a few years younger. 'He'll be so pleased. And Sarah will be too. They're in this evening's paper actually, talking about that new disability rights campaign.'

Jess nodded. 'Oh really? That's great. Is Brian here?'

'He's not I'm afraid. He's at Homerton Hospital for Sarah's physio.'

Jess frowned. She could give the money to Laura, but what if she forgot to pass it on to Brian before the end of the day? Would it still count as a good deed that might help her out of the time loop?

'I was really hoping to catch him,' Jess said.

'Well, he'll be at the hospital for most of today if you want to try and find him. He usually waits for her out front when it's sunny, so he shouldn't be hard to spot. This will really cheer him up.' Laura reached out and squeezed her arm, making Jess feel even worse. Being thanked for doing something she should have done months ago made her burn with shame.

'Nice meeting you,' Jess mumbled, heading back towards the gates. Looking back over her shoulder as she stepped back outside, Jess saw Laura still standing on the step, waving goodbye.

As her bus pulled up outside Homerton Hospital, Jess saw Brian sitting on a bench, a Costa Coffee cup clutched in one hand and a pen in the other. A book was perched on his lap, which he was frowning at with concentration.

As Jess hopped off the bus and got closer, she saw it was a sudoku puzzle book. He was wearing a short-sleeved checked shirt tucked into some beige slacks, his greying hair blowing wispily across his head. His mobile phone was in an old-fashioned case clipped to his belt, and his wire-rimmed glasses glinted gold in the sunshine.

The thing about picturing your landlord as a cigar-smoking fat cat is that the illusion is quite easily shattered when you're forced to confront reality.

'Mr Parker?' Jess said, and Brian jumped, causing the book to fall off his knee and onto the floor. Picking it up, Jess shook the dust off it and handed it to him. He squinted at her, then his face cleared.

'Hello, Jess! What are you doing here?' he said, looking behind him.

'I'm here to see you, actually. Your wife told me you'd be here. Do you mind if I sit?'

Brian shuffled along the concrete bench to make space for her, and she sat down.

'I just wanted to say sorry, and to give you this,' she said, pulling the envelope out of her bag. She'd panicked a bit in the bank and asked for the cash in £10 notes, so the envelope was bulging. Opening it, Brian let out a little 'Oh!' of surprise, then his shoulders visibly relaxed.

'Is this your rent money, Jess? This is wonderful, thank you.'

'There's the last two months' rent in there, and it'll be on time every month from now on. Pinky promise. I set up a direct debit,' she added proudly.

'Thank you. I hope your dog is OK now?'

'Sorry . . . my dog?'

'The one who got run over last month, and needed wheels fitted to replace his "poor shattered little legs". That's how you put it, wasn't it?'

'Oh yes,' Jess blushed. 'He . . . he's fine, thanks.'

'You don't say?' Brian said, pushing up his glasses. 'If you're turning over a new leaf when it comes to paying your rent, does that mean you'll stop smoking in the flat too? I suppose I can ignore all the dog hair if you'll do that for me. Especially seeing as he's so tragically disabled.'

Jess blushed. 'It's a deal.' Brian nodded, stuffing the envelope in his back pocket – rather carelessly, Jess thought, considering how much money was in it.

'And will you say sorry to Sarah for me too?' Jess said, standing up. 'I didn't mean to make life more difficult for either of you. And if she ever needs any advice on getting into journalism . . . Well, I might only work for a trashy weekly magazine, but if I can do it, literally anyone can. I'd be happy to help.'

'How did you know she was studying journalism?'

Jess panicked. She forgot the newspaper article wasn't actually out yet. 'I, er, saw a very early edition of the *Standard*,' she muttered, waving goodbye and turning towards the bus stop before Brian could ask any more awkward questions.

A few feet from the bench, Jess paused to light a cigarette, waving her hand in front of her face to disperse the cloud of smoke from her first puff. As it drifted away, she stared, frozen to the spot, before jumping behind a large hospital sign on her left just in time.

Her heart thumping, Jess pulled her phone out of her bag. It was ten to eleven, which meant right about now Mel should be on her way to the mysterious meeting she'd not wanted to tell her about. Except Mel was here: stepping out of a cab, slamming the door, and walking towards the hospital, a look of grim determination on her face.

Her footsteps getting closer, Jess held her breath as Mel paused in front of the sign she was hiding behind.

Jess looked down and recognised Mel's pristine black ballet pumps, and the tip of her purple cane. She hoped Mel didn't feel the urge to look down too, as she was bound to recognise the battered red Converse Jess wore almost every day.

After a short pause, Mel strode towards the hospital.

As quickly as she could, Jess opened her texts, tapped out a message and hit Send.

Hey Mel, good luck with your meeting xxx

Jess saw Mel pause at the reception entrance, pull out her phone, and read her message, frowning. Rubbing her eyes, she seemed to let out a deep sigh, before stuffing her phone back in her bag and heading inside, leaving Jess staring at thin air.

Chapter 30

September 2006, the abandoned house

As Jess stretched her fingertips to reach Mel's, a voice called out behind her.

'Get away from there,' the male voice said. 'You don't want to fall too, do you? Come on.'

'I'll be right here, OK?' Jess promised Mel, reluctantly withdrawing her arm and shuffling backwards. Above Mel, where she lay at the bottom of the hole she'd plunged through, Jess's face was quickly joined by that of a gentle-looking man in his early sixties.

'You've got yourself in quite a pickle, haven't you?' he said, kindly.

'I think I might have done,' Mel said, slowly. She was struggling to keep her eyes open.

'Don't lie down now, will you?' the man said briskly. 'I'm George, and we're going to have a chat until the ambulance gets here. Then you'll be getting a cast for your leg for all your friends to sign. Not bad, eh? What's your name, love?'

'Mel,' she said, softly. Everything was going a bit fuzzy around the edges, but she couldn't stop glancing at the bright-white bone emerging from her leg like a blood-stained glacier.

'Hello, Mel. Why don't you look at me instead of that poor leg of yours, and we'll be out of here in a jiffy.'

Within fifteen minutes, two paramedics clad in fluorescent yellow and green had gently moved Jess away from the hole and taken over George's soothing monologue. Mel was still awake, but barely, and she hadn't been able to resist lying back on the floor of the basement, despite George urging her not to.

After being given strong painkillers, Mel's leg was firmly strapped up, and she was eased out of the hole, onto a stretcher and out of the bungalow. Jess hovered in the background, clenching her fists in anguish, looking for ways to help. While the paramedics had been taping up Mel's leg, George had helped take the front door off its hinges so they could get her outside causing as little pain as possible.

As they carried her out, Jess heard an anguished yell as Mel's mum and dad arrived and gathered around their daughter. Behind them, George stood next to the ambulance, still clutching his screwdriver and talking to a girl who was about the same age as Jess and Mel.

Jess had spoken to her briefly when she'd run to the house next door, screaming for help. Aya was George's lodger, and due to start her medical degree after the summer holidays, so she'd promised Jess she'd call Mel's parents and tell them about the accident.

'Don't worry, they'll just be glad she's OK,' Aya promised, rubbing Jess's shoulder with concern as she sobbed in fear. But Jess had just cried even harder. How could this stranger know how Mel's parents would react when they found out that Jess had broken their only daughter?

And now, as they gripped their daughter's thin, pale hand, their faces etched with worry as she was fed into the mouth of an ambulance, Jess felt sick. She'd always got a buzz out of narrowly dodging trouble, but Mel had never felt the same as her. And there was no doubt about it: this would never have happened if it wasn't for Jess.

She'd completely ignored Mel's protests, knowing she could be persuaded to do anything if Jess pushed hard enough. And now Mel's race tomorrow was ruined. And many more races after that too, probably.

As Mel was driven to Homerton Hospital, her parents drove behind the ambulance, Jess sitting in the back seat. The car was silent, apart from the sound of Mel's mum crying softly.

'She'll be OK, won't she? They'll be able to fix it, won't they?' Jess asked desperately. But they just ignored her, the car somehow feeling cold despite the sun streaming through the windows.

Reaching the hospital, Mel's parents haphazardly parked their car before rushing into A&E where Mel was being examined. As soon as they arrived, they were ushered into a family room by a nurse.

'Mel is being checked over now, but it looks like she might need emergency surgery,' she said gently, provoking Mel's mum to sob even more loudly. 'A doctor will be with you soon to discuss it.'

Jess felt invisible as Mel's parents sat holding each other, their heads touching, whispering to each other. Fear and guilt competed for her attention, and she felt like clawing off her skin and growing a new one. Anything to get rid of this awful feeling. There was no escape from her conscience here, in this sterile, bare room. Feeling suffocated, like the walls were closing in on her, she knew she had to get out.

'I'm just going to . . . ' Jess said, standing up, but Mel's parents didn't even look up. She might as well be a ghost.

Mel and Jess were family. Mel had said so herself. Except now, Jess had hurt her more than anyone else ever had. She'd forced her into doing something she didn't want to do and had shattered her leg. It was all Jess's fault. Surely Mel wouldn't want to see her, or even look at her, after what she'd done? What if she went into her hospital room and Jess saw the loathing she felt for herself reflected in Mel's face? She wouldn't be able to handle it.

Feeling like she could hardly breathe, she stumbled towards the hospital exit. Outside, she leant her palms on her knees, and retched, thin bile spilling onto the pavement. She couldn't go back in and face what she'd done. So instead, she turned towards the road that led away from the hospital and towards home, and started running.

Chapter 31

As her phone bleeped insistently in the background, Jess wrapped her pillow around her head. Then she threw out her arm, turned the alarm off and pushed her phone off the bedside table.

'What's new, Pussycat? You tell me,' she muttered into her pillow. Yesterday had sent her mind into a complete tailspin. She'd finally discovered a part of what Mel was hiding from her – and it was more serious than Jess had imagined.

Mel had been to hospital plenty of times over the fifteen years since the accident, for treatment on her leg. But she'd always told Jess about it before – as far as she knew, anyway. She even went to appointments with her when she could. So did that mean this was something beyond a routine check-up?

She thought back to the huge bunch of flowers Aya had bought Mel the night she'd spent at their flat, and the times, even before the time loop, that she'd noticed Mel looking tired or lost in thought. Her stomach rolled with possibilities, none of them good. She felt awful that she'd spent the last five weeks wrapped up in her own problems, while trying to avoid thinking too hard about what Mel had been hiding from her, scared of what she might discover. What if it was something that meant their friendship would never be the same again?

Flipping the pillow off her head, she pulled her ashtray onto her chest, lit a cigarette and blew clouds of smoke towards the ceiling, stroking Alfie on the pillow beside hers with her free hand.

Was Mel ill? Like, *really* ill?

Was it something to do with her leg?

Perhaps she was pregnant? Mel had always wanted children.

Or maybe it was something else that Jess's imagination, virile as it was, couldn't quite conjure up.

Whatever it was, it was something Mel wasn't ready to tell her about.

'She'll do anything to avoid having a serious conversation about her problems.'

'That makes two of you, doesn't it?'

'I'll talk to her when the time's right.'

So what exactly was Mel hiding?

Jess's mind drifted towards Donna Wilson and her friend Jane Doe.

Donna didn't begrudge her old friend her new happiness. She'd been lonely and had gone out there to find a better life for herself too, instead of dwelling on the past. But Jess was sure Donna would have been happier if she'd been less stubborn and had just apologised when it mattered the most. She certainly would have been less likely to end up with a sleaze like Alejandro with a good friend in her corner.

If Mel was hiding something big from Jess, did this mean their friendship was coming to an end, like Donna and Jane's had? That a day would come when they wouldn't hang out any more? Having walked side by side since the day they'd met, the accident had sent them each down different paths.

Mel had met Aya, had given up running, and endured years of gruelling physiotherapy. Jess had never forgiven herself for what she'd done and she'd learned to silence her guilty feelings by telling herself it wasn't her fault, that running away from the hospital that day hadn't mattered, that it had been worth it for Mel in the end . . . And, when that didn't work, she silenced them with a bottle of white wine instead. But Jess had always thought they'd remained as close as ever – until she'd discovered Mel was hiding something.

She needed to find out what was going on, to challenge Mel directly, but she also had to tread carefully. Mel might not remember their conversation if things got heated, but Jess would never forget it. *Bijou* magazine always said that tricky conversations, like break-ups, should be done somewhere neutral – somewhere public without too many memories attached, where things couldn't get too heated.

Jess would ask Mel to meet her tonight, knowing she'd say yes. And she already knew the perfect place.

'Hey, diddle, diddle, can you work out this riddle?'

A depressingly upbeat jester was leaping around on top of a table furnished with an upside-down tea set.

'How did the cow jump over the moon, and why did the dish run away with the spoon? Solve this quiz, and you will find, an adventure room to blow your mind! Can I get a hey, diddle, diddle, guys?'

'Hey, diddle, diddle,' Jess muttered, furiously.

'Aww look how much you're enjoying yourself,' Mel said. 'And you were worried this would be shit.'

Jess adjusted her top hat and scowled. Although Mel had always wanted to take part in an immersive theatre show, Jess had quickly realised that choosing this nursery-themed nightmare as a 'neutral, public environment' to chat in had been a terrible decision.

Set underneath some old railway arches, the venue somehow managed to be freezing cold inside, despite the warmth of the evening, and Jess shivered in her Oscar the Grouch-coloured cardigan.

After being told no phones or bags were allowed 'on set' (£2 for the cloakroom, on top of £35 a ticket), they were ushered into a black-lit room by a man who seemed to be dressed as a small, muddy hill.

'I'm a tuffet,' he'd said, shrugging.

Inside, piles of junk were painted in garish fluorescent paint, making them glow in the black light, threatening to give the audience a massive collective migraine. When a man wearing a cheap-looking jester's outfit decorated with an offensive number of bells had leapt out from behind a pile of rakes and waggled his marotte in her face, Jess had tried to run back through the exit, until Mel had gently steered her back into the room.

Jess looked on in horror as the jester contorted his way around the junk, 'ha-ha-ha!' and 'tee-hee-hee!'-ing his way through his introductory speech. It was delivered with all the manic enthusiasm of a man who was starting to realise that playing 'Riddles the Rhyming Jester, Master of Mayhem and Giggler of Gags!' was unlikely to lead to a place at RADA.

'Come on, it'll be fun if we get stuck in,' Mel whispered, as everyone applauded excitedly, before hunting enthusiastically for items that were props from well-known nursery rhymes. 'This thing has had amazing reviews.'

'Do you think there might be a gun in here?' Jess asked, picking up a plate of bread and honey made out of polystyrene. 'Maybe the Queen of Hearts used a Glock?'

'Come on, it might be better than you think,' Mel said.

But by the time they were tasked with searching the upside-down tea set for clues to Riddles' latest challenge, even Mel was beginning to flag.

'I thought the point of the theatre was that you sit down with a lovely drink and are entertained?' she said, picking up a teapot that had a cow crudely drawn on the side. 'How come we're doing all the work?'

'You brought this on yourself. Although I did think there would be more sitting down involved, to be honest. Is your leg OK?' Jess had noticed that Mel's limp was more pronounced than ever.

'I'll survive,' Mel said grimly. Jess looked around the room and wondered when the next drink was coming. Even if a G&T did cost £9, she could really do with several right now.

Jess had been searching for the right time to ask Mel about her hospital appointment, and now her enthusiasm for immersive theatre had been well and truly crushed for ever, she decided it was now or never.

'Hey, how was your appointment today?' she asked lightly, pretending to examine a toast rack.

'My ... what? It was just a meeting. About next year's schedules,' Mel said, leaning down and adjusting her dress so her hair fell across her face. 'And it was fine.'

Jess swallowed. She was about to open a box she wouldn't be able to close again, even if she wanted to. 'Oh really?

I don't know why, but I got the impression that it was an appointment. And I wondered if you might have something you might want to talk to me about?'

'Time's running out, of that you should have no doubt!' Riddles shouted from his spot sitting cross-legged on top of a grandfather clock. 'The faster you solve the puzzle, the less Riddles has to hustle!'

'That doesn't even rhyme,' Mel muttered, taking off her bonnet. She turned to Jess, looking tired. 'What do you think I might want to talk to you about?'

'I'm not sure. But lately I've felt like we're not as close as before. Almost like we're two different trains on two different tracks, and the tracks are gradually getting further and further apart.' Mel blinked in surprise. 'And I wondered if you might have something you want to tell me. Maybe you're waiting for the right time. And I thought perhaps that time might be now.' Jess looked around her at the pastel-hued room they were in, and realised that now was definitely not the best time. But she'd finally found the courage to ask Mel the question, and couldn't dodge it any longer.

'Have you been talking to Aya?'

'No, nothing like that. I wouldn't talk about you behind your back.' Mel had the good grace to blush. 'Let's call it intuition.'

Jess clutched the toast rack, her heart pounding at what Mel might have to say next. What if she'd decided Jess wasn't worth having as a friend? What if she'd realised that Jess didn't deserve her friendship and wanted to ease herself out of her chaotic orbit?

'I suppose we do lead quite different lives these days,' Mel said carefully, 'but just because I'm doing new stuff now, that doesn't mean I don't want to hang out with you. You're still like family to me. Although there is something I need to talk to you about. I have tried a couple of times, but it's been difficult when everything's so hectic. You're struggling with money, dealing with Maggie, grappling with the grand New York dating experiment. You don't need to hear my stuff on top of yours.'

'I do though,' Jess said, feeling sick. 'You can tell me anything.'

'Can I get a hey, diddle, diddle, guys?' Riddles yelled.

'Oh, fuck off!' Jess said.

'I'm not sure now is the time, is it?' Mel said, as the crowd yelled back, and Jess's heart sank. 'This has been fun, and I'm really grateful for you buying the tickets. It's one thing to tick off the bucket list and never ever return to, anyway.'

'Now's the perfect time,' Jess said, growing desperate. 'If you don't want to do it here, we could go to the Bush, have a drink. Or five.' She laughed nervously.

Mel paused, then shook her head and put her bonnet back on her head.

'I'm far too tired now, and we've got a riddle to solve. How about we talk about this tomorrow?'

Chapter 32

As her bus pulled up outside Homerton Hospital, Jess saw Brian sitting on a bench, a Costa cup clutched in one hand and a pen in the other. A book was perched on his lap, which he was frowning at with concentration.

This time, when she hopped off the bus, she didn't head for Brian's bench. Instead, she sat on a seat at the other side of the turning circle where taxis and worried relatives dropped off and picked up their passengers. Her legs like jelly, she sat down and waited, trying not to catch Brian's attention as he concentrated on his sudoku puzzles.

After the night at the theatre, Jess had wracked her brain for a way to get Mel to open up about what was going on. She'd tried to get her to talk, but Mel needed more time. Something Jess had in abundance, but Mel had no more of until Jess leapt out of the time loop. She realised that the only way to get Mel to talk to her today might be to approach her at the hospital. That way she couldn't deny that she'd lied to Jess about her meeting, and might be persuaded to talk.

Jess's last three afternoons had each panned out the same

way. She'd leave Alfie at home happily munching on some treats, sit on the bench opposite Brian and wait for Mel to emerge through the reception doors after her appointment. She'd lean heavily against the wall outside, looking like she'd been crying. Pulling her phone out of her bag, she'd hold it up to her face, squinting as she moved it left and right – checking her make-up in the camera.

This was always the moment Jess tried to approach her. She'd will herself to stand up, walk towards Mel, and ask her what was going on. But each time her courage failed her. She was too scared of what she might discover, and with infinite chances to get it right the next time, it was all too easy to put it off until tomorrow. But this was bigger than everything else – than her job, than Tom, than her flat. And she had to face her fears and do something about it.

After a nervous wait on the bench, Jess watched as Mel finally emerged from the hospital. She leaned against the wall outside and pulled out her phone. And this time, Jess willed her legs to pick her up and put one foot in front of the other, until she was standing in front of her best friend, her stomach turning terrified somersaults.

'Hey,' she said, and Mel pulled down her phone and gasped.

'Oh!' she said, clutching her phone to her chest. 'What are you doing here?'

Jess took a deep breath and launched into the speech she'd spent every moment of her vigil on the bench rehearsing in her head.

'I'm here because we need to talk. About the appointment you just had and what it was about, and why you've been hiding it from me. I know you feel like we're growing apart, which is why you couldn't talk to me about it. But maybe if you tell me what's going on, I can help. Or at least be there for you. Because whatever it is, I'm your best friend – your family – and you can tell me anything.'

'Shit,' Mel muttered, wiping her face with her hand, as Jess let out a shaky breath. 'Can't this wait until tomorrow, Jess? I get what you're saying, and maybe I should have talked to you. But it's already been a really long day. I'm not sure I can deal with this right now.'

'It can't wait, trust me,' Jess said, holding Mel's hand and looking at her intently. 'I know it's hurting you to have to do this here and now, but we have to. I just can't explain why – not yet, anyway.'

'OK,' Mel sighed. 'Let's find a seat.'

Jess's legs shook as they headed back to her bench. 'I'm listening,' she said, once they were sitting down.

Mel squeezed her eyes shut, then opened them and turned to face Jess. 'So this is hard to talk about. And I wasn't sure how you'd react, which is why I didn't tell you. Or maybe I *was* sure and didn't want to have to deal with it. But . . . you know I've been having a lot of pain in my leg lately?' Jess nodded mutely. 'It's been getting worse and worse over the last few months – years, even – and my consultant has been working on a few things to try and help me.'

'I knew your leg was hurting you, but I didn't realise it was getting worse.'

Or rather you were too wrapped up in your car crash of a life to notice, Jess told herself.

'It's something called CRPS,' Mel continued, haltingly. 'It's a syndrome that causes people with injuries like mine pain. I've been getting sores on my calf too, which sometimes get infected. And it's got to the stage where there are no more treatments left to try.' Mel swallowed hard, her eyes glistening with fresh tears. She sniffed and swiped at her nose. 'Anyway, they had a consultation about it, after my latest round of treatment failed, and . . . you see . . . today's appointment was to talk about a last resort.'

'Which is?' Jess said, forcing the words out as a tight lump formed in her throat.

'There's nothing they can do about the pain any more. So the next step, if I decide to go ahead with it, is amputation below the knee. It's risky, and will mean wearing a prosthetic for the rest of my life. But it should stop hurting me for good. I might even be able to throw away my cane.'

'They want to remove your *leg*?' Jess said, tears suddenly spilling from her eyes. 'But that's *huge*. Why didn't you tell me about all those appointments? Or about any of this? You know I would have been here for you.'

'I was worried you might not be able to cope. Or that you might . . . run away.'

Jess shook her head. 'I wouldn't run away. Of course I wouldn't.'

Mel looked at her hands, and Jess felt a prickly wave of understanding flowing through her.

'So that's what this is about – what happened after the accident? You're still angry with me for leaving while you were in hospital?'

'No, of course not,' Mel said hurriedly. 'I was just worried about how you might react if it was bad news, that's all. I suppose I didn't want you to feel guilty.'

'Why were you worried I'd feel guilty?' Jess said, her heart thumping. 'Is it because you blame me for the accident?'

'God no, of course not, Jess,' Mel said, taking her hand. 'I've never blamed you, you know that.'

Jess slowly pulled her hand away. 'But you do deep down, don't you? Otherwise why would you worry about me feeling guilty? I knew you thought it was my fault all this time.'

Jess tugged at her hair. Part of her had always known this moment was coming – the moment when she'd find out what Mel had really thought of Jess since that day in the bungalow. And now her worst fears were being realised.

Mel frowned, shaking her head. 'Where have you got that idea from? Don't be silly. '

Jess felt something dark uncurling in her chest. She nodded to herself, as if the answer to a puzzle she'd struggled to work out was finally becoming clear. Why would Mel hide all this from her unless she secretly blamed Jess for what had happened, every bit as much as she blamed herself?

'I knew you blamed me,' Jess said, blinking back tears. 'Everyone did. I saw the way your parents looked at me that night, and I could see it in the teachers' faces when I got back to school, too. Everybody thought I'd ruined your life.'

'Why would they think that? Why would *I*?' Mel said, looking bewildered.

'Because you were the future star, the one who was going to be a huge success,' Jess said, her voice wavering. 'While I was rejected by my parents, then rejected by my best friend. When I met you, I fooled myself that I was worthy of you. But I wasn't, was I? I was the bad influence, so whatever really happened in the bungalow, everyone was going to think the accident had to be all my fault. I just didn't think you were one of them. You must regret ever meeting me.'

Mel shook her head. 'Jess, of course I don't. I love you. We're family, remember?'

She reached her hand out to Jess, but she flinched away.

'I never blamed you. Never. I just didn't tell you about all this because I didn't want you to feel bad about it.'

'So you thought I'd feel "bad", but at the same time you don't secretly think your injury is my fault? How does that work?' Jess said, hotly.

Mel sighed, and rubbed her face. 'I'm not blind, Jess. I can see how you feel, even though we barely ever talk about the accident. You never mention it, and I can't, because of how you react. I know that deep down you blame yourself for what happened. But it doesn't follow that I blame you too.'

'Maybe you don't know me that well after all,' Jess said, her cheeks burning. 'Because actually, I *don't* blame myself. You're the one who had running practice the next day. You could have tried a bit harder to stop me. Or . . . or carried on being the well-behaved one, and gone home. I didn't shove you in there at gunpoint, or rot those floorboards.'

Even after years of telling herself the same stories about that night, over and over again, the words sounded painfully hollow in Jess's ears. Cruel, even.

Mel's cheeks pinkened and she raised her voice. 'I *did* try to stop you, if you remember. Several times, in fact. But doing crazy things was part of the fun of being your friend. So I honestly never thought it was your fault. Not once. Not out loud, not even in my head. But can you truly say the same about yourself?'

Jess covered her face and started crying, great waves of guilt crashing through her.

'This is ridiculous, Jess,' Mel said, shaking her head. 'I actually really wanted you to be here with me today. And Aya wanted you here too. She nagged and nagged me to tell you because she's in surgery and couldn't come. But I was worried that if the doctors decided I needed an amputation, I'd end up looking after you instead of the other way around. And it's starting to look like I was right.'

'I find it hard to believe you'd want the person who ruined your life holding your hand,' Jess said, monstrous guilt thundering through her chest so hard, she'd lost all control over her own, bitter words.

'Have you ever thought that it might do you good to just *talk* about this stuff, rather than brushing it under the carpet like you do with everything else?' Mel asked. 'Then maybe we can get through this together.'

Jess shook her head helplessly.

'Then I'm not sure I can do this any more. Not today,' Mel said quietly, looking defeated. Gingerly, she pushed herself up from the bench using her cane. 'But maybe if you apologised, instead of acting like I secretly hate you, we can fix this tomorrow.'

There was a long pause. Then slowly, Jess shook her head. Mel was right about all of it. She'd avoided talking about the accident for all these years, out of blind terror that one day, Mel would realise Jess wasn't worthy of her friendship and leave. But apologising meant breaking apart the lies that had calcified over fifteen years of retelling, and accepting a responsibility she'd spent most of her life running away from. The words wouldn't come, stuck fast in her throat.

'I can't,' she croaked.

'Then I think we need to take a break, Jess, don't you?' Mel said, her voice catching on the words. 'I can't be around you if you're going to be like this. I can't take away your guilt, or make you see things the way I see them. And why should I be the one to exhaust myself trying when you won't? I think I've been punished enough already, don't you?'

With that, Mel walked stiffly away. Jess could see, even from behind, that Mel was trying to hide her limp, knowing that Jess might see her very pain as an imagined accusation.

She sank her head heavily into her hands, feeling like she'd just been hit by a bulldozer. Every nerve was screaming, her stomach was rolling, and she was trembling all over.

She could barely process what had just happened. She'd promised to listen to Mel, to be there for her. But instead of telling Mel how genuinely sorry she was, she'd hurt her best friend unimaginably on one of the hardest days of her life. Rubbing her forehead with a shaking hand, Jess tried to work out how everything had gone so wrong. She'd thought the time loop had given her a chance to make her life better. But now, her life was a bigger mess than ever.

Chapter 33

Mel was sitting in a wheelchair facing the window when Jess crept into her room, clutching a bunch of lilies. The room smelt of antiseptic, with an unpleasant metallic background tang, and everything in it was light green, cream or beige. Apart from the hospital's family room, Jess didn't think she'd ever been anywhere more depressing.

'If you were looking out onto a windswept beach instead of a car park, you'd be the spitting image of that sickly woman out of *Beaches*,' Jess said, smiling nervously.

When Mel spun around to face her, Jess tried to cover her shock. It had been a week since she'd seen her best friend, but she seemed to have lost weight from her already-thin frame, and her face was even paler than when she'd been lying underneath the floorboards, staring up at her in pain. Her leg was propped straight in front of her, covered by a blanket.

'Is that supposed to be a compliment?' Mel said, wheeling herself towards the bed. 'I suppose you do look like Bette

Midler with all that hair and those enormous bazongas of yours. Are those for me?'

'No, I've just started carrying flowers around with me for a laugh. Of course they're for you.'

Mel smiled, but it didn't reach her eyes. She looked exhausted and scared. Jess put the flowers down on the small wheeled table that sat beside Mel's bed, which was rigged up with a range of medieval-looking pulleys.

'You've come at the right time, anyway,' Mel sighed. 'I'm only allowed out of bed for half an hour a day unless I'm having tests done. Bloody bastards. Which you'd know, by the way, if you'd actually been here. Where the hell have you been, Jess? Mum said you were with them in the family room when I was brought in, but then you just vanished. What was so important that you couldn't come and see me? Even Aya popped in to check how I'm doing.'

'Who?' Jess frowned.

'Never mind,' Mel sighed.

Jess swallowed hard. 'I've just been really busy. You know, with the police wanting to know what happened, and Nan telling them to fuck off and stuff. They wanted to charge us with trespassing, but Nan wasn't having any of it. You should have seen her, it was hilarious . . .'

An uncomfortable silence fell over the room. Mel looked like she wanted to say something, but Jess knew she had to make sure she didn't get the chance. She could easily imagine what Mel wanted to say to her, but it wasn't anything she hadn't said to herself every waking minute of the past week.

'This is all your fault.'

'You've ruined my life.'

268

'*Why would I still want to be friends with you?*'

She'd decided that if she just ploughed ahead and behaved as if the accident wasn't her fault, perhaps Mel would eventually believe that too. After all, she was a grown woman, wasn't she? Jess hadn't *forced* her to go into that house. Meanwhile, she'd do everything she could to make it up to her and hope that eventually it would all be forgotten.

'Anyway, another thing I've been doing has been looking for exercises you can do at home, while your leg heals,' Jess said, quickly. 'I found a book about physiotherapy in the library. And it was totally Dullsville, but I read it all. And apparently there are ways of keeping your fitness levels up, even if you can't walk for a bit. Hang on.'

Jess felt desperation rising in her chest as she pulled the heavy book out of her backpack and opened it up at the page she'd carefully folded over.

'See, you can do strengthening exercises while you're sitting down, so your muscles don't go all floppy. Then when you're ready to run again, you'll be good to go. Well, almost. You won't be back to how you were before, not at first. But eventually.'

Jess handed Mel the book, tapping a photo of an elderly man sitting in a chair bicycling his legs in the air.

'Thanks,' Mel said, shutting the book and throwing it onto the bed, 'but I'm not going to be running again any time soon, or any time *ever* by the looks of it. My leg's totally shattered, Jess. I've already had an operation on it, and I'm going to need more. Maybe lots more. It's over.'

'Oh shit, Mel,' Jess said, swallowing hard. 'What are you going to do?'

'It'll be fine.' Mel shrugged, busying herself with the

flowers by tearing open their thin plastic wrapping. 'There's a lot of pressure in racing. Not having to go to all that training will be a relief, if anything. I never get to sit down, but now look.' Mel gestured at her chair. 'And as for my glittering running career . . . There's plenty of other stuff I can do. I've always wanted to get into TV, and now I'm gay *and* disabled, I reckon I'll be a shoo-in.'

Jess giggled, then pressed her palm over her mouth. 'Well then. I guess all's well that ends well, right?'

'Sure,' Mel said, although she wasn't smiling. 'And anyway, it was my own fault,' she added, looking at Jess carefully. 'I shouldn't have gone into that house in the first place, should I?'

Jess blinked, then swallowed hard.

'Yeah, it was a bit dumb when you had a race the next day. And those floorboards were obviously rotten. Why didn't you just jump over them?'

'I'm just careless, I guess. That's what I told the doctor, and my parents. That it was all my own fault.'

'Right,' Jess nodded, and Mel's shoulders drooped.

An apology was hovering on her lips, but she swallowed it down. If she tried hard enough, perhaps she could make Mel see that the accident wasn't so bad after all. Because if Jess's stubbornness had ruined her best friend's life, how could she ever live with herself?

'You know I love you,' Jess said, reaching across the bed and grabbing Mel's hand.

'I love you too. Family, right?'

'Family,' Jess agreed. 'Although there is one thing we need to talk about.'

'What is it?'

'Have you wet yourself?'

Tentatively, Mel sniffed the air around her bed.

'It's not me, it's these lilies. You've basically bought me a bunch of piss. Thanks a bloody lot.'

As they burst out laughing, Jess tried to hide her relief and ignore the knot of guilt that had settled in her stomach and slowly, inexorably, began tightening.

Chapter 34

For the hundredth time, as she jerked awake, Jess wished that she'd got stuck in a time loop on a Saturday. Or any other day when her stupid, sodding, poxy alarm wouldn't go off at 7.45 a.m. Picking up her phone, she stroked a finger over Mel's morning text, and felt a pang of sadness that only seemed to get worse with each passing day.

Mel: What's new, Pussycat?

As well as missing her friend terribly, Jess had discovered that time doesn't heal all wounds. It had been months of Fridays ago since she'd confronted Mel at the hospital, but thinking about it still hit her like a punch to the stomach.

Alfie leapt onto the pillow beside her head as she grabbed her ashtray and balanced it on her chest. Lighting a cigarette, she blew a perfect smoke ring towards the ceiling, followed by a smaller one that sailed straight through the first. She'd read somewhere that it takes 10,000 hours of practise to become an expert at any skill, but it had only taken her about 1,000 or so to finally nail smoke rings. Take that, Anders Ericsson.

After her argument with Mel, Jess had stopped trying to work out how to escape the time loop. Perhaps, she'd realised, it hadn't been sent to help her fix her problems after all. Perhaps it was simply the universe's way of protecting the people in her life from her own, disastrous influence – including staying away from Mel and leaving her to process the news about her leg without barging in and making it a million times worse. Even so, at first she'd found it almost impossible to stay away more than a couple of weeks at a time. Hoping to erase the terrible memory of the conversation they'd had outside the hospital, she'd tried several times to pluck up the courage to redo it and try to make things right. But each time she saw her friend standing outside the hospital, looking as vulnerable as Jess had ever seen her, haltingly checking her make-up in her phone, she lost her courage.

What if she lost control and hurt Mel the way she'd hurt her before, all over again?

She couldn't bear it.

So instead, Jess avoided Mel, hoping to at least not make things any worse.

Each morning she made sure to hide Nate's pants, played a hand or two of poker or arranged an overdraft with the bank so she could transfer the money she owed into Brian's account, and deleted the email she'd sent Donna.

Luckily, it had only taken three Fridays of being locked out of Donna's email account to eventually work out her password. Pulling the photo of Donna and Alejandro sipping from a fish bowl cocktail from her handbag, she'd realised that the caption – 'Donna + Alejandro 4 Eva!!!' – hit the sweet spot of capital letters, symbols and numbers beloved by email providers everywhere.

She also made sure she distracted Beth and Inkblot before they reached her road each evening, so the moped mugger didn't have a chance to attack them. But apart from her routine of patching up the problems she'd caused, and making sure she didn't manage to hurt anyone else in the process, she'd frittered her time away as if it was worthless. She'd been quite disappointed to answer her own question about what she'd do with eternity, which turned out to be: nothing much.

At first, she'd spent a few weeks in bed feeling sorry for herself, chain-smoking and listening to Tom pleading at her through the chained front door. Next, she'd lived through a few months of Fridays that she'd actually quite enjoyed. She'd treated it a bit like a holiday, spending her days doing all the touristy things around London she'd never got around to doing, and eating £300 scrambled egg and caviar breakfasts at The Ritz.

Sometimes, she waited until Tom arrived at her flat, and dragged him out with her. They'd gone on day trips to nearby places, making the most of the sunshine on Brighton Beach and eating nothing but ice cream all day. Jess had discovered she hated surfing, but quite liked hang-gliding, while Tom apparently had a weird thing for aquariums. Possibly because it was the ideal place to gather more facts.

She'd eaten a lot of exotic foods, including that puffer fish that can kill you if it's not prepared properly, and had fun seeing how many calories she could eat in twenty-four hours without throwing up, which turned out to be a delicate balancing act (her personal record being 9,672).

During one memorable fortnight of Fridays, she'd found a

driving instructor who was willing to ditch her clients that day in exchange for £1,500 cash. Jess was pretty sure she could pass her test now, if she ever escaped the loop.

Buoyed by her success, there was a period about three months in – or was it four? – when she'd tried a spot of self-improvement, learning some Italian, making seventeen inedible loaves of bread, and trying to master some card tricks, before coming to her senses and remembering that she thought magicians were seriously creepy.

She'd read all the chunky novels in her flat, watched all the films at the cinema, and seen pretty much everything with a Rotten Tomatoes Fresh rating of 40% or above on her subscription channels, smashing her TV screen (again), this time with a well-aimed empty wine bottle, when Ilsa chose Laszlo at the end of *Casablanca*.

She'd also spent a lot of time with her nan. Although, before the time loop, she'd had both good days and bad, today had been a good day, and Jess had made the very most of it, getting her to recall memories of her mum and dad, and tell wild stories of her youth until Jess had memorised every word.

If she ever escaped the loop, she planned to turn them into a book.

She'd definitely had some fun along the way, but she knew deep down that a life without consequences or any lasting impact on other humans, or on the world, was pointless.

Although she loved spending time with Tom, every morning after their days out she woke up to an empty flat, both Tom and her purchases vanished. They were building memories together, but only one of them would ever actually remember them.

She could drive, but she couldn't travel anywhere that took

her past 6.45 in the morning. If she tried, she'd simply find herself suddenly back home in bed, hoping that in some other parallel universe a suddenly driverless car wasn't careering into a load of pedestrians.

There were no birthdays or Christmases or parties, no snow or rain, no changes to her face or body. The time loop felt safe, without any nasty surprises or, by being very careful, guilt over new things she'd said or done. But having always tried to wring the most excitement possible out of life, she yearned for a return to unpredictability, even if that sometimes meant things going wrong. When you could throw time away without any repercussions, making the most of it became harder.

Yes, she could better herself, but she had no way of applying any of what she'd learned beyond a single day of her life. She could master Italian, but never go to Italy. She could practise long enough to become the world's best magician, but would never get the chance to make Simon Cowell pull his surprised face on *Britain's Got Talent*.

And even as she slowly fell in love with Tom, and realised she had almost thrown away the most incredible thing in her life, she would always have slept with Nate just the day before.

Gradually, as she ran out of new experiences to help make her feel alive, her world had shrunk to just her flat and its tiny garden, as she was unable to find the energy to go anywhere else.

What was the point?

Stubbing her cigarette out, Jess covered her eyes with a forearm. And suddenly, she realised she couldn't bear to go through another identical day. It was just too much. Killing herself to try to break the loop wasn't an option, because what if she didn't survive? And falling asleep only gave herself a moment's respite before she woke up on Friday morning again.

What she really needed was to reach slow oblivion.

'What do you think, boy?' she asked Alfie. 'Shall we go shopping, then to the Bush?'

Holding up her palm, Alfie slapped it with his tiny paw and woofed.

Chapter 35

Nan: Is Monty Don married?

Jess was pushing her way into the Polski Sklep on the corner to top up her depleted alcohol supplies. As the buzzer let off its ear-splitting shriek, Jess jumped out of her skin for the millionth time. Even with infinity on her side, she'd never get used to it.

'That fucking thing,' she muttered, her heart pounding as she stomped towards the vodka aisle.

As she shuffled down the aisle, trying to decide between gin, vodka and wine, and looking in vain for a new flavour of Pot Noodle she might not have tried yet, Borys tapped his watch, as he had done every time she'd ventured into the Polski Sklep during work hours over the past months of Fridays.

'Half past ten? This isn't your usual time, Jess. Have you been fired from your job? Or are you taking what they call a duvet day? I say, feckless lazy-arse day, more like, yes?'

'I see your sarcasm hasn't changed, then, Borys,' Jess said flatly.

'Me, sarcastic? That's xenophobic, I think,' Borys said, gravely.

'You can't pretend things are xenophobic just to win arguments,' Jess said, throwing three Pot Noodles and a frozen pepperoni pizza into her basket, then adding two bottles of white wine. 'And besides, sarcasm is universal.'

Grabbing a bottle of extra-hot sauce from a bottom shelf, Jess stood up, paused, and frowned.

Something was bugging her about what Borys had just said.

Half past ten.

Jess's mind slowly clicked the puzzle pieces into place. Then her stomach lurched wildly and she dropped her basket on the floor, one of the wine bottles shattering on impact.

'Oh fuck. Tom!' she yelled, running out of the shop, leaving Borys's startled face peering around the counter in shock.

Having run out of booze earlier than usual that morning, Jess had forgotten all about hiding Nate's underwear. It was still in her bedroom, tucked under her pillow, and she wasn't in her flat to intercept Tom and stop him finding it. Which meant right about now, he'd be surrounded by scattered rose petals and wondering who on earth a tiny pair of palm-tree decorated pants belonged to.

Running up the steps to her flat, Jess's hands were shaking so hard, she struggled to get the key into the lock. She couldn't handle this again. Not after everything she and Tom had been through together.

'Tom! Are you in there? It's Jess, stop whatever you're doing, I need to talk to you, *now*,' she called, as she threw open the door. 'Tom? Where are you? Tom?' she said, flying into the bedroom. Then froze as she saw him sitting on the edge of the bed, staring at the pair of unfamiliar blue shorts he'd just pulled out from underneath Jess's pillow.

She saw that he had already written 'WILL YOU BE' in petals, and her heart cracked. The first time she'd seen Tom's reaction to finding out she was cheating, she had been able to convince herself that she'd done nothing wrong. Nothing *really* wrong, at least. But so much had changed since Friday the First, and the days she'd spent with Tom during the time loop were some of the best of her life.

Even though he couldn't remember their trips to the seaside, or sharing chilli hot dogs, or clinking drinks on the sofa wearing wedding outfits, Jess felt completely differently about him to the way she had done the first time she had seen this scene play out. But now, there was nothing she could do to stop it happening all over again.

As she watched the face that had become so familiar and so precious to her crumpling in realisation at what she'd done, Jess remembered trying to persuade Tom that he should be happy to 'share' her with Nate and felt like crying. What had she been thinking? Now, she'd give anything in the world to avoid hurting him.

'I can explain, Tom. I can explain everything,' she said from the doorway, her eyes filling with tears. Her heart thudded painfully, aching at the same time.

'Can you?' he said, softly, his voice catching in his throat. Jess couldn't answer. He looked up at her with such sadness, she could barely breathe. 'I thought we had something special here, Jess. I know you think I'm a bit of a nerd, but I really like you. Whatever you think about yourself, I think you're brilliant. You're bright and hilarious and talented. And I was kind of hoping that if I liked you enough, you'd start to like yourself, too.'

'I do like myself. And I like *you*,' Jess said, desperately.

'Very much. This was just some ... stupid mistake. Please don't be upset.'

'If that's true, and you really like me, then that makes this even harder to understand,' Tom said, gesturing at the bed. 'You're obviously into open relationships, or something. But I'm not up for it. Not at all. I like you far too much for that. Liked, I suppose. I guess I'm going now. Sorry about the mess. Have fun with Tiny Hollister Pants Guy,' he added bitterly.

'Please. Please, Tom. Don't go,' Jess begged. 'Let me explain.'

Taking a deep breath, Tom pushed past Jess, who had tears running down her cheeks. As she heard him opening the front door, then softly closing it behind him, she wanted to call out to him, to bring him back.

She wanted to tell him how sorry she was. To tell him that he had become one of the most important people in her life. That she knew he saw her for the person she was not the one she pretended to be.

She wanted to tell him she could only hope one day to deserve someone as special as him, and that she would do everything she could to be that person. She wanted to beg him to stay, because she'd been blind, and an idiot and that that Jess was long gone. But most of all she wanted to remind him that he was falling for her, no matter how ridiculous that seemed – and to tell him that long ago, she had fallen in love with him.

But she didn't say any of those things.

Just as her apology to Mel had been, the words were trapped in her throat like a rock. Her chest felt like there were stones inside her lungs, and her legs had gone completely numb. As the flat descended into silence, she stared at the bed, where Tom had carefully stacked up piles of plucked red petals.

Sinking onto the bed, Jess lay on top of them, buried her head in the pillow, and started to cry.

Chapter 36

Swaying gently on her stool, Jess squeezed one eye shut and held her glass up to the light from the lamp perched at the end of the bar. It was shaped like a Hawaiian hula dancer, her skirt made from real grass, most of which was broken and bent from years of drunk punters trying to see what was up there.

'I give this whisky a three out of ten,' she said, her tongue feeling as rough as tree bark, and slightly too big for her mouth. 'Write that down, Mark, so I don't forget. I'm going to become a whisky afficia . . . afficia . . . expert. It's gonna be my new thing. My next new *talent*.'

Sighing, Mark plucked a stub of pencil from behind his ear and drew a squiggle on his notepad.

'Are you sure you don't want to get Mel down here?' Mark said, glancing at the clock behind him. It was creeping towards 9 p.m., and Jess had been slouching across his bar since early this afternoon. 'Or that Paddington-looking fella? What's his name?'

'He's called Tom,' Jess said, sniffing lustily. 'And I love him. But he doesn't love me, because . . . well, I'm me. And

Mel, too. We had an argument. A huge one. She doesn't want to be my friend any more and I can't blame her. It's not her fault, is it? It's all mine. All my fault. Who would want to be friends with someone like me? It's no wonder she doesn't believe me about the time loop even though it's all true. All of it. Watch this.'

Pulling her cigarettes from her bag, Jess lit one at the bar.

'Hey, you can't do that,' Mark hissed. 'I'll get fined. It's over a grand if customers smoke indoors.'

'Don't worry about it, I can pay that. Remember when I paid two grand for the quiz machine?' Jess frowned. 'No, of course you don't. Nobody remembers anything I do any more. It's like being a ghost.'

Blowing a perfect smoke ring, Jess blew another, smaller smoke ring straight through it.

'See?'

'Yes, very impressive,' Mark said, snatching the cigarette from Jess's fingers and running it under the tap beneath the bar. 'Look, I'm sure Mel does want to be your friend. You two are tight. Maybe she just needs a break.'

'Yes! That's what she meant. I hope, anyway. That we need a break. Like Ross and Rachel, so she can go and get a new best friend.' Jess raised her glass to John Travolta, who was staring intently out of a *Pulp Fiction* poster stuck up with yellowing Sellotape behind the bar.

'How long have you worked here, Mark? Mark, Mark, Mark? Marky Mark-Mark?'

'About twenty years, I reckon. It's a solid job, nice regulars. When they don't get too smashed, anyway.' He raised an eyebrow at Jess.

'But nothing changes in here, does it? Everything is always

the same. Arthur doesn't even seem to age. How do you cope with nothing ever changing?'

'It's not *always* the same. I got a new ale in last week. And some rosemary and thyme flavoured crisp things. Although Christ knows why anyone would want to eat them.'

'You know what I mean,' Jess said, slapping the bar. 'You see the same customers all the time. The same tourists asking how to get to Primark. We've had the same argument about your stairs a million times.'

'I can't install a lift, Jess.'

'Whatever. That's not the point. The point is, how do you not get bored? When every day is the same, time goes all ... floopy. So what do you do? How do you make your life *count*?'

'I guess I try new things whenever I can. I don't actually live here, you know. I have a home, and hobbies. I like cooking. I made a banging roast dinner the other day.'

'I've tried that. But I'm still bored,' Jess said, ruefully. Mark sighed and shook his head. Sticking out her tongue, she poured the last drop of her whisky onto it. 'Luckily, I've discovered a great solution for boredom. Booze, and lots of it. Which whisky is next then?'

'You've tried them all, pretty much,' Mark said, scanning the bottles behind the bar and scratching the back of his neck. 'And I really think you should get home, Jess. Can I call you an Uber? My treat.'

'You're probably right, as usual. You were right the last time I got hammered in here, too. And the time before that,' Jess sniffed, swiping at her nose with the palm of her hand as she clambered off her bar stool and clipped Alfie's lead to his collar. Mark grimaced and passed her a black napkin from the pile on the bar. 'But no Uber. Fresh air will do me good. Tube train is good. All good.'

Mark sighed, looking worried. 'OK, but be careful getting home, please?'

'Oh, I'll be careful, definitely. No getting mugged for me! No-sirree! And you be careful with that glass.'

'Eh?' Mark said, then dropped the pint glass he was polishing with a tea towel. 'Oh, bollocks.'

'Every time,' Jess said.

'Stay safe, Jess,' Mark said, crunching over the shards of broken glass behind the bar and steering her towards the door.

'Let me guess, you want to see me in one piece on Saturday afternoon?'

'Well ... yes, that's exactly what I was going to say,' Mark said, holding the door open and gently angling her towards the Tube. 'I will see you tomorrow, won't I?'

'Don't count on it,' Jess said softly, stepping out into the warm evening air.

Chapter 37

By the time she reached her Tube stop, Jess realised that, despite her past best efforts, she'd never been quite this drunk before. She'd spent the last few stops on the train with her handbag unzipped and open on her lap just in case she needed it, concentrating hard on not being sick.

She clung to the escalator handrail, Alfie nestled against her chest, picturing her comfy bed and the clear head she'd be treated to when she woke up in the morning, to stop herself from simply lying on the floor of the Tube station and waiting to be dragged home by the police. Although, what difference would it really make if she did that?

She sent up a small prayer of thanks that she hadn't got this epically drunk on Thursday night. If she'd had to live through eternity with a hangover like the one that was currently brewing, she wasn't sure she'd have made it.

'Five more minutes and you'll be in bed. We can do this, right, Alfie?' she muttered as she walked carefully along the pavement, grabbing uselessly at twigs sticking out from the bushes she passed, as if they'd help break her fall if she stumbled.

As she reached her road, she saw a woman ahead of her walking a small black dog, like a shadow at her heels.

Frowning, Jess realised she was too late to intercept Beth and Inkblot before they reached her road.

'Beth! Inkblot! It's me, Jess!' she shouted, waving her arms. 'Be careful, OK?'

Beth turned around and looked with alarm at the stranger shouting her name and weaving up the pavement towards her. She squinted, trying to work out if it was someone she knew. Then her eyes widened as she was lit up by a white light shining behind Jess, which was quickly getting brighter. Jess heard a roaring sound behind her, and Beth screamed something she couldn't understand.

'Shit,' Jess muttered, trying to swerve to her left. Losing her balance and stumbling sideways instead, the wheel of the moped smashed into Jess's right leg, followed by the handlebars crashing into her back, sending her flying through the air, dragging Alfie behind her.

Feeling like everything was happening in slow motion, she landed in a crumpled heap on the pavement.

The moped screeched to a halt. She heard the moped rider swearing to himself in panic, before revving his engine and tearing away up the road.

There was a moment of stillness before Jess opened her eyes, and her body exploded in a riot of pain, her back and ribs feeling like they were being chopped with a meat cleaver. She could tell without looking that her leg was twisted at an unnatural angle, and she'd hit her head and could feel warm blood spreading underneath it. A few feet away, Alfie was lying on the pavement, spots of red blood in his white fur. He was whining softly, and Jess desperately reached out a hand towards him. She tried to shuffle nearer to him, but found her body wouldn't obey her brain's commands to move.

'Alfie,' she croaked, a tear sliding out of her right eye and down her cheek.

Then her forehead creased, even though her whole face hurt. Something about this felt familiar. That first Friday, when she'd been hit by the moped. This had happened back then, too – only she'd forgotten all about it.

'Help! Help us!' she heard Beth screaming hoarsely as she ran towards Jess. She crouched over her, her hands shaking wildly, tears spilling down her face as she pulled her phone out of her bag and called an ambulance. Behind her, Inkblot was gently nudging Alfie with his nose, whimpering.

The terror on Beth's face told Jess all she needed to know about how bad she must look. But she felt strangely calm. She was only worried about Alfie. Watching his chest rising and falling as he panted, Jess half-listened to Beth talking to the emergency services operator.

'Please, come quickly ... ' she said urgently, giving their location. ' ... She's awake, but ... Yes, yes. Thank you.'

'Please help Alfie,' Jess said thickly. 'He's such a good boy.'

'Oh god, I'm so sorry, this is all my fault,' Beth babbled, hovering over Jess. 'I should have seen the bike sooner!' Gradually, more people appeared behind Beth. Their worried faces bent towards Jess, then towards each other, whispering, the invisible membrane that exists between strangers in London suddenly broken by the drama.

I must look pretty grim, Jess thought vaguely, remembering Beth's story of the man who'd asked her for directions as she lay on the floor after being mugged. Around these parts, things had to get pretty bad before people started actually worrying about someone they didn't know.

Jess smiled at everyone benignly. Things were hurting a lot less already, like the pain was being gently wrapped in cotton wool. Alfie had stopped whimpering too, which had to be good, right?

'It's not your fault. Everything's my fault. Everything,' Jess told Beth thickly. She tried to lift her arm to comfort her, but for some reason it wouldn't listen. 'Don't let Inkblot run off. He's such a good boy too . . .'

'Here, Inkblot,' Beth sobbed, grabbing her dog's lead. Scooping him up, she pressed her face against his fur as he whimpered, straining to go back to Alfie's side, and held Jess's hand.

Jess watched with strange detachment as the group of faces hovering over her shone flashing blue. She was so very tired; she just wanted to sleep. And maybe that would be good too. She would wake up on Friday right as rain. Except something told Jess this sleep might not be the same as the others. That maybe, if she succumbed to it, she wouldn't wake up at all.

Struggling to keep her eyes open, the crowd parted and a paramedic dressed in green and yellow appeared. Jess wondered if this is how Mel felt, trapped in the jagged hole beneath the bungalow's rotted living-room floor.

'Keep your eyes open for me, love,' the paramedic urged. She had a lovely voice, Jess thought. 'Can you tell me your name?'

'Jess,' she managed, although she wasn't sure she'd said it out loud. 'Alfie,' she said, trying to point towards him.

'Stay with us, please. Don't close your eyes. Try and talk to me.'

Just like when Mel had her accident, Jess thought, vaguely.

It was comforting, knowing her best friend knew exactly how she felt. Except they weren't best friends any more, were they? Mel had realised who Jess really was, just like she'd always known she would, eventually.

The contents of Jess's handbag had been scattered across the pavement as she fell. While the paramedic injected her with morphine she really didn't need, as the pain was all gone now, Jess spotted the photo of Donna and Alejandro on holiday resting on the pavement a few inches from her face.

They were still happily sipping from a fishbowl cocktail, Donna's face lit up with hope and happiness.

I've got to tell Donna about Alejandro, Jess thought. *She deserves to be happy. I'll tell her tomorrow.*

As she was gently eased onto a stretcher, she watched the photograph being lifted by a breeze, blown over Alfie's now-still body, and into the night air.

Chapter 38

As her alarm went off, Jess shot bolt upright, panting, her heart pounding hard in her chest. Picking up her phone with shaking hands, she hoped, for the first time, to see the same thing she always saw.

Friday 13 August

Mel: What's new, Pussycat?

Looking over the side of the bed in relief, she scooped Alfie into her arms. He licked her face, clearly only interested in the fact that now she was awake, breakfast was on its way.

'Oh, thank god. Thank *god*!' Jess cried, her tears soaking into Alfie's fur as she kissed his little face over and over again. Poking her feet into her unicorn slippers, with Alfie still clutched in her arms, she shuffled into the bathroom and stared at her face in the mirror.

'I'm still here. *You're* still here,' Jess told Alfie, touching her face to check she wasn't dreaming.

Last night, after being taken into the ambulance, Jess had drifted in and out of consciousness, only aware of small snatches of what happened next.

She remembered a shocking jolt rippling through her as the trolley she was lying on crashed feet-first through some doors.

She remembered being annoyed by some bright lights above her, thinking for a moment that she was at home, the sun punching its way through her thin bedroom curtains.

She remembered thinking about Tom and Mel, and hoping they knew how sorry she was for everything she'd done.

She remembered wondering if Alfie was still on the pavement, a cold hand of fear clutching her heart.

She remembered fighting against the feeling of darkness that had started creeping through her body, no matter how peaceful it felt, knowing that this sleep was one she might not wake up from at 7.45 a.m.

And she remembered the panicked voices of the medics around her as the machines she was attached to began bleeping out desperate warnings.

This can't be the end. I didn't fix things, she'd thought, trying to open her eyes. If she could just explain to them how important it was that she lived – that she needed another go at Friday, to protect Alfie, tell Tom that she loved him, and to make things right with Mel – then everything would be OK.

But as the edges of her vision slowly went black, she'd realised it was too late.

Until now, she'd only remembered being hit by the moped on Friday the First, and nothing more. But now, she remembered Beth rushing over to help her, Alfie laying on the pavement beside her, and everything that had happened afterwards.

Now, the same as last time, she'd woken up without a scratch on her. But even so, she knew the terrible truth.

I didn't survive the accident.

I didn't survive it on Friday the First, and I didn't survive it last night. But somehow, I'm still here.

Shaking all over, her wobbly legs deposited her, with a bump, onto the floor. On the first day of the time loop, she'd been given the second chance to beat all second chances, but she'd completely blown it over and over again.

Her last thoughts yesterday, before everything had faded into darkness, had been about the hurt she'd caused the people around her. She'd spent months stuck in the time loop looking for an easy way out, sticking a plaster over her mistakes without ever trying to fix things beneath the surface, because that would mean finally facing up to her greatest fear.

She'd spent her life running from accountability, under the guise of being carefree and having the time of her life. But the truth was that ever since Mel's accident, taking responsibility for her actions had felt like an impossible hurdle to overcome. It meant facing up to the one thing she couldn't bear to acknowledge: that her reckless behaviour didn't just get herself into trouble.

In a single day, Mel and Tom, Donna and Brian – and even Alfie – had all been impacted by her recklessness. But at last, her past had caught up with her. There was nowhere left to run – and now, she had to turn around and face it.

Holding her face in her hands, Jess started sobbing, with relief and with guilt.

It might take time to prepare, but she was ready to fix things – properly this time. At last, she was ready to do what she should have done a long, long time ago.

Chapter 39

'Twice in two days? And before lunchtime, too. To what do I owe the pleasure?' Mark said as Jess walked into the Bush and nodded at Arthur in his spot in the window.

'You're just super lucky, I guess,' Jess said, hopping onto a bar stool. 'Can I get a bottle of white wine, two glasses and a blue WKD please?'

'Ah, let me guess. You're meeting Mel and that fella who looks like he's out of *Paddington*?'

'Tom, yes. You'll probably be seeing a lot more of him after today – well, maybe – so you might want to stop saying that. Although you won't remember this anyway, will you?'

'Eh?'

'Never mind.'

As Mark pulled a bottle of WKD out of the fridge, Jess tilted her head at the poster of John Travolta dancing intently to 'You Never Can Tell' at Jack Rabbit Slim's.

'What is it about *Pulp Fiction* you love so much anyway, Mark?' she asked, surprised that in all the Fridays she'd spent at the Bush, she'd never asked that question.

'It's not actually *Pulp Fiction* per se; it's John Travolta I like,' Mark said, scooping ice into a bucket. 'Truth be told, *Grease* is my favourite of his films, but I'm not likely to get away with putting pictures of that up, am I? The lads would tear me a new one. Especially Arthur. He got up to all sorts back in the day and has a reputation to protect. Isn't that right, Arthur?'

Arthur raised his pint in agreement.

'I really should introduce him to my nan,' Jess said thoughtfully. 'Anyway, your *Grease*-y secret's safe with me. What's so good about Travolta, then?'

'What's *not* so good about him, more like. His films are all bangers. Apart from *Look Who's Talking*, obviously. But what I really like is that he pulled himself up from rock bottom, you know? One minute he's playing a talking sperm, before he plunges into obscurity. Everyone assumes that's it for his once-illustrious career.

'Then BOOM!' Jess jumped in her seat. 'Tarantino rediscovers him and suddenly he's a bit fatter and older, but cooler than Christmas. I like that. It's hopeful, innit?' Mark looked sadly down at his beer gut.

'Is Christmas that cool? It's got terrible jumpers.'

'It's cool *figuratively*. You did ask.'

Upstairs, Jess nodded to the boys in the corner of the room. 'Happy birthday, Tez,' she called. 'I've put a round for you behind the bar. Just a small warning, though – if you drink too much and decide to climb the lamp post outside Aldi on the way home, don't, OK? No good will come of it.'

'You what?' Tez said, turning around in his seat and looking at Jess in confusion.

'Never mind, you'll understand later. Just be careful. And maybe google "degloving" before you go off playing Spider-Man.'

Placing her drinks on the table by the window, Alfie curled underneath it, Jess folded a single beer mat into quarters, ripped a small layer off one corner, and pushed it under the back left leg.

Soon after, Jess heard the familiar sound of Mel making her way carefully up the stairs. As she always did on Friday 13th, she looked tired, and her eyes were pink from crying. Jess couldn't believe she hadn't noticed from that very first Friday. Leaping up from her chair, Jess wrapped her in a huge hug and squeezed her tight.

'Hey, what's this in aid of?' Mel laughed over her shoulder, nuzzling into it.

'I just haven't seen you for ages, that's all,' Jess said, a tear rolling down her cheeks and soaking into Mel's yellow diaphanous Friday Dress.

'Dude, you saw me yesterday. Calm down.'

'Saying "dude" is generational appropriation,' Jess said primly, pulling Mel's chair out for her as she dumped her bags and cane under the windowsill. It was so good to see her again.

Mel laughed. 'So what's the emergency then? I'm knackered.'

'I know, and I'm really sorry to drag you out,' Jess said. 'Look, here's Tom. I can tell you both at the same time. I wonder why he looks so pleased with himself? It's almost like he's been in *cahoots* with someone ...' Jess raised her eyebrows at Mel, who blushed.

Tom bounded up the stairs grinning, and Jess's heart did a loop-the-loop at the sight of his familiar green jumper and sticky-up hair.

'Hey, Mel, hi, Jess. Wow, you look stunning!'

'Thanks,' Jess said modestly, kissing Tom's cheek and grabbing him for a huge hug as Alfie dashed out from under the table to lick his ankles. Whether Tom knew it or not, the pair had become firm friends over the past months of the time loop.

On Jess's way to the pub, she'd picked up the olive-green mini dress and black-wool biker jacket she'd bought on one of her very first Fridays, enjoying how grown-up it made her feel. Although they didn't go with the outfit, she'd added the posh red shoes she loved so much, and, thanks to plenty of practise, could now walk in as comfortably as if they were her favourite Converse.

Standing up, she gave Tom and Mel a twirl, before stalking to the stairs doing her best model-walk and blowing a kiss at them over her shoulder.

'Shit. How are you doing that?' Mel marvelled. 'You normally fall over in flip-flops.'

'Ah, now, that's what we're here to talk about,' Jess said, sitting down next to Tom. As a balled-up paper napkin suddenly flew towards her head, she snatched it from mid-air without even looking.

'Nice one,' the group of boys across the pub cheered.

'How did you do that?' Mel frowned.

'Well, here's the thing. I'm certain you're not going to believe me, because why would you? But I want you to keep an open mind and not run away, or assume I've been drinking. Just . . . listen.'

Jess took a deep breath, watching their expectant faces as she began her speech. 'The truth is, I've been living through a time loop for what feels like for ever now. Every morning I wake up on Friday 13th, and unless I change things, every day is exactly the same. You go to your appointment

298

at the hospital, Mel. Which I'm so, so sorry you had to go through alone.'

Mel opened her mouth in shock, then shut it again.

'Tom goes to my flat in the morning, and spells, "WILL YOU BE MY GIRLFRIEND?" in red rose petals on my bed. And although at the beginning it seemed beyond cheesy, and the thought of being anyone's girlfriend was an absolute no, when I live through a rose-petals day now, I always say yes.'

'Wow. Really?' Tom said, unable to stop himself smiling.

'Yep. I've even read all the *Lord of the Rings* books and seen the films. And if that's not a sign that I'm into you, I'm not sure what is.'

'You've done what?'

'I know, amazing, right? And look! Almost as good as Gandalf.' Jess grabbed the cigarette she'd stuck behind her ear, lit it with her pink plastic lighter, and started blowing a series of perfect smoke rings, each new one sailing through the last.

Mel and Tom stared at Jess, then at each other, dumbstruck.

'What the fuck?' Mel muttered. 'Have you been practising in secret?'

'And you think I could hide a talent like that from you, instead of constantly showing off, do you?' Jess asked, and Mel shook her head.

Jess was almost starting to enjoy herself.

'The films are utter garbage, of course, apart from Gandalf's smoke-ring-boat thing, but I really enjoyed the books. I can definitely relate to creatures who eat that many meals. Although I couldn't believe it when they got back to Hobbiton and Saruman had destroyed it. All that stuff they added into the films, and they left out the most jaw-dropping bit!'

'I don't understand. You hate fantasy novels,' Tom said, ruffling the hair at the back of his head.

'I knew they were your favourites, but I always thought life was too short for that shit,' Jess shrugged. 'Then Friday suddenly turned into an eternity, and I couldn't think of a good enough excuse not to bother. Isn't that right, Alfie?' Jess said.

Leaning under the table and holding up her palm, Mel and Tom looked even more startled as Alfie high-fived Jess back.

'See, Alfie got hit by the moped on Friday the First too, so I think he's trapped in the time loop with me. Poor old Alfie. Although it does mean he's gained a *lot* of dog years, and learned a few new tricks of his own.'

'Sorry, who got hit by a what now?' Mel said, looking shaken.

'Never mind that. The point is that I'm bored of eternity now. I can't even die, and once – or maybe twice – was quite enough anyway, thank you very much. So you really don't have to believe me when I tell you time loops exist, but I'm tired of pretending that everything's OK and not having anyone to talk to about it. So how about you just pretend that I'm having some weird breakdown that you'll worry about tomorrow, and keep me company for now?'

'It does sound a bit mad, Jess,' Mel said, warily.

'And that's fine, as long as you stay. Because you might have seen me yesterday, Mel, and you saw me on Wednesday, Tom. But I haven't seen either of you for weeks. Not properly, anyway. And I miss you guys so much. And I think I've finally worked out what I need to do to leap out of the time loop. But I kind of need your help to do it. So will you? Help me, that is?'

Mel and Tom went quiet. Then they glanced at each other. There was a long silence.

'OK,' Mel said. 'What do you need us to do?'

Chapter 40

When her alarm went off, Jess slapped it off on its first tinny note and swung her legs out of bed. Grabbing her notebook and pen from underneath it, she wrote out her plan of action, moment by moment. She'd gone through it over and over again, and everything had to be timed to the minute. It would be a close call to get it all done, but she'd worked it all out minutely and had practised some of the harder parts over the past few Fridays.

She knew she could do it – she just had to stay focused.

First, she deleted her email to Donna, and set up a new, anonymous email address. Bringing up the website links she'd researched and memorised, she copied and pasted the relevant parts into a fresh email from her new account, wrote a short message, and hit Send.

Grabbing Nate's pants from underneath her pillow, she held them over the metal wastepaper basket under her dresser, grabbed her lighter, and set the flame against one of the palm trees on the waistband. It wasn't strictly necessary, but felt cathartic.

Once they were burning enthusiastically, she threw them into the bin and headed for the shower.

Throwing on her vintage T-shirt, baggy jeans and slouchy Oscar-the-Grouch-coloured cardigan, she topped her Friday Outfit off with the bee necklace Mel had given her for her eighteenth birthday. Looking in the mirror, she twirled it between her fingers, hoping that after today everything would be different for her, and for Mel. She'd shoved herself in a cage of her own making, and Mel was suffering too because of it. But it was time to set them both free.

And to do some washing, because this look was starting to feel a bit samey and she didn't have time to hit Covent Garden today.

Snapping a photo of herself wearing the necklace and grinning widely, she sent it in reply to Mel's morning text.

> **I BEES great, thank you! Hope your meeting goes**
> **OK today. Love you xxx**

Next, she tapped out a reply to Tom, whose message made her heart flip at the thought of what she had to do.

> **Tom: See you later.**
> **Looking forward to our date! xxx**

> **Me too. I can't wait. But we have to talk.**
> **Please don't wig out worrying about it Xxx**

Letting Alfie outside and filling his dog bowl, she grabbed a handful of marshmallows from the bag in the kitchen for her own breakfast, sat on the sofa, and dug the remote control out from between the cushions. Switching on the TV, she pushed down the volume. She had a phone call to make, but found the sight of Naga's familiar face, winking away at bad jokes about Morris dancers, strangely soothing.

They'd been through a lot together, even if Naga didn't know it.

Jess didn't want to leave anything about today to chance, which meant she had to dial Jane Doe's number in exactly three minutes. That would give her enough time to say what she needed to say, and leave the flat right on schedule.

As she waited for 8 a.m. to arrive, Jess threw three marshmallows into the air and caught them all in her mouth – yet another useless talent she'd acquired during her time in eternity.

Knowing Jane was a PR in Hove had made her easy enough to track down, and, during her months of doing nothing much, Jess had whiled away a good afternoon or two stalking her on Instagram, Twitter and Facebook.

Seeing how happy she seemed, with her Boden-clad kids and veneer-toothed husband, had made Jess feel even sadder when she thought about Donna and her predicament. She deserved that kind of happiness too – but thanks to one mistake, she'd ended up with creepy old Alejandro in her life instead of a supportive best friend.

Now, hitting the mobile number listed on Jane Doe's website, Jess took a deep breath, hoping she could remember what she'd said in her successful practise call to Jane. She knew that even a small variation in their conversation could send this part of the plan, and everything else too, careering in a different direction.

If the time loop had taught her anything, it was that the butterfly effect was a real drag.

Jane answered after three rings, exactly as Jess had known she would.

'Hello, Jane Doe PR,' the voice at the other end said.

'Hello, Jane,' Jess said, clearing her throat. 'My name's Jess, and I'm a journalist for *Real Talk!* magazine.'

'Oh, hello there,' Jane said, sounding interested. 'How can I help?'

While *Real Talk!* might not attract the same calibre of advertisers as *Bijou* magazine, it sold thousands of copies each week. A call from Jess was considered something of a holy grail for people like Jane, who promoted the products *Real Talk!* readers really wanted to read about: everything from super-mops to sunny holidays.

'I'm calling about someone you know, actually. Donna Wilson?'

'Donna Wilson? Oh my goodness, how is she? I haven't heard from her for years. Is she OK?' Suddenly, Jane sounded worried.

'She's absolutely fine, don't worry. But I've got something important to ask you, and I'm hoping you'll hear me out . . .'

Hanging up the phone ten minutes later, Jess resisted punching the air with both fists. She couldn't take anything about today for granted. Not until every last thing was in place. Waiting impatiently for Alfie to finish his breakfast, she clipped his lead to his collar, grabbed her handbag, and headed for Borys's shop.

'Four pounds twenty-five, please,' he said, smiling, after she'd piled her papers and chocolate onto the counter.

'And what do I owe you for my tab?' Jess asked, waving her debit card.

'You want to pay off your card?' Borys frowned. 'Are you

sick? I think you must be dying, yes? You must be dead soon, otherwise payment never come. This is goodbye?'

'What if I actually was dying, Borys? That joke wouldn't be very funny then, would it?'

'Shop go out of business. Close for ever,' Borys said, seriously. 'You're my best customer for ready meal for one. Plus wine. Lots of scratch cards on pay day. Very lucrative for Borys.'

Jess laughed. 'OK, Borys, don't rub it in. Just take the bloody money. And while you're at it, how much would you want for your super-irritating door buzzer?'

'Door buzzer? Thing that buzz when customer come in?'

'Yes, that. You don't really need it, do you, let's face it. You're literally always here.' In all the times she'd been into the shop, Jess had never once seen the counter empty. Apparently, Borys never went for a wee, which was a mystery she was happy never to solve.

Borys shrugged. 'Twenty pounds?'

'Deal. I'll pay for that now, too.'

On her way out of the shop, Jess grabbed the broom propped behind Borys's counter, gave the box that housed the nerve-shredding buzz a single, hard jab with the handle, and caught it in her outstretched hand. Borys looked impressed.

'Not my first time,' she said with a shrug, before taking Alfie for his walk around the block, dropping the buzzer in the bin on the way.

As she walked, she had one last call to make, and, if she'd timed it correctly, she should still hit the Tube right on time.

As planned, after ending her call, Jess found herself standing on the escalator behind Beth, Inkblot's shiny black nose peering back over her shoulder.

Delighted to see him again, Alfie started barking happily, straining his nose towards him for a friendly sniff.

'Woah there, what's got into you, little fluffer?' Beth laughed, turning to look over her shoulder at Alfie.

'Don't mind him, he just isn't used to the existence of other dogs yet. Even though it's been years. What's yours called? He's absolutely gorgeous, although I bet you spend all day being told that.'

'He's only little, so it's still lovely when people say it,' Beth beamed, turning around. 'I'm sure I'll get bored of it eventually, but not yet. Isn't he cute?'

'He's adorable,' Jess agreed, stroking Inkblot's nose with two fingers. He beamed at her happily, licking her fingers.

'This is Inkblot, and I'm Beth. Say hello, Inkblot.'

'I'm Jess. Hello Inkblot, and hello Beth. Have you found that having a puppy is a bit like having a baby? You're the one doing all the hard work, but they're the ones who get all the attention?'

'You're not wrong,' Beth laughed, stepping off the escalator. Jess followed her onto the platform. 'Not that I want to come off all stalkery, but I think I've seen you walking Inkblot near mine. Just past the Polski Sklep on the corner?'

'Yes, that's me. You wouldn't believe how much walking he needs. He's like a furry whirlwind. I've started taking him into the office so the girls can walk him at lunch. He's pretty popular. Aren't you, boy?' Inkblot woofed his agreement.

'Well, I can't blame them. Maybe I'll see you around and I can give you a hand too? Like those babysitting pools people set up, but with our pooches.'

'That sounds like a great idea. They're cute but tiring, right?'

Jess chatted to Beth until she stepped off the carriage a few stops later, Inkblot snuggled in her arms. Jess hoped she'd done enough to make sure Beth remembered her later on.

'See you around,' Jess waved, marvelling at how not-awful she felt talking to strangers on the Tube once she'd tried it. It was the one new thing she hadn't bothered trying over the last however many months, but it was a lot less horrible than she'd expected.

By skipping Alfie's pre-work snuffle around Hoxton Square, firmly promising to take him out to bother pigeons later, Jess arrived at the office a few minutes early.

As they slid from the edge of the photocopier where Jasmit had balanced them, Jess grabbed the box of paperclips.

'I'll take these and you can have these,' she said, handing Jasmit her pile of newspapers and chocolate.

'Aww, you shouldn't have. Thanks, Jess.'

'Can we have a quick chat? It's urgent.'

'Sofas?'

'Please.'

Jasmit clutched her bump as they walked – and waddled – their way to the sofas laid out in the corner of the office, where visiting dignitaries waited for Maggie to deign to meet them, and staff came to cry after being screamed at by her.

'What have you done now?' Jasmit asked.

Jess took a deep breath. 'We can't run Donna and Alejandro's story. The one Maggie calls the Halloween Heifer. But I think I've got a plan to fill the pages that will make everyone happy. Even her.'

'Why can't we run the story? What did you do?' Jasmit frowned.

Jess explained about Alejandro's wandering hands. 'I can't go ahead with the story knowing Donna's going to get hurt

307

and Alejandro is going to be paid for lying through his teeth. It's just not right.' Across the office, Jess heard cheering and a cry of 'Eleven!' as June finished her impressive bout of sneezing.

'I know you've got a surprisingly acute guilt complex, Jess, but since when did you start worrying about our punters' feelings more than having an actual job? You know Maggie's going to go ballistic, right?'

'Since this morning. Technically. But I've worked out a way of making sure Donna knows what she's getting herself into without getting us into trouble. I just need your help bagging the replacement story, which I'm hoping Maggie will like as much as the original. Maybe even more.'

Jess explained her idea, and what she needed Jasmit to do to make it happen.

'OK. That might actually work,' Jasmit said, thoughtfully. 'I'm pretty impressed you've pulled this together so fast – what have you done with Jess? The one who'll do almost anything to shy away from taking responsibility for her many magnificent fuck-ups?'

'Ha bloody ha.'

'Although, why do I have to get involved? Shouldn't you be overseeing all this, seeing as it's your cunning plan?'

'Well, that's the other thing. I need the afternoon off. And for you to look after Alfie for a bit. I honestly wouldn't ask if it wasn't a matter of life and death,' Jess said, pulling a pleading face.

'Life and death? Seriously?'

'In a way, yeah. But I've planned this really carefully, so it should all go smoothly for you. I'm actually a bit jealous that you'll be the one to see how it all pans out.'

'OK,' Jasmit sighed, rubbing her bump. 'This stress can't be good for the twins, you know.'

'Unlike the double espresso you have every morning?'

'A fair point. But at least stay until after the story falls through. Just because you've replaced it doesn't mean Maggie won't go nuts about it. I need you to act as my human shield. If a delicious brie can harm the twins, imagine what her evil vibes could do to them?'

'Deal. Pinky promise,' Jess said.

'Here, help me up, would you?'

Jess grabbed Jasmit's hands, leaned back on her heels, and pulled her to her feet, just as Ashleigh stomped over to the sofas, Donna and Alejandro in tow.

'These two are yours, I presume? I found them in reception, completely failing to work out how to use the lifts,' Ashleigh said archly, glaring at Jess before stalking off.

'Thanks, love!' Donna said, smiling at Ashleigh's retreating back.

'What a lovely girl, eh?' Jess said.

'That's exactly what I was going to say,' Donna beamed.

'Anyway, it's lovely to see you both!' Jess smiled brightly, pushing away her nerves. 'Let me introduce you to Terrence and he'll give you your costumes. I really think you're going to like them.'

Back at her desk, Jess nibbled her nails as she waited for Terrence to bring the pair back to her desk, Donna's Elvira wig in hand and Alejandro's plastic teeth inserted.

'*Hola, señorita*,' Alejandro said to Jasmit through his plastic teeth. She pulled a face as Maggie stepped out of her office chirping, 'Ah, this must be our two lovebirds!' right on cue, shooting Jess a dirty look as she clocked Donna's wig.

Alejandro slipped his teeth out and grabbed Maggie's hand to kiss it, while Jess watched Donna intently.

There was no reason for her to do things any differently this time around, was there? Jess hadn't rehearsed this part of the plan, but Donna had found Jess's other, horrible email the same way every single time, so there was no reason it would be different for this new one, was there?

Except that everything was hanging on this one moment and, so far, Friday 13th hadn't exactly proved to be Jess's lucky day.

Her heart thudded and she barely dared to breathe as she heard a muffled 'ping' coming from the direction of Donna's bag, followed by her cheerful, 'That'll be my reminder to check my lottery numbers.' Jess watched Donna pull her phone from her bag, tap open her email app, then freeze as she found the email Jess had sent her that morning.

It was hard to watch, knowing exactly what she was reading.

From: Truthteller12345
To: Donna Wilson
Subject: The TRUTH about Alejandro!

Hello Donna,

You don't know me, but I'm hoping you'll believe me when I tell you I'm a friend. This is going to be hard to hear, but I've found out a few things about your fiancé that I think you deserve to know.

What you do with this information is entirely up to you, but whatever you decide, please believe this: you deserve a lot better, and you will find happiness.

At the bottom of the email, Jess had attached a series of screen grabs from local newspapers about Alejandro being handed a jail sentence for a spate of robberies in South Yorkshire, three years earlier. He wasn't even Spanish – his real name was Alan, and he was from Barnsley. No wonder his '*Ah, mi amore!*' continental-style theatrics had felt so fake.

She'd also included links to chat rooms filled with women who had been conned by Alejandro – or rather, Alan – in the past. Headed things like 'DO NOT TRUST THIS MAN!!!' and 'I lost a thousand pounds – help me expose this love rat!', some of the posts included photos of Alan with his arm around different women. Each of them had believed his lies, and they'd all been left heartbroken and out of pocket, most of them too ashamed and hurt to report what he'd done to the police.

Jess braced herself for Donna to start sobbing. But instead, she did something much, much better. She swung her hand-bag round and smashed it over Alan's head.

'You complete and utter love-rat BASTARD!' she yelled, grabbing Alan's cape and tugging him around so he was facing her. 'You . . . you complete ARSEHOLE!'

'What have I done, *mi amore*?' Alan stuttered, turning his face into a picture of bewildered innocence. Which rapidly turned into a picture of smashed-in pain when, to Jess's horror and delight, Donna curled her hand into a fist and punched him right in the middle of his handsome nose.

Alan crumpled to the floor and started whimpering in a decidedly un-macho manner.

'To think I believed you, you lying . . . *turd!*' Donna screamed at him, as he clutched his nose, blood pouring through his fingers. Across the office, the food editor had

311

opened a bag of popcorn sent to her by a PR, and was watching in amazement, while Ian had already whipped out his phone and started recording.

'All those promises. "Ohh, I love you, *mi amore*, you're not like the others, *dulzura*." What a load of phoney nonsense. You're dumped, Dracula. Or should I call you *Alan*? Go back to Barnsley, you contemptible little creep.'

'You've broken my fucking nose, you mad fat bitch,' Alan wailed, in a distinctly un-Spanish accent.

'Do *not* call her fat, you bastard,' Jess said, stepping pointedly on Alan's hand as she moved towards Donna and wrapped a protective arm around her. 'She might not be a size ten, but she's worth ten of you.'

Growling as ferociously as he could, Alfie grabbed Alan's cape between his teeth and started wriggling back and forth, trying to drag him towards the lifts, without much success.

'Why don't you come over here and sit with me, Donna?' Jess said, guiding her towards the sofa and raising her eyebrows at Jasmit. 'Ian will make you a cuppa, won't you, Ian? Milk, two sugars, isn't it?'

'I'll make you all the tea you want because that was amazing,' Ian muttered, finally putting his phone down.

As Jess led Donna to the sofas, she heard Jasmit behind her asking to talk to Maggie in her office.

'Tell that horrible slimeball he's got until five o'clock to be out of my flat and gone from my life for good,' Donna sniffed, her eyes red. Jess handed her a tissue. 'I never want to hear from him again.'

'Of course. Anything you want. Bloody shitbag.'

After delivering the message to a sulky, blood-spattered Alan who was sitting at Jess's desk clutching the bridge of his nose and scowling, Alfie yapping angrily at his feet, Jess went back to the sofa and held Donna's hand as she wept about her broken heart.

Meanwhile, she kept half an anxious eye on Maggie's office door, until Jasmit finally emerged and hurried – as far as she could hurry in any meaningful way any more – over to the sofas.

'Maggie wants a quick word, then you'd best get going,' she said. 'I'll look after Donna.' Jasmit turned to her. 'How about some lunch, my treat?' Donna gave Jasmit a wobbly smile and nodded.

'Good idea,' Jess agreed. 'I'm sure we can keep Donna occupied until five, can't we, Jas? Then you won't have to see that git ever again. Good luck, Donna,' she added, grabbing her in a hug. 'It was lovely getting to know you. And I'm sorry about what happened; you really don't deserve it.'

As Jess cautiously poked her head around the door to Maggie's office, she caught the editor prowling behind her desk like a caged tiger.

'Jasmit says you've got a plan to fill those four pages that have just been completely fucking ruined,' Maggie snapped, before Jess had even had a chance to shut the door behind her. 'And admittedly, if you pull it off, this half-arsed "plan" of yours could work. *Just*. But what I really want to know is how you so magically predicted this story was going to go tits-up in the first place? It's a bit of an odd coincidence that someone sent the Halloween Heifer an email about her other half's wrongdoings on the very morning of a shoot no one except the people in this office knew about, don't you think?'

'She's called Donna, not the Halloween Heifer,' Jess said firmly, and Maggie's eyebrows shot up in surprise. 'And yes, it is a strange coincidence. But I think this new story could be really good. And at least it will be the truth, which is usually more interesting than a load of lies anyway.'

'Couldn't you have developed a conscience some other time?' Maggie hissed. 'We're pulling together one of our biggest-ever Halloween issues and I'm having a nightmare trying to keep our budgets intact. You'd better hope this works or I might have to launch an inquiry into today's incident, and ask IT to trace the IP address that email to Donna came from. And I'm not sure that would go too well for you, would it?'

'I'd survive. But actually, it's all going to be OK.'

Smiling serenely, she left a furious-looking Maggie behind her and breezed out of the office.

Chapter 41

By the time Jess had stopped off at the bank and made her way to the hospital, her timetable had started unravelling slightly. It was almost 11.a.m, and Jess had hoped to catch Mel as she walked into the hospital, but she'd already be inside by now. She didn't have as much time as she'd have liked, but it would have to do.

Hurriedly, she gave Brian his money in a bulging envelope, apologised for the stress she'd caused him, and explained that she'd set up a direct debit to pay her rent on time in future. Then she handed him a tattered business card.

'Please apologise to Sarah for me too. If she ever needs any advice on getting into journalism, or a work experience placement, I'd be happy to help. I might only work for a trashy weekly magazine, but we actually do some pretty good stuff, you know?'

'How did you—' Brian started to ask, but Jess had already started running towards the hospital doors.

She knew exactly where to go. On Alfie's walk that morning, she'd phoned Aya. 'I know all about today's appointment.

The one Mel has about her leg,' she'd said. 'And I know you can't be there, because you're busy being amazing and saving children's lives and stuff, so I really want to be with her instead. Only I might not make it in time if I can't get off work and I don't want to disappoint her if I can't be there. So can you tell me which department she'll be in, so I can just go straight there? And not tell her I'm coming?'

'Wow,' Aya had said, sounding shocked. 'I don't want you to take this the wrong way, but . . . see, we didn't want to tell you because Mel was worried you'd be upset. She thought . . . she thought you might think she was blaming you somehow.'

'Because I never talk about the accident, I know. And actually, I would deserve the blame if Mel ever gave it to me. The accident *was* my fault. I forced Mel into that house. And she's right, I would have taken it badly if she'd told me about today's appointment. I would have thrown a shit-fit, in fact. But it's time for me to grow up a bit now, don't you think? She deserves a better friend than the one I've been lately.'

'I'm so glad you're going to be there for her, Jess. It'll mean the world to her. And to me, too,' Aya said, sounding relieved.

'Well, she shouldn't have to go through this alone. You don't know how lucky you are, you know. Will you hurry up and propose to her already?'

Aya laughed. 'I think I do know how lucky I am, thanks very much. I was actually planning on winning you over a bit more before popping the question. You're not exactly my number-one fan and she's always considering your feelings before her own. It's really annoying. Does this mean you'd be OK with me doing it? Popping the question, I mean?'

'Absolutely. Get it done,' Jess said. 'And thanks for making her happy. I know I haven't done that great a job of it lately.

Maybe after today we can both work on that one together. Oh, and Aya?'

'Yes?'

'Mel doesn't like lilies, OK? Maybe stick to peonies from now on.'

And like the heroines in her favourite movies, she'd hung up without saying goodbye.

Aya had told her Mel would be at the pain management clinic at the hospital, which Jess had looked up on a map she'd found online. Running up the stairs, she was out of breath by the time she flew through the doors.

Mel was sitting on a plastic chair under a sign that told patients and visitors to TURN OFF YOUR MOBILE NOW! Her shoulders were rounded downwards and her chin jutted defiantly upwards, just like the first time Jess had set eyes on her at Langley High. She was anxiously playing with the floaty material of her dress, trying to feel brave while making herself look as small as possible.

The sight of her made Jess's heart crack.

She felt a rush of shame realising that it had taken something as huge as the time loop to make her look beyond her own petty problems – problems entirely of her own making – and see how badly she had let down her friend.

Slipping into the chair beside her, Jess took Mel's hand in hers. As she looked up, shock broke across her face, before it transformed into a brilliant smile, her face flooding with relief. Leaning over, she wrapped Jess in a hug.

'I thought I could do this on my own, but I'm so glad you're here,' she said.

'I love you,' Jess said, burying her face in Mel's shoulder and squeezing her tight. 'And I'm so, so sorry for everything. For the accident, for running away, and for never letting you talk about any of it. And I swear things are going to be different – really different, not just patched over like usual – starting from today.'

Beneath her arms, Mel's body shook with tears, and Jess knew that even if she had to spend an eternity of Fridays in this hospital waiting room, she'd never let Mel go through this day alone again.

Jess held her hand the whole way through her appointment, gently squeezing it as Mel heard that the doctors couldn't do anything more to relieve her pain, stroking her arm as she was told her only option was an amputation, and holding her as she sobbed outside the ward.

Knowing what was coming meant Jess was able to find the strength to be the person Mel needed her to be at her darkest moment, without crumbling herself. It hurt to think of all the times Mel had gone through this day alone thanks to the time loop. Especially when she'd been dragged to the pub afterwards to make Jess feel better about being fired and dumped by Tom, both of which she'd only had herself to blame for.

What must she have thought of me? Jess wondered.

Except she already knew: Mel would have been thinking that she wanted to help her friend through a hard time, no matter what she was going through herself, and been happy to put her first.

That was just the way Mel was. And it was time to start levelling the playing field.

'So what do you want to do now?' Jess asked, as she sat beside Mel on the bench where, unbeknownst to Mel, they'd had their big argument. It already felt like a lifetime ago.

'We can do anything you like. I can drop you off home or leave you the hell alone. Whatever will help you the most right now.'

Mel had finally stopped crying and looked completely drained. She closed her eyes and raised her face to the sun, before turning to face Jess.

She swiped a finger under her eye. 'What's my make-up looking like?'

'Absolute disaster.'

'Bush then?' she said, managing a small smile.

'Bush it is,' Jess nodded. 'Can we just make one quick stop along the way? Then drinks are on me. If Mark's lucky, I might even pay off my tab.'

'Twice in two days? To what do I owe the pleasure?' Mark said, as Jess pushed open the door to the pub. 'And you as well?' he added as Mel appeared behind her. 'Don't either of you have jobs to go to?'

'Hmm, well, I'm hoping I still do. I'll find out soon enough,' Jess said, checking the time on her phone. Her plan should be underway by now, and sure enough, Jasmit had sent a text to The Devil Wears Primark group while Jess had been busy running her latest errand.

> **Jasmit:** The eagle has landed: repeat, the eagle has landed. You're going to have to tell me exactly how you pulled this off later, Doctor Mysterio. I'll let you know how it goes

'What's up?' Mel frowned.

'It's a very long story, and not one for you to worry about

right now. Mark, can we get a bottle of white? Oh, and I got you a present.'

She handed Mark a carrier bag, and he put the wine bottle down on the bar, and peered inside.

'Hey! This is amazing, thank you,' he grinned, pulling out a signed photo of John Travolta. He was standing next to a glossy-looking Olivia Newton-John, his hair sharply slicked back, his chin dimple going for miles.

'Maybe it's time to forget what the haters think and admit *Grease* is your favourite John Travolta film rather than *Pulp Fiction*? Arthur wouldn't make fun of you, would you, Arthur?'

'*Grease* is a proper banger,' Arthur agreed from his seat by the window, raising his pint.

'How did you know I love *Grease*?' Mark said, carefully putting the print back in its bag and grabbing two wine glasses.

'You wouldn't believe me even if I told you,' Jess grinned. As Mel headed for the stairs, Jess stuck out her arm to stop her. 'Give me two minutes,' she said, and headed towards Arthur's seat.

Jess bent her head and started earnestly talking to Arthur. A few moments later, he shrugged, and headed for the stairs, climbing them creakily one at a time.

'You need to install a bloody lift in here,' he grumbled as he reached the top, and Jess hid a splutter of laughter behind her hand.

'Your throne, madam,' Jess said, gesturing towards the spot by the window.

'How the hell did you manage that?' Mel said, placing her bag and cane reverentially underneath the windowsill. 'It doesn't even wobble!'

Alfie shuffled under the table then barked, clearly not warming to their new spot.

'I can be very persuasive when I want to be,' Jess said, mysteriously. Actually, she'd been working on Arthur for days, trying to find out what his weakness was. At first, she'd tried appealing to his better nature, but it turned out he didn't have one.

In the end, a promise that she'd put enough money behind the bar for him to buy a pint of Guinness and some salt and vinegar crisps every single day, as long as they could have the downstairs window table any time they needed it, did the trick.

Jess would just have to cut down smoking – which was a shame now she'd mastered smoke rings, but probably for the best for her lungs. She'd also promised to introduce Arthur to her nan, who was apparently quite famous in his circle of East End pensioners, which could potentially turn out to be an even bigger sacrifice.

When they were comfortably settled, Mel reached over and held Jess's hands.

'Thank you again for coming today. It really meant a lot,' she said. 'And I'm really sorry I didn't tell you about all this before. I thought ... never mind what I thought. But I was obviously wrong.'

'Don't say another word,' Jess said, tears springing into her eyes. 'I know how I've behaved these last few years. Decades, even. Avoiding talking about your leg, getting drunk when I could see it was hurting you. Never letting you talk about the accident. We vowed never to let each other down, but I've done it every day without even seeing it. And all this time you've been nothing but amazing.'

Mel looked like she was going to say something, but then changed her mind. Instead, she squeezed Jess's hands tight, tears filling her eyes.

'I swear I'm never going take you for granted again,' Jess continued. 'Something's happened to me lately – I can't explain what. But I'm different. And I'm going to get my act together from now on. I want us to be totally honest with each other. I won't hide anything from you, and you've got to tell me when I'm being a dick.'

'I did try . . .'

'OK, I'll give you that,' Jess laughed. 'But I'm really hoping to bring my being-a-dick average down after today.'

'When you say you won't hide anything from me . . . Does that mean there's something to tell?' Mel asked, sipping her wine.

'Well . . . this might come as a bit of a surprise. But I've fallen in love with Tom.'

'You're kidding me?' Mel squealed. 'It's only been, what . . . six weeks? And didn't you shag Nate, like, yesterday? How can you be in *love*?'

'Go hard or go home, right?' Jess said, ruefully. 'I know I've behaved ridiculously. And that Tom really likes me back. But I'm going to end it with Nate and tell Tom all about it. I owe him that, at least. Then he can decide if he still wants to ask me to be his girlfriend in a flurry of red bloody rose petals. Thanks for trying to dissuade him from that, by the way. It really is a disgustingly sappy idea. I mean rose petals . . . honestly.'

'I won't ask how you know about that. My brain's hurting enough already. But it sounds like you're doing the right thing. What's this sudden burst of honesty all about?'

'Well, I've come to realise I've become a bit of a car wreck. And, shock horror, it's not just me getting hurt – other people are being hurled around the car at the same time. I reckon it's time to face up to things for a change, instead of running away. It can't hurt, right?'

Raising her glass, she clinked hers against Mel's, at the same time as they heard someone yelling 'Sorry, mate!' from above them, followed by Arthur's outraged voice floating down the stairs.

'Oi! I don't give a shit about the three-second rule, or if it's your bloody birthday. Get downstairs and buy me a new pint, you little bastards.'

Chapter 42

'What are you two doing downstairs? Arthur didn't die, did he?' Aya asked, a huge bunch of peonies arriving through the door a few seconds ahead of her.

Jess and Mel had been chatting for hours, and as the afternoon had spooled out, Jess had felt the growing gap between them finally closing. Although it hadn't fully disappeared, the gnawing feeling in the pit of her stomach felt like it had shrunk. Just a little for now – but enough.

'Aya!' Mel grinned, twisting around in her chair to give her a hug. 'How did you know I was here?'

'A little bird told me,' she said, raising her eyebrows at Jess as she kissed Mel on the cheek and handed her the flowers.

'I've got to go and face the music with Tom, but I didn't want to leave you on your own,' Jess said, standing up and draping her cardigan over her arm. 'Have a great evening, guys. And thank you both for all your support, and the offers to stay in your spare room. I know it doesn't seem like it, but I appreciate it. I really do.'

Mel and Aya shot each other a confused look, before Mel stood to hug Jess.

'I'll see you soon,' Jess promised. 'Love you.'

'Love you too, and good luck with Tom,' Mel said. 'And sorry for giving him your front door keys.'

'Weirdly, I think you did us both a favour, actually,' Jess said, and headed outside.

Pacing outside the pub, she pulled out her phone, lit a cigarette, and blew one perfect smoke ring after another as she waited nervously for Jasmit to answer her call.

'There you are,' Jasmit said, 'I've been trying to get hold of you.'

'Sorry, I was dealing with my emergency. Which, by the way, is going way better than expected so far. How did it go at your end?'

'It was amazing. Terrence *actually* cried – although he reckoned it was his hay fever playing up – and I swear Maggie almost smiled. Like, a real one rather than that demented Joker-style thing she does when she wants stuff.'

That morning, Jess had told Jane Doe about Alejandro and his despicable past. Then, she'd explained how Donna had described their friendship, and what it had meant to her.

'I've been through something similar with my friend Mel recently, and it just feels wrong to think that two friends who were so close could grow apart and never see each other again,' Jess had explained. 'Donna told me how much she regrets not patching things up with you. And her face when she spoke about you ... well, you remember how it shines when she's happy?'

'I do,' Jane had said softly.

'Well, she was just beaming. It was nothing like the looks

325

she gives this Alan fella. You were really special to her. And I just think if you could come and see her and talk it through . . . maybe you could be friends again. If you wanted to be. It would mean the world to her. She really misses you.'

'I miss Donna too,' Jane had sighed. 'Our lives went in such different directions, but you're always the same person inside, aren't you? She was a bit of a mess back then, but underneath it all she was always so kind, and really funny. I've never met anyone quite like her since.'

'Then I've got a proposal. And without wanting to sound mercenary, it could be good for your business, too. You do the PR for SomeSuch, which makes household stuff like mops and things, don't you?'

'For my sins. It's not quite as glamorous as running a Chanel campaign, I can tell you that much.'

'Tell me about it,' Jess had laughed. 'I run a tips page that's just full to bursting with products like yours, and I've got a producer friend who just happens to work for *Wakey, Wakey, Britain!* and has agreed to meet up with you and chat through your client list. Then perhaps we can do something for you in return . . .'

On the Friday Jess had asked for Mel's help getting out of the time loop, she'd agreed that she could promote Jane's products on the show without too much trouble, and given Jess permission to arrange a meeting, if it would help.

Using the carrot Mel had generously promised her, Jess had persuaded Jane to come to Aevum House that afternoon to meet Donna and have a chat. And if a photographer and writer just happened to be there to capture the emotional reunion . . . Well, it wouldn't do any harm at all, would it?

Jasmit carried on telling Jess what had happened when Jane

arrived at the office, where Donna was still being treated like royalty after the morning's drama.

'I was expecting awkward handshakes and a gradual thawing out, but as soon as Donna and Jane set eyes on each other, they both burst into tears and started hugging. Once they started chatting, they didn't want to stop. We caught it all on camera, they're happy for us to use the footage, and you can interview them both properly on Monday to get all the background stuff on their friendship for the story. Even Maggie agreed it was better than the Halloween Hunk piece, especially as we've got it on film. Plus, of course, Ian caught Donna smacking Alan in the mush and his accent suddenly disappearing, which will make another brilliant front-pager for the next issue. Rachel reckons there's a great chance it'll go viral, too. We've already watched the video about ten times; it's amazing.'

'Good for Donna,' Jess grinned. 'Please tell me Maggie isn't going to destroy the story with one of her terrible headlines?'

'Amazingly, no. She wants to make it the main cover line for Halloween, and she's going to call it, "Our Friendship Came Back ... From the DEAD!".'

'Of course she is,' Jess said.

Jess saw Tom waiting for her outside the Tube station before he spotted her, and paused for a moment to watch him. He was pacing nervously up and down, like an expectant dad on a maternity ward in a 1950s film.

At the very sight of him, her face lit up, her heart swooped and her stomach twisted all at once. How could she ever have held him in the same esteem as Nate? She could no longer see it at all.

327

'Swit swoo!' Tom exclaimed when Jess tapped him on the shoulder. She was wearing her Covent Garden outfit, complete with ridiculous, but drop-dead sexy, red shoes. Blowing smoke rings and learning how to walk in heels might not be the best-ever uses for eternity, but at that moment, Jess was happy with her life choices.

Tom smiled brightly. 'Shall we go, then?' he said, chirpily.

'You're absolutely bricking it about what I've got to say to you, aren't you?' Jess said.

Tom nodded. 'Couldn't be more terrified.'

'Let's get to it, then,' she said, and let him lead the way to Hot Stuff, where she pretended – quite convincingly, she thought – to be shocked and delighted. In some ways, being stuck in a time loop was like an endless surprise party you'd found out about weeks ago.

Inside, Jess gently guided Tom towards choosing the dishes she'd learned were his favourites. Then, as they placed their orders, she leant back in her chair and caught an iPad in mid-air, which had been knocked over by a baby whose face was covered in barbecue sauce.

'Thanks,' the baby's grateful mum said, looking impressed. Jess wouldn't miss many things about the time loop, but a moment like that, when she felt like a sexy psychic ninja, was one of them.

Taking a sip of Diet Coke, she rested her palms on the table, and took a deep breath.

'OK. So I've got something to tell you,' she said. 'And it's pretty horrible, but I want you to hear me out, all the way to the end without interrupting or walking away. Can you do that?'

Tom nodded mutely. Jess wished Old Jess could be having

this conversation instead of her. It would be so much easier if she could make up a lame excuse for her behaviour to get out of apologising sincerely. But, unfortunately for her, New Jess was facing up to her problems from now on, no matter how difficult it was.

'When we met that night down the Bush, I was already seeing someone else. He's called Nate, and I'd been dating him for a few days. When I met you, I'd just read an article in *Bijou* magazine about New York dating, where you try on a couple of guys for size before moving on. I decided you and Nate would be perfect candidates, so I started seeing you both at once.'

'Oh,' Tom said, his face crumpling.

Jess took a deep breath. 'That's not all. We carried on seeing each other the whole time you and I were dating. And we carried on sleeping together. I convinced myself that you didn't care very much about me, and ... no, that's not right.' Jess paused and rubbed her face. 'I knew you cared about me. Maybe I didn't know how much. But I knew. I just chose not to see it.' Jess let out a shaky breath as she realised she was giving herself a talking to, at the same time she was confessing to Tom.

'It was easier to keep you both at arm's-length, and to tell myself what I was doing was harmless because we weren't proper couples. But it wasn't harmless, was it? You actually like me. And, even if you didn't, what I did was pretty shoddy behaviour. You don't treat people like that unless everyone's on the same page. I hid Nate's existence from you, but we were together, and you should have been able to trust me.'

Jess let out a wobbly breath. This was even harder than she'd thought.

'But since then, I've realised I really care about you, Tom. You're funny and kind. You've got an interesting fact for everything, which I pretend is annoying, but just shows how curious you are about the world. You wear ridiculous jumpers even in summer, which make you a really excellent hugger, and I think you'd even enjoy *Love or Dare* if you'd give it a chance. And you see me for who I am. You *like* me for who I am. And being with someone like you is something I'd really like to try on for size. Much more than New York dating.'

'OK,' Tom said, swallowing hard. 'This is a lot to take in. I'm not sure what to say. Maybe . . . why?'

'There is no proper reason why. I have no excuse for what I did, apart from willingly being blind to your feelings so I could have fun. You don't deserve to be treated like that, and I don't deserve your forgiveness. But I'm telling you this now because I wanted you to hear it from me rather than finding out some other way. And I want, more than anything, to be given a second chance to do things right and be the girlfriend you deserve.'

Tom blushed pink, then frowned. 'When did you last sleep with this Nate person?'

Jess paused. She'd known this question was coming, and there were two answers. She'd gone months now without seeing Nate. But Tom deserved the truth as it existed on his timeline, not hers.

'Yesterday morning,' she said, letting out a shaky breath. 'But it's over for good now.'

Across the table, Tom closed his eyes in pain.

'Here you go, guys!' the waiter said brightly, setting down the plates in front of them, and setting a bowl of plain chicken under the table for Alfie.

'Thanks so much,' Jess said, smiling at the waiter. As he left, an uncomfortable silence settled over the table.

'Please say something,' Jess said. 'Even if it's "Bog off, you harlot".'

'Why are you telling me this now?' Tom said, struggling to keep his voice steady. 'I don't understand what's changed?'

'It's hard to explain. But I guess, in summary, I'm falling in love with you. And I know you're falling for me too. Although everyone knows what that really means is that you're in love already, but you just don't want to say it out loud yet in case the other person isn't on the same page. So I guess what I mean to say is: I love you, Tom. And it seemed important to start telling the truth. Then maybe we can move onto the fun bits, like ... well, whatever sappy things people in love do with each other. I don't really know, I've never done it before.'

Tom couldn't help a smile creeping onto his lips, and Jess breathed out in relief. Her revelation had shocked him, but it had definitely helped that it had come with a side helping of 'I love you'.

'What kind of things do you *think* couples get up to?' Tom asked, folding his arms.

'I don't know ... mooning over rainbows, gasping at puppies in pet shop windows, talking to other people on holiday. That kind of thing.'

'And when did you last see an actual puppy in a real pet shop window?'

'All right. But you know what I mean,' Jess said, risking a smile.

'I'm not sure what to say,' Tom said, looking at his food like it was from an alien planet. Jess's revelation had thoroughly dazed him. After a long pause, he took a deep breath and said, 'You're right. I do really care for you, Jess. And, normally, cheating would be a total dealbreaker for me because relationships should always be based on trust ... But at the same time, you could easily have just stopped seeing Nate and not told me, and I never would have known about him. So that's something, I guess?'

Jess sighed. 'I've realised I can't keep putting off dealing with my problems. Facing up to stuff is my new ... thing. Along with drinking Diet Coke whenever I feel guilty, instead of too much wine.' She waggled her glass.

'I can see that,' Tom said, ruffling the back of his hair. 'And I do appreciate it. I can't say I'm thrilled to know you've been seeing someone else. Especially someone called Nate – I'm imagining some *Love or Dare*-style hunk impressing you with his youthful moves now, which isn't great. But that you've told me at all is important, I guess.'

Jess nodded, feeling shaky with relief.

'And you've also told me this other huge thing,' Tom added. 'I'm not actually sure my brain is up to processing so much and digesting this much meat at the same time, to be honest,' he added, prodding a fork into his chilli dog.

'I know this is loads to take in, and I can't expect you to make a decision right now,' Jess said, thinking it was lucky Tom didn't know time travel was real as well, in case his head exploded. 'How about we just put this aside for a couple of hours, and enjoy our dinner? Maybe, by the end of the night, you'll have a better idea of what you want to do. Of what you want *us* to do.'

'Ideally, I'd rewind and we'd get to enjoy our food first before you told me you'd been bedding someone else and are in love with me,' Tom said, ruefully.

Jess struggled to keep a straight face at 'bedding'; he really was adorable.

'But this hot dog looks delicious, so you've got yourself a deal.'

Chapter 43

'Oh my god. I think my dinner baby might be triplets,' Jess groaned, rubbing her stomach as she and Tom emerged from the Tube after dinner.

'I can't wait to meet you, kids,' Tom said, leaning over and kissing the bulge of her tummy.

By the end of what Jess hoped would be her last-ever meal at Hot Stuff, she and Tom had managed to get back into their usual rhythm of exchanging stories and making each other laugh. Tom had cackled loudly when Jess had related the tale about Donna punching Alan, and held Jess's hand when she told him about Mel's hospital appointment.

'She's pretty amazing, isn't she?' Tom had said. 'Poor Mel. Do you know what she'll do?'

'I think she'll go for the amputation,' Jess had replied. 'She's got a long road ahead of her and I want to make sure I'm there every step of the way. If you'll excuse the pun.'

Tom had laughed, despite himself. And, as they'd stepped out of the restaurant and into the warm evening air, and Jess had tentatively asked if he'd see her home, he'd readily agreed.

Now, glancing nervously at her phone, Jess quickened her pace.

'Come on, let's get back quickly,' she said. 'I need to, er, defrost some chicken.'

'How can you think about food after the meal we've just eaten?' Tom groaned.

'Get used to it. It's my special power,' Jess said.

As they rounded the corner onto her street, they heard barking behind them. Inkblot was crossing the road, snuffling his way towards them, Beth close behind him, looking at her phone.

'Beth, isn't it?' Jess said, turning around. 'And Inkblot?'

'Oh hi, Jess, hi, Alfie,' Beth said, looking up and smiling as Alfie trotted over to Inkblot and started yapping at him delightedly.

Jess was relieved Beth recognised them both. 'I thought you said you weren't stalking me?'

'Dammit, I'm terrible at this. I knew I should have reread *Stalking for Dummies*,' Jess laughed. 'Tom, this is Beth and Inkblot. Inkblot's the one with the fur. And Beth, this is my ... Tom.'

'Her boyfriend. Nice to meet you,' Tom nodded, while Jess's heart seemed to swell two sizes. 'And nice to meet you too,' he added, crouching down to stroke Inkblot, who was delighted by the attention. 'You're a GOOD boy, aren't you? Such a GOOD boy,' he told him, while Jess smiled fondly at them both.

Jess looked down the road behind Beth, then frowned as she saw a single headlight and heard the roar of an engine getting closer. Surely it couldn't be ...

'Careful!' she yelled, leaping between Beth and the road.

She squeezed her eyes shut as the moped roared by, a girl riding on the back whooping and waving at them as it passed.

'Why are you being so weird?' Tom said, straightening up, as Jess opened her eyes and stared at the moped zooming off into the distance, her arms still spread protectively in front of Beth.

Jess pressed a hand to her chest and felt her heart hammering. Then she paused and strained to listen.

Something felt different, as if a noise that had been thrumming in the background – a quiet noise, the kind you barely noticed – had been switched off.

Suddenly, she could feel the absence of something she hadn't even been completely aware of until now.

Realising Tom and Beth were staring at her, she shook her head and laughed. 'Sorry, there's been a spate of muggings around here lately. They've even hurt a few people quite badly. I panicked for a second there.'

'You literally flung yourself in front of me to save me,' Beth laughed. 'I'm dead impressed – I feel like Joey's sandwich. Although you don't need to worry – it says in the paper that the police caught those guys just this morning. Look.'

Handing Inkblot's lead to Tom, Beth pulled a copy of the *Evening Standard* out of her bag. Flicking through the pages, she found what she was looking for, folded the paper in half and handed it to Jess.

The headline that had once read, POLICE FRUSTRATED BY MUGGING GANG, now said, TIP-OFF HELPS POLICE FOIL MOPED MUGGERS.

Police have credited an anonymous tipster after the successful arrest of a gang of muggers targeting women in East

London. The gang had stolen over £20,000 of property during their crime spree, including a series of drive-by moped robberies.

Police revealed an anonymous tip-off led to the arrest of the gang's ringleader, who revealed the whereabouts of his accomplices in exchange for a deal.

Police Superintendent Timothy Stone said: 'We received a call at approximately 9.25 a.m. this morning apprising us of a number plate alleged to belong to one of the criminals the Metropolitan Police has been hunting. A raid of the suspect's home uncovered several items of stolen property, and we were able to apprehend the suspect and take him into custody.'

'Well, will you look at that?' Jess said, smiling to herself. 'Justice is served. Whoever put that tip in is a true hero, I reckon. Deserves some kind of medal. Or a pizza. Maybe both.'

Tom looked at her oddly. 'Shall we get you home? It was lovely to meet you, Beth. And Inkblot.' Tom bent down and tried to shake Inkblot's paw. He looked at it with his head cocked and licked it.

'Give him about fifty hours of practise and he'll nail it, I promise,' Jess said.

Beth laughed. 'See you around, Jess. Come on, stinker,' she said, tugging Inkblot gently towards her house, a shadow trotting at her heels.

'That was pretty impressive,' Tom said as they climbed the steps to Jess's flat. 'Protecting a stranger from a dastardly mugger, *and* in sexy heels. You really have turned over a new leaf, haven't you?'

Reaching her front door, Jess turned to Tom and took his hands in hers. 'Listen, Tom. I know tonight has been a lot—'

'A *lot* a lot,' he agreed.

'—but if you can forgive me for what I did, I'll do my best to be everything you deserve. Or at least try to be – I don't come with a three-year guarantee, I'm not a washing machine. I even burned a pair of Nate's stinky pants this morning to prove it's over, and I'm really, truly sorry. I can't say much more than that. The rest is up to you.'

'You set fire to his pants? Isn't that a bit OTT? I wondered what that smell was, but just assumed you'd been cooking your specialty of toast a la burnt bits,' Tom said. Then slapped a hand over his mouth.

'Don't worry, I know all about your breaking and entering,' Jess grinned. 'Please promise me you'll never go into cat burglary instead of book-binding as a career, because you're really terrible at it.

'And, if you still want me after everything that's happened, the answer to the question written on my bed in red rose petals is yes. Of course, yes. I would be honoured to be your girlfriend. I'll even consider giving up smoking and eating a few vegetables.'

Tom closed one eye and looked at Jess. 'There's something very different about you today. And not just the shoes and outfit, which are incredible, by the way. I'm not sure what it is, but I'm planning on finding out. So I guess we should give this a go, shouldn't we? Just to check.'

'Just to check,' Jess nodded.

Tom leaned in and kissed her. It was a different kind of kiss to all the ones they'd shared before. It was the kind of kiss Jess had never received from anyone, but definitely the kind she was keen to experience over and over again, exactly like the first one.

'So,' Jess said, pressing her nose against Tom's, 'what shall we do tomorrow?'

Acknowledgements

This should really be an apologies page: I would be surprised if, in the whole history of fiction, anyone has made more of a fuss about writing a light-hearted comic novel than me, so I'm sorry to everyone who had to listen to me whinge. But I also need to thank some people too, as is traditional.

Thanks to Mum and Dad for absolutely everything (why did you *have* me?). Sorry for still being a pest.

Thanks to Dookie for persevering on the Twitter-stalking front, and for keeping me laughing, even through the five-cry days. Your programming is really coming along nicely.

Thanks to Jo Unwin of JULA for taking a chance on me, having my back, and sending me 22-point-font emails of encouragement when I needed them.

Thanks to everyone at Little, Brown who helped make this book what it is, especially Darcy Nicholson for the rigorous editing, unwaveringly positive feedback, and for letting me keep my ending.

Thanks to Luke Chilton for the annoying advice, which was always right, and for replying to every lengthy text, even if he's way too fond of voice notes. And to Sian Griffiths for being a beta reader who never leaves you hanging, and pulls no punches.

Thanks to Thread for putting up with it all (poor Dookie), to Katie Espiner for the friendship, Real Talk and Vogues, and to Adam Kay for the Champagne, advice, and soothing words.

And thanks to me, aged 14, for adding, 'Write a book' to my five-point life-goals plan. You absolute idiot.

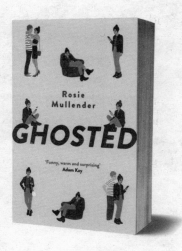

How badly have you been ghosted? No, literally.

A year ago, Emily was ghosted.

But it's fine, she's over it. And Andy was never part of the plan anyway. She's working on Project New Emily – New Emily goes to cocktail bars, wears ankle-breaking heels and has her life together. She's looking for a new man to match; Andy's old Converse and bad jokes were never going to work.

Thoughts about Andy are firmly in the past – until his name is spelled out on a Ouija board at a party. Emily discovers that Andy didn't ghost her – he died. And just as she's trying to work out how she feels, Andy turns up in her flat as a ghost. A ghost. In her flat.

Once she's over the shock, Emily realises she needs to get rid of this ghost of dating past so she can focus on the new man in her sights – and that the only way she can do that is to help Andy solve the mystery of his death. But as she spends more time with him, she remembers how nice it was to let her guard down and just be Old Emily sometimes.

Emily must choose between her new life and the past that's come back to haunt her. But she soon discovers that when it comes to putting her ghosts to rest, it's not as easy as she might think . . .